JASC

INCARNATION

WANDERING STARS VOLUME ONE

fourshadow publishing

Scripture quotations from the *Authorized King James Version*, Public Domain, 1611

Quotations from the *Book of Enoch*, Not in Copyright, Translation by R. H. Charles, 1917

Quotations from *The Prose Edda of Snorri Sturlson*, Public Domain, Translation by Arthur Gilchrist Brodeur, 1916

Cover design and artwork by Mike Heath at Magnus Creative
www.magnus-creative.com

Maps, diagrams, and page layout by Jason Tesar
www.jasontesar.com

Published by
4shadow, LLC

ISBN-13: 978-1477655153
ISBN-10: 1477655158

Grace, my reading companion
I will always treasure the magnificent journeys we took
Venturing into other worlds through the pages of a book

ADDITIONAL CONTENTS

THE REALM OF TIMA

S. A. 692-693, THE INCARNATION ERA

DA-MAYIM

• SENVIDAR
ARAGATSIYR

G R E A T   W A T E R S

ARMAYIM
ARAR
OAHV

BAHYITH •
BOKHAR   EHREVHAR

SAHVEYIM

DALEN
A-SORGUD

MUDENA DEL-EDHA • HARAGDEH

MALAKIYR
PARDEYA

GONGUR
KHANOK

• KHELRUSA

AD-DANYIM   NE-DANYIM

N O W D

CADOL
HAR-MARAH
KATAN MURAKSZHUG
HAR-MARAH

• SEDEKIYR

NAGAH

NORDUR

VESTUR   AUSTUR

SUDUR

300 MI
500 KM

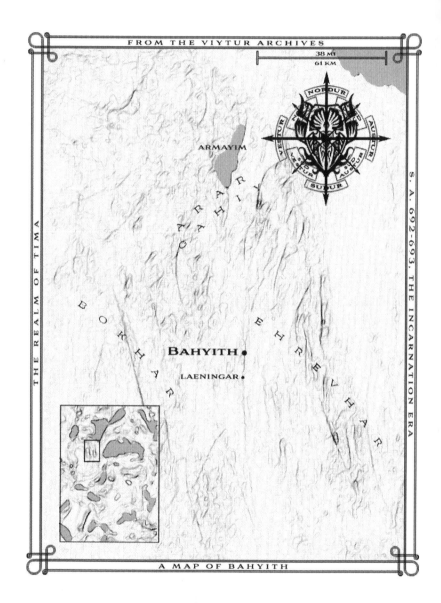

38 MI
61 KM

NORDUR
VESTUR
AUSTUR
SUDUR

ARMAYIM

GARARIY GAHIRIY

BOKHAR

EHREVHAR

BAHYITH •

LAENINGAR •

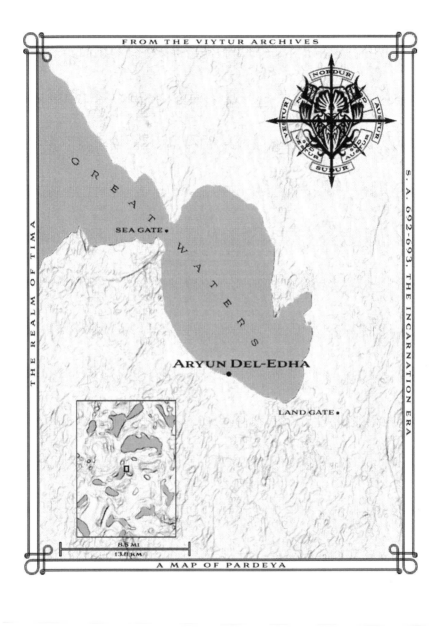

NORDUR

AUSTUR

VESTUR

SUDUR

S. A. 692-693, THE INCARNATION ERA

THE REALM OF TIMA

GREAT WATERS

SEA GATE •

ARYUN DEL-EDHA
•

LAND GATE •

8.5 MI
13.8 KM

A MAP OF PARDEYA

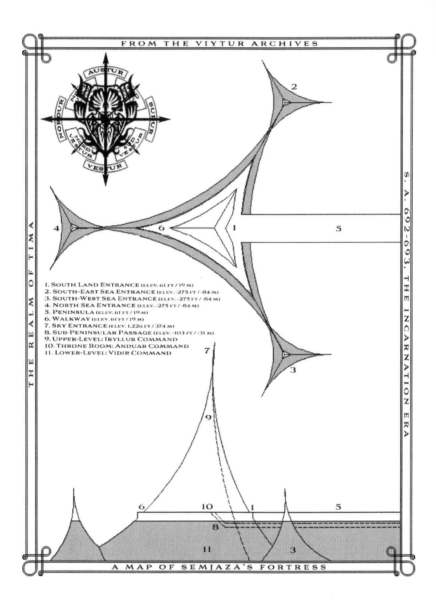

THE REALM OF TIMA

S. A. 692-693, THE INCARNATION ERA

1. **SOUTH LAND ENTRANCE** (ELEV. 61 FT / 19 M)
2. **SOUTH-EAST SEA ENTRANCE** (ELEV. -275 FT / -84 M)
3. **SOUTH-WEST SEA ENTRANCE** (ELEV. -275 FT / -84 M)
4. **NORTH SEA ENTRANCE** (ELEV. -275 FT / -84 M)
5. **PENINSULA** (ELEV. 61 FT / 19 M)
6. **WALKWAY** (ELEV. 61 FT / 19 M)
7. **SKY ENTRANCE** (ELEV. 1,226 FT / 374 M)
8. **SUB-PENINSULAR PASSAGE** (ELEV. -103 FT / -31 M)
9. **UPPER-LEVEL: IRYLLUR COMMAND**
10. **THRONE ROOM: ANDUAR COMMAND**
11. **LOWER-LEVEL: VIDIR COMMAND**

...the angels which kept not their first estate, but left their own habitation, he hath reserved in everlasting chains under darkness unto the judgment of the great day...wandering stars, to whom is reserved the blackness of darkness forever.[1]

1

Shards of light were scattered like wounds across a crimson sky, converging over the western horizon. The vibrant display was all that remained of the Holy One's manifestation in this place along creation's spectrum. Somewhere beyond those jagged peaks, past a multitude of worlds invisible from this perspective, the city of the Holy One marked the end of the Eternal Realm where the blazing illumination of His righteousness dwelled. But here, on the Borderland before the Temporal Realm, the nothingness of the Evil One cloaked the land in darkness.

The desolate terrain below passed by in a blur. Ahead, the glowing forms of the winged Iryllurym moved silently through the mist which clung to the recesses of the landscape. Their ethereal bodies were nearly motionless; gliding with a gracefulness that defied the blinding speed at which they flew.

At the rear of the formation, Sariel nodded to his own soldiers, giving the silent order to ready their weapons. Through the eye holes of his sleek helmet, he inspected the indistinct structure of his gauntlets and breastplate. At other points along the spectrum, the luminescent armor would have a more substantial existence. The Borderland, however, had long ago become a place of loosely-contained shapes and colors. Reaching to the small of his back, he unsheathed a pair of *vaepkir*, the famed weapon of the angelic soldiers of the sky. Each elegantly curved blade now ran across the outside edge of

his forearms, extending beyond his clenched fists at the front
and his elbows at the back.

All around him, Sariel's soldiers indicated their readiness,
but he could feel uncertainty hanging in the air like a suffocating
fog. Their unanswered questions still rang in his ears and they
were looking to him now to make sense of what they were about
to do.   One wing of Iryllurym, forty-nine in all, had been
assigned to this joint operation. They were to fly low and fast
into enemy territory and come about to approach the demons
from behind. Meanwhile, the ground forces of the Anduarym
would meet the enemy head on. It seemed simple enough. But
Sariel's seven-member special operations team was normally
assigned to smaller, strategic missions.   Their quick-strike
capability was better suited for removing enemy sentries and
laying the foundation for advancing ground troops, not for a
standard military action such as this. Like many recent orders
he'd been given, he knew it wasn't an intelligent one.

The larger formation began banking to the left and Sariel
followed, struggling to shove his emotions and insubordinate
thoughts back into a place where no one could see them. What
his soldiers needed now was confidence and assurance. Behind
the protective barrier of his helmet, Sariel opened his mouth.
The air around him seemed to come alive as a single tone,
crystal clear, grew in volume until it filled the spaces between
him and his soldiers. One by one, each winged angel added a
harmonic tone, joining the Skalagid, a Song of Understanding.
Immediately, their thoughts were melded together in a form of
group-communication far more efficient than words.

"Stay close to me," he told them. "Do what you do best. Fly
fast. Strike hard. Eliminate the enemy. Give them a taste of
your *vaepkir* and let the Marotru regret their unfaithfulness to
the Holy One!"

At once, the spirits of his friends were lifted. Their wings
seemed to move with greater agility. The tension drained from
their muscles, even as the grip on their weapons tightened. And
now it was Sariel's turn to experience the benefit of
empowerment that came with shared understanding. For ages,

they had relied on one another; fought side by side in countless battles. Through it all, the strength of their conviction and the solidarity of their purpose is what had kept them alive. Sariel now felt invincible, just as they did. Up ahead, the mist parted into two swirling vortexes in the wake of the wing leader, an instant before the remainder of the attack group entered the cover of darkness.

For a moment, all seemed silent and still.

When they exited the concealing fog, the stillness was gone. The rear lines of the demonic army could just be seen across the wide valley. Their writhing mass appeared as a blotch of shadows, consuming any remnants of ambient light that struggled for existence in this harsh environment. In stark contrast, the radiant forms of the Anduarym shone through the enemy silhouettes like a sunrise in the Temporal Realm. The wingless ground soldiers were already engaging the demons.

At the center of the enemy formation were the Nin-Myndarym. Protected by lesser demons on all sides, these Unshapers were the heart of the army's power, the dark fulcrum around which every shadow pivoted. As the polar opposites of the Myndarym, Sariel reserved a special hatred for these evil creatures. He locked his eyes on his objective and brought his arms forward, clasping his *vaepkir* together into a rigid, bladed frame that would act as a ramming weapon.

In seconds, the warriors of the sky closed the distance. Keeping low to the terrain, the formation of Iryllurym struck at the center of the Marotru army, banking left and right at the last moment to fracture the rear guard in two. The ranks of lesser demons parted like a cleft in a mountain, exposing the Unshapers.

Sariel braced himself.

His arms jolted violently as his *vaepkir* sliced through alternating spaces of air and the negative mass of the Nin-Myndarym bodies. Each density change brought a rapid succession of glaring lights that illuminated grotesque faces, crooked limbs, and gaunt torsos. With his momentum slowing and his weapons threatening to tear away from his grip, Sariel pulled up just before reaching the front lines.

His massive wings now stabbed upward, seizing large quantities of air before thrusting them downward, propelling his body into the sky. The other six members of his team followed closely as they gained altitude and readied themselves for the next attack. Below, traces of light still lingered, marking the path of the Iryllur attack. They appeared as a braided cord of pale colors, unraveling at one end, with the individual threads radiating outward along the rear of the enemy ranks. Hundreds of demons had perished in a matter of seconds. Some were still disappearing into brilliant explosions of whiteness.

Gradually, but with an exponential increase in volume, a low rumble emerged from the sounds of battle. It rose quickly to a thunderous roar, drowning out all others. The chaotic jumble of light and shadows on the battlefield below seemed to calm as soldiers on both sides of the conflict ceased fighting.

Then the Anduarym began to fall.

The ground beneath their feet dissolved, opening into a gaping hole like the mouth of a colossal monster. It started at the back of the angelic force, rippling forward to engulf the soldiers, and finally the front lines of the demonic horde as well. When the last angelic points of light were swallowed into the belly of the earth, Sariel realized that the battle was over.

In just a few seconds, the entire Anduar army had vanished.

Only when he saw movement at the edges of the crater did Sariel realize what had happened. At first, a dozen tentacles appeared. Then it was thousands, as the Nedaret began crawling from their subterranean domain. The massive demons moved with an unnatural gait. Folded, snakelike appendages shot out, then unfurled to the extent of their reach, heaving the weight of the demons' upper bodies along the ground. It was disgusting enough to encounter these burrowing abominations in their own domain, even more so above ground.

With his eyes fixed on the swarming shadows emerging onto the battlefield, Sariel didn't see the counter attack until one of his soldiers abruptly plummeted from the formation, spiraling downward in the smothering embrace of a winged demon. Looking up, he only had time to flinch as the descending cloud of fangs and claws engulfed all that remained of the angelic forces.

*   *   *   *

The sky overhead loomed black, fading to the deepest blue as it reached the horizon. The dark silhouette of mountains marked the end of one realm and the beginning of another. All was enveloped in a blanket of silence. Within the endless expanse of the firmament, small points of light pierced the darkness. Scattered against the backdrop of nothingness, their light swelled in intensity until their multitudes covered the heavens. Their brilliant whiteness pulsed, sometimes in unison, sometimes individually. In the moments between pulses, hints of color played around their edges.

Gradually, some stars dimmed, showing their distinct colors as their brightness decreased. Drifting closer to each other, they began to draw inward and spiral around a vortex; their speed increasing with proximity to the large, fiery star at their center. Quickly, they coalesced into one multi-colored orb.

In reaction to this movement, the remaining points of light parted and momentarily hovered as if confused, making way for this new spectacle. They encircled the orb from a safe distance and were joined, one by one, with white stars from farther away. Slowly the stars arranged themselves in concentric circles around the rapidly spinning orb.

And still, all was silent.

The core of the orb flared red with fire, seeming to issue a challenge to the hovering circle of stars as it expanded to occupy more space.

The challenge was answered by a collective brightening of the white stars, driving back the darkness of the night and washing the sky with their intensity. Altogether, their brilliance was twice that of their dimmer counterparts.

Without warning the orb burst, scattering millions of prismatic colors in all directions.

At the same instant, the Bright Stars converged upon the Dim Ones, moving to swallow the force of their expansion. At the moment of impact, the two groups became one. Time, itself, seemed to stretch out as if all of creation held its breath.

In a blinding flash, the explosion sent a bolt of light to the earth. Sparks were hurled in all directions; skipping across the ground, arcing through the air, burning through everything in their paths and leaving charred wounds upon the soil and vegetation. Ages seemed to pass until the remnants of the Dim Ones faded entirely and only blotches of shadow endured; holes in the earth that appeared darker than the nothingness of the sky, now ashen by comparison.

But the deadly shadows were not defeated. They changed shape, attaching themselves to the trees and animals of the earth. Everywhere they touched, darkness spread like a poison. Every being they touched became withered and distorted, perverted from its original form by the hatred of the Dark Ones.

And the earth trembled.

The righteous wrath of the Bright Ones flared. Heat radiated from their blinding light as they descended to the earth.

The wicked fury of the Dark Ones seethed. Bitter cold emanated from their nothingness as they moved to intercept their descending enemies.

Dark Ones were incinerated in flashes of light, and Bright Ones were engulfed in shadow, never to return.

In the distance, almost unnoticeable at first, more Bright Ones descended. Separated from the battle they came to the earth gently, taking the form of creatures that move through the land, sea, and sky. Everywhere they touched, the spreading flow of poison from the Dark Ones was stemmed. The earth began to heal as its form was altered. When their work was complete, the stars ascended into the sky while the battle raged on the horizon.

And the earth shuddered.

But not all ascended. Some stayed behind, wandering among creation, continuing their work. And as their light began to dim and spread throughout the earth, it enveloped creatures of the land, sea, and sky, swirling into disparate bands of color. From within the dance of vibrant hues came billowing clouds of darkness that grew into new beings, large and powerful. They emerged in somber colors that defied the light from which they were born. Their forms were twisted perversions of the creatures of the earth. They opened their mouths and began to feed upon the world as their very existence depended on laying waste to creation and consuming the creatures of the land, sea, and sky.

The people fled in terror, their cries rising to the sky as smoke. And, as the people perished, their blood spilled onto the land, flowing to the low places, seeping into the cracks and crevices.

And the earth shook.

And the shuddering increased until the foundations of the earth collapsed. Where blood had flowed, great cracks now opened, releasing the fountains of the deep. The land was suddenly lifted to the sky and the earth was rent in two. The waters of the abyss escaped from beneath the earth and covered the sky with darkness, raining down in torrents. On the horizon the shadow of the abyss rose like mountains and swept across the land as an insatiable demon, devouring all created things.

Growing.

Moving closer.

Rising until nothing else could be seen.

Enoch sat upright and inhaled sharply. His heart beat loudly in his ears, a stark contrast to the surrounding silence.

"Are you alright?" came a weary whisper from his left.

Enoch simply exhaled, trying to calm himself.

"What's wrong?" the voice repeated, clearer and louder this time, but cracking slightly at the edges. "Was it a vision?" said the voice, after a long pause. This time, the words were steady.

Enoch turned to his wife, Zacol, and nodded, still not ready for words of his own.

A soft whimper came from the other side of the room and Zacol rose to check on their son. She carefully pulled a cover over the boy and waited to make sure he fell asleep again. When the small room was silent once more, she turned and walked quickly out the door.

Enoch hunched forward and put his face in his hands, gently massaging his eye sockets with his fingertips.

After all this time, her first reaction is still anger. I thought we had grown beyond this!

Enoch opened his eyes slowly and let his hands slide down his face. With a deep breath, he rose to his feet and followed Zacol outside.

She stood with her arms crossed, her back to him.

Enoch ducked under the edge of their thatched roof and stepped out into the night. Over Zacol's shoulder, a broad expanse of grasslands extended as far as the eye could see. A short distance away, hundreds of tiny huts, just like their own, were huddled in the bright moonlight. Theirs was the only one separated from the rest of the tribe.

"Why won't He leave you alone?" she said softly without turning.

Enoch walked forward a few steps and clasped his hands behind his back. "It's a privilege that He speaks to me at all."

Zacol's head dropped. "It feels like a curse sometimes."

Enoch gritted his teeth to keep from saying something that would only make the situation worse. Looking down at the blades of soft grass between his toes, he had to admit that his wife was only saying what he sometimes felt himself. By the time his clenched jaw finally relaxed, he was able to say the words that they both needed to hear.

"He speaks out of love for us, even if the message is not always pleasant. And we know the consequences of ignoring what He reveals are borne by everyone."

Zacol turned around slowly. Instead of a stern expression, she had tears in her eyes. "What did you see this time?"

Enoch took a breath, then reached up and gently wiped the tears from her check with the back of his fingers.

"Something bad?" she probed.

Enoch simply nodded.

"And what are you supposed to do?" she asked, trying as always to get to the point as quickly as possible.

Enoch glanced down at the grass again, suddenly unable to look into her eyes. He wished he didn't have to say it. "I have to go away for a while." A moment of silence passed before he looked up again.

Zacol's eyes were closed and her head was lifted slightly. She pursed her lips, but remained silent. Without another word, she stepped past him and walked away.

2

A luminescent trail of blood meandered along the soil. Its path was erratic; disturbed occasionally by footprints on one side and lateral scuff marks on the other. Sariel tried his best to deny the fact that somewhere, on the other end of the glowing line of evidence they were leaving behind, the demonic hordes were tracking them. It would hardly be a difficult task.

The liquid light that coursed through angelic veins would have been lost against the radiant backdrop of their own territory. But they were now behind enemy lines, and the dark, barren soil of this place only made their presence blatantly obvious.

"Come on," Sariel said, bearing almost all of Amthardel's weight.

The Iryllur was looking paler by the second. His legs were covered in his own blood, spilling freely from the gash on the left side of his abdomen.

They both knew it was fatal. But Sariel didn't want Amthardel dying in a place like this. As he hefted the soldier across the rough soil, he looked down into the valley to the north, seeking solace in the iridescent forest now less than a mile away.

"It's beautiful. You'll see," he assured his friend.

Painful seconds lengthened into excruciating minutes while the two soldiers hobbled across the land. In this Eternal Realm, where even light and sound were immortal and the passage of time was irrelevant, Sariel was oddly aware of every moment. It truly felt like an eternity before they crossed the line that separated the territory of the Holy from the Unholy. Finally leaving behind the desolate, shadowy realm of the demons, the two Iryllurym descended into the protection of the towering trees.

Thick grasses grew tall around the water that roamed peacefully through the flat lands below, fed by an underground spring. From the rich soil, the surrounding trees grew massive, like giant sentinels keeping watch over the glen. Their leaves danced in the breeze, the shimmering outlines scattering a multitude of green hues in every direction. In concert with this rhythmic motion were the lingering echoes of songs that seemed intertwined with the very spirit of this sacred place. As the gentle passage of air rippled the surface of the lake, melodies were stirred up and tossed along the glassy swells, colliding with harmonies that had been lying dormant for years.

But all of this, Sariel had seen countless times before. Now, in the last moments of Amthardel's life, the only thing he noticed was the distant look in the eyes of the Iryllur sitting next to him.

"You were right," Amthardel said. "This is a good place to die."

Sariel clenched his fists, but kept his eyes fixed on the face of his soldier.

Amthardel took a deep breath, then winced. "Don't let them win," he said, turning his head. For a brief moment, his eyes seemed to brighten with clarity and that faraway look disappeared.

Sariel wanted to say something. But words were insufficient. Instead, he closed his mouth and nodded—a silent promise. Then, they both turned and looked out over the waters of Laeningar, the Valley of Healing.

Why do we keep doing this? How long are we supposed to watch each other die? Is there even victory on the other side of this war?

One after another, faces sprang into Sariel's mind. Iryllur. Anduar. Vidir. Soldiers. Friends. He closed his eyes, but the memories only became more vivid. Ages of loss concentrated into one moment. When he opened his eyes, tears rolled down his cheeks.

Amthardel was leaning more heavily on him now. Gently, Sariel pulled his arm out from underneath his friend's and leaned away to look into the face of the soldier who had been with him through countless battles. The angel's eyes were closed and the pale light that shone beneath his skin only moments ago had now faded.

In the distance, a faint howl sounded. It echoed through the valley, a chilling reminder of the enemy's relentless aggression.

Sariel remained seated on the shore, holding the last member of his team. Despite the peaceful rhythm of dancing leaves and soothing melodies of trickling water, this sacred valley failed to ease his constricted throat. He could still see the confused faces of his soldiers. Their innocent questions reverberated in his ears.

And what did I tell them? That everything would be fine. That this mission was just like all the rest.

These were all the same words that Sariel had heard from his own superiors. He regurgitated them just as a loyal soldier ought. And in the end, they turned out to be lies. As he gently lowered Amthardel's body to the grass, he noticed the cuts and scrapes on his own forearms.

Why was I spared?

Why were his injuries so miniscule by comparison? Why was he the only survivor when he was the one who led them to their deaths?

Another howl echoed through the valley.

Reaching down, Sariel pried a *vaepkir* from the now stiff fingers of his friend. Amthardel had clutched it tight until the very end, a testament to his unwavering determination to fight. Lifting the weapon from the pool of blood beside his soldier, Sariel held it tight and felt the weight of it in his hand. He examined the three sharpened talons that diverged from the primary blade to cover his knuckles.   Even in the near formlessness of the Borderland, the weapon still appeared graceful.   On the other end, at the very tip of the deadly instrument of war, the dark stains of demon blood marred its otherwise gleaming surface.

Another howl sounded. It was only a few hundred feet away and now accompanied by snorting and heavy breathing.

Sariel stood up and walked a few paces away from the water, facing the direction of the forest where the howling had come from. He realized now that his silent promise to Amthardel only moments ago might also have been a lie.

Don't let them win. Don't let the demons win. But I can't control the outcome. I promised all of them that it would be just like every other mission. And I couldn't control that either!

What he would normally push aside for a more convenient time, he allowed himself to feel. It had been a pointless battle; an utter failure and a staggering waste of resources. He and his soldiers had no business being pulled into that operation. Now, he was the only one left of a highly-trained and specialized group of soldiers.   More than that, they had been his last remaining friends—the only ones he had trusted, and the only ones who had trusted him. And now, he was alone.

Sariel's hand began to shake. Only then did he notice the bulging knuckles and strained tendons of the fingers that had unconsciously tightened around the hilt of the weapon—a blade that had ended the tortured lives of innumerable demons.

Shadows moved between the trees, keeping just out of sight. They were waiting for something.

Sariel remained still. His body, rigorously trained by ages of conflict, reacted with a simple determination. There would be no more running. Amthardel had died in a place of peace and beauty; not in the wasteland of the demons. That objective had been met. And now, while his thoughts were consumed, his winged, warrior form readied itself for its last stand. This would be the end.

Suddenly, the whole forest darkened. Demons poured from between the dense trees and came into the open in one coordinated movement, blocking the radiance of the woods with their emptiness. Their bodies were collections of nothingness, reflecting no light. Instead, as the negative mass of each demon moved in front of an object, the light around it distorted and bent inward.

Small shapes crawled over the ground on four legs. Their talons dug into the soil as their elongated snouts inhaled loudly, taking in the scent of their prey. In the trees above, larger, flying creatures settled on the branches, extending their angular wings to either side. In between the darker sections of structural bone, the thin membranes that made up their wings absorbed less light, giving a pale appearance.

Sariel's eyes narrowed at seeing the demonic counterpart to the Iryllurym—the soldiers of the Marotru who had descended upon his team from above. But eventually, his gaze landed on the largest and darkest creatures; the ones who destroyed the angelic army from beneath. The Nedaret moved now across the grassy surface with barbed tentacles, hard as stone, raking the fertile soil for traction.

The entire formation slowed to a stop. Though Sariel had eliminated hundreds of them on the battlefield this day, the enemy's reluctance to attack was not due to fear. Instead, they relished the fact that they had the lone angel surrounded.

With his back to the water, Sariel looked out upon one after another of his enemies. There was no escape. The odds were impossible. He stared at his own death and couldn't help the defiant grin that overtook his face.

The winged demons took to the air.

The small ones scrambled forward along the ground.

The massive ones lurched into motion.

Sariel crouched forward with his *vaepkir* ready to strike. But something inside him hesitated.

Your function is not to think, but to act! he remembered, as the words of his superior came to memory. The words spoken just before the battle.

Yes, my Rada!

In that single, obedient response, Sariel had committed his soldiers to their deaths.

This is what they'd want. For me to act. For me to fight!

The smaller, faster demons had now come within striking distance. Two sprang from the ground with their claws ready to rip his stomach open.

His lightning-quick reflex cut through both shadows in one swift movement and the demons vanished into a brilliant flash.

Think! What would they not want you to do?

Spinning to face three more demons, his reflexes took over now. His muscled limbs propelled him through a dance of death, hacking and slashing his way through the infestation of darkness.

Go where it is forbidden. Where the demons cannot follow. Regroup.

Sariel sprang from the ground as his wings thrust him upward into the nearest shadow.

The blade of the demon came down on him. Its serrated edge glanced off his *vaepkir*, leaving behind crimson sparks that perished into swirls of smoke.

Sariel plowed through the absence of light and brought the protruding tip of his own blade across the demon's neck. Pale green and purple flashed as the enemy slipped by, spiraling downward to its death.

The Temporal Realm!

In a small pocket of safety before the next winged demon, Sariel cast his weapon away and willed his body to *shift*. Though he wore the winged form of an Iryllur, he was not bound by their limitations. He was one of the Myndarym—the race of angels who could *shift* their existence to any point along the spectrum of creation.

What had once appeared as a cloud of winged shadows and snarling fangs suddenly became a dizzying array of swirling ashes—a mixture of pale and dark, colorless blotches that quickly gave way to empty air. The sky, once deep orange, drained of color before it took on shades of blue. In the distance, the brilliance of the trees dimmed and the green hues seemed to become encased in more distinct forms.

As Sariel moved through the layers of the creation spectrum, he could almost feel the confusion among the ranks of the Marotru. A Shaper masquerading as a soldier was rare enough, but even his own kind would have been shocked. The Temporal Realm had long ago become forbidden to those who used to *shape* it. Though it was a violation of the laws of his realm, he kept pushing himself until he felt the firm lift of air beneath his feathered wings.

* * * *

Sheyir sat on a low, flat rock, dangling her feet in the still water of the pond. It felt cool between her toes and gave her a momentary distraction from her frustration. It shouldn't have come as a surprise when her father announced the forthcoming betrothal to her uncle, but it did anyway. She had many uncles, but it seemed as though she would have to marry the most repulsive one. Unfortunately, her father didn't have much say in the matter; such things were dictated by the customs of her people. Nevertheless, she wasn't comforted by this. It only made her angry to think about the fact that there wasn't another option. Someday this would all seem more bearable, someday when she had given up hope for something different.

But now was not that time. Now, she wasn't able to bear it. And the feel of the water wasn't able to dispel her feelings. In fact, the whole valley felt different today. The trees around her looked strange and dull, like the life had been drained out of them. Had something happened, or was it just her own situation that had changed? Since she was a child, she'd been coming to this place to be alone and to sing. But she didn't feel much like singing now.

As she glanced around at her surroundings, something on the edge of her vision caught her attention. Sheyir turned and looked up, noticing something strange about the trees just a few yards away. She squinted, but the perplexing vision only intensified. One section of the forest seemed to bulge outward as if she were looking at it through a dew drop. The subtle green and brown hues of the vegetation slowly separated into bands of more intense color. She watched, fascinated by the beautiful, but unexplained event.

And then, it was there—a massive, winged creature hovering in the air, facing away from her. Sheyir was instantly paralyzed with fear and the only thing she could hear above the powerful beat of its white wings was the pounding of her own heart.

The creature pivoted slowly toward her as it descended to the earth. When its human-shaped body touched the ground, the feathered wings, dappled with bands of gold and reddish-brown, came to rest. If it hadn't noticed her presence before, it did now with large, deep-set, animal eyes, blue in color. The prominent eyebrows gave it a look of intensity, as if it was able to see into her very soul. Its face and head were covered in white, shaggy hair, swept back from its large, sharp nose as if blown by the wind. But the rest of the creature's tan skin was hairless.

Sheyir willed her body to move, but it was frozen in place, melded with the rock beneath her.

The creature, whose body seemed to be made entirely of muscle, took a step forward.

Sheyir instantly grew cold while her face flushed with heat. Even though it stood a stone's throw away, it seemed as though the creature's vast wings could reach out and encircle her.

Instead, the creature retracted them and tucked them behind its shoulders.

Suddenly, Sheyir felt control of her body return. Without pausing even a moment to make sense of the situation, she fled in terror. As her bare feet dug into the wet sand of the shoreline, she could almost feel its breath on her skin. In her mind, she could still see those giant wings and knew that it would take but two thrusts for the creature to catch her. But she ran anyway, blind with panic.

The thick foliage of the trees slapped her face and body as she finally reached the forest, feeling instantly safer among the confined space that would inhibit flying creatures from attacking. She kept running until she couldn't breathe and her legs wouldn't move any longer. She stumbled and fell into the mud. Crawling now on her hands and knees, she wondered why she hadn't already been taken from the ground and carried off into the sky. Risking a look behind, she was surprised to see nothing.

The creature was not there.

She looked up quickly, expecting to see it descending upon her, but neither was it in the sky above. In fact, there was no sign of it; only the broken reeds and bent blades of grass disturbed by her passage. Her lungs burned and her heart raced, obstructing her ears from listening for signs of pursuit.

Where is it?

Sheyir stood motionless, her chest heaving, for what seemed like an eternity. Slowly, her heart grew quieter and she thought she could hear something. More seconds passed and the sound of singing drifted to her. It was the most clear, brilliant tone she'd ever heard. Increasing in volume, it pierced the air and rumbled the ground beneath her feet, all at once. What was more startling was the melody—a song she used to sing as a child.

How could it know? What does it want?

Slowly, the vines parted on the other side of the clearing.

Sheyir remained still, too exhausted to run any longer.

From between the broad leaves, a man stepped through into the light. Even at this distance, she could see that he was several heads taller than she. Only a tattered white loincloth covered his tan skin. His white, shaggy hair and beard were unmistakable. Though smaller and without wings, she knew it was still the same creature.

"Please don't go, Sheyir," he said in her language. "I've come a long way to see you."

She backed away carefully, feeling more cautious than afraid now.

How does it know my name?

The man, *the creature*, extended its hand toward her in a pleading gesture.

Sheyir stepped slowly backward into a tangle of thick vines until broad leaves blocked her vision of the strange man. Immediately, she felt shielded from the power of his gaze. Her body was her own once more. Turning, she ran toward her village as quickly as her legs would carry her.

3

The midmorning sun was bright, making the dew on the grass sparkle. The elders and most of the inhabitants of Sedekiyr were gathered in the center of the village, watching Enoch and his family from a distance.

Zacol slid a leaf-wrapped bundle of nuts and dried berries into an already full animal skin bag. "There," she said as she lifted the bag and hung it across Enoch's shoulders. "That should keep you for a few days. Then you'll have to gather what you can along the way."

"Thank you," Enoch replied, trying to make eye contact with his wife. She was doing her best to ignore the implications of this journey. But he didn't want her to keep silent. He wanted her to voice her frustrations so they wouldn't gnaw at her while he was gone.

"They look more curious than anything," he offered, looking over her shoulder at the rest of their tribe.

Zacol looked up suddenly with her head tilted slightly. "Of course they are. What did you expect?"

Enoch squinted. At least she was talking now. "...nothing, I guess. But I hoped that someone would show some concern. They're just standing there."

"Maybe they want to give you some time alone with your family."

Enoch shrugged his shoulders.

"We're making progress," Zacol assured him.

Enoch looked down and rubbed the scars on his wrists, permanent reminders of what he'd endured over the years; how far he'd come. "And now I'm leaving."

Zacol's head dropped. Her voice lowered to a whisper. "When you come back, we'll just have to start over."

Enoch quickly placed his hands on Zacol's shoulders. "I will come back. And we will start over."

Zacol looked up again and her red-rimmed eyes were starting to well up. All she could do was nod her head.

Enoch shifted the weight of his bag and looked over to his son, Methushelak, who was hunched over in the grass nearby.[4] The boy was always fascinated by the creatures crawling through the soil.

"You still haven't told me where you're going."

Enoch grinned and looked back to his wife. "You still haven't asked."

Now it was Zacol who smiled, and tilted her head. "Where are you going?"

"I thought you'd never ask," he continued, enjoying the brief moment of humor amid the heavy circumstances.

Zacol waited with raised eyebrows.

"In my dream, I was above the land, like a bird of the sky. In the distance, I saw a tall mountain. And I could see the land between here and there, and where the water was situated. The mountain was the one I've heard described by people who've passed through the land of Nowd."[2]

"Nowd? Why would He send you to those murderers?" she asked, looking more worried than before.

"Their father was a murderer," he corrected. "That doesn't mean all of them are."

Zacol's face softened. It was obvious that she didn't want to spend their last minutes together in confrontation.

"And besides," Enoch continued. "My message is not for them."

Zacol's eyes narrowed. "Who is it for, then?"

Enoch looked up to the sky. The mist was keeping low to the plains this day, and the deep blue overhead was unusually clear.5 "I saw the stars fall from the sky. I saw the Children of Heaven abandon their home and come to ours. And I felt His heart breaking—" he replied, trailing off as he remembered the waters of the abyss rushing across the land.

Zacol's eyebrows rose quickly. "Has this already happened?"

Enoch was silent for a moment. "Some of it has happened and some is yet to come."

Zacol turned away and shook her head. "And what are you supposed to do about it? Tell the Children of Heaven to go back? Warn the *haragam*? Can any of it be changed anyway?"

Enoch cringed at his wife's use of the derogatory term for the Kahyin tribe. Even though their patriarch had murdered his brother, Enoch refused to believe that any person or tribe was above another. The Kahyin were simply lost, prevented from knowing the Holy One by the guilt of their father. And as much as his own tribe would hate to admit it, every human was descended from the same father and mother.

"I will tell the Children of Heaven what the Holy One has shown me. I don't know if I can prevent anything. He asks only for my obedience in following His voice."

Zacol's eyebrows smoothed until she wore a blank expression.

It was difficult for Enoch to make others understand what he had been learning his whole life, and what he was only now starting to comprehend. It had always been this way. Ever since he was a child, people treated him differently because he could hear the voice of the Holy One. Many thought he was crazy. Others said he was a liar. Some even wanted so much to deny the presence of the Holy One, that they resorted to violence to keep Enoch from speaking the truth. Zacol was the only one who listened; the only one who truly believed.

"How long will you be gone?" she asked softly.

Her beauty was radiant this morning. Her black, straight hair moved slightly in the breeze. Her dark brown eyes, normally intense, were softened by her emotional brokenness.

"I don't know," he said softly. With resignation, he added, "...as long as it takes."

"Ahva, ahva," came a small voice at his leg.

Enoch looked down to his son who was holding something up for his father to see.

"What is it?" Enoch asked, bending down.

"I found a rock," the boy answered.

"Methu," Enoch started, placing a hand on his son's shoulder. "You're going to be a strong man someday. But the most important thing is, if the Holy One speaks to you, you listen to Him. Do you understand?"

"Uh huh. See, it's from the moving waters, but I found it in the grass."

Enoch smiled and stood up.

Zacol's eyes were filled with tears again. "We'll miss you. Please come back as soon as you can."

Enoch slowly wrapped his arms around his wife and pulled her close until her head was laid against his chest. He tried to savor a moment that certainly would not come again for a long while. "I will, my love," he whispered into Zacol's ear.

* * * *

Why did I say that?

Sariel still had his hand outstretched in the direction Sheyir had run. The branches and leaves still swayed from her passage, but she was gone. He slowly curled his fingers inward and lowered his arm.

I just came here to escape. To regroup. Didn't I?

But his words to Sheyir still hung in the air, revealing a deeper motive that he himself wasn't aware of until the moment it took the form of words.

I've come a long way to see you.

Sariel lowered his gaze to the ground beside him while he searched his memory for confirmation or denial of what he'd just spoken. Laeningar had become a place of refuge for him in recent times. In the Eternal Realm, there was a sharp contrast between it and the territory of the Evil One. Even among the luminescent terrain of his own territory, the Valley of Healing stood out as a special place. It had drawn his attention at first sight, but what succeeded in capturing his fascination was the realization that it had all been created by a human woman. Never before had such a thing occurred. Humans, as a species, hadn't yet learned the art of song. But it was there waiting for them, because it pleased the Holy One to create such things, even ideas, for humans to discover. And the humans were His most cherished creation.

When Sariel had first seen her, he had known why. She had been the most beautiful thing he'd ever encountered. Her tiny frame—half the size of Sariel's—appeared as an intricate tapestry of sparkling, multi-colored threads, shifting from one family of hues to another with each emotion. Over the years, he watched her grow from a child into a woman. She always had songs in her heart, even before she could speak. And when she discovered them, and gave them voice, she sang as though she were a gifted Shaper who had been taught the deepest knowledge of Songs from the Holy One. Without knowing what she was doing, she created healing, and established peace. But Sariel knew what she was doing. He could see it. He could see the effect of her melodies, how they drifted to the ground and took root. In this place where he now stood, he could still hear the lingering songs from years past, blending with the harmonies that she had sung only days before. In his spirit, Sariel could feel the way her songs calmed the storms of his troubled mind.

I didn't come here to escape the demons. I didn't even come to think about my next course of action. It was instinct. I didn't want to die because there's still something worth living for.

And it wasn't the Valley of Healing that still held worth in his eyes; it was the one who had created it, the one who sang it into existence.

I love her, he admitted to himself.

I've always loved her.

But could he be with Sheyir? Could he live in her world, as a human? Was he ready to do what was forbidden? Was he ready to risk ruining what was perfect in his mind? Would she love him in return? Or would this last, beautiful idea die like everything else in his life?

The stream flowing from Laeningar wound through wide grasslands and dense forests. Mist rose from the earth, clinging heavily to the thick vegetation where the air was still. In other places, where a slight breeze had cleared away the moisture, bright sunlight came down in great, silver columns, warming the earth. Surrounded by the buzzing of insects and a seemingly infinite variety of chirps and whistles from brightly-colored birds, Sariel waded through the shallows of the stream. He was in no hurry. Once he'd come to understand his true motivation for entering the Temporal Realm, and had made peace with it, he found himself thoroughly enjoying his new home. The feel of the cool water between his toes. The alternating stone and sand terrain beneath his feet. The way each step brought swirling plumes of silt off the bottom, to be swept downstream by the mild current.

The Temporal Realm shared many similarities with the Eternal, though the differences were fascinating. Colors were duller, but shapes seemed more defined. Sounds didn't linger into eternity, but were more crisp and vibrant. Sariel inhaled the sweet fragrance of the flowers that bloomed everywhere, smiling at the lack of subtlety. Existence, it seemed, was more real in this place; perhaps intensified by the loss of immortality.

And to think, all of creation was once a combination of both attributes.

When his thoughts returned to Sheyir, he shook his head at his own stupidity. He hadn't ever planned on revealing himself to her in bodily form, but now that he had, he regretted the way it happened. The form he'd maintained during his recent age as a soldier was nothing like any person or animal she would ever have come in contact with. In the blindness of the moment, he came into her realm and took on the nearest temporal equivalent to an Iryllur. Only when he saw the terror on her face did he realize his mistake. And then she ran.

So, what do I do now? She seemed less afraid after I shaped into a human, but she still left.

Sariel thought about her tribe and what he'd observed over the years. Even though he had watched her almost exclusively, he had unconsciously gathered other information along the way, including learning her language.

As he went back through his memory, he saw something hidden beneath her reaction to his human form, something he'd missed until just this moment.

A hint of intrigue mingled with her uncertainty?

Among the Chatsiyram, women were responsible for gathering and preparing food, tending to the men, and performing nearly every physical task required to maintain the village, with the exception of building shelters. They weren't physically abused, but they were ignored and disproportionately burdened. When the work for the day was finished, most of the women tended to gather together to share stories, eat, and talk about other women. Sometimes, when they talked about each other's husbands, the conversation turned ugly. The women could be just as unfriendly as the men of the tribe. This was why Sheyir spent most of her free time alone.

And then, after years of isolating yourself from women— ignored by men; never pursued or even engaged in conversation—a man tells you that he's come a long way to see you. Yes. She's intrigued. She must be!

Seeing now the mixture of emotions in her reaction, a strategy began to form in Sariel's mind—one that occupied his thoughts for the remainder of his journey.

Rounding a bend, the stream widened into a shallow pool with a sandy bottom. Several small children waded in the water. Some were splashing; others were poking sticks into the sand and watching the silt billow toward the surface.

"Hello, children."

The small, dark faces looked up. The girls stood motionless with curiosity. The boys instantly smiled and began to make their way over.

Sariel kept moving slowly forward. "Are you playing a game?"

"Why do you look strange?" one of the boys asked, without a hint of embarrassment.

Sariel smiled. Even wearing a human form, his pale features still marked him as a stranger. "Everyone in my tribe looks like me. But my tribe is very far away."

"You're tall," one boy observed.

Another boy came close and touched Sariel's arm, as if checking to see that he was real.

"Can I play your game too?" he asked the children.

"No," an older girl answered quickly.

"Yes, you can play with us," a boy corrected.

"Thank you. And what are you playing?"

The girl answered again. "The boys are looking for fish."

"And you are splashing?" Sariel asked.

"No," the girl corrected. "We are trying to catch the fish when they find one."

"Oh, I see," Sariel replied.

One of the boys put a stick onto Sariel's hand and pushed his fingers closed.

"No, he doesn't want to look for fish," the girl corrected.

Sariel looked down at the boy whose eyes seemed a bit larger than before. "What if I was the fish?" he said, suddenly sitting down in the water.

All the children laughed, even the oldest girl.

Sariel laughed too, knowing he must look ridiculous to them. He could see the excitement in their faces and knew that none of them had ever played with an adult. Adults didn't play with children in the Chatsiyr tribe and the little ones learned quickly to keep to themselves if they wanted to have any fun.

At the most, they might have a caretaker watching them.

As soon as the thought came to him, Sariel began to scan the nearby trees. It took only a moment to locate a terror-stricken female face, peering at him through the leaves. And then the face was gone.

Sariel stood up. "Do your parents live nearby?"

The oldest girl nodded.

"Can you take me to see them?"

The boy who had put the stick in Sariel's hand now grabbed two of his fingers and began to pull him toward the shore. He looked up at Sariel and squinted in bright sunlight reflecting from the water. "Can we play after you talk to them?"

Sariel smiled again. "I would like that very much." *Though I doubt I'll get the opportunity.*

The children led him away from the stream and into the trees, seeming to follow a memorized path, though none of the vegetation was worn away or gave any indication of regular travel. Minutes later, the grass gave way to bare soil and a village appeared almost out of nothing. Several large grass huts were roughly arranged between the trees, around what appeared to be a central meeting area. The huts had thatch roofs, but no walls, and were supported by thick wooden poles set into the ground. A ring of stones lay at the center of the meeting area, seating for the men of the tribe during the evening meal.

Several adult women could be seen in the distance, but Sariel's attention was immediately drawn to a commotion on his right. The woman who'd seen him by the stream was now talking to a man and pointing in his direction. Within seconds, two more males appeared, each carrying a *khafar*—a crude digging instrument that could function as a short spear in times of necessity.

"Children," he said, letting go of the boy's hand. "I think this is as far as I should go. Thank you for playing with me. I had fun."

The children looked across the meeting area at the approaching men and instinctively backed away.

Sariel held his hands out to either side and waited, trying to look as non-threatening as possible.

"Shulek! Shulek!" one young man shouted, approaching at a brisk pace. He looked much like a male version of Sheyir, with short, black hair and earthen skin. His thin frame was covered at the waist with a dull, brown loincloth. His eyes had the intense look of a frightened animal, as he commanded Sariel to be gone.

"I mean you no harm," Sariel offered.

"You are not welcome here. Shulek!" said another, louder than the first. Three young men now stood in front of Sariel, *khafars* held at their sides.

Sariel noted that they weren't yet holding their building implements in a two-handed grip, indicating that, although they were wary, the situation hadn't yet escalated to the point of violence. The Chatsiyram were a peaceful people by upbringing, abhorring aggression in every circumstance except defense of their homes or families. The short spears were actually little more than arm-length sticks with a flattened spade end for digging. They looked much more innocent than the weapons Sariel usually faced, but he kept an eye on them anyway.

"Why have you come?" they persisted.

Sariel looked past them, scanning the gathering crowd for Sheyir's face, but he didn't see her. Neither did he see her father. "I've come on a journey from far away."

One of the men grabbed his spear with both hands and tightened his grip.

There aren't enough of them. This isn't going to work. It needs to be bigger.

Seeing his strategy beginning to disintegrate, Sariel took a step backward, still keeping his hands out and visible.

"You are not welcome here!" one of the men repeated.

Sariel nodded and continued to step backward. When the men lowered their weapons, he turned his back to them and walked away.

4

From his home city of Sedekiyr, Enoch had traveled due north. Somewhere beyond the eastern horizon lay the mountains of Nagah, but Enoch kept the shores of Da-Mayim visible on his western side as he picked his way carefully through the grassy plains. Traveling at a pace that he knew would be sustainable for quite some time, he moved only by the light of day, continuing on a straight route for three weeks until he reached a body of water that spread to the north, east, and west as far as his eye could see. Turning westward, he kept the shoreline on his right side for another three days until the land narrowed between it and another body of water to the west. Across this strip of land, which he named Ad-Banyim, he traveled with relative ease until the shorelines on either side began to widen and the terrain began to slope upward. In his mind, he could still see clearly the path that had been laid out before him. And with confidence, he kept to the right-hand shoreline as it gradually swung north, then east again, over the course of the following week. The land here sloped sharply from the mountains to the water, and passage was difficult and slow across the rocky terrain.[11] Having long ago used up his provisions, he was now grazing as he moved, collecting fruit and anything else edible along the way.

His breathing was coming in ragged gasps now, as he expended precious energy to reach the bush growing in the dark soil between the jagged rocks of the slope.

It looked bigger from below, he thought as he slumped to the ground beside it. Within minutes, he had picked all the bright red clumps from the leaves and put most of them away in his bag. After eating a handful of the tart berries, he loosened the ties and removed the skins covering the bottoms of his feet. The soft grasses that had been stuffed inside were matted and wet with blood.

He hissed softly as he probed the sensitive skin with his fingers. His feet had toughened considerably over the past weeks, but the cut on his left heel seemed to be getting worse.

Too much walking. Holy One, please protect the feet of the one who goes to deliver your message.

Reclining against the rocks, Enoch looked out over the terrain ahead. The shoreline below continued to swing eastward and it appeared that the steep slopes would lessen in the coming days. Already, dense groupings of trees were becoming more common in the spaces between the crags of stone. Far ahead, a group of dark shapes were clustered together in a flat clearing before the water—a herd grazing on the thick grass. Enoch watched their lazy movements and it reminded him of the animals of the plains near Sedekiyr.

Suddenly, a massive shape burst from the wall of trees to the north. It ran on two powerful hind legs and kept its enormous head low to the ground. Even in this posture, the dull green creature was roughly four times taller than any of the grazing animals.

The herd scattered immediately. Loud, mournful bellows escaped the frightened animals as they ran in all directions. A few hobbled awkwardly for the water and plunged in without hesitating. When the predator reached them, they were floundering wildly and unable to escape.

Enoch crouched low and held his stomach as he watched the attacker rush into the shallow water with its jaws open, its head tilted to the side.

The creature clamped down on the nearest animal and shook its head violently from side to side. The water foamed white, then red. A harsh growl cut through the panicked splashing.

Seconds later, the smaller animal was nothing more than a limp shape hanging from the jaws of the predator that carried it back into the trees.

Enoch crawled backward on his hands and knees and lowered himself to the ground when he was out of sight. His heart pounded in his chest. The rock felt cold against his face and the smell of wet soil filled his nostrils.

I was headed there! And I still have to walk through that place! How am I going to survive this terrible land?

At once, his heart slowed and the tension left his muscles. He felt the presence of the Holy One. Beyond his hand lying flat against the moss-covered rocks, he saw the bush that he'd picked bare of its fruit—the bush that had seemed so important only a few minutes ago, but turned out to be not worth the effort. He smiled when he realized what had just happened.

Holy One, it is Your guidance which sustains me. Not my own. Forgive my fearful heart.

* * * *

"What did he say?"

"I mean you no harm," the young man answered.

Another leaned forward. "He said he came on a journey from far away."

The conversation of the males was almost too faint to hear. Sheyir picked up a bundle of wide-bladed strands of grass and submerged them in water, pretending to be occupied by the work at hand. But she listened intently to the discussion taking place nearby.

"He was very big, like the stories of the murderers from the east. But his skin was pale and his hair was white."

"His eyes were like the deep waters," another young man pointed out.

Sheyir's father crossed his arms and leaned back from the circle. As the elder of the tribe, it was his responsibility to interpret the signs and give direction to his people.

Like the other Chatsiyram, Sheyir's fate rested solely on the wisdom of her father. With the exception of his choice of husband for his daughter, he usually made good decisions. But Sheyir already knew what her father's reaction would be to a visitation by such a strange and intimidating man. What surprised her, however, was the way her heart began to beat faster when she thought of him. And though he wasn't human and could fly away at any moment, she nevertheless feared that the Chatsiyr males would somehow hurt him.

"I do not like the words you tell me," her father responded finally.

Sheyir pushed another bundle beneath the water and kept her eyes down. But her ears strained to hear her father's judgment.

"You will take the young men and find where he went. You will kill him so he cannot bring trouble to our people."

Sheyir suddenly turned her head in the opposite direction and squeezed her eyes shut. She imagined the stranger again and the melody he sang. She remembered his words.

Please don't go, Sheyir. I've come a long way to see you.

"Fly away," she whispered to the stranger. "Wherever you are, fly far away."

* * * *

Sariel waited patiently on a flat rock in the center of shallow water, downstream from the Chatsiyr village. In the fading light of dusk, he sat motionless, listening. He wondered how long it would take for the men of the village to discuss the matter, reach a consensus, and decide to track the strange man who had shown up unannounced and invaded their privacy. With his eyes closed, his ears became attuned to the concert of sounds— insects buzzing, water trickling, birds chirping. Then he heard it—a faint sound that was out of place amid the persistent noises of the jungle. A swish of grass that didn't follow the rhythm of the breeze drifting through the stream bed.

Sariel rose to his feet and readied himself for the coming confrontation. Somewhere, out in the darkness, the Chatsiyr men were closing in to eliminate a threat. Even though he was expecting them, it was still quite startling to see the empty riverbed gently reflecting the last of the daylight, suddenly populated with dozens of silhouettes. Though they weren't hunters, they certainly would have been up to the challenge. They moved quietly for a group of herbivores.

More young men appeared in the grass along the opposite bank of the stream. And he knew that if he were to turn around, he'd see still more behind him. Casually crossing his arms, Sariel waited as the men moved closer, now only a hundred feet away.

They continued to close in, tightening the circle, holding their spears either in a two-handed grip or above the shoulder, ready to throw.

Just a little closer. There, that should work just fine.

Keeping his body in the Temporal Realm, Sariel began to *shift* his consciousness toward the Eternal, just enough to escape the limitation of the evening darkness. From this new vantage point, where the existence of all living beings could be seen as glowing orbs with tendrils stretching toward the Eternal, Sariel watched a simple melody expand from his lips and drift through the air, bursting into tiny points of light when it reached the Chatsiyr men. Though inaudible within the boundaries of the Temporal Realm, he could still watch the results as he *shifted* his consciousness back to where his body remained.

All of a sudden, birds dropped from the evening sky, diving for the insects that their senses told them were there.

The Chatsiyr men flinched, as the small, winged creatures apparently swooped to attack them. As the men moved closer to the pale stranger who stood confidently upon the river, the birds' movements became more aggressive. Finally, they stopped and began to back away.

Sariel smiled to himself as he watched them retreat. Surely they would be awestruck by the power of someone able to command the creatures of the sky. He'd shown them mystical influence with restraint. No one had been hurt. With any luck, the Chatsiyr elder would hear the incredible story from his subjects, and would see this stranger not as a threat, but as a potential ally.

One step closer to Sheyir.

5

The following morning, Sariel had more visitors. He knew the previous night's confrontation would have one of two outcomes. Either the men of the village would return in greater numbers, hoping to overwhelm him by force, or they would come peaceably, bringing their elder to make an alliance with the powerful stranger. Sariel hoped the latter was true and that his demonstration was sufficient to prevent any further attempts at violence. When he saw the small group of Chatsiyram traveling in the open, his hope increased.

They walked slowly beside the stream, understandably cautious. The youngest men with smooth faces walked in front. They carried *khafars* in their clenched fists. Older males followed closely behind, with close-cropped, bearded faces that shifted continually, looking for additional signs of danger. When they were within speaking distance, the group halted. The young men in front parted into two groups.

The elder, whose beard fell well past his chest, moved forward from the back of the group. His hair and beard were braided and adorned with long blades of grass that made a swishing sound as he moved. He was slightly shorter and thicker than the rest, but his movements were still agile. Stepping to the front of the small delegation, the elder stood with his arms relaxed at his sides. He carried no weapon and remained silent. His eyes scanned Sariel from head to toe, but his face betrayed no emotion.

"Welcome," Sariel greeted. "I have food. Will you join me for a meal?"

The elder's eyes narrowed slightly.

A meal was a clear peace offering in their culture, but it was usually prepared by the women. Sariel was alone, and clearly not a female.

"We will eat with you," the elder replied after a long silence.

Sariel nodded and turned, motioning for them to follow. He led them slowly toward his temporary dwelling where he had a small pile of fruit arranged on the ground, atop a bed of broad leaves. It represented a few hours of morning gathering.

The Chatsiyr males quickly gathered in a circle around the food and seated themselves on the ground. Without any formalities, each young man reached forward and took one piece. The man on the elder's right side grabbed two and handed one to the tribe's leader.

"You mean us no harm," the elder said, accepting the cone-shaped fruit. Then, without taking his gaze from Sariel, he expertly peeled the firm, red skin to reveal the edible flesh inside.

Sariel couldn't tell from the inflection whether this was a question or statement, but he thought it was a good place to start the conversation either way. "This is true," he replied.

"Why are you here?" the elder asked, then took a bite of his food.

"I have journeyed from far away. I came to help you and your people."

The elder stopped chewing and his eyebrows shot upward, then quickly plummeted. "Who sent you?"

"No one," Sariel admitted. "I am only traveling through your land. And if I am able, I will help anyone who has need."

"...because you have *dathrah*," the elder stated.

Sariel had heard this word only once before, but he remembered it well. Any wisdom or ability not common to the typical tribe member was seen as supernatural in origin, or *dathrah*. "Yes," he admitted.

"How did you learn this *dathrah*?"

Sariel thought for a moment. "It was given to me a very long time ago. But I see you have *dathrah*, as well." Having reached the first milestone of the conversation—getting the elder to recognize his powers—Sariel now wanted to move on to the next objective. "You can see what others cannot."

"Yes," the elder confirmed. His eyebrows lowered slowly while the rest of his face remained unmoving. "How do you know this?"

With his confrontational style of communication, the elder was making it difficult to steer the conversation. Though Sariel wanted his powers to be established in their minds, he didn't want them to dwell on it. Instead, he hoped to progress to an understanding of their needs and how he might help. If they invited him into their village, regardless of the terms, he would have a better chance of establishing a relationship with them and thereby gain access to regular contact with Sheyir.

"...because you came to me without a *khafar*. I can see that you care about the safety of your people. Tell me, are your people protected? What have you seen with your *dathrah*?"

The elder was silent for a moment.

Perhaps I've gone too fast. I should have waited before questioning his weaknesses.

"You will come to our village and we will talk more."

He blatantly avoided the question, but Sariel was pleased nonetheless. The invitation alone showed an extraordinary amount of progress in such a short time. Though tempted as he was to celebrate, he still had a long way to go. The elder hadn't yet introduced himself. When names were finally exchanged, then he would know that he had accomplished something significant with Sheyir's father. And that accomplishment would lead him to his ultimate goal.

* * * *

The steep, rocky terrain gave way to lush fields and forests again as Enoch moved eastward, still keeping the shoreline on his right side. In the silence of this solitary journey, it was the whispers of the Holy One that kept him going, fueling his tired body. But the sightings of large beasts roaming the land were becoming more frequent. They were a constant reminder that he was not alone or safe from danger.

Another eight days brought him to a second narrow stretch of land between two bodies of water, which he named Ne-Banyim. As he moved through this area and away from the water, the land rose again. Enoch's progress slowed considerably as he encountered hill after hill, and he found his energy sapped before the end of each day. Eating as much as he could find to maintain his strength, he continued pushing eastward. After nearly two weeks through this tiresome land he crested a hill and caught the first glimpse of the mountains from his dream. Katan Har-Marah they would be called from that day forward—the Lesser Mountains of My Vision. Having finally reached the land of Nowd, Enoch stopped early that day and rested to regain his strength. After spending the night atop the knoll with the mountains in the distance, he turned northeast and began the last leg of his journey with renewed vigor.

The grassy plains were gone now, replaced by dense forests which dotted the landscape. The mist rising from the ground was thicker here than in Sedekiyr, and seemed to prefer lodging itself in the trees. Moving carefully through the foreign terrain, Enoch turned gradually to the north. Using the memory of his vision, he kept the water always within sight to serve as a reference. After a week, the taller mountain of his dream loomed on the northeastern horizon.

"Gadol Har-Marah," he said aloud. The sound of his own voice after so many days of silence was almost startling. He stood for a moment, looking at the great uprising of land. Mist obscured the peak, making the mountain seem all the more ominous. And somewhere on the other side of it was the city of Khanok, home of the Kahyin tribe. As he stared into the distance, he lifted a piece of green fruit to his lips and took a bite. It was bitter, but it was something to fill his stomach.

The low screech of an animal brought him out of his thoughts and reminded him that he needed to keep moving. He began walking again and heard the same sound from a different direction this time.

Mating call?

When he heard a third call from yet another direction, his hand tightened around the walking stick he'd acquired only days after leaving Sedekiyr.

Hunting party!

Glancing around, he searched for shelter—a tree to climb, a ravine to cross. Unfortunately, he was surrounded by nothing but knee-high grasses and the occasional tall bush. The nearest trees were several minutes run from where he stood.

Where are they?

From what he'd seen in the last few weeks, predatory pack animals were usually larger than knee-high. So he was immediately suspicious of the surrounding bushes. To the north, the land dropped into a wide clearing free of bushes or any tall vegetation. He began to run without another thought.

Instantly, other screeches sounded from multiple directions behind him, clearly audible above the swish of the wet grasses slapping at his legs as he ran. He changed his grip on his walking stick and was now greatly relieved to have something that could be used as a weapon.

Descending the hill at a rapid pace, he reached the flat land within seconds and began hacking his way through the waist-high grass. Only a few strides away from the shallower vegetation, Enoch flinched when a creature, larger than himself, rose into view. Instinctively, he swung his walking stick.

The creature quickly dodged to the side and swung something in retaliation.

Enoch caught the blow on the side of his head and his vision went black.

When he regained consciousness, he was lying face-down in the grass, hands tied behind his back. His head throbbed with pain and he could feel something wet covering the side of his head and shoulders.

"Luh, Luh. Wu-selema el muhadis arushida," one of his attackers stated emphatically.

Enoch couldn't see anything but dirt and the thick roots of some grass stalks. His initial confusion was just beginning to dissipate as he considered the possibility that these animals were, in fact, human.

Someone spoke again in a language Enoch didn't understand and another man replied quickly with agitation in his voice, as if they were arguing. Something strong clamped his arm and pulled Enoch painfully to his feet. His shoulder threatened to rip from its socket and, for a moment, the pain in his head was forgotten. Enoch stifled a scream, trying his best to be compliant and somehow survive whatever was about to happen to him.

For the first time, Enoch now saw his attackers face to face—people of the Kahyin tribe. They were all nearly a full head taller than he, with skin much darker than his own. Their size and muscular forms were made more intimidating by the disturbing animal skins they wore. The empty skull and jagged teeth of some reptilian creature protected their heads and hung down in front of their faces. Across their shoulders and backs they wore thick, mottled hides, embedded with rows of spines. The rest of their bodies were naked, and they showed no hint of shame about it. In their hands they each carried a short wooden club with half of its length covered by the tail-skin of the same creature—tiny, dull spines that grew tighter and shorter until they ended at a bulbous, bludgeoning instrument. Judging by the way it swung from the men's grasp, it appeared to have the weight of stone.

Enoch presumed that he had already been on the receiving end of this weapon and would do anything to prevent it from happening again.

"Siyeruh," one of the men said, nodding his head to the north.

Looking into the man's eyes, which were almost black, Enoch understood exactly what to do, even though he didn't understand their language. With his hands fastened behind him, he began to carefully make his way through the grass.

One of the men ran ahead and Enoch paused to see what he was doing. This only provoked another man to jab his weapon into Enoch's back.

"Siyeruh," the man behind him repeated.

Enoch saw now that the man in front was leading the way, and picked up his pace to match him.

6

Sariel sat on one of the rocks arranged in a circle at the center of the Chatsiyr village. Across from him sat the elder and his brothers, the other senior members of the tribe. The pale orange of the setting sun carved out shadows among their stern faces, making them appear even less friendly than during their previous visit. As was customary, the women of the tribe waited on the men, bringing the evening meal wrapped in a thick, broad leaf, tied into a bundle with a long strand of grass.

How quickly things change!

Despite their earlier hostility, the hospitality of the Chatsiyram was lavish when one was invited by the elder. Earlier in the morning, from the moment Sariel entered the village, he was treated like a cherished object. The children ran up to him and began to touch the skin of his arms and legs, wondering at his paleness. He recognized some of them from their playtime at the nearby stream. The same boy, who had originally led him into the village, again took his hand and seemed content to just walk alongside. Sariel instantly took a liking to the child.

After the children were shooed away, the men casually led Sariel around their village, showing him how things were arranged. They enjoyed bragging to him about their building skills which were, indeed, impressive. Their living structures, set back from the central meeting area, were also made entirely from trees and grasses, but were more elaborate, with windows and multiple rooms. The men held back from discussing anything important, but Sariel knew that the time would eventually come.

After a few hours, he was then entrusted to the care of the women where he observed their food gathering responsibilities. Being herbivores, they foraged in the nearby forests, fields, and riverbanks for anything edible. Whatever they gathered, they brought back to the village to be prepared later in the evening.

Sariel sat now with the result of this work in his hands, given to him by one of the elder's other daughters. Normally, the wives and daughters would work together, with all the females attending to the needs of the patriarch of each immediate family. But with a guest among them, the responsibilities of the elder's daughters were conferred upon Sariel. It was a custom that should have excited him. But there was no sign of Sheyir. He'd felt distracted all day, constantly looking over his shoulder to catch a glimpse of her. Now, he was beginning to wonder if she had been locked away somewhere, punished for making contact with a stranger before the elder had allowed it.

Sariel looked methodically from face to face among the crowd that had gathered around them, searching while he waited for the men to initiate the meal.

The elder began to untie the bundle.

Sariel momentarily gave up looking to concentrate on the task at hand, mimicking the actions of the tribe leader. The dark green leaf slowly unwound to reveal a moist clump of vegetables that had been soaked in water, then mashed. Sprinkled over the top were small pieces of dried fruits and nuts.

The men dug their fingers into the paste and lifted it to their mouths.

Sariel watched, then followed their example. When the paste entered his mouth, his tongue exploded with various sensations he'd never experienced before. In the Eternal Realm, all things were sustained by the Spirit of the Holy One. But in the Temporal, other methods had to be devised for maintaining life—food was a necessity here. Sariel moved the sticky substance around in his mouth to experience it more fully, then swallowed it quickly. He wasn't sure if the tastes were pleasurable, but they were vivid.

Looking up, he realized that the seniors of the tribe were staring intently at him, presumably waiting for his approval or disapproval of their food. He smiled in return and dug his fingers into the clump for another bite.

Without warning, Sheyir stepped from behind him and held out a cup of liquid. Her long, black hair caught the last rays of the sun like the shimmering surface of a lake. Her smooth, young skin was earthen in color, with warm undertones. Like the rest of the females in the Chatsiyr tribe, her body was clothed in a sleeveless, knee-length covering, expertly woven from plant fibers.

Sariel felt his face flush. He quickly reached up and took the drink, moving it immediately to his lips to cover up the expression on his face that must have been obvious to everyone sitting around the circle. He closed his eyes briefly, trying to compose himself while the cold liquid slid down his throat. When he was finished, he handed the cup back to Sheyir and nodded with the same dismissive expression that he'd observed in every male and female interaction throughout the day. Then he proceeded to take another bite, trying very hard not to notice when Sheyir turned and left the group.

When the moment had passed, Sariel looked up.

The elder and the other men were just finishing their food. Their faces wore the same expressions. The movements of their bodies were unchanged. No one had seemed to notice.

The elder wiped the food from his mouth and beard with the back of his hand, then set down his leaf which had been scraped clean. He proceeded to clear his throat and then wait for the women to remove the remains of the meal. The women worked efficiently with the commonplace task and when the men were the only ones left around the ring of stones, the elder turned to Sariel. The sun was halfway below the horizon now and his face was nearly lost in the darkness, with only his eyes and the upper part of his face reflecting the orange light.

"You asked me what my *dathrah* has shown me."

Sariel leaned forward and nodded his head.

"I have seen that some things are within my control, and some things are not."

Sariel waited patiently for the man to make his point, which seemed like it would be a long time coming.

"I have seen *tehrah* that is beyond my strength. This is a danger to my people."

Evil? Sariel translated to himself.

Sheyir's father paused now, perhaps choosing his words carefully, or taking one last opportunity to assess the stranger. His expressionless face was difficult to read.

"The young men have seen your *dathrah*. If you do not mean us harm...if you speak truth when you say you have come to help, then I have a task for you."

I like where this is going. Sariel nodded again.

The elder continued. "At the end of these mountains, where they stretch toward the water, is a place called Arar Gahiy, the Valley of the Curse. In this valley is Armayim, the Lake of the Curse. In this place we can no longer walk; I have forbidden it. It is too dangerous for my people. In the morning, the young men will take you. They will not go into Arar Gahiy. You will go alone. You will see if your *dathrah* shows you what I have seen. Then you will return and tell me what you saw. You will tell me if your *dathrah* is strong enough to help my people."

Sariel waited for a moment to make sure that the elder was finished talking. After a brief silence, he responded. "Thank you for your trust. I will do as you ask and if there is a way to help your people, I will."

The elder neither smiled, nor frowned. Without breaking eye contact, he stood up, apparently satisfied with the conclusion of the discussion. The other senior tribe members rose with him and Sariel stood as well.

"You have been shown where you will sleep." the elder stated.

"Yes," Sariel replied, assuming it was a question. "But I will stay here for a while and think on the things you have told me."

This time, the elder nodded, then turned and walked into the darkness.

When the men were gone, Sariel sat down again and leaned forward, resting his elbows on his knees.

Valley of the Curse? I wonder what he means. ...an evil that is beyond my strength?

While he meditated on the discussion, a presence nearby interrupted his thoughts. Turning, he could barely make out the form of someone standing a short distance away.

"I did not tell them," she said softly.

Sheyir!

Her voice was like the song of water gliding over smooth stones in a creek. It was gentle, clear, and complex. "...about our first meeting?" he clarified.

"Yes," she replied simply.

"I must apologize to you. I didn't mean to frighten you. That is the last thing I want."

Sheyir's faint silhouette came a step closer. She remained quiet for a moment while her head turned from side to side. "You said you have come a long way to see me."

"Yes, that's correct."

"Men do not seek after women," she countered softly, almost in a whisper.

Sariel smiled. "Not among the Chatsiyram. But I am not from your tribe...and you already know that I am not a man."

His statement seemed to hang in the air for an eternity, without a response.

"Do you know what I am?" he asked finally.

"My people tell stories of the Baynor. They used to walk the earth, but not for many years."

Children of Light, he translated to himself, smiling at the confident way she presented her opinions, not unlike her father. "It is not far from the truth," he admitted. "And what do the rest of your people think I am?"

Sariel could almost feel a change in her demeanor. Though he couldn't see it, he imagined she was smiling. And in that tiny fraction of time, he promised himself that he would give his life to make her smile more often.

"They say that you are an elder without a tribe."

"This is also not far from the truth," he replied.

Sheyir's head lowered for a moment, then came up again. Slowly, her outline backed away until it melded with the darkness.

Sariel listened to the faint sound of her feet retreating, unhurriedly, across the soil. He smiled to himself as he looked up to the night sky, now beginning to sparkle with the appearance of the stars. It seemed that so much had transpired in such a short amount of time. But that was the way of things in the Temporal Realm. So far, he liked his new home.

* * * *

Through the mist, the ominous silhouette of Gadol Har-Marah darkened the northeastern horizon. As Enoch moved through the cold, wet grass, a shiver moved through his body. It wasn't the chill in the air that filled him with fear, but the oppressive aura of the dense forest that loomed overhead, blocking the sky.

With hands tied behind his back, he trudged onward, following the lead of his captors as he had for the last day and a half. No one had said more than a few words and Enoch knew better than to speak to them. Instead, he kept his head down, his feet moving, and his thoughts inclined toward the Holy One.

Then, just as he had settled into this routine, odd shapes began to emerge from the fog and the men began to speak amongst each other. As they drew near, Enoch realized that the conical structures dotting the landscape were dwellings. It was a village. The homes, perhaps a hundred in all, consisted of long, wooden poles leaned against one another and wrapped in the same reptile hide as the sparse clothing his captives wore. From the openings at their peaks, thin lines of smoke rose into the sky.

Almost immediately, the village inhabitants came out to greet the small procession. The women were naked except for necklaces of long, pointed teeth that radiated about their necks. Around their wrists and ankles, they wore an assortment of bones strung together with strips of hide. Their hair was long, black, and coarse, gathered into a single braid that ran down to the lower back.

Embarrassed by their immodesty, Enoch kept his eyes on the ground, wondering if the men would untie him now that they had arrived. Abruptly, something hard glanced off his leg. Enoch quickly looked up at the gathering crowd of women and noticed that most of them were holding rocks or sticks. As one of the men pushed him forward through the crowd, another rock hit him in the cheek and he flinched.

This show of fear was met with a growing chorus of vibrating screeches that cut through the air. The women appeared to be growing more agitated by the second. Then, the stones began to fly through the air. Enoch tucked his face toward his shoulder, but it was no use. He couldn't stop the rocks from pelting his skin. Between the small, sharp jabs cutting into his flesh, he also felt the heavier impact of the sticks against his arms and legs. Within seconds, the pain was unbearable.

He started to fall and felt a powerful grip on his arm suddenly lift him back to his feet and force him forward. With his eyes closed and his head turned, he struggled through a mass of tangled limbs until he bumped into something more solid.

A large man towered above the women. He stared hard into Enoch's eyes for a moment, then struck him in the face.

Enoch felt his legs go limp and he crashed to the ground. Dozens of other blows glanced off his extremities, feeling weak by comparison, until someone kicked his exposed ribs, making his body spasm in pain.

When the beating finally stopped, Enoch's feet were lifted off the ground. Too weak to resist, he simply opened his eyes and watched as the hunters proceeded to drag him. But the intense pain of his skin grinding across the rough soil brought him instantly out of his stupor. Fighting to sit up, he flopped from his side onto his back and tried to use his hands to push his body away from the jagged rocks that were tearing at his flesh.

Holy One, save me!

The men finally stopped in front of a larger dwelling encased in more colorful reptilian hides than those around it.

The hunters dropped his legs and Enoch rolled onto his side and rested his head on the bare earth. Breathing heavily and wincing at the pain, he feared what would happen next.

From inside the tent, the muffled sound of speaking could be heard. Moments later, a large flap of hide was pushed open and smoke billowed from the opening. One of the hunters came out, followed by an older man whose skin was painted white with ash. Circling his head was a crown of fanged teeth, stabbing upward toward the sky. When the older man spoke, his voice seemed rough and distant. The hunters replied quickly, perhaps answering his question.

Enoch struggled to make out anything intelligible from their speech, but their language was entirely foreign. He recognized one phrase that he also heard them speak after his capture, but he didn't know the meaning of it.

The leader of the hunting party knelt down and pulled on the cords that bound Enoch's hands. Laying a curved, sharpened bone against them, he severed the cords with a quick, violent movement.

Immediately, Enoch felt a rush of blood return to his fingers. He wondered briefly if the hunter had cut his skin, but when he pulled his hands in front of him and flexed his joints, he could see that the only wounds were the abrasions on his wrists and the cuts and scrapes on his palms from being dragged across the ground.

Before he could comprehend the sudden change in behavior of his captors, the hunter gently lifted him to his feet and led him toward a nearby stream.

Oh no; they're going to drown me!

The hunting party sat him in the shallow water of a small pool.

Immediately, Enoch closed his eyes. *Most Holy One of Heaven,* he prayed silently. *Let not Your servant perish at the hands of these ignorant people. Preserve my life so that I may continue to follow You. Cover me with the protection of Your hand.*

When he opened his eyes, several women had gathered around him.

What are they doing?

They began to softly scoop up the cool water and pour it on his skin. One of the women took his hands and submerged them, gently stroking his palms to clean away the blood.

"What are you doing to me?" he asked aloud. But no one answered. The women just quietly cleansed his body, while in the distance, the hunting party stood with their arms crossed.

7

With the sun rising over Bokhar—Morning Mountain, as it is called among the Chatsiyram—Sariel and three young men set out from the village and headed north along the river. Most of the people were already awake and had gathered along the banks to see them off, but Sheyir wasn't among them. Sariel followed the lead of the others who moved across a field and into another stand of trees, then turned abruptly to the west and into the river. As they stepped into the cool, shallow water and waded across to the western shore where passage would be easier, Sariel couldn't help but look back. To his relief, Sheyir was standing on the bank. The sun illuminated her from behind and she appeared as an ethereal being, as when Sariel had watched her from the Eternal Realm. He smiled and she smiled in return. It was a simple exchange, but enough to satisfy his need for some communication before their momentary parting. Hopefully, she understood that he was thinking about her, and would continue to do so until they saw each other again.

Turning around, Sariel set his mind to the task at hand and followed the young men through the water. For the next four days, they trekked downstream across rolling, grassy foothills. With few obstructions, they made quick progress through the valley that ran between Bokhar to the east, and Ehrevhar to the west. With the sun nearing the Evening Mountain on its descent, the men crossed back to the east side of the river at a wide ford and made their way into the foothills of Bokhar. As they ascended, the grassy lowlands gave way to thick tangles of trees which slowed their speed considerably. Just before sunset, they reached the summit of a rock outcropping that jutted from the dense vegetation and overlooked the valley to the north. From this vantage point, Sariel could see that the river turned slightly to the northeast and broke into dozens of streams until they rejoined at a large lake. The valley itself widened as it left the confines of the mountains.

"This is Arar Gahiy?" he asked his guides.

"Yes. Reeds grow tall near the water. Good for building roofs," one of the men answered. "We will sleep here tonight and you will go in the morning."

"Very well," Sariel replied, anxious to get started despite the growing anxiety with each step closer to this mysterious place.

After a fitful night's sleep, Sariel rose early and sat on the rocks overlooking the valley. He was still trying to get used to the human form he wore. He had never slept before coming to the Temporal Realm, but found that his body tired quickly in this habitation, so it was a necessity. So too was food, as his body grew hungry after only a short time without nourishment. He knew all these things, of course, before crossing over. But knowing and experiencing were very different.

When his companions woke, they handed him a small bag with some dried fruit.

Sariel understood this to mean that he was expected to leave, so he did. Making his way down the mountainside, he moved slowly through the forests until he reached the grassy foothills again, nibbling on some food to fight off the hunger. By midmorning, he reached the east side of Armayim, the Lake of the Curse. He could see what the young men meant about the reeds. Standing at twice his height, the thick green shoots were clustered densely in the shallows at the water's edge. He walked casually, regularly *shifting* his consciousness slightly toward the Eternal, giving himself the best opportunity to discover what inhabited this area and what might be out of place. He wasn't sure what he was supposed to be looking for; Sheyir's father didn't say why he considered the valley to be cursed. Sariel had questioned the younger men during their journey, but all he was able to ascertain was that this valley used to be a place where the young men came to gather building materials. The Chatsiyram knew something that they weren't sharing, and this was Sariel's test. If he really did possess *dathrah*, as they thought, then he should be able to tell them why the valley is cursed.

Shortly after mid-day, Sariel was moving around the northern end of the lake when he saw a flicker of shadow among the reeds. Moving cautiously toward the water's edge, he found a sandy shore that had been cleared of vegetation. It appeared that the reeds had been harvested from this side of the lake some time ago. Looking left and right along the shore, he found nothing. Then he noticed something sticking out of the water a few yards in.

Choosing his steps carefully, he waded out into the shallows. It didn't take long before he found something that he'd never seen before and it gave him a sickening feeling in his stomach. Just below the surface, human bones lay half-embedded in the sand. Their lifeless skulls looked eternally up at the sky through hollow eye sockets. The long, narrow bones of hands reached outward, as if pleading for someone to bring them back to life.

Sariel shivered. He had seen many deaths among the angelic races, but never a dead human. Though not immortal, their lifespan was still nearly a thousand years. In fact, the first humans were still alive to this day. He'd only heard of them dying by accident and had never seen it first-hand. Yet now he looked down on several and it broke his heart. Sariel slowly *shifted* his consciousness toward the Eternal and immediately, his body went rigid.

All around him, demons swarmed, screaming and wailing with mournful cries.

He backed up a few paces and stared in disbelief.

Their appendages were thin, their abdomens distended, and they flailed about as if in pain. Their coloring, which was normally blacker than the darkest night, looked sickly gray with blotches of white and pale green.

"Ikthier manom hatda!   Ikthier manom hatda!" they screamed in discordant unison.

Baffled by their use of the Kahyin language, and their presence in this realm, Sariel remained silent for a moment, watching them swarm over the human skeletons like flies over refuse.

"What are you doing here?" he demanded finally.

The demons shrank back in fear, but their initial reaction quickly changed. "We might ask you the same question," one retorted.

"Yes, what are you doing here, Child of Light?" another asked. "This is not your home."

Sariel ignored the questions. "You have been banned from this realm," he stated.

First one, then the rest began to laugh. It was a grotesque sound, like a wheezing bark.

Even without their cooperation, Sariel was gleaning useful information. He noted that the creatures' movements, though awkward by their perverted nature, also seemed confined to a certain location. As their spiderous forms crawled, then floated through the air with the look of dissipating smoke, each one moved through a space that roughly coincided with one of the human bodies. They passed through the air and even down into the water and earth beneath the bones, but never elsewhere.

Their starved appearance also suggested that the source of their strength was depleted. Sariel looked again to the dead humans lying beneath the water.

Impossible!

Long ago, the demons were prevented from existing in the same realm as humans. From that point forward, their only interaction with the Temporal came through manipulation of a being's spirit, which existed in a realm partially accessible to them. But no human would, or even could, consciously yield their bodily existence to a demon. Humans simply didn't have control over their own spirit in that way, and most weren't even aware of this part of themselves.

Pick them up! Pick them up!

The demons' words echoed in Sariel's mind as his gaze remained fixed on the bones. Just then, something in the sand caught the light of the midday sun. Sariel squinted at the reflection, then quickly pulled a short, thin reed out of the marsh by its roots. Snapping the stalk, he used the makeshift pole to reach toward the sand beneath the water.

"No. No!" the demons screamed. "Take it for yourself. You don't need a stick. Are you afraid? Is the Child of Light afraid of a shiny rock?" they mocked.

Probing in the sand, Sariel brought something golden to the surface. It shined like nothing else around it. He took one careful step forward and peered down into the water to see a small figurine fashioned from gold, in the form of a predatory land animal.

Humans don't yet know the art of working metal! Someone made it for them. Or showed them how to craft it for themselves. Which means—

Sariel's mind raced to conclusions which contradicted what he already knew to be true. As his mind struggled to comprehend what he was observing, he also noticed a braided thread that was strung through a hole in the top of the statue. Pushing his reed into the sand, he lifted the golden object by its thong and held it in the air, where it swung and rotated, catching the light of the sun.

Immediately, one of the demons rushed forward and tried to hold it, though its hands passed through it like mist through a forest.

"Take it," it said. "You can have it if you want. The humans don't need it anymore," it sneered.

Interesting.

Without touching the figurine, Sariel used the reed to fling the cursed object far out into the field, away from the lake.

Just as he suspected, one demon was forcefully dragged through the air, leaving traces of putrid green swirls in its wake. The figurine landed with a bounce among the tall grasses while the demon involuntarily mirrored the movement, jolting and tumbling as it went. When the figurine came to a stop, the demon tried to regain its bearings, shifting its gaze quickly around the new territory with an excited but disoriented look in its dark eyes.

Sariel spun around to face the others, who looked as though the pleasure of their secret was just stolen. "Who are you working with?"

The demons shrank back in fear, but remained silent.

"Who made these?" he demanded, assuming there were more figurines beneath the sand.

One small voice replied, almost a whisper. "We don't have to tell you anything."

Sariel locked eyes with the creature and scowled. "Of course you don't have to. You always have a choice. But I can affect your choices. Tell me what I want to know, or I will make your already pathetic existence even more painful."

The demons weren't moving anymore. Their sharpened claws were embedded in the sand; their silent forms crouched as if ready to attack.

"WHO ARE YOU WORKING WITH?"

Their faces slowly distorted; fanged mouths stretching into smiles of pleasure.

Sariel gritted his teeth. It seemed that while he had been fighting futile, but straightforward battles in the Eternal Realm, the war had spread to the Temporal. The questions racing through his mind, and the creatures facing him now, were confirmation of the fear that had been growing exponentially in his heart. This war was already far more complex than the Amatru was willing to admit.

Ending the existence of these horrid beings would have been as simple as *shifting* into their location along the spectrum and crushing their fragile bodies with his bare hands. But these demons represented something significant, even if he didn't yet know what it was. His days of acting before thinking were over.

Backing away, Sariel *shifted* his consciousness fully into the Temporal and watched the sickly bodies fade, replaced by the calming vision of the rippled water on the lake surface.

* * * *

Enoch wasn't sure what the elder had said to the hunters. But whatever it was, it made a big difference in how they treated him. After being hunted like an animal, tied, beaten, and stripped of his clothing, they now bathed him, dressed his wounds, and fed him. After several confusing days of this behavior, they painted his skin in white ash like the elder, with large swatches of red river clay around his neck and abdomen. Then, he and another group of men set out from the village and marched east toward the mountain. This time, his wrists weren't bound, and he wasn't poked and prodded like an animal. Instead, they showed him honor as if he were a special guest.

For more than a week, Enoch traveled with three men in front of him and three behind. They no longer wore the head coverings of their hunting dress, but a simple draping of reptile hide over their shoulders, which fell across their chests and backs. Amidst dense thickets and tall trees, they pushed through the rolling landscape, always climbing in elevation toward Gadol Har-Marah. On the eighth day, the land jutted upward at a sharp angle, signaling that they had reached the base of the mountain. Then, they began to climb, single-file, up a winding path worn into the packed soil. Sometimes it was necessary to climb on hands and feet over boulders and up large cracks in the side of the cliffs. By the time the path leveled out, the sun was already beginning its descent and Enoch was exhausted.

The men simply smiled, patted him on the back, and continued forward into the trees. Passage was easier now that the land was level. And when the forest overhead parted enough to see the sky, Enoch could make out a thin line of white water meandering down the sheer face of the mountain. From somewhere, the faint sound of rushing water could be heard.

"Where are we going?" he asked again.

"Hetha thud-eyuk. Hetha thud-eyuk," they repeated for the hundredth time, waving him forward.

Minutes later, the forest began to clear as they approached a small lake that butted up against a sheer rock face on the east side. Against the dark, gray stone was a white swath of water, cascading down from the heights above and falling into the lake. Though little could be heard above the rushing water, Enoch knew that all else was silent. This place was special; he could feel it.

One of the hunters spoke to him again and Enoch nodded his head and smiled, understanding nothing except that they wanted to keep moving. Then something caught his attention and he abruptly stopped walking. A short distance ahead, the southern shoreline of the lake sloped gently toward the water except for a large, flat area of rock which stood several feet above the waterline. At the center of this area, a thick, wooden pole rose from the ground, the diameter of a man's body. Whether it was a tree without limbs growing from the stone, or a pole planted by human hands, the ropes hanging from it revealed its purpose. The blood-stained rock beneath it and the shallow trench leading toward the water made his body go weak in the knees.

"Hetha thud-eyuk," they said, looking back at him.

Enoch couldn't believe his eyes, or prevent his head from swaying side to side. "No," he whispered.

"Nuhana heya dakribun honekha," one man said with a furrowed brow.

Without warning, Enoch was pushed from behind.

"NO!" he screamed, as he slipped on the loose soil and fell.

At once, several hands were on him, restraining his flailing arms, lifting him from the ground. They were incredibly strong, and Enoch could do nothing as they carried him to the pole and tied his wrists with the rope.

Once Enoch was fastened in place, the men backed away, frowning as if confused by Enoch's reaction.

Enoch hung from his wrists. His toes barely touched the ground, not enough to support the weight of his body. Everywhere he looked, he saw the dark brown stains of blood. On the pole. In the crevices of the rock beneath him. On the rope. Old blood, shed over the course of years. He knew now that he was to be a sacrifice to whatever spirit they hoped to appease. Out of instinct, perhaps out of spite, Enoch immediately closed his eyes.

Holy One of Heaven. Do not forsake Your servant, he pleaded. *You have always been with me, even when I was a child. You spoke to me and I listened. I have come into this strange land, among these strange people, at Your request. I wish only to be obedient to You. If it is Your will that I die in this way, then so be it. But how could You be honored with actions such as theirs?*

Enoch opened his eyes, expecting to see a weapon of some kind. Instead, the men just backed away toward the trees, their faces now without expression.

Certainly, they do not worship You, but some other thing? Certainly, You are not pleased with their actions? Their wickedness is proof of their ignorance. Does this not bring You to anger? Save me. Do not let me die at the hands of these lost people. They practice wickedness because they do not know You. Do not let them slay me, for they will have learned nothing but to continue in their wickedness.

A sharp screech cut through the air. Reverberating off the water and stone, it brought an end to Enoch's prayer and clouded his mind with fear. Like the calls of the hunting party when they took him captive, and the shrill cries of the women when he entered their village, this noise conveyed meaning. Something terrible was about to happen. But this sound was stronger, purer, clearer. And now he realized that the calls of the Kahyin people were only pale imitations of this sound. In his mind, he saw the hides on their backs, the spines protruding from beneath the skin. He could see the length of the teeth in the necklaces that the women wore around their necks. He could see the fanged skulls that the hunting party wore on their heads.

In the trees across the lake, something moved.

Enoch's imaginings were gone now as his eyes scanned the tree line, looking for a very real threat. Again, he caught a glimpse of something farther to the south.

It was moving.

Craning his neck to see past the arms that blocked his vision, Enoch looked behind him. The men were gone. But in their place were two large reptilian creatures, slightly larger than a man. They walked on four powerful legs and looked agile enough to leap the entire seventy feet between them. The scales of their hides were interrupted by pointed spines which ran in rows down their backs and tails.

Enoch suddenly couldn't breathe, choked by his own fear.

The creature on the right raised its long, narrow snout and sniffed the air. Two quick and loud inhalations.

"AHHHH!" Enoch screamed, louder than he'd ever screamed in his life.

The creatures began to stalk forward.

Enoch continued to scream.

Their putrid stench entered his nostrils, making him gag and cough repeatedly.

They were within reach now, circling slowly. The one on the left raised its angular head and opened a wickedly fanged mouth, letting out a wail that could have been heard all the way back to the Kahyin village.

With his body shaking, Enoch closed his eyes again.

Holy One. The time is now at hand. Do not leave me in my time of need, for I am about to endure the most difficult task of any that You have set before me. Stay with me, for I will also be with You soon.

The hot, humid breath of one creature could be felt on his legs.

Enoch kept his eyes shut and held his own breath, trying to keep down the bile that was rising in his throat.

All of a sudden, a barrage of noise ripped through the air, sounding like a mixture of a howl and a snarl.

In the resulting silence, Enoch opened his eyes.

On the shore was another creature. Thick, gray hair covered its entire body. Its long snout was curled up into a snarl, revealing sharp teeth. Its bright, golden eyes held an intensity that seemed to look right through Enoch's soul. Even crouching in an attack posture, this four-legged mammal was obviously much larger than the reptiles.

Holy One. Save me from these foul beasts!

With the interruption of their meal, the reptiles turned and moved away from each other. Spreading out, they cautiously approached the threat, hissing and clicking to each other as they moved forward.

Enoch glanced from the reptiles to the third creature, then back again, wondering which would end up tearing the flesh from his bones.

The gray-haired animal howled again and pounded its front paws on the ground, refusing to give ground to the reptiles.

In response, the reptiles exchanged a rapid series of clicking noises, then unexpectedly leaped in unison.

The mammal dodged quickly to the left and reared up to the nearest attacker. Their jaws just missed each other as the mammal sank its teeth into the neck of the reptile and spun, using its larger weight and the momentum of the attacker to throw the reptile toward the shore and into the path of the other.

The scaled beast on the left came to a sliding halt on the stone, its neck torn open. Blood poured from mangled flesh and spilled out, staining the bare rock. The remaining reptile floundered as it tried to step over, then around the body of its fallen partner.

The gray-haired beast raised its head and loosed another howl that shook the earth.

In the face of such power, the other creature backed away toward the shore, then burst into a run as soon as its claws touched soil.

In the ensuing silence, Enoch could hear the loud beating of his own heart.

Holy One. Save me!

Still facing the shoreline, the head of the mammal turned. As gore dripped from its chin, the animal stared into Enoch's eyes. Then, it slowly opened a mouth full of sharpened teeth, each as long as Enoch's hand.

"Olathe heya elhet?" The deep, guttural noise sounded like the language of the Kahyin, but like many people speaking at once.

Enoch stared in disbelief. "Holy One.   Save me," he whimpered aloud, now fighting back tears.

"Are you Shayeth?" the voice of the animal boomed.[3]

Enoch was speechless.

"Who are you?" the beast growled, perfectly enunciating the words in the Shayeth language.

Enoch opened his mouth. "H... How are you able—"

"WHO ARE YOU?" the animal interrupted.

"My name is Enoch," he answered quickly, pulling himself up by his wrists.

"You are different than the rest of these humans."

Enoch stared at the creature, unable to comprehend the thought of an animal speaking. He answered almost without thinking. "I am not from the same tribe as these people. They captured me and brought me here."

"NO!" the animal barked. It was now only a few of its long strides away from Enoch. "You misunderstand me. I can see that you carry the presence of another with you.

Enoch's heart, which had been beating rapidly to this point, seemed to slow. Immediately, he felt a rush of peace. The change in his composure must have been drastic, because the beast's piercing golden eyes widened.

"It is the presence of the Holy One."

The animal walked closer. Even on all fours, its back stood taller that Enoch's head. It circled once, sniffing as it went. When it came back around, it turned directly toward Enoch and looked him in the eyes. "What are you doing here?"

Enoch thought he'd already explained that. Then he realized what the animal was really asking. "I was shown a vision by the Holy One. And now I'm trying to deliver a message from Him."

"What is your message and whom is it for?" it asked, surprisingly quiet.

Enoch took a slow breath and adjusted his wrists. "It is for the Wandering Stars of Heaven. The ones who shape creation."

The animal took a step back and its gaze drifted to the ground beside it. When it looked up again, its golden eyes seemed to glisten. "Go on," it said quietly.

Enoch cleared his throat. "He told me that they have broken His heart. 'You have abandoned your home and have brought great wickedness upon the earth,' He told me. He showed me what they've done and I saw His tears of sorrow fill the earth. He wants them to repent of their disobedience and return to Him."

The animal now stared out across the lake. Its eyes narrowed.

"Please. Let me go. I must find them and deliver my message."

Beneath the terrible face before him, something intangible shifted. It was more than an emotion, something deeper. And for a long moment the beast remained silent, hopefully considering Enoch's plea. Finally it looked back to Enoch, opened its mouth, and leaned forward.

Enoch recoiled in fear.

The massive teeth plunged deep into the wood of the pole, severing clean the ropes that bound his wrists.

Immediately, Enoch slumped to the stone below, too scared to support his own weight. For a moment, he simply leaned against the wood and massaged his wrists, unable to look up into the terrifying gaze of the creature.

"Come with me, Prophet," a deep, gentle voice spoke.

Enoch looked up slowly.

"There is someone you need to meet," it added. "Get up."

Enoch obediently pushed himself up to standing, ignoring his body's protests.

The animal crouched low. "Climb on my back."

Enoch stood motionless, afraid to touch the animal.

"Hurry up. We don't have much time," it warned. "Grab my fur and climb up."

Gently, Enoch gripped fistfuls of the coarse, gray hair and pulled himself up. Once atop the massive beast, he could feel its heat and strength. His legs were nearly lost in the depth of its fur.

"Lean forward and hold on tight," it said.

Enoch barely managed to follow the orders before the animal leaped into action, bounding into the trees with only a few strides of its powerful legs.

8

"Go on ahead," Sariel called. "I'll catch up."

After reconnecting with his escorts, he was now only a few hours away from the Chatsiyr village. His traveling companions had stopped walking, their foreheads furrowed.

"I need to arrange my thoughts before meeting with the elder," he explained.

The men exchanged glances among themselves, then turned and continued walking south without any discussion.

When they were out of sight, Sariel looked up into the foothills of Ehrevhar and waited. After a few minutes, an immense, winged figure came out from the foliage and walked down the slope. He was comparable in size to Sariel's angelic form, but his mottled coloring was comprised of browns, reds, and tans. Like most Iryllurym, his chestnut colored hair was finger-length, and swept back from his face. But it was his large, golden eyes that Sariel would always remember. For many years, they were the eyes of the only friend he had. But in recent times, they'd gone separate ways and lost contact with each other.

Moving upslope into the waist-deep grass, Sariel approached the soldier and looked up. "Welcome," he said as soon as they met.

Stepping sideways until he was downslope, the angel still towered over Sariel's human form.

"I thought that was you. What are you doing here?" Tarsaeel asked calmly.

"I should ask you the same. How did you find me?" Sariel countered.

Tarsaeel's lowered eyebrows revealed concern, which only made Sariel more alarmed.

"I was notified when you didn't report back," the angel replied. "I checked with Batna, but they didn't find your body on the battlefield. I knew you'd die before being taken prisoner, so I figured—"

Sariel nodded.

"What are you doing here Sariel?"

"...trying to help."

"No. What you're doing is forbidden."

"Is it?" Sariel asked. "How is this different from the early days? These people still need our help."

Tarsaeel dropped his head. "The difference is that it was necessary then. Now you're operating in disobedience."

Sariel breathed heavily without letting his gaze leave the eyes of his former friend. "I'm not going back. There is too much to do. And here...I'm actually making a difference."

Tarsaeel exhaled. "Look. Everyone knows it was a mistake to put your unit in that battle."

Sariel squinted. "Everyone except my commanding officers, you mean."

"They just needed bodies," Tarsaeel offered. "We knew you'd be outnumbered."

"That's exactly my point," Sariel replied, louder than he intended. When he spoke again, he lowered his voice. "Something's wrong. I can't explain it. But something is wrong with the execution of our mission. And with your responsibilities, you can probably see it better than anyone. Our leadership is going down the wrong path."

"Are you suggesting that we become like the enemy? That we fight like them? Deceit? Treachery?"

"No," Sariel replied. "Perhaps. I don't know," he said finally with a wave of his hand. "It just seems like the enemy is willing to go to greater lengths to win. Meanwhile, we have to play by all the rules. Any they just keep reinventing the conflict. How can we win against that?"

Tarsaeel's jaw clinched and his face went rigid. "We can win because we're on the right side! Or some of us are."

Sariel immediately forgave the insult. He understood the soldier's anger. He would have said the same thing just a few years ago. "Look," he said putting his hand up in a gesture of submission. "I haven't abandoned the cause. I'm just putting my efforts to better use."

Tarsaeel slowly shook his head from side to side. "You deceive yourself. Omynd is over. This realm is self-sufficient. And your emotions are swayed by lust."

It took Sariel a moment to realize that the angel spoke of Sheyir. "Lust? Is that what you think it is?"

"How could it be anything else?" Tarsaeel said dismissively. "We are not human. They are the ones who must mate in order for their species to survive. But we are not like them."

"To hear you reduce it to such a base level tells me that you really never understood what we were doing," Sariel said. Now he was the one who was disappointed. "It's called love. And obviously, you've never experienced it. But, as unfortunate as that is, it doesn't matter anyway because she has nothing to do with this. The real issue is that, while there's a war going on and we're busy killing each other in that realm, there are casualties in this realm. People are suffering here. Creation is changing here and people are dying. But we don't get to see the result of our actions. We're prevented from seeing how our ineffective strategy is actually failing."

"She has everything to do with this," Tarsaeel said quietly, suddenly changing the tone of the argument. "You have no idea what you're getting yourself into."

These last words caused a surge of apprehension in Sariel's heart. Rarely had Tarsaeel ever spoken with such a melancholy warning. Holding the rank of Sau-Rada in the Viytur, the Intelligence arm of the Amatru, Tarsaeel had access to information that few were authorized to know.

"What do you mean?" Sariel asked, now very concerned.

"You'll know soon enough. Anyway..." he said dismissively. "...I'm not at liberty to discuss such things with you. I came to warn you of a coming conflict."

Sariel ran his fingers through his hair. His mind was still reeling from the enigmatic words about Sheyir, but it was clear that he wouldn't get any more information.

"...a conflict? Here?" Sariel asked.

"Yes. You're not the only one to have crossed over. Have you heard of Semjaza?"

"No."

Tarsaeel continued. "He's a Pri-Rada of a joint operations group, or he used be. He crossed over years ago with three divisions of Anduarym, Iryllurym, and Vidirym. He's already set up his own earthly kingdom and has quite a strong position."[8]

Sariel opened his mouth, then shut it again and looked to the sky in frustration. "This is what I'm talking about. So we didn't do anything about it when he crossed over. But now that he's established himself, we're trying to plan something?"

Tarsaeel shrugged. "You know as well as I do that there just aren't enough resources to address every problem."

"Yeah," Sariel replied, not bothering to hide the anger in his voice.

"Look at it this way," Tarsaeel continued, leaning forward to tower over Sariel's shorter, human form. "That very same lack of resources is precisely why the Amatru hasn't invaded this place and dragged you back to the Eternal realm."

"Why are you telling me this anyway?"

"Because your Pri-Rada is coordinating with a mission to pay him a visit. I expect it'll be bloody, and I'd hate for you to be mistaken for one of them."

"I didn't think that mattered to you anymore," Sariel replied, turning to look out across the valley to Bokhar.

"You're not the only one here," Tarsaeel said flatly. "Are you sure you still want to make it your home? It's not too late to come back."

Sariel looked up into Tarsaeel's eyes. In that instant, he saw the uncountable number of wars they'd faced together. He saw the faces of his fellow soldiers dying in agony. He saw the beauty of creation reduced to a wasteland. Then he saw Sheyir; her vulnerability. Who would protect her? Who would love her? Who else was even capable of knowing her?

"I'm sorry, I truly am. But I can't go back."

Tarsaeel's eyes closed slowly. "Be safe," he said simply, when they opened again.

In his voice, Sariel could hear something that he hadn't heard in ages—the farewell of someone who didn't expect him to survive what he was about to face. As Tarsaeel turned and walked up the hill, disappearing into the trees, his warning echoed in Sariel's ears.

You have no idea what you're getting yourself into.

Deep in his spirit, Sariel was inclined to agree. But that had never stopped him before. And the thought of leaving Sheyir was unbearable. So, he watched his former friend go and wondered if it was the last time they'd see each other.

* * * *

What had taken Enoch most of the day to climb, the animal on which he rode descended by the time the sun had set. With the orange light now behind the horizon, the sky began to darken quickly. Running effortlessly, the beast moved west, then north along the base of Gadol Har-Marah.

Enoch's legs were cramped from trying to hold tight to the animal's abdomen. And the passing night air against his naked skin chilled him to the bone. Tucking down into the thick fur, he sought the warmth of the animal's body as he watched the terrain slip past at unbelievable speeds. Within an hour the creature began to slow, then stopped altogether.

Enoch sat up to take note of his surroundings. The air was clear of the usual mist and the stars seemed bright overhead. To the west, moonlight glittered on the surface of a large body of water. To the southeast, a pale orange glow illuminated the base of Gadol Har-Marah.

"What is that?" Enoch whispered, mostly to himself.

"The inhabitants call it Khelrusa. I believe your people call it Khanok," the beast answered.

"I've never seen it before."

"And you won't tonight," it replied. "We're going this way."

Enoch looked down and realized that the animal was standing in the middle of a wide path of bare soil, which cut across the grasslands. The path ran toward Khanok in one direction and toward the water in the other direction.

"Hold on," the beast cautioned. "I'll be moving faster now."

Faster? I thought we were already moving faster.

The animal lunged into motion and Enoch ducked down, gripping the fur with all the strength left in his hands. A short while later, a mountain range of jagged rock rose from the horizon. Seeming out of place among the grass-covered flatlands, Enoch marveled at its unusual appearance. Gradually, the path began to climb into the mountains, but the beast maintained his extraordinary pace, never showing any signs of tiring.

Holding tight for safety and warmth, Enoch watched the crude stone pass by, its irregular silhouette looking menacing against the night sky.

After rounding numerous corners and changing directions multiple times, the beast slowed to a trot, then a walk. "It's time to use your legs again," it said, finally stopping.

As it crouched, Enoch slid over the side of its back and collapsed as soon as his feet touched the ground. His legs were numb from the ride. As he sat in the rough dirt, massaging his useless limbs, stars began to swim at the edge of his vision. He quickly rubbed his eyes, then realized that the light wasn't an apparition. All around him, the air was filled with tiny sparks of light, drifting outward from the glowing body of the creature who towered above him. Its form seemed to dissolve slowly as more pieces of light ventured into the air.

Enoch slid backward, terrified and excited by its beauty at the same time.

Without warning, the points of light reversed their direction and rapidly converged on the creature who seemed much taller than before.

Enoch covered his eyes and braced himself, expecting something horrible to happen. When nothing did, he slowly dropped his hands from his eyes.

Where the animal stood only a moment before, there was now a magnificent creature that looked much more familiar. In form, it seemed human. But Enoch knew this to be impossible for it stood at twice his height. Even in the darkness, he could see its beauty and gracefulness.

"What are you?" he asked.

"A Wandering Star of Heaven," he replied. "One of the Myndarym—the ones who *shape* creation."

Enoch put a hand to his mouth as he realized he'd already delivered his message to one of the intended recipients.

"We have farther to go, but you'll need to travel on foot," he said, turning to walk up the path.

Enoch quickly rose to his feet and ran to catch up, which proved difficult with the angel's long strides. He followed at a short distance, now feeling more awkward than he did sitting on the back of an animal. They continued in silence for a while, until Enoch worked up enough courage to ask a question.

"What is your name?" His voice seemed to violate some unspoken law of silence in this eerie place.

"Ananel," the angel replied without turning.

Moments later, they rounded a gentle bend and Enoch found himself facing yet another extraordinary sight. The path widened greatly, running straight into a sheer wall of stone that stood a hundred feet tall and many times as wide. At each end, where the vertical surface met with the jagged protrusions of the mountain sides, the stone rose to a point. Like two spines from the back of those horrid reptiles, these structures looked just as deadly. Each had three faces, like an angular version of the Kahyin dwelling.

"How could such a thing be crafted from stone?" he marveled.

Ananel quickly looked back with a smirk on his face, then continued walking toward the center of the path where it led through an open section of the wall.

On either side of the path, two more angels stood with arms crossed at their chests. They were easily three heads taller than Ananel, and their build was wider and more muscular. They each wore a simple loincloth that fell to the mid-thigh, but were otherwise naked. Even beneath the night sky, Enoch could tell that their skin and hair were darker. Their eyes, possibly black, remained fixed toward the distance behind him. And Enoch was grateful, for his body was already shaking and he dared not think about what would happen if they looked directly at him.

As Ananel neared, the gaze of the taller angels turned toward him.

He simply nodded in acknowledgement.

"Menn eru inte leyft i a stad," one of the guards bellowed. Though loud and commanding, his voice sounded more human than Ananel's.

Ananel replied in the same language and both the guards suddenly looked down at the human intruder.

Enoch felt his legs go limp and he had to avert his eyes to keep from falling over. From the corner of his vision, he saw the angels nod. Ananel stepped forward and Enoch followed, keeping his eyes on the ground. As he passed by the guards, he could almost feel heat coming from their eyes.

With the wall towering overhead, casting a shadow in the moonlight, Enoch followed his angelic escort through the passage until it widened at the crest of a hill. Feeling confident enough to lift his head once more, Enoch looked out over miles of water encircled by jagged mountains that appeared as the teeth of a ravenous animal. If the mountains were its gaping, deadly jaw threatening to rend the sky, the water was its endless throat ready to swallow it.

"The Kahyin call it Mudena Del-Edha, City of the Gods," Ananel said, anticipating Enoch's question.

Enoch just nodded, struggling to grasp the vastness of what his eyes were witnessing. Without being told, he knew that this place had been constructed, but he couldn't comprehend how such a thing was possible. Around the inside of the mountains, where they descended into the water, a wide road circled the valley and disappeared into the mist clinging to the shoreline. As his eyes followed the route that they were obviously taking, his vision settled upon something which exceeded anything else he'd yet witnessed. Rising from the mist and water on the south end of the valley was a tower, shaped like those flanking the entrance they'd just come through. Only this one was so wide and tall that Enoch couldn't really tell how far away it was. His eyes made him believe that it rose even above the surrounding mountains, but the thought seemed impossible.

"...and that?" he asked the Ananel.

"Aryun Del-Edha. Eyes of the Gods."

Enoch was silent for a moment, lost in the grandeur of the peak that seemed impossibly high.

"Let's go," Ananel said, interrupting the moment.

For the better part of an hour, the two walked along the road which traversed the base of the southern mountains. The wide lake was still and menacing. Above its dark surface, a gray mist floated, with tiny swirls developing where it met the water. Minutes passed while they grew closer and closer to the tower. With each step, its height seemed more dramatic; less real. Finally, they reached a narrow peninsula of stone that extended out into the water, connecting the tower to the southern shore.

As Enoch followed Ananel across the land bridge, he noted three lesser towers protruding from the water to the north, east, and west. Each bore the same look, with three steep faces that eventually converged at a peak. Enoch thought about the simple habitations of his tribe, made of wood, thatch, and animal skins. These massive structures were something entirely different.

The path on which they walked ran straight toward the southern face of the tower, into which was carved a gigantic doorway of the same triangular shape. The path also diverged at this point and appeared to encircle the base of the tower, but

Enoch's attention was drawn to the guards posted at either side of the doorway.

This time, the menacing angels remained silent and still.

Ananel walked past them without slowing and Enoch followed as closely as he could, trying his best to look like he belonged in this foreign place.

The inside of the tower was just as grand as its exterior. As he looked across the cavernous interior and to the ceiling far above, Enoch thought that he might be able to fit the entire Shayeth village into the first level. Fires burned in small bowls carved into the walls, casting a flickering yellow light throughout. As he followed, he watched Ananel's shadow slide across the stone and land on numerous surfaces and details graven into the rock.

At the center of the room, a wedge-shaped wall rose from the floor to the ceiling. Ananel circled it and Enoch hung back, afraid of what he might see. To his astonishment, the floor on the other side seemed to rise in a series of platforms that extended toward a triangular-shaped doorway in the ceiling. Just as confusion began to set in, Ananel stepped onto the first platform.

"Don't be afraid," he said. Then he turned and began to climb the stairs.

Enoch couldn't help but be afraid. He'd never seen anything like it in all his years.

Holy One, go before me as I tread upon the path of the unknown!

Ananel disappeared through the doorway at the top.

Enoch took a deep breath, then climbed quickly to catch up. At the top of the stairs, he could see that the doorway was actually a tunnel twice his own height, which cut through the ceiling of the first level, and in turn, became the floor of the second chamber. Sound moved differently through this level as the ceiling was nowhere to be found. It might as well have been open to the sky above. This chamber was more brightly lit than the previous one, and slightly smaller. The walls and floor were constructed of a stone that Enoch had never seen. They were almost transparent, like water, but with veins of different colors running throughout. All of this, Enoch noticed in an instant. For an instant was all the time he had before a deafening noise attacked him from behind, shattering the silence and bringing an end to all thought.

"VAD AR A UTTRYKK AV DETTA VALDSHU?"

Enoch grabbed his ears and fell to the stone stairs. Already, his head was pounding in the aftermath of the noise. But through his tightly held grip, the muffled sound of Ananel's voice could still be heard.

"The outrage is that your supposedly careful plans have failed."

Enoch uncovered his ears carefully and looked up to Ananel who had reached the top of the stairs and was facing the other direction.

"Hvorfor gera du tala i a tunga av a Shayetham?" the voice replied, quieter this time.

Enoch instantly recognized the name of his tribe.

Ananel looked down to him. "Get up and turn around."

Enoch turned his head as he slowly rose to his feet and climbed the last few steps. At the far end of the chamber, the floor was elevated by another flight of steps. At the top, a massive figure sat upon a throne carved from stone darker than the night sky. Its surface was covered in facets, each reflecting the fire light so that it gleamed with a dark radiance. The angel who sat upon the throne looked similar to the guards, but larger, with skin that held a reddish hue beneath its earthen tone. His black hair fell almost to his shoulders. His eyes burned with the color of the embers from a fire. And like the guards, he wore nothing except a loincloth of pure white, smoother than any clothing Enoch had ever seen.

As if the sight of this angel weren't intimidating enough, he was flanked by four others.

Standing before the left side of the throne were two winged angels who appeared similar in height to Ananel. Each had two massive wings sprouting from his upper back, and two smaller wings below that. The one whose skin was darkest had sleek, black feathers and piercing, red eyes. The other had a mottled brown appearance, with softer looking feathers.

Seated on the steps to the right side of the throne, were two wingless angels of brown and gray tones. Their elongated facial features reminded Enoch of Ananel's animal form.[22]

"This is Enoch, a prophet of the Shayetham. I met him yesterday on the southern slopes of Murakszhug. One of the smaller Kahyin tribes was trying to offer him as a sacrifice to the Akila Lena Lahaema. You can see as well as I that he is different from any other human. And when I asked him what he was doing so far away from his people, he told me he had been given a message from the Holy One—a message to the Wandering Stars of Heaven!"

The angel upon the throne suddenly leaned forward.

"...the ones who *shaped* creation," Ananel clarified. "Isn't that right, Enoch?"

Enoch nodded, then looked to the angel on the throne. He couldn't be sure, for he was not yet familiar with these beings, but he felt some tension between Ananel and the one on the throne.

The large angel slowly turned his fierce eyes from Ananel to Enoch. "Come here, little one."

Enoch obeyed immediately, but slowed his pace as he neared the steps.

"What is this message?"

Enoch swallowed. His throat now seemed too tight to allow the passage of air. But he tried to ignore it. This was the moment he'd been meditating on since he left Sedekiyr. All those weeks of reflecting on the vision he had been given, had eventually turned into words in his mind. Words that he knew, without a doubt, had been placed there by the Holy One. He also knew that this message was currently keeping him alive in city that seemed to be forbidden to humans. And he feared that when it was delivered, he'd no longer be needed. But stronger than any of these realizations was the knowledge that his duty was to obey the voice of the Holy One, so he continued.

"The Holy One gave me a vision of what you have done, what you are doing, and what the result will be if you continue on this path." The words coming out of Enoch's mouth were filled with conviction, though he was inwardly paralyzed by fear. "I saw the stars, the angels of heaven, descend to the earth and transform it to keep it from dying by the poison of the Dark Ones. When their work was finished not all of them returned to their home. Some stayed behind and inhabited the earth. They were no longer doing the work of the Holy One, but they continued to shape creation as they saw fit. They were deceived by their own pride. They took wives from among the children of men and from the creatures of the earth. To these were born abominations that filled the earth with evil—"

"What is he talking about?" Ananel, whose eyes had been fixed on Enoch, glared at the angel upon the throne.

The other simply held up his hand in protest. "Continue," he said to Enoch.

"Then I felt His heart breaking. I saw His tears of sorrow fill the whole earth. And everything was destroyed. Everything. If you continue in your wickedness, none of us will survive!"

When Enoch was finished, his words seem to hang in the air. Silence filled the stone chamber for what seemed an eternity.

Finally, Ananel broke the silence. "You set us up. You used us, then you betrayed us!"

"I did nothing of the sort," the other replied calmly.

Ananel cocked his head slightly. "He spoke nothing of you or your soldiers. ONLY THE MYNDARYM!"

The other remained silent, while those near the throne turned to face Ananel, obviously positioning themselves to protect their superior. The tension in the room was increasing and Enoch wished that he could leave, now that his message had been delivered.

"...taking wives?"

"That's none of your concern," the other angel replied.

"It's absolutely my concern!" Ananel shot back. "Since you couldn't do it without our help. This was not the plan we agreed on. Who is helping you?"

Suddenly, all of the angels looked up as if they'd heard something.

Enoch followed their gaze and saw a winged angel silently descending through the open air of the tower above. It came from the shadows, the firelight barely illuminating its massive wings until it was almost on top of them. Enoch cowered in fear.

The angel landed quickly and gently upon the floor of the throne room, while the fires moved erratically and threatened to blow out from the sudden rush of wind. Instantly, the dark angel faced the throne and knelt, pulling his wings around himself like a cloak.

As he and the one upon the throne began to exchange words, Enoch whispered to Ananel. "What's happening?"

Ananel inclined his head without taking his gaze from the one on the throne. "A Speaker of the armies of Heaven is at the gate, seeking council with Semjaza."

Semjaza looked past the winged angel. "You see, Ananel. It is not just the Myndarym. In fact, He sent only a prophet to you, while he sent an army for me."

"Vad skal ag ger, minn Rada?" the winged messenger asked.

Semjaza looked slowly from the messenger to Ananel, then to Enoch and back before answering.

"Ja, Rada min," the angel replied. Then he rose, unfurled his massive wings, and leaped into the air. As his wings thrust downward, several of the fires set into the walls blew out. In an instant, the angel disappeared into the shadows above the chamber.

"What's happening?" Enoch asked again.

Ananel kept his eyes on Semjaza and only held up a finger to Enoch, indicating that he should wait.

"Little one," Semjaza said. "Since you claim to know the voice of the Holy One, and have shown faithfulness in delivering His message, you will now deliver a message for me."

Enoch looked quickly to Ananel, whose face was now unreadable.

"Go to the Speaker at the gate. Tell him that I repent of my disobedience. I will need time to meditate upon my actions, but I will take council at the break of daylight. Then I will be ready to accept whatever terms he is offering. Do you understand all of this?"

Enoch nodded.

"Good. Ananel will escort you to the gate."

Ananel's face still showed no emotion as he descended the steps through the doorway in the floor.

Enoch looked once more at the angel upon the throne and his guards, then hurried to catch up to Ananel.

Once outside, Ananel's pace quickened and Enoch was running again to keep up.

"Who is this Speaker?"

Ananel stopped and turned around. Kneeling, he looked straight into Enoch's eyes. "Prophet, you're going to have to do this on your own."

"Wh— You're not going with me?"

"No. I'm afraid not. I have more pressing matters. Just follow the road the way we came in. When you get to the gate, announce yourself as the prophet who speaks for Semjaza. They'll be expecting you."

Before Enoch could reply, Ananel's form began to dissolve into a multitude of embers, drifting into the air. When they converged, they took the shimmering form of a four-legged animal. Then the radiance subsided and a massive wolf stood in its place. "Good luck," it growled, then burst into a run along the land bridge, moving faster than at any time during the previous hours.

When Ananel was gone, Enoch looked up to the sky.

What have I gotten myself into? Holy One of Heaven, I am beyond my capacity to understand what You've laid before me. Give me Your wisdom and Your strength to discern what is right. Give me the words to speak, for fear holds my tongue captive.

With a deep breath, Enoch put one foot in front of the other and began to make his way back in the direction he'd come.

9

When Sariel crossed the shallow stream, dozens of the Chatsiyram were gathered on the shore. His leaving to investigate the cursed valley was an unusual event in the life of the tribe, and now they waited eagerly to hear what he'd found. Unfortunately, Sariel didn't have good news to report. In fact, between what he found at the lake and his conversation with Tarsaeel, he was deeply troubled about the way events were unfolding. He must have worn this concern on his face, because when he caught Sheyir's beautiful gaze, the smile drained from her face.

Once across the knee-deep pool, Sariel headed straight for Sheyir's father who stood in the shade of a nearby tree.

The elder looked Sariel up and down, then leaned from side to side, inspecting him. Apparently satisfied, he raised his eyebrows, but remained silent.

"We have much to talk about," Sariel said.

The man nodded. "We will go to the place of meeting and talk about what you found." Without another word, the elder turned and began to walk toward the village.

Sariel followed in silence, trying to avoid the stares of the other tribe members.

The *place of meeting* turned out to be one of the large hut structures located near the center of the village. Without walls, its columns of thick tree trunks supported a massive thatched roof which could easily shelter one hundred people from the heat of the day. On this day however, it seemed that every man, woman, and child in the village was present and there wasn't enough room for everyone.

At the center of this crowd, Sariel sat on the ground, across from Sheyir's father and the other senior members of the tribe. Looking at the eager faces of the men around him and the women behind, Sariel was reluctant to start. "Is there somewhere more private that we can talk?"

The elder looked around and his eyes grew stern. "I have no secrets from my people."

This seemed to contradict their previous meetings where only the men participated. Sariel had apparently misjudged the tribe's custom on the matter.

In the absence of discussion, the elder tried to initiate something. "You were taken to the valley and you stayed until the evening."

"That's correct," Sariel replied. "How long have you known about the curse?"

The elder's eyes went wide and he glanced quickly to the men sitting on either side of him. "Two years," he answered with a scowl.

"And how did you know that the valley was cursed? Did you see it with your *dathrah*?"

The elder leaned forward. "No. I sent a gathering party to take reeds from the lake. Only three men came back. They told me that the others had killed each other, or killed themselves. They looked sick. I didn't want their sickness to spread to the rest of my people. I put them away."

"Put them away?" Sariel asked. "What does that mean? Are they still alive?"

"...only one. He is very sick. We keep him outside of the village. No one is allowed to go near him, except for the one who brings him food."

"Can I see him?" Sariel asked quickly.

"I want to know what you found in Arar Gahiy," the elder stated, getting straight to the point.

Sariel sighed. "I found those who cursed your people. But I need to speak with the man to understand how they were cursed and how to keep their sickness from spreading to others."

"The sickness will not spread," the elder assured with a wave of his hand.

"How do you know that it won't unless you understand what the curse is?"

The elder thought for a moment. "Very well. The one who feeds him will take you. Then you will tell me what you found."

Sariel nodded in agreement.

*   *   *   *

It was now well into the middle of the night and Enoch was thoroughly exhausted. The weeks of walking, dodging danger, foraging for food, and troubled sleep had worn down his courage and sapped his strength. He'd delivered his message, perhaps narrowly escaping death, only to be drawn further into this strange and complex culture where he always seemed out of place. Each day, each hour, presented some new challenge. And now, as he neared the gate that marked the boundary of Semjaza's city, he wondered if the Speaker would consider him just a messenger or part of Semjaza's rebellion.

The passage through the wall was darker than before, as the moon sat lower in the sky. With a sense of foreboding, Enoch approached the entrance, knowing that the guards were somewhere near. But toward the end, his fears seemed to dissipate, replaced by a sense of calm. By the time he exited the gate, he realized why.

Standing boldly at the center of the clearing before the gate, was another angel. Instead of the darker features that he'd seen from the others, this one had radiant, amber skin and white hair, with burning golden eyes. It wore a covering of pure white cloth that fell to its feet, with a wide belt slung across its chest, made of an unknown material that seemed to glow with bands of gold and amber. Enoch couldn't tell whether it was male or female. And though it was similar to Ananel, Enoch immediately sensed something different about this one.

"Du eru a spaumadurinn sem Semjaza sandir i hans stadur?"

Without Ananel to interpret for him, Enoch was left to wonder what the words meant. "I am Enoch of the Shayetham. Are you the Speaker?"

"I am. And you are the human Semjaza sends to speak in his stead?" the angel repeated, in perfect execution of Enoch's own language.

"I am," Enoch replied.

The angel eyed him suspiciously, then took a few steps forward. "You are acquainted with the Holy One, and yet you keep company with criminals. How is it that you find yourself speaking on behalf of a traitor?"

Enoch quickly glanced behind, but the guards gave no indication of being offended. "The Holy One gave me a vision which led me to this place. Now Semjaza sends me to—"

"Come with me," the angel interrupted. "We will speak somewhere more comfortable.

Although twice the height of Enoch, the Speaker walked slowly enough for him to keep pace. As soon as they rounded the bend and were out of sight of the main gate, two other angels stepped out from behind the jagged rocks. Their darker brown tones made them blend in with the cliffs more so than the Speaker.

Retracing the steps that Ananel had taken earlier, the small group descended the mountain pass until it opened onto the grassy plains. To the west side of the road, several massive figures waited. Being evening, Enoch expected to see tents or temporary shelters of some kind. But the angels, who all bore the same radiant look and calming presence, stood in the open. Perhaps they didn't expect their task to take long or else they didn't need to sleep. Enoch thought it was probably the latter.

"This way," the Speaker said, heading between the others until he and Enoch were standing on the other side of them.

"I bring Enoch, prophet of the Shayetham. As you can see, he knows the Holy One."

A murmur of curiosity arose from the crowd.

Enoch wondered how these beings could *see* that he knew the Holy One. If he were back home in Sedekiyr, this question would consume his thoughts for days. In the back of his mind, he knew that there would be time to consider these events in greater depth, but for now he tried his best to maintain concentration on the present.

"Tell us, Prophet. Now that you are among friends, how have you come to speak on behalf of Semjaza?"

At this, the crowd was silent.

Enoch looked up to the eyes of those gathered and saw a mixture of curiosity and concern. Surprisingly absent was the judgment he expected. "The Holy One gave me a vision of things that have already passed, and some that are yet to come. From this vision came a message, which I was to deliver to the Wandering Stars. And in doing so, I was brought to the throne room of Semjaza. While there, one of his guards announced your presence at the gate. So, he sent me to deliver a message to you."

The Speaker's eyebrows dropped as he looked to the other angels, but everyone kept silent.

"Do you wish to know the vision that I was given?"

"No," the Speaker replied. "That is not meant for our ears. Just tell us Semjaza's message."

"He told me, 'I repent of my disobedience. I will need time to meditate upon my actions, but I will take council at the break of daylight. Then I will be ready to accept whatever terms he is offering.'"

The Speaker knelt to the ground so he could look eye-to-eye with Enoch. "Is that all he said?"

"Yes," Enoch answered, now worried that he'd left something out. "I... He didn't say anything else. But if you want to know anything, I would be pleased to answer whatever you ask."

"It's too easy," another angel said, speaking over Enoch.

"Agreed," the Speaker replied.

"What should we do now?" another asked.

The Speaker thought for a moment. "It is the way of the enemy to think the worst. For now, we will take him at his word. If he is indeed willing to repent of his actions, we will expect him to comply with our orders."

The Speaker turned now to Enoch. "Enoch, will you return into the city and deliver a message to Semjaza?"

"I will."

"Good. Tell him that I accept his repentance and the terms of peace that govern it. Forgiveness is not for me to decide. But we will safely escort him and all of those under his command or influence to the Eternal Realm for judgment. We will wait until the rising of the sun to hear his decision."

Enoch nodded. "Shall I go now?"

"Yes," the Speaker replied. "These two will escort you back to the gate."

The other angels who accompanied the Speaker only moments ago now stepped forward. One took the lead and began to walk back along the road that led into the mountains. Enoch wanted, more than anything, to stay in the company of so many of the holy angels, to talk with them and ask them about their world and about the Holy One. Instead, he obediently turned and followed, with the second angel taking the rear.

The next hours passed in silence with Enoch lost in his thoughts. He wondered how Semjaza would react to the Speaker's message. He felt a growing sense of dread at returning to the throne room. Suddenly, his stomach dropped. He had been with Ananel on his first visit. Would the guards allow him entry into the city this time? Would the escorts accompany him?

As they neared the gate, Enoch saw that Semjaza's guards weren't at their posts. It seemed strange, but he was immediately distracted by the realization that his escorts had stopped walking and he was now in front. "Are you not coming?" he asked, turning around.

"No, little one," the angel on the left answered. "We will not enter the city."

Enoch felt his brow wrinkle and tried to quickly smooth it. "Are you not permitted?"

"Our reasons are quite complicated. Our answer should suff—"

The angel on the left looked quickly to the other escort.

Unexpectedly, they both rushed toward Enoch and lifted him from the road. They pushed him into a crevice in the sheer face of the nearby cliff. It happened so quickly that Enoch didn't even have time to resist; though it wouldn't have mattered if he did. Their enormous bodies pinned him against the rock and he was helpless. But in the few seconds of stillness that followed, Enoch realized that their actions were meant for his protection.

A low rumble moved through the ground and he could feel the vibration in the rock pressed against his face. Through a small opening between the cliff and the angel's limbs, Enoch barely glimpsed numerous silhouettes shooting through the sky, their dark shapes only slightly lighter than the backdrop. Slower in speed, but closer in proximity, more tall figures rushed by the crevice opening along the ground.

"Stay quiet little one," one of the escorts whispered.

But Enoch didn't need the instruction. He knew by instinct to keep silent.

When the commotion had passed, the angels released their grip on Enoch and pushed themselves out of the narrow crevice.

Enoch leaned away from the rock and followed his escorts back to the road. "What was that?"

"We must move quickly," one replied.

"It looks like Semjaza only sent you to stall for time," the other one said with disgust.

Enoch backed away, now realizing that Semjaza had only asked him to go to the Speaker because he couldn't move quickly with his tiny legs. "But... I..." he stammered, trying to find the words to express his own disgust.

"It's not your fault little one." The nearest angel stepped behind Enoch and lifted him off the ground, holding him securely with one massive arm across his chest.

Amid a dizzying cloud of sparks that swirled, then pulled inward, Enoch felt himself suddenly thrust upward into the air. The road and cliffs passed beneath him in disorienting blur. His head swam and his stomach threatened to heave until he noticed the other escort, who now looked like one of the winged angels he'd seen earlier, was flying beside him. Then he realized that he was being carried by angels who could change their forms like Ananel. That's when the adventurous side of him, the part that took delight in experiencing the beauty of the Holy One's ways, could hardly contain his excitement.

I'm flying. Like a bird of the sky!

10

They kept the cursed man on the western outskirts of the village, in a small valley in the foothills of Ehrevhar. The one responsible for feeding him was the man's wife, whose emotions were unreadable to Sariel. She walked at a brisk pace, while Sariel wondered what she had endured over the past two years. He imagined himself in her place and what it would feel like to have your husband return from a gathering expedition with a sickness. He is then forced to live outside of the village, which meant that you would also have to accompany him. With your status among the Chatsiyram dependent on your husband, your life would also have changed in an instant.

"Where are the wives of the other men?" Sariel asked, as soon as the thought came to him.

"They are dead," she replied flatly.

"Oh," Sariel mumbled. "I'm sorry. Did they become sick also?"

The woman stopped walking for a moment and turned around. Her eyes looked to be on the verge of tears, but the rest of her face remained expressionless. "They got too close and the men killed them."

"The sick men?" Sariel clarified.

"Yes. They killed their own wives," she answered, then turned and began to walk again.

"You saw this happen?" Sariel asked, not wanting to be disrespectful, but needing to understand the nature of the sickness.

"Yes," she replied, picking up her pace.

"And now that the other men are dead, it's just you and your husband. And you haven't touched each other in all this time?"

"He's not my husband anymore," she said softly without turning around. Her voice cracked a little with these last words.

Sariel stopped asking questions after this and they continued in silence for half an hour before descending a hill into a wide meadow. Sariel scanned the terrain, looking for a tent or structure of some sort.

"Where does he live?" he asked, finally breaking the silence.

"This way," she replied simply without breaking her stride. Following a worn path through the knee-high grass, she walked with the confidence of someone who had made this trip many times before.

Gradually, the peacefulness of the valley became disturbed by an odd screeching and moaning sound that grew louder as they trekked across the meadow. It sounded like a wounded animal.

"Is that your husband?" Sariel asked cautiously.

"He's not my husband anymore," she repeated.

"Of course. I'm sorry."

"He is always like this," she offered, speaking the first words of their trip that were not in response to one of Sariel's questions. "I believe that the sickness is angry to be trapped in his body."

Sariel nodded slowly. *I believe you're more correct than you know.*

Suddenly, the woman stopped walking. In front of her, the grass had been worn down to the earth and only the deep brown soil remained. The path widened slightly and turned around a bend. She looked at Sariel and inclined her head toward the widened path.

"Is this it?" Sariel asked, lifting his head to peer over the grass.

"Yes. I don't know what you think you can do for him. But be careful not to touch him. If he lays his hands on you he will kill you."

"Thank you," Sariel replied to the woman, then stepped past her to follow the worn trail.

It continued to widen around the bend until it opened into a small clearing of bare earth, perhaps fifty feet in diameter. At the center of the clearing, a low platform of latticed saplings was spread across a hole in the ground and fastened to thicker poles embedded in the earth around the perimeter. Sariel realized instantly what he was looking at, and was disgusted at the thought.

The moaning and screeching was loud now as Sariel approached the pit. Inching cautiously forward, he could see that the hole was roughly ten feet deep and twenty feet in diameter. The latticed lid was constructed of tree branches as thick as a man's forearm, lashed together at their intersections with long strands of grass.

Caged like a dangerous animal.

Abruptly, a hand shot out from the edge and swiped at the air in front of Sariel's feet. On instinct, he jumped backward. The skin of the arm and hand was a sickly, yellow hue, covered in dirt. The fingernails were long and jagged, nearly black. Beneath the gaunt skin, bone and sinew could be seen in great detail. Then, the arm retracted and gripped the cage. Something else pressed against the wood and the sound of sniffing could be heard.

Sariel closed his eyes for a moment to compose himself. When he was ready, he circled around to the south side of the hole to get a better look at the man. As soon as he found a good vantage point, the screaming stopped.

There, clinging to the lid and the earthen wall on the side of the pit, was a creature that only vaguely looked human. Its long, thin limbs stuck out at odd angles, clinging like a spider to the boundary of its confines.

As Sariel moved slowly around the perimeter, dark and lifeless eyes tracked his every movement from a bulbous head that swiveled in a cocked position, like a poisonous insect. Its naked and hairless body was cut and bleeding in multiple places, appearing little healthier than the skeletons by the lake of reeds.

"What do you want with us, Child of Light," it said calmly, with a complicated sound of several people trying to speak over each other. "Have you come to destroy us?"

Sariel *shifted* his consciousness slightly toward the Eternal Realm to see what he was really dealing with. Instantly, the structured existence of the Temporal faded away, revealing three demons that crawled over the spirit of the man, like spiders over the carcass of an insect. They looked slightly stronger than their counterparts by the lake, no doubt due to their living host.

"What business do you have with this man?" Sariel asked, taking a step forward.

"You cannot have him!" they screamed in unison. "He yielded to us," one of them replied alone.

Sariel looked over the man's body, seeking a figurine, but he was naked.

It's in his stomach, along with the two from the other men!

Sariel clenched his fists. "Swallowing a figurine does not constitute yielding your will."

One demon chuckled with a raspy cough.

Another crawled to the front of the man's chest, its barbed talons digging in as it moved. "The Amatru will never prevail, because they refuse to see the limitations of their own laws."

This only angered Sariel more. He had trained for years and fought under the principle that the ways of the enemy were evil, through and through. Yet, he had also lived through countless wars and seen millions of his fellow angels slaughtered. And through the dizzying chaos, he'd come to resent the limitations that were placed on them.

The limitations we placed on ourselves.

This resentment eventually turned into wondering how far each side was willing to go to achieve victory. And hearing the demons words only stirred up the conflicting feelings of resentment and loyalty in his heart.

Sariel took a breath to calm himself, then stared hard at the demons. "I'm going to give you one chance to yield your authority over this man. When I return, if I find that you are still here, I will send you all to the void."

One demon snickered at this.

Another peeked out from behind the man. "If you were capable, you would already have done it."

The third simply smiled, its grotesque face distorting into an unnatural expression.

With his mind racing to provide an explanation for this madness, years of training and experience overtook Sariel's thoughts and focused them on what must be done to correct the problem. Without another word, he turned and left.

*   *   *   *

Enoch's excitement lasted only a few seconds, before the escorts left the mountainous terrain and descended toward the grassy plains beside the road. As they glided to a soft and silent landing, Enoch could already see that the gathering of angels was much larger than before, comprised of both Semjaza's soldiers and the Speaker's escorts. When their feet touched the ground, the one holding Enoch stayed in a crouching position and lowered him gently to the grass.

The other advanced cautiously on foot.

Semjaza and his wingless soldiers encircled the Speaker and his angels, outnumbering them four to one. The unexplainable difference that Enoch felt when in the presence of each was now contrasted in a vivid way. The Speaker and his angels looked out of place. Their smaller, homogeneous group appeared more colorful and orderly, standing out against the nighttime backdrop of the fields. Fully clothed, without weapons of any kind, they appeared vulnerable. Those under Semjaza's rule were darker and muted in color. Their bare forms were more muscular and varied greatly in size. The parts of their bodies that were covered were clothed in protective raiment that reminded Enoch of the reptilian creatures that nearly ended his life. In their hands they carried a variety of weapons that looked even more deadly than the clubs carried by the Kahyin. These angels were at home in this Temporal environment and, by their advancing steps, it was obvious that they were aware of their advantage.

"Dar ar din Pri-Rada?" Semjaza asked. His mouth was curled up into a deadly grin.

The muscles along the Speaker's jaw flexed while he backed slowly away in a hunched position. He replied to Semjaza's question with his hands out to his sides.

Enoch wished desperately that he knew their language so he could understand what was happening.

Semjaza's response sounded cold. He moved a few paces forward, his bladed spear now within striking distance.

The Speaker took one quick step backward and held up one hand in front of himself, pleading with narrowed eyes. His voice was thick with desperation."

Suddenly, the night sky overhead grew darker as large sections of the stars were blotted out.

Enoch's escort quickly let go of him and burst into the air with a powerful rush of wind.

Enoch dropped lower onto his stomach. From between the blades of grass, he saw sparks shoot outward from the Speaker's escorts as they tried to change form. Only a few managed to take to the air just as a swarm of dark shapes fell upon them from the sky above. In the moonlight, the grassy expanse erupted with movement as Semjaza's ground soldiers closed in. Arms flailed and wings beat erratically. Harsh grunts and screams cut through the night air. With his tiny frame hidden by the tall vegetation, Enoch watched in horror as the Speaker's escorts fell from the sky around him, their limp bodies jolting abruptly when they hit the ground. Everywhere he looked, he saw another image that was more frightening than the first. One of the Speaker's soldiers broke through the fray, but immediately arched his back as a spear came through his chest. Enoch flinched as he watched the soldier pitch forward and land only feet away from where he hid.

And then silence covered everything.

Rising slightly, Enoch parted the grass.

The Speaker was on the ground, trying to crawl backwards away from Semjaza who stood over him. His face and chest were covered in lacerations.

Two of Semjaza's ground soldiers stood on each of the Speaker's arms, pinning him to the ground while the tips of their spears hovered near his face.

Someone handed Semjaza a weapon with a long handle on one end and a wide blade on the other. Semjaza took it, keeping his gaze fixed on his enemy. Without warning he swung the blade downward where it landed with a sickening thud.

The Speaker screamed in agony and flailed violently, now only held down by his one remaining arm. The other, severed from his body, lay still in the grass.

Enoch clasped a hand over his mouth to keep from screaming. He'd never seen anything so violent and grotesque in all his years upon the earth. As the tears poured from his eyes, he wished that the Holy One would end this madness.

The Speaker's screams eventually lessened into moans of pain, and then silence altogether.

Semjaza stood calmly over the wounded angel, smiling. He spoke again in the same unintelligible language, then glanced back to his soldiers.

The Speaker looked up with tears streaming down his face. His final words were barely above a whisper.

Semjaza nodded and his ground soldier stepped off the Speaker's arm.

Slowly, the grass, the dark sky, and the stars along the horizon appeared to bend inward toward the Speaker. Then he was gone.

11

Sariel sat across from Sheyir's father and the other Chatsiyr elders. It was now dusk and the whole tribe had gathered again at the place of meeting following the meal. Sariel had put off his explanation as long as possible and was now ready to disclose what he had discovered.

"In Arar Gahiy, on the north end of Armayim, I found the remains of men from another tribe. They had been dead for quite some time."

The elder's posture straightened as he glanced quickly to the men near him. "This can't be. For generations, we have had an understanding with the People of the Trees. We do not leave the land between the mountains and they do not come into our land."

"Nevertheless, I found them there at the edge of the water. Among the bones I also found a small, graven image."

The elder's forehead wrinkled.

How do I describe this to them? "Like the flowers and leaves that you wear on your bodies, but this object was made by hands, and did not grow from the ground."

The elder pushed his lips together and stared at the ground.

Sariel waited until it seemed that his words were understood. "This thing is owned by someone, just as you own or possess this land. This graven image carries with it an evil spirit."

"This is not true!" Sheyir's father replied quickly.

Sariel took a breath and sighed in frustration. Taking a moment to choose his words carefully, he tried again. "The People of the Grass..." Sariel started slowly, interpreting the name of the Chatsiyr tribe, "...know that there is another world beyond this one."

Sheyir's father nodded slowly.

"In this other world, spirits live."

Again, he nodded.

"Sometimes," Sariel continued, "...these spirits come into this world."

"Yes. They live inside some animals and cause them to kill others."

Sariel looked up to the sky that was growing darker with every second. This concept was incredibly vast and difficult to explain with such a limited vocabulary as theirs, or to a people whose only interaction with the Eternal Realm was the occasional possession of an animal by a demon. Technically, it didn't happen often. But the Chatsiyram were herbivores trying to make sense of the brutality of the animals around them. He decided to let the elder's comments pass. At least the man was following his logic up to this point.

"This object was crafted to defy the laws governing the interaction of these two worlds. It was crafted to deceive men. Whoever possesses this object unknowingly allows the evil spirit to live inside him."

At this, the elder's eyebrows lifted. "How can you know this?"

"My *dathrah* has shown this to me."

"This is a powerful *dathrah*," the elder replied.

"Yes," Sariel answered with a nod.

"How did you get this *dathrah*?" he asked, going back to the same conversation they had at their first meeting.

"We have all been given different abilities; this is the one I have been given," Sariel answered quickly, trying to get the conversation back on course. "I have also been to see the man with sickness. I saw three evil spirits that live inside him. I believe he took one of the graven images from the lake, and then took two from the other sick men who were with him. These spirits were not meant to live in this world," he paused, noting the irony of his own situation.

"They are angry at being confined to his body, yet they do not have authority to go anywhere else. They move about in a manner that they are accustomed to, but his body does not move as theirs. They care not for food or other things that we find necessary. They think different thoughts and speak with different words. This is why he is starved and injured. This is why he yells and moans like an animal. This is why he appears to be sick."

The elder sat back and looked down at the dirt, perhaps trying to comprehend Sariel's explanation or else make it fit with what he already believed. Finally, he spoke. "Can he be helped?"

Sariel smiled. "Yes, I believe he can. But I will need everyone in this village to participate."

The elder looked to his brothers and received nods of affirmation. "We will help," he replied. "Then you will tell me more about this other world."

Sariel agreed with a slight nod.

* * * *

Enoch stood in the knee-deep grass looking down at the Speaker's severed arm. In the pale light emerging from the eastern sky, he could see splatters of blood everywhere. Bodies were strewn across the ground; some whole and some in pieces. Every time he looked at one of their expressions, whether twisted into grimaces of torture, or resting with the peacefulness of sleep, all he could see were Zacol and Methu. As if their beautiful faces were somehow attached to the lifeless bodies of the Speaker's angels. Despite the silence, only broken by the occasional whisper of wind passing over plains, Enoch's heart was racing. The two people he loved more than life itself were far beyond the southwestern horizon, with no one to protect them.

A faint rustle in the grass behind suddenly jolted him from his stupor. Turning quickly, he saw the dissolving form of a massive wolf, accompanied by dozens of other creatures. With heavy eyes, he blinked slowly, wishing that he was at home with his family. When his eyes opened again, the tall, graceful creatures around him were closer than expected, as if he'd slept in that instant.

"What happened here?" Ananel asked softly.

Enoch opened his mouth, but nothing came out. Tears rolled down his cheeks as he looked up at the angel.

Ananel stared down at Enoch, while the others moved about the field, pointing, kneeling, and whispering to each other.

"I—can't— can't understand what they said," he managed.

Ananel knelt and cautiously placed his hand on Enoch's shoulder. "If you will permit me to look through your eyes, I will reveal it to you."

Enoch nodded, not even understanding what he was agreeing to.

Ananel closed his eyes.

Everything was dark except a sliver of night sky and road visible through the crevice to the left. Semjaza's Iryllurym flew past the opening, followed by the marching Anduarym.

Suddenly, Enoch was flying. The mountains passed beneath his feet. The rough terrain slowly turned to smooth fields. The massive arm across his chest, held him securely in the air.

Enoch's feet touched the solid earth again, and he felt his body gently lowered to the grass.

"Where is your Pri-Rada?" Semjaza asked, though the grin on his face said he already knew the answer.

The Speaker backed away slowly. His body was tense with the anticipation of violence, but he held his hands out to either side in a gesture of submission. "Unlike you and your treacherous ways, my Pri-Rada expected a civil meeting. He sent only a small delegation."

"Then he is an incompetent fool," Semjaza replied, advancing with his vandrekt in a ready position.

The Speaker jumped back suddenly as he realized that Semjaza wasn't simply trying to intimidate him—he was going to attack. In a desperate, but pointless act, the Speaker put his hand up as if it would protect him. "Are you so foolish as to attack the Amatru? It would be an act of war!"

The stars were darkened as the formation of Iryllurym dove from the sky.

The Speaker's escorts began to shape into flying angels, but only a few made it off the ground and even their efforts were wasted. The blades of the Iryllurym cut through their unguarded flesh with deadly precision.

Enoch flinched in horror.

Semjaza lunged forward and thrust his vandrekt into the Speaker's shoulder. The pain distracted the angel and kept him from shifting.

All around, the Anduarym attacked the unarmed escorts. Most were impaled where they stood.

One ran straight for Enoch. His body suddenly straightened, then arched backward.

Enoch flinched.

The escort dropped forward to the grass.

Enoch was frozen with fear. He kept his head down for a moment until the grunts and screams eventually died down to silence.

The Speaker was on the ground. He'd been stabbed multiple times in the torso, but none of the wounds were fatal. Blood poured down his face from a laceration high on his head. It was obvious that Semjaza was only toying with him.

Two Anduarym stood on the Speaker's arms, pinning him to the ground.

Semjaza accepted a svvard from one of his ground soldiers. His gaze remained fixed on the speaker as he brought the blade *suddenly downward. The sharpened metal cut through skin and bone in one movement, until it lay embedded in the soil.*

The Speaker screamed in agony and writhed on the ground.

The larger and stronger Anduar who stood on his remaining arm had to bring all of his weight to bear in order to contain the flailing angel.

Then, in a bold act of courage, the Speaker silenced himself. Though his pain must have been unbearable, he refused to allow Semjaza to take pleasure in his suffering.

Semjaza leaned over him. "Go back to your world and tell Ganisheel that this is my realm. I consider his presence here to be an act of war. If I even hear a rumor of the Amatru coming here again, I'll bring the war to him. And he has no idea what I'm capable of or what I have at my disposal."

Semjaza looked away briefly to revel in the strength of the soldiers at his command. Then he turned back to the Speaker. "If he persists, I'll show him the depth of his incompetence."

The Speaker tried to compose himself, staring defiantly into Semjaza's eyes. But his body was weaker than his spirit. Tears fell from his eyes and blood poured from the stump where his arm used to be. "You can't come back from this," he whispered.

Semjaza nodded, and his Anduarym released the Speaker.

Without hesitation, the angel shifted into the Eternal Realm.

Ananel removed his hand from Enoch's shoulder.

Suddenly, it was morning again and the other Myndarym were now gathered around Ananel. "Semjaza used the prophet to stall and distract the Speaker while he gathered his army. They slew the delegation, in direct violation of the terms of peace which govern such a meeting."

"Why would he react so rashly?" someone asked.

Ananel turned. "He seemed offended when we talked in the throne room—that the Holy One sent a prophet to us, but an army to him. This was a show of force. He sent the Speaker away with a warning for his Pri-Rada to never enter this realm again."

Upon hearing Ananel's summary, some of the Myndarym expressed disbelief, others disapproval. Still others kept silent.

"Isn't this what he was supposed to do? To protect us, if necessary?" someone asked.

"He wasn't protecting us," someone else countered.

"The Amatru were never supposed to know about us," another offered.

"He's declared war on the Amatru!"

Ananel held up his hands. "Please. Please," he stated, bringing the group to silence. "We all feared this day would eventually come. Semjaza has betrayed his end of our agreement. All of this is proof that he was incapable of keeping things quiet."

"What about him," someone asked.

Suddenly, all eyes were on Enoch.

Ananel spoke quietly. "I had hoped that you could all hear his message for yourselves. But I don't think that matters anymore. Semjaza has just sealed our fate. The Amatru will hold us partially responsible for what happened here."

"Can't we send someone to plead for us?" Make amends?"

Ananel shook his head. "I doubt they'll be willing to discuss anything after such an egregious violation."

"What are we to do then?"

Silence followed. Enoch suddenly felt very small and insignificant—nothing more than an unwelcomed visitor.

"We've all felt this change coming," Ananel continued. "I, for one, expected it to come sooner than this day. Nevertheless, it's here. And now we have a choice to make. Either we submit to Semjaza's rule and give up our hopes of attaining freedom, or we go our own way. Right now!"

"But he'll come looking for us," someone said.

"Where would we go?" another asked.

Ananel nodded slowly, with a determined look in his eyes. "Wherever we want. This is our land, even more than it is his. And he's going to be busy preparing for war."

A breeze had picked up and was causing the blades of grass to wave in unison. The curling mist drifting over the plains seemed to emphasize the silence that had fallen on the group.

One by one, the Myndarym began to go their separate ways. Without another word, Ananel *shaped* into his animal form and set off to the north with most of the Myndarym following him. Within seconds, Enoch found himself standing alone on a battlefield, surrounded by the corpses of slain angels.

*   *   *   *

"...but men don't sing," the elder argued.

Not in this tribe they don't, Sariel thought. "The women do."

"Yes. And my youngest daughter is the most talented."

The recognition of Sheyir's ability seemed awkward in his mouth. It was probably the only time he'd ever expressed anything resembling pride or even approval of a female in his tribe. Sariel wondered if he'd even heard Sheyir sing, or was his proclamation based on second-hand information?

"Alright. Then I'll need the men to move to one side, and the women to the other."

The elder turned to the rest of the tribe gathered around the uncovered meeting area at the center of the village. He gave the order and they split and reassembled as instructed—with the men now on the west side of the clearing; the women on the east.

"If you're willing, this would be easier if you gave me authority to instruct them myself," Sariel suggested.

The elder's eyebrows dropped, but relaxed after a moment of hesitation. "Everyone will obey the visitor until I say otherwise," he told the crowd.

"Thank you," Sariel said. "Now, will all the women please step forward and assemble into one line." He waited for them to follow his command, then walked to Sheyir at the front of the line. "I want you to sing the same sounds as I do."

Sheyir nodded.

Sariel sang one note, then waited as Sheyir mimicked it perfectly.

Sariel then sang two notes at a higher pitch.

Again, Sheyir repeated the sounds.

"Good. Now a simple melody," Sariel responded, singing several notes in a series, alternating up and down.

Sheyir mimicked it effortlessly.

"Thank you," he said with a smile. "Please step over to the side."

Sheyir moved closer to her father.

Sariel stepped in front of the next woman and repeated the test with different notes. This woman was able to mimic up to two notes, but couldn't follow the melody. After three tries, Sariel asked her to step to the other side of the elder and wait.

By mid-afternoon, he'd made his way through the remaining females of the tribe. There were a total of one hundred and thirty who could sing, or at least discern the differences between sounds. From there, he spent more time with each one as they sang through a multitude of sounds and combinations of tones. As the last rays of sunlight disappeared over Ehrevhar, Sariel had the women separated into groups of similar abilities, based on the range of their vocal chords. When the sun was finally set, the elder pronounced their work complete for the day. Since the women had been occupied with other tasks, the evening meal would be much smaller than usual.

Sitting across the clearing from the elders, it appeared that everyone was tired from the day's activities and in no mood to talk. Sheyir was the only one of the tribe who seemed more energized than exhausted. But Sariel pretended not to notice. It was critical that he keep his feelings for Sheyir a secret from the rest of the tribe until he'd established himself as a person worthy of their respect. And in order to keep his body from betraying his feelings, he tried to concentrate instead on his overall plan and how to make the best use of the men, given the limitations imposed by the elder.

It's going to be a busy few months, he thought, feeling sleep pulling at his exhausted body. As he contemplated the frailty of this new existence, he felt something at the back of his mind.

Beneath the surface of thought, a nagging fear clung to him, whispering that he wouldn't be able to save the man. And if he couldn't do it, then all his hopes would be lost. He would never be accepted among the Chatsiyram.

He would never be Sheyir's, and Sheyir would never be his.

12

Sheyir's eyes darted from one feature to another. First his lips. He pronounced each word carefully, as if he tasted it the moment before it left his tongue. Then his eyes. The deepest, clearest blue she'd ever seen. There was kindness and gentleness there. But also a fierce sadness that spoke of hidden tragedy. His skin was smooth, like a child's; with the warm tones of pale sand along the banks of a stream.

She watched Sariel as if he were a dream come to life. The fear that paralyzed her at their first meeting was but a distant memory. Though it lingered at the back of her thoughts, whispering to her that she would soon wake from the dream, it was restrained by what her other senses told her. Others may have reason to fear this man, this creature. But there was no danger for her.

"Long ago, our worlds were one with each other. But there began a great war among my kind and creation was stretched. It pulled all of us apart, such that we could only live in the place where we remained. Those whom we fought were forbidden from your realm. But one found a way to cross the void and he brought death with him. That's when this realm began to drift away," he said, looking up at the trees overhead.

Sheyir followed his gaze. And when she looked at the leaves dancing in the breeze, it was as if she were looking through different eyes. Her world, though beautiful at times, had always seemed somehow broken. Sariel's words lifted the mist that blocked her sight, revealing what she had always known to be true.

"Thus, the Temporal Realm was born as it separated from the Eternal."

"Why are you called Myndarym?" Sheyir asked.

Sariel smiled and the corners of his eyes wrinkled. "It means Shapers. We have always had the ability to change our form. It enables us to carry out our purpose—to sustain all that was created. But when your world was separated from mine, our purpose was changed. We were entrusted with Baerlagid—the Songs of Creation. We used this knowledge to *shape* your world so that it could survive on its own. So, it is really a double-meaning. We have both the ability to change our form and the ability to change the form of others."

"And this is what you did before you came here?" she probed, fascinated by his explanations.

"At one time," he clarified. "Though we were all involved in the Shaping, many were reassigned to other tasks as your world became self-sufficient. That's when I became a soldier."

Sheyir looked from his lips to his eyes. "What is a soldier?"

He squinted, then glanced down at the rock on which they sat. After a long pause, his eyes met hers again. "Has your tribe ever fought with another?"

Sheyir nodded. "I have never seen it, but it happened in my father's time, when he was young."

"In my world, there is a very powerful tribe that seeks to destroy all others. And just as it is the women's task among the Chatsiyram to gather food, it is the task among some of my kind to fight against this tribe."

Sheyir's gaze now drifted down to Sariel's forearm. The cuts and scrapes that had been there were healing well. Most were only light scars now, the skin slightly pinker that its surroundings. But a few scabs were still present where the injuries had been more severe. "This is why your arms were wounded when you first appeared to me," she stated, reaching to touch his skin.

She wasn't sure what compelled her to do this. She almost expected him to flinch or at least pull his arm back, but he kept still. Maybe she was challenging him. Or was she challenging her own fears, confronting the voice at the back of her thoughts that promised her this man was dangerous?

Whatever the reason, his eyes never even blinked.

"If you can change your form, can you not *shape* your arms?"

Sariel looked down and clenched his fist, but the rest of his body remained still. "I will keep the scars so that I don't forget."

"But you can heal yourself?"

"Yes," he replied with a smile.

"Then you cannot die."

Sariel lifted his head and closed his eyes for a brief moment. "I wish that were the case. Sometimes, we are wounded faster than we can heal. Sometimes we die."

Sheyir reached out again. But this time, instead of just touching his forearm, she laid her hand there and felt the warmth exchanged between their touch. "Sometimes we die also."

A swishing of grass behind them startled Sheyir.

Sariel pulled his arm away and sat upright. "So you must follow my lead," he said loudly. "I will have to react quickly to whatever I encounter and I will need you to sing—"

Sheyir turned to see a boy who was standing in the dense vines on the edge of the forest.

"Yes, what is it?" Sariel asked.

The boy stepped shyly toward them and extended the bundle in his hands.

Sariel reached up and took the cloth from the child. Unrolling it, he held it up to the light reflecting from the river. With a few sharp tugs, he pulled the fine weaving taut and seemed pleased at its strength. Then he handed it back to the boy. "Tell them it will do fine."

The boy smiled and ran off into the trees.

* * * *

Enoch ran as fast as his legs would carry him. The sound of his feet hitting the soggy earth seemed incredibly loud. He was trying desperately to keep quiet, but each labored stride brought a great sucking noise as he struggled to maintain his speed and keep his feet from being pulled under. Plowing through a field of waist-high blades of bright-green vegetation, he was thankful for the dense root system which felt more solid beneath his feet, even as the sharp edges sliced through his skin.

He glanced quickly over his shoulder and scanned the blue sky above the trees, but it wasn't there. His breath was coming in rapid spasms now. His lungs burned in his chest, but he ran anyway.

Suddenly, a dark shape appeared just over the trees to his left. It had changed direction and was now attacking from the side.

Enoch pushed himself harder, expending the last of his energy to escape. With each step across the sodden earth, he pulled hard against the sticky substance which slowed him down. And then, there was nothing beneath him.

He was falling forward.

A rippled surface rose quickly to meet him. Before he could react, he hit the water with a violent splash and slipped under. The current was strong and immediately pulled him to the right as he struggled to turn his body over. Water slipped in through his nose and he fought the urge to cough, knowing it would only force the remaining air from his lungs.

Clawing through the turbulent environment, he reached the surface and immediately gasped for air. The current had already dragged him a good distance to the east and across to the northern bank where a tangle of wide-leafed vines grew thick into an overhang. Enoch reached up and grabbed hold of the exposed roots and pulled himself under the shadows.

With nothing but the sound of water in his ears, Enoch waited, feeling his heart still pounding in his chest.

A moment later, a shadow slid across the water. Through the leaves above, he watched a massive creature pass overhead. Its long and narrow head turned to the side as it scanned the river for its prey.

Enoch remained still and silent.

With wings as large as an Iryllur, the brightly-colored reptile glided beyond the far bank of the river and out of sight past the tall grasses.

Enoch waited for several minutes before coughing to expel the liquid in his lungs. Then he turned toward the bank and reached up to pull himself out of the water. Before his hands were hundreds of large, purple blossoms sprouting from the dark green vines. Their intricate, spiraling petals were veined with a brilliant, pink color that brought a smile to Enoch's face. Then, he noticed thin, pale leaves of another plant sticking out below it, near the waterline. This vegetation was plainer in appearance and nearly dead as it was being smothered by the flowering plant. Even its roots seemed choked by the other.

Enoch paused for moment, then breathed deeply.

Holy One. I see what You have meant for me to see. You let me fall into the river so that I would be hidden from the hunter of the air. What I mistook for peril, was your provision. And now you remind me through flowers that your angels should not be here. Though they are beautiful and powerful, they are not meant to live with us. Their cities will grow taller and overshadow ours. Their accomplishments will appear brighter and more beautiful than ours. And we will strive to adopt their ways until our foundation rests upon them. And they will choke the life from us.

Enoch wearily pulled himself out of the water and stood, dripping, while he scanned the terrain for any sign of predators. Once again, he was by himself. Though each day had brought some proof that he was not alone.

Stepping away from the water, Enoch continued north in search of the Myndarym.

13

After months of investigation, trials, training, and practice, Sariel and the entire Chatsiyr tribe were ready. In the pale yellow of the sunrise, they stood in a circle around the pit where the sick man was caged. Everyone seemed quite nervous despite the excessive preparations. Sariel had spent the last hour giving final instructions to the various groups of men and women, pointing to the symbols that he'd scratched into the dirt in front of them, all the while trying to be heard over the screams and moans of the man beneath their feet. Finally, he stepped toward the cage, just out of the tortured man's reach. With a deep breath, he *shifted* his consciousness toward the Eternal Realm.

"I see that you did not heed my warning," he said to the demons, now digging their claws into the man's flesh as if they were prepared to tear it from his body.

"Leave us alone!" they screamed.

"I promise to leave you alone when you leave this man alone."

"No. No," they replied. "He wants us."

"At one time he may have. But how can you know this now? You've subverted his will so that it is no longer distinguishable from your own."

"It makes no difference," one countered. "You don't have the authority to make us leave, Child of Light. You are dim now. And you have no weapons."

Sariel lifted his chin and straightened his stance.

He opened his mouth and sang a single, clear note and held it for many seconds. When he stopped and restarted the note, Sheyir accompanied him with a slightly lower sound. The simple harmony caused the demons' eyes to flare wide.

Sariel *shifted* his consciousness back to the Temporal and kept singing. Each time he stopped and restarted, another voice joined in until, after several minutes, all one hundred and thirty women were singing. In the Temporal Realm, the earth vibrated under their feet and the blades of grass seemed to bow down, resonating with the powerful sound.

Inside the Eternal existence, the sounds passed through the air in brightly colored waves, filling the spaces between the tribe and the demons. The visible currents radiated from each human mouth and collided with the evil spirits who clung to the frail spirit of the human. With every impact, the waves of sound scattered; reflections and refractions that gave Sariel an understanding of their true names. He could see what they were made of. He could see their true nature. He adjusted his pitch downward and was pleased when the Chatsiyram followed his lead, the lower notes giving clarity to his knowledge of the enemy. By the time he explored the range of sounds available to him, he was confident that he could name the demons. He was confident that the sum of voices gathered this day would be sufficient to sing Navlagid, a Song of Naming.

Focusing on the core of the demons' existence, he began a melody which the tribe could mimic. Then, moving his own pitch to cover the lowest, unrepresented tones, he began to sing a counter melody which forced that portion of the demon's existence to resonate with it.

The demons understood immediately what was happening. They began to scream out with shrill cries, attempting to disrupt the harmony among the Chatsiyram. But Sariel's rigorous training prevailed and the people repeated the melody, hitting their notes without wavering.

In his physical body, Sariel pointed to one of the groups of men. After a few seconds, he lifted his hand and let it drop. The loud boom of a drum coordinated perfectly with the movement of his hand. He repeated the motion a few more times, then let the men continue beating out the timing he'd established. This signaled to the tribe that the Song of Naming had begun.

Each group of women now sang a variant of the melody that Sariel had established, repeating it in time with the beating of the drum. Now he was free to adjust his voice across the spectrum of sounds and fill in the gaps, to sing the unrepresented notes. He felt a power welling up inside him that had been absent for as long as he could remember. It was the feeling that he got when he had first started *shaping* creation.

Within ten cycles of the melody and numerous harmonies, the demons were becoming compliant, powerless against the music that now defined their beings.

With the tribe continuing to sing, Sariel pointed to another group of men, each bearing a different length of reed cut at an angle on one end. The men lifted the crude flutes to their lips and waited for Sariel's direction.

He pointed at one man in particular, then at the woman whose note he was supposed to replace. Sariel lifted his hand and let it drop, signaling the timing of that man's note within the melody. One by one, he transferred responsibility for representing the melody from the singing women to the men with their instruments. The transition was smooth.

Having now freed up the singers while maintaining control over the demons, Sariel began to sing Tanklagid, a Song of Idea. Remembering the way the human's body reacted to the initial notes, Sariel breathed a soft melody, injecting it into the rhythm of the Song of Naming. It floated toward the demons and was partially absorbed by the body of the human. The part that was not absorbed reflected from the man and appeared to originate from within him.

Pointing at Sheyir, Sariel transferred this responsibility to her and moved his attention to another target. With a low, throated moan, he sent another melody into the earth below the man's feet. It too reflected the Song and Sariel immediately enlisted another woman to support this part of the Idea. When the man, ground, air, and grass in the immediate area were all singing with reflected ideas, Sariel carefully spoke a fragment of a harmonious language that he could reproduce with his human vocal chords. With this ancient language, he inserted the Idea that this existence wasn't worth the effort it required to hold on to it.

Within seconds, the demons began to see that the earth was dry and desolate, the air suffocating. The blades of grass threatened to reach out and strangle them. And the human beneath their taloned grasp seemed pathetic and weak.

Is this existence really better than our last?

Wouldn't it be better to go back and regain our former status?

This man is dying. His fragile body cannot sustain us. His weakness is limiting.

We are meant for greater things.

He cannot even move us from one end of this prison to the other without losing his breath.

Aren't we better than this?

Shouldn't we just let go?

Won't we just slip into the Eternal?

It would better—

Suddenly, one of the demons lost its grip and was immediately sucked through the Void—the chasm that separated the Temporal Realm from the territory of the Evil One. It was a place of nothingness, where no being or object could exist. And having done so, the demon forfeited its hold on the inadequate physical existence it had been clinging to for so long. In an instant, it was transported to the far end of the spectrum, where nothing that has been made can be unmade.

Sariel kept singing, but inwardly he smiled at the thought that one more demon had just been put into the Place of Holding. And he trusted what he had been told—one day, that existence would become a punishment that could not be escaped.

After several more iterations of the Song of Idea, it was clear that the other two demons were either stronger, or had learned from the mistake of the first. It was time to change tactics.

With half the men still playing their instruments, maintaining the Song of Naming, Sariel now enlisted the remainder of the men. Pointing at them individually, he signaled which drums to beat as well as their timing. Some used large, hollowed tree stumps with cloth stretched over the opening, while others beat rocks against smaller reeds that hung from thread around their wrists. Gradually, they constructed a percussive wall of sound that stretched from the lowest, earth-rumbling boom to the highest, ear-piercing report.

The demons, already doubled over in pain, now glanced nervously around, seeking the source of their fear.

Sariel pointed to the groups of women, then clenched his fist, signaling Vinlagid, a Song of Force. Suddenly, he shouted a string of monotone notes arranged in a specific rhythm. The next time he shouted, all one hundred and thirty women matched the sound perfectly. On the next cycle, he sang a long and complicated melody over the shouting, which spanned the limits of his ability. And when he repeated the phrase, Sheyir wove a harmony through his melody that was so beautiful, Sariel almost lost his concentration. Immediately, tears welled up in his eyes as his earthly body struggled with the overwhelming emotions that the combined Songs caused inside him.

The relentless waves of sound crashed against the demons, shaking their footing and forcing them backward. As their talons began to slide backward over the surface of the man's spirit, gouges opened up along the flesh of his physical body, spilling blood down his shoulders and arms. One demon extended its fanged snout and clamped down on the man's head, desperate to somehow maintain its grip.

The man suddenly reached up and grabbed both sides of his head, screaming now with his own voice.

"Leave me," he shouted, with a harsh rasp.

Instantly, the demons were flung into the void, their shrieks leaving a trail of echoes.

Sariel waved both his hands in the air, and at once, the tribe was silent.

In the following stillness, the man in the pit fell forward, collapsing in the mud at his knees.

Sariel exhaled and wiped the tears from his face. "Remove this," he said gently, kneeling down and placing his hand on the latticed lid.

Obediently, the men of the tribe dropped their instruments and began to untie the chords that fastened the lid. It seemed to take an eternity. While he waited, Sariel *shifted* toward the Eternal and was relieved to find that a dim light remained at the core of the being in the pit. It was faint, and flickered like a flame on the verge of ceasing.

"Hurry," he told the men.

No sooner had he said the words than the men lifted the lid off the pit.

Sariel put his hands on the earth and swung his legs over the edge, dropping down into the hole that smelled of urine and feces. Trudging through the shallow muck, he knelt and picked up the frail man, lifting him as easily as a child.

He was pale and starved, but he was alive. Looking up into the sky, Sariel noted that the sun was already nearing the western horizon. Apparently, they'd been singing all day long, though it seemed only minutes. But the fatigue in his own throat and muscles, and the weariness in his eyes confirmed what he saw. Now the tears began to fall from his eyes as his physical body released the emotion it had been trying to hold in. With blurred vision, he looked up and saw the man's wife standing on the edge of the pit.

Her face bore streaks where tears had washed away the dirt. Her eyes were rimmed with red. But behind her physical appearance, there was something else. Something intangible.

Shifting to the perspective of the Eternal Realm, Sariel recognized it immediately. Where once had been despair, the woman's core radiated with hope.

*   *   *   *

The setting sun cast silver shafts of light across the path, looking as tangible as tree trunks that had been bent over by the wind. Sheyir walked slowly across the damp soil, enjoying the alternating light and shadows falling across her face as she passed through the silent forest. Now that preparations were ready for the celebration, she was going inform her father that the people were expecting his arrival.

But her feet moved slowly, hesitantly. She wasn't in a hurry to begin the celebration like the rest of her people, for this type of occasion was usually when a betrothal would be announced. While Sariel's recent success was sure to have impressed her father, the elder had no knowledge of their feelings for each other. In time, Sariel would gain the respect of her father, but she doubted it would happen before her impending marriage to her uncle. Still, her father had not yet announced their engagement and she wondered if it might be because he was holding back to see how events would transpire with this newcomer to the Chatsiyr tribe.

I hope that's the reason!

Her father's house slowly came into view. It was a massive structure of thick tree trunks and intricately woven saplings, with a tall, thatch roof. She'd grown up within its walls, but now that she lived elsewhere with the older children, it seemed just as foreign and distant as her father. The sight of it, looming in the mist, seemed to remind her that her father was often unpredictable; as if the house itself were telling her, *you'll be married before Sariel can do anything about it!*

Sheyir stopped just before the raised platform that served as the floor. Her body seemed unwilling to go forward. It refused to walk into a future that left her bound to someone she didn't love. Her ears didn't want to hear the words that would change her life forever. And yet, over her throbbing heart, voices rang clear.

"You only care for power! For *dathrah*, not tradition!" It was her uncle's voice.

"I will do as I wish, and you will obey it," her father replied. "That is tradition."

A quick silence followed and Sheyir cautiously removed her foot from the first step leading up to the door.

"He's not one of us. But you have decided already."

"I have decided nothing! I have only told you to wait," her father replied. "Why does it matter so much to you? You have many wives."

There was a long pause this time and Sheyir leaned forward to hear her uncle's answer, but there was no reply.

A series of rapid footsteps suddenly grew louder.

Sheyir backed away from the steps.

An instant later, her uncle came through the doorway. His head snapped to the side and his angry glare settled on her, while his wide body lumbered down the steps. When he reached the ground, he exhaled quickly through his nose and stomped off into the trees, heading away from the village.

Sheyir swallowed hard and watched him go. The look on his face had been terrifying. But it seemed that Sariel's efforts were having an effect. At least for tonight, she didn't have to worry about an announcement.

And this thought caused a smile to slowly spread across her face.

* * * *

It had been three days since the tribe had freed the sick man from the evil spirits that inhabited his body. Already, he was looking healthier. Color had returned to his skin and his gaunt frame had begun to thicken each day with regular meals. His wife, once an outcast, was enjoying the restoration of her family's status among the tribe.

In the spirit of the celebration that Sheyir's father decreed, Sariel thought it was the perfect time to introduce the Chatsiyram to something that many other human tribes had already discovered for themselves—fire. After instructing the tribe not to be alarmed at the dangerous, but useful element, he enlisted the men's help in digging a pit in the center of the meeting place. Using some old thatch from a run-down shelter, Sariel showed the men how to use friction to generate embers which could be coaxed into a flame. Once lit, he explained that adding denser materials would prevent it from burning itself out. Being expert builders, the men took quickly to the concepts and marveled at Sariel's vast wisdom.

Now, under an evening sky, the tribe gathered around the blaze and enjoyed its mesmerizing appearance and the warmth it provided. While the children danced in the background, the women roasted a variety of fruits as Sariel had shown them. When the meal was ready, Sariel watched the expressions on the men's faces as they tasted the intensified, sweetened flavors. It seemed that this new technique would be popular among the tribe.

"In all the three hundred and twelve cycles of the sun that I've lived, I've never seen or heard anything of its kind," Sheyir's father said.

Sariel turned around quickly, startled by the older man's stealthy approach. "I'm pleased you like it."

"Ha!" the old man barked, as he came alongside and lowered himself to the ground. "I don't mean the dancing light or the food," he corrected. "What you did about the sickness. You have great *dathrah*, beyond anything I know."

Sariel smiled. "I told you I came to help."

The elder turned his gaze to the dancing light, as he called it, and his eyes seemed to look past the flames. After a moment, his face widened into a grin. "My name is Yeduah. And I'm honored to meet you."

Over Yeduah's hunched silhouette, Sheyir stood a few paces back, illuminated by the dancing flames. She placed a hand over her mouth and turned away, her eyes glistening with tears.

"My name is Sariel. And I'm honored to meet you," he replied.

14

Pri-Rada Himel of the Iryllur stood with his arms crossed, overlooking an immense valley of lush forests and meadows. Between the patches of brilliant green hues, a river of crisp blue cut across the landscape, breaking into smaller tributaries as it neared the horizon. Himel's six wings lay against his back in resting position; but even retracted, their enormous size was intimidating.

The Pri-Rada turned his head and looked back over his shoulder as Sariel approached. "Join me," he said quietly.

After looking back at the two massive guards standing a few paces away on each flank, Sariel stepped up to the edge of the cliff and joined his superior.

"It's beautiful, isn't it," Himel asked softly.

Sariel knew the Iryllur was leading up to something—making a point, but he decided to play along anyway. "Yes, my Rada."

"Would you have this valley given over to the Marotru?"

"No, my Rada. Of course not."

The Pri-Rada continued to stare out across the vastness of the tranquil beauty before them. "Then why have you come to me instead of working through your immediate superior, unless to voice your disagreement with the mission to a higher authority?"

There's the point, Sariel thought. "My Rada. I do, indeed, disagree with the mission. But it is not because I want to see the enemy win. I am Iryllur, just as you are. I remain faithful."

"But you are not...just as I," the Pri-Rada countered, without raising his voice. He turned his head to look at Sariel and his numerous wings flexed slightly. "The higher orders have been tasked with thinking, and the lower orders with doing."

Sariel felt suddenly aware of his own wings—inferior in both size and quantity. He looked to the ground for a moment, then turned to the Pri-Rada. "Then why did you agree to meet, if not to hear my concerns?"

The superior turned his gaze back to the valley and crossed his arms. "...because I have concerns of my own. When someone under my authority voices opposition to our mission, it is a problem—"

"Regardless of the reason?" Sariel asked quickly.

The Pri-Rada inhaled slowly, pausing for a moment before answering. "Regardless..."

Sariel could see his superior's irritation mounting, but his own frustration was quickly becoming more of a concern.

"The Viytur gather and analyze the intelligence. Myself, and the other Pri-Radas, turn the intelligence into useable information. And you soldiers act on it," he explained calmly, as if to a new recruit.

"I know the process!" Sariel blurted out, unable to control himself in the face of such ridicule. "I'm questioning the intelligence. Why are you assigning my strike team to this operation?"

Himel turned his body to face Sariel and all six of his wings flared out to the extent of their reach. "Are you afraid of your mission?"

Sariel stepped backward and suddenly noticed that the guards had come a few steps forward. "No, my Rada."

"Are you one of the Marotru?"

"No, my Rada!"

"Are you faithful to the Holy One?"

"YES, MY RADA!"

"ARE YOU A SOLDIER?"

"YES, MY RADA!"

"I CAN'T HEAR YOU!"

"RADA TALAD!"

Sariel's body shook as he woke. His skin was damp with sweat. He was lying on the ground, looking up at the inside of a thatched roof. He lay still for a moment, breathing deeply as if fear and anger were things that this body could rid itself of with each exhale. When he composed himself, he climbed to his feet and walked out of the shelter into the morning light.

* * * *

"Come back soon and tell me what you find," Sheyir heard her father say.

Yeduah and Sariel were standing on the outskirts of the village, speaking in private. Sheyir's heart was racing as she hid among the trees, listening to the exchange between the two men.

Why is he leaving?

She had not spied on anyone since her childhood, but it seemed to be a regular occurrence lately. She wished it wasn't necessary, but since Sariel had arrived, many unusual things were happening in her village and she couldn't contain her curiosity. Reaching up, she parted the vines and peered through the leaves.

Sariel nodded, then turned and walked into the trees to the north.

Where is he going?

Sheyir waited until her father moved back toward the village before she left her hiding place. Running as swiftly and quietly as possible, she paralleled the path that Sariel had taken. A moment later, she stood on the eastern bank of the stream that flowed from Bahyith toward Arar Gahiy. In her haste, she had passed him, and now searched in panic until she saw him coming along the shore.

Sariel walked with his head down, seemingly unaware of his surroundings.

Sheyir's heart beat frantically in her chest as she moved upstream toward him.

Sariel finally looked up when Sheyir was nearly close enough to touch him. His forehead smoothed and his lips curled into a smile.

"Weren't you going to say goodbye?" she asked above the sound of the water. His bright blue eyes almost looked as if he'd been crying.

"I was hoping you'd follow me out here," he said quietly, looking over his shoulder. "You know I cannot express my feelings for you openly. At least, not yet."

Sheyir's heart leaped to hear the word *feelings*. "Where are you going?"

Sariel reached out with both hands and pulled her closer. "Your father gave me his name last night," he said, looking down into her eyes.

"Yes. I know," she replied with a smile. The feeling of his touch was exhilarating, but his leaving and the look in his eyes were deeply troubling.

"I'm making great progress toward gaining Yeduah's trust," he continued. "But he will never allow us to marry until I'm fully accepted into the tribe. I must have his complete trust."

Sheyir's face suddenly felt hot. She and Sariel had spent a considerable amount of time together in the past few months and had exchanged many tender moments. But they'd never spoken of marriage. Nor had they even spoken directly about their feelings for one another. It was assumed, but never voiced until this moment.

"...to marry?" she repeated.

"That is, of course, only if you're willing," Sariel added.

Now tears welled up in Sheyir's eyes. To hear a man speak so passionately was utterly foreign to her. But she loved it. In fact, every conversation with this man was more exciting than the last. And even the simplest moments between them—times they sat in silence and watched the flow of the river—were more thrilling than the best times she'd experienced before they met. "I'm willing," she said softly.

With his strong arms around her, he leaned down and brought his face close to hers. For a moment, she could feel his breath against her lips. "I love you Sheyir," he said. Then he kissed her softly.

Sheyir knew instantly that she'd treasure this moment for as long as she lived. She laid her head against his chest, and listened to the beat of his heart. Finally, she looked up again. "Why do you have to go? Is he not satisfied with what you've already done?"

Sariel pulled away slightly to see her face. "It's not really a question of being satisfied. I have an ability that he finds useful. It is in the best interest of his people to gain as much benefit as possible from it. Either someone powerful made those figurines or taught those men to make them for themselves.[10] Your father and I both know that either possibility is only a signal of a grave threat to your people."

"Can't you ignore it? Why do you seek out danger?" she pleaded.

Suddenly, something behind Sariel's eyes flashed. There were no visual clues or changes in expression. But something passed over him in an instant that he immediately concealed. Something that made Sheyir think she'd wounded him deeply.

He blinked heavily before speaking. "The last time I ignored my intuition, people died."

Sheyir stared into his eyes, wondering when the day would come when he would tell her what had happened. She was suddenly aware of how little she knew of him. *How many lives he must have lived. How many things he must have seen.*

"I'm going to find the source of this threat and learn anything that your father would consider useful. And I'll continue to help him for as long as it takes. Eventually I will be considered one of the Chatsiyram."

Sheyir laid her head against Sariel's chest again and watched the stream flow by, soaking in the comfort and safety of his love. In that moment, whatever doubts were clinging to the back of her mind drifted away. And all that was left was confidence that she wanted to be with this man, this Baynor, for the rest of her life.

"We could just run away," Sheyir offered, not realizing what she had said until the words came out of her mouth.

"It would not be right for me to take you away from your people. I want to do this the honorable way."

Sheyir smiled at this, moved by Sariel's unwavering dedication and enjoying being the object of it. "Then go. But guard yourself and come back safely to me."

"I will," he answered. "And thoughts of you will sustain me."

15

Enoch leaned against a tree, breathing heavily after cresting a hill. It was now late in the afternoon, but the shade of the forest kept the air cool. As his heart slowed to a comfortable pace, he began to look around him and take in the view. The ridge on which he stood looked to be the southernmost of a chain of peaks that grew in height as they extended to the north. Each peak protruded from the low-lying mist like islands from water.

After leaving Haragdeh, the Fields of Slaughter as he would remember them, Enoch reverted to the habit that had been formed during his long journey from Sedekiyr. He awoke, gathered food, ate, and looked for shelter. Every day, he asked the Holy One for guidance and listened carefully. And day after day, he received some sign or message that confirmed his purpose—to find the Myndarym. But direction continued to be a source of confusion.

Weeks later, he reached a narrow strip of land between two bodies of water. After crossing this, he spent the next week and a half exploring a parcel of land that was surrounded by water and attached to the mainland on three sides by land bridges. This place, he named Sahveyim. After crossing the western land bridge, Enoch wandered along the shore of what he called the Great Waters, for they seemed to have no end. Eventually leaving the shore, he continued north as it passed from sight into the east. Gradually, the flat terrain began to steepen until he reached the chain of mountain peaks where he now stood.

Throughout his journey, with plenty of time to meditate on the events he witnessed at Mudena Del-Edha, Enoch realized that Semjaza and his soldiers were not Myndarym. They never changed their forms. They moved and even spoke with more confidence. Perhaps pride or arrogance. But they seemed altogether graceless and inelegant compared to the Myndarym. Enoch could still hear the complexity of Ananel's voice and see the way he moved across the land. He was agile even when not in his animal form.

If Enoch's message was only for the Myndarym, then the Holy One would deal separately with Semjaza. This realization lifted a weight from Enoch's shoulders and focused his thoughts once again on the ones who *shape* creation. Though the Myndarym weren't part of Semjaza's open defiance, they still held themselves partially responsible for what happened to the Speaker and his escorts.

Wait. That's not true. They don't hold themselves responsible at all. They believe that the armies of Heaven will hold them responsible. And that is not repentance. That's fear of judgment.

Now Enoch saw the challenge in his mission. These magnificent creatures were still in defiance, but theirs was different from Semjaza's. Theirs was inward. The kind that causes them to lie to themselves.

Denial!

This kind of defiance was far more difficult to correct. Enoch was sure of this, for it was the same problem that he'd been battling among his own tribe for years. The Shayeth were a stubborn people who had lost their knowledge of the Holy One. After years of concerning themselves with only what they could see and touch and taste, their willful ignorance of the unseen had become their way of life. Now Enoch realized why he had been chosen to speak to the Myndarym.

Holy One. Your thoughts are high above mine. After all this time, I finally see a glimpse of what You have been preparing me for. And may You also use this task to teach me something that I can carry back to my people. Show me how to open their stubborn hearts.

Just as his thoughts turned to the Shayeth, he pictured Zacol and Methu. Tears came instantly to his eyes as he thought about them, alone, living on the outskirts of Sedekiyr, treated as people who were barely tolerable. It was Enoch's fault that they would never have a normal life. They were forced to live with the consequences of Enoch's choices. And now, he wasn't even there to help them.

Suddenly, Enoch felt his stomach tighten and his skin became sensitive.

Is it my family? Holy One, are you telling me something about them? Please protect them and provide for them.

Enoch now felt an overwhelming sense that something was watching him. He turned quickly, but the forest was still and silent.

No predators!

He looked to the sky.

No flying creatures!

Just as he exhaled in relief, he noticed something through the trees. His throat tightened at the same time his heart began to beat loudly.

In the shadows of a rock outcropping, a massive figure of hair and teeth blended almost perfectly with the surroundings.

Enoch held his breath, unable to even scream. Then a flicker of recognition brought an abrupt end to his fear.

The wolfen form stepped silently from the rocks. The creature whose back stood several feet taller than Enoch's head began to shimmer. Its coarse, gray fur dissolved into tiny strands of light which grew in intensity, expanding until they broke apart into millions of sparks. Quickly, they reassembled into the silhouette of a human, two times taller than Enoch. As the shimmering faded, the recognizable face of Ananel remained.

"How did you find us, Prophet?" the Myndar asked in a soft, yet powerful voice.

Enoch felt a surge of exhaustion, then relief in the aftermath of the fear. He inhaled deeply. "It was the Holy One." All of a sudden, Enoch realized that Ananel had spoken in the angelic language. And he had understood the words, and replied in the same language.

How can I—? Oh! That's what he did to me at Haragdeh, when he saw through my eyes!

Ananel's eyebrows narrowed. "Do you have another message for us?"

Enoch pushed himself away from the tree and stood straightened. "No. The same message."

Ananel made a low noise in his throat, like a growl, but quieter. "Your presence here is troubling."

Enoch remained silent.

"Very well. Come with me. I'll take you to the others," the angel replied. Again, his body began to shimmer as he *shaped* himself back into an animal. When he was finished, he crouched low to the ground.

Enoch recognized the cue and climbed onto his back. Within minutes, they had descended the hilltop and entered the misty forest below. Even at Ananel's easy pace, he still managed to cover incredible distance compared to Enoch's slow wanderings. Quickly settling into the rhythm of Ananel's trot, Enoch's mind began to wander. His thoughts returned to the differences he had noted between Ananel and Semjaza.

"This thing you do—changing into an animal; can all angels do this?"

"No," Ananel replied. "But the Myndarym can." There was hint of amusement in his voice.

"Semjaza and his followers had different forms, some with wings. Are they Myndar, as well?"

Ananel chuckled now. "No. But I will forgive the insult because of your ignorance."

Even though he already suspected the answer, Enoch still felt embarrassed. "What are they?"

"The winged ones are called Iryllurym. Semjaza and the others without wings are called Anduarym. And there is also a third kind under his rule. They are called Vidirym. They live and move beneath the water."

"Hmm," Enoch mumbled. After a moment of silence, he worked up the courage to ask the question that had been running through his mind since that fearful day in the Haragdeh. "Why did they attack the Speaker and his angels?"

"It seems a rash move, I know. But Semjaza is no fool. There is strategy in everything he does."

"Oh. Um. What I meant was, I don't even understand the reason for their conflict."

"Ah. I see," Ananel said, gracefully side-stepping a tree. "Semjaza is a soldier. He was a Pri-Rada in the Saman. In your tongue, that would be Third Rule of Joint Operations, which is like an elder who is in authority over men who fight with other tribes. When he came to this world, he did so in violation of the laws that govern our kind. Not only is his presence here forbidden, but to establish his own kingdom in this realm is willful disobedience of the highest order. The Speaker came to make it evident that the other elders are aware of what Semjaza is doing here."

Enoch noted the hypocrisy in Ananel's explanation, but decided not to speak of it yet. "But wouldn't his actions only anger the elders even further?"

"Perhaps. But Semjaza knows that they are too busy fighting other wars. So he sent a very clear message. He will not go without a fight. And that fight will be costly to the elders."

"Is there much fighting where you come from?" he asked the angel.

"Yes. It has been that way from the beginning."

Enoch paused for a moment, trying to make sense of all that he heard. Watching the trees pass by in the afternoon light, he was struck with the beauty of his own world. Yet, somewhere invisible to his eyes was another realm that sounded both amazing and sad at the same time. When these thoughts passed, Enoch decided it was time.

"And what about you? If you know it is forbidden to be here, why did you come?"

Ananel didn't answer right away. In fact, Enoch wondered whether or not he had heard the question. But Ananel's canine ears seemed capable of hearing much more than his own, so he remained quiet.

"The Myndarym are not soldiers," he said finally. "We are— Do you have people among your tribe who make things— craftsmen, builders, and such?"

"Yes," Enoch replied, amused at the thought of an angel of heaven trying hard to relate his world to that of a human.

"And do you have people among your tribe who make things, not just to be used, but simply for the pleasure of others?"

Enoch thought hard to find the equivalent among the Shayetham. "Sometimes, my wife puts flowers in her hair. There is no purpose in this other than to give me pleasure when I look at her."

"Yes," Ananel replied. "Among the Myndarym, we build many things, including those which only serve to give pleasure. In this way, we understand your world and your kind far better than Semjaza and his soldiers ever will. But a short while ago, at least by our accounting of time, some of us were placed under his leadership."

"I see," Enoch replied. The sun was almost set now and he wondered how Ananel could see where he was going. "How far must we travel before we reach the others?"

"We're nearly there now," he replied.

Enoch couldn't see anything ahead, but trusted that Ananel told the truth. "So, is your disagreement with Semjaza due to your different tribes?" Enoch asked, trying to make sense of the conversations and actions he'd witnessed.

"I suppose that is one way to explain it. It is not only our tribes, as you say, but our very natures. The Myndarym see the beauty in creation. We enjoy making new things and fixing things that are broken. We take pleasure in seeing and knowing how something is constructed. Soldiers tend to see things differently. I suppose it is to be expected, but Semjaza and his angels have learned to see creation in terms of leverage, in terms of power."

"What do you mean?" Enoch asked, embarrassed again that he was unfamiliar with these terms.

"All of Semjaza's relationships to others have been defined by authority. Who has authority over me? Over whom do I have authority? And because of their purpose, their relationship to the enemy is defined by the power to fight. Who is more powerful than I? Whom can I conquer? These are the questions they ask themselves."

"And the Myndarym resent his authority?" Enoch asked.

"Yes." Ananel leaped effortlessly up a short bank of rocks.

"...because he misuses it?" Enoch probed further.

"We are here," Ananel announced, abruptly ending the conversation.

The trees opened to reveal a shallow, wide valley in the western foothills of the mountains that they'd been paralleling. A gentle river wound its way from the higher elevation and emptied into a larger body of water to the west. In the fading light, Enoch could barely make out a tall forest of trees that seemed unnatural among the otherwise grassy valley.

A moment later, Ananel's long strides brought them close to the forest and Enoch realized that it was no ordinary stand of trees. These reached higher into the air than any others he'd ever seen. And what appeared unnatural from afar was now simply breathtaking. The trunks and limbs were intertwined with each other, as if they were threads making up a cloth. But there were no signs of splintering or breakage among the branches. It was as if they had grown this way from seedlings. Above the towering wall of interwoven branches, the upper portion of the forest was thick with leaves and flowering blossoms. It was the most beautiful thing Enoch had ever seen.

"It has only been a few months and already you've created this?" he asked in amazement.

"As I said, we are builders."

As he stared, a question came to Enoch's mind and he couldn't resist asking it. Though he already knew the answer, he wanted Ananel to ponder it further. "You said my presence here troubles you. Why?"

Ananel stopped and crouched low, while Enoch climbed to the ground.

Shaping to his angelic form, Ananel continued toward a doorway formed by the meeting of two arched tree trunks. Moving now on two legs, he looked back at Enoch without stopping.

"This is what we must discuss in the presence of the Myndarym. Come with me."

Since leaving Sedekiyr, each day had brought Enoch something different. Whether it was new food to eat, large and vicious creatures, or dangerous tribes of people, each new experience forced him to adapt. But this moment was different. Instead of danger or fear of something new, he took pleasure in everything his eyes touched. The inside of the Myndar city was even more extraordinary than the outside. The bending and weaving of trees was a theme throughout, only now he walked through the beautiful complexity, beneath covered passages that led from one gigantic room to another. The ceilings seemed impossibly high, and were thatched so tightly that neither the stars nor the moon shone through. But this didn't impede travel through the city, for the interior was illuminated by the glowing stalks of some unknown vines that wove through the other structures. In his mind, he named it Aragatsiyr, City of Woven Trees.

Ananel led Enoch to the uncovered center of the city where a gentle pool of water was gathered, fed by a diverted stream from the nearby river. Everywhere Enoch looked he saw such extraordinary sights that his mind reeled from the effort of comprehension. Those things that he did understand caused him to think of how to incorporate them into his village. Slowly, the growing presence of Myndarym entering the uncovered area from passages around the perimeter, and their skeptical stares began to erode his fascination. Finally, a powerful voice cut through the murmur of the crowd.

"Fellow Myndarym. Once again I bring to you Enoch of the Shayetham."

Now the murmur rose to a din as the other angels expressed their confusion about the presence of a human within their city.

"I found him standing on a ridge to the south of our city. He apparently found his way here through no means other than direction from the Holy One."

"Did you bring us another message?" someone asked.

"No," Ananel answered quickly, before Enoch could say anything. "He brings the same message, but now that we are free of the complications of Semjaza, we will hear him."

In the awkward silence, Enoch looked around at the surrounding faces and recognized some of them from months ago. But now he felt better-equipped to understand what he saw and noticed more details. All of them were large, but thinner and less muscular than Semjaza's soldiers. He saw a variety of skin and hair color, vibrant and diverse compared to humans. Blues and greens, oranges and yellows. Eyes brighter than the color of flowers. Their graceful beauty was beyond anything he'd ever witnessed. And most surprising was the presence of several who appeared to be female. The perfect shape of their faces made Enoch stare in disbelief. Their long, flowing hair seemed to move as if blown by the wind, though the air was perfectly still. Beneath their loose flowing clothing, Enoch caught brief glimpses of their outlines as they moved, sending shivers through his body that made him blush. Immediately, he thought of Zacol and Methu and closed his eyes in shame, trying to shut out the visions of perfection before him. He wondered if these magnificent creatures ever married and had families of their own.

When he opened his eyes again, the Myndarym were assembled around the perimeter of the meeting area. Enoch felt their perceiving gaze staring into his very spirit.

"Enoch of the Shayetham," one of the women began.

Enoch immediately averted his eyes to keep from being distracted.

"...you must know that Semjaza lied to us."

Her voice seemed to soothe every part of him, washing away months of exhaustion. He took a slow breath and tried to compose himself. "This is what I've heard, but I do not understand the nature of your relationship with him."

The voice of another joined the conversation, this one decidedly male. "We all wished to live in the Temporal Realm. He offered us a way to come in secret in exchange for our help. But now the Amatru know we're here. And we will be held responsible for what Semjaza has done."

Again, Enoch heard the shifting of blame to Semjaza, but there was clearly more to the situation than what they were revealing. When he looked out across the faces in the crowd, he found pleading, distraught looks. "Please. I am merely a human who listens for the voice of the Holy One," he begged in return. "I know very little of your world or the things you've done. I don't wish to show you disrespect, but I don't understand what you are telling me. Please make your speech plain so that I may understand and answer you accordingly."

Ananel stepped forward from his place beside Enoch. "I have a suggestion. This Prophet has told me that the Holy One gives him visions."

Immediately, a look of understanding crossed the faces staring at Enoch. Again, he seemed to be the only one who was confused.

"Perhaps even the angelic language of this realm is insufficient."

Enoch shrugged his shoulders, unsure if he was supposed to respond.

Ananel knelt down and looked Enoch directly in the eye. "Would you allow us to speak to you in another way, and to make that way known to you?"

"I... Yes, I suppose," Enoch replied cautiously. "Like the language we are using now?"

"No," the angel replied with a reassuring smile. "This other way is quite different."

Enoch nodded.

Ananel stood up and opened his mouth. Slowly, the meeting area was filled with the sweetest of sounds, a gentle song that drifted among the blades of grass and the gently swirling water of the pool. It gradually built in volume and complexity as others joined in.

Enoch felt a blanket of peace cover him, and the strong need to close his eyes, which he promptly obeyed. One moment, he was thinking how beautiful their singing was, and the next he found himself seeing, feeling, hearing, touching, and even tasting things that he was sure he had never experienced. It lasted only a few minutes, but when the sensation passed, he understood exactly what had happened.

In the following silence, Enoch opened his eyes. "This is your language which cannot be spoken in this realm. How then did you speak it to me and how did I understand it?"

Ananel, now standing at his full height, looked down. "Though our realms have drifted apart, there is a portion of the Eternal still attached to the Temporal. We moved you into this place where our language can be spoken. We opened your ears by singing a Song of Understanding."

Enoch looked down at the soft grass beneath his feet and slowly rubbed his palms together. His mind now raced with ideas that had been planted in his mind—memories so complete that he felt as though they were his experiences. Now he understood that words were but a pale shadow of how these creatures communicated. Spoken language seemed terribly inadequate. But he gave them words anyway.

"Semjaza wanted to come to this realm, but he was held back by the limitations of his own ability. He and his soldiers are not Myndarym. They could not *shift*."

Enoch could see nods of affirmation from the Myndarym as he began pacing, the thoughts coming more quickly than he could speak.

"He desired to set up an earthly kingdom without opposition and needed your help to get here, and your knowledge of humans to gain control of the Kahyin people. Your role as Shapers had already come to an end and you were facing military service under his leadership. He offered to give you another existence among the creation you knew so well, to take you along and make it appear as if you perished in battle. But he failed in this. My coming, and that of the Speaker, revealed that the Holy One and the Amatru knew what had transpired, and what Semjaza was attempting to do."

Enoch slowly looked up at the faces he once feared. Now, as he wiped the tears from his eyes, he no longer feared them, but feared for them.

"You are not supposed to be here. The heart of the Holy One is broken by your actions. His tears come now from my eyes," Enoch whispered.

"You can see now that we have hid nothing from you," Ananel admitted. "And this is our plea to you—that you take our petition for forgiveness before the Holy One. Present it to Him and make Him understand our unfortunate position. We desire peace and not war. We do not align ourselves with Semjaza any longer."[12]

Enoch opened his mouth to speak, but nothing came out. There were too many conflicting thoughts and emotions. Again and again, he heard the Myndarym's refusal to accept their own disobedience.   Again and again, they shifted the blame to Semjaza. And now they asked him to go before the Holy One and *make Him understand,* as if He needed to. As if His perspective was wrong and He needed some missing piece of information to reach a just conclusion. And yet, Enoch also shared their memory of Semjaza's manipulation. By what they placed into his mind, he experienced their betrayal. He felt their helplessness and he sympathized with their situation. Finally, he managed a few words.

"I don't know how to take your petition before Him."

Ananel knelt down again. "You said He speaks to you. Don't you also speak with Him?"

"Yes," Enoch admitted. "But it's not the same as we are now speaking."

Ananel hung his head. "We do not understand the fullness of the Holy One's love for your kind. From the beginning, He has favored humans above all other creations. Even above us. None of the Myndarym have ever spoken or heard directly from Him. Yet you experience this daily. We can see that you are special, even among humans. If you are unable to take our petition before Him, then surely all is lost. We are without hope."

Enoch looked from Ananel to the other faces among the meeting area. He couldn't stand to see them this way. For such magnificent creatures, they now appeared pathetic. From some unknown place inside him, confidence welled up—a confidence propelled by mercy. "I will try," he offered. "I will try."

16

Sariel traveled north along the stream, following the same path that he'd taken previously to Arar Gahiy, but this time he was alone. The day after leaving Bahyith, he *shaped* into his Iryllur form and flew east into the foothills of Bokhar. Crossing over the Morning Mountain, he descended into flatlands that were choked with towering trees and dense undergrowth. According to Yeduah's instructions, the People of the Trees lived in the forests which grew thickest between the eastern slope of Bokhar and the Great Waters.

For several days, Sariel flew in a methodical search pattern over the land, always *shifting* his consciousness toward the Eternal and back. Each time he perceived the glow of a living being's spirit he descended to the trees for a closer look with his physical eyes. But he found nothing except animals of all kinds—reptiles, and mammals—moving in herds, or at other times alone. Occasionally, a school of fish swimming through the abundant streams would appear from high above as a gathering of human spirits. But the Aytsam were nowhere to be found.

Gradually, Sariel made his way south and east. There, on the narrowest section of land that separated the Great Waters from another body of water to its northwest, he noticed a difference in the pattern of the trees. With caution, he landed and approached the area on foot.

What he had barely noticed from above turned out to be human dwellings suspended in the thick braches. Platforms of bundled saplings were connected by rope bridges, creating an entire village high overhead, just beneath the underhanging foliage. But it was deserted. Sariel flew up to the braches and walked along the platforms, looking for clues. Then he searched the ground beneath the village, but it looked as if it hadn't been used in months.

A brief flicker of movement in the distance suddenly caught his attention.

Sariel stopped and peered through the congested throng of massive tree trunks.

Did I imagine it?

Just then, a flash of dark, earthy skin flitted between trees to his right. Something was moving south.

Sariel *shaped* into his human form and started off at a run. Vines threatened to strangle him as he dodged between the undergrowth, heading southeast on a course that would bring him into contact with whatever was out there. A few minutes later, he reached a clearing where thick grass grew up around a boulder. Without breaking his stride, he leaped onto the side of the rock and scrambled to its top. With his breath now coming in heaves, he watched and listened, hoping that his prey hadn't deviated from the direction it had been moving.

Just when he began to lose hope, he saw something else. This time, he was sure that it was more than one person. They were still moving south and he had been moving parallel with them and was now slightly behind. They were quicker than he thought.

The People of the Trees!

Sprinting from his vantage point, Sariel dodged between bushes and quickly made his way through the waist-high grass and out of the clearing. Under another stand of trees, the grasses gave way to wet soil and rotting leaves. Though unpleasant, he moved quicker over this terrain. By the time he reached the next clearing, he was sure that he'd gained ground, expecting them to be directly east of him, perhaps a little to the south.

His eyes scanned the opposite tree line and his ears struggled to hear over the beating of his heart. But nothing was there.

Did I miss something?

Suddenly, he heard a faint scraping noise that sounded different from the other jungle noises. It came from the southeast.

There you are.

Sariel quickly left the trees and crossed another meadow, swinging eastward to bring himself directly behind his prey. He quickly found that the terrain they were moving over offered easier passage than his own, which explained part of their speed. The soil was compacted on either side of a stream. And he was certain now they'd spotted him, which would explain the reason for their haste.

Skirting wide around a shallow pool, Sariel broke through the brush and stopped dead in his tracks. There, a hundred feet before him, stood a gigantic feline. Even in its crouched position, its massive head was level with Sariel's, while its back stood slightly taller. Its pale orange fur was flecked with brown spots and a few vertical stripes running along its back. The creature's face was scrunched into a snarl, revealing a massive jaw of flesh-rending teeth, two of which were longer than Sariel's hands. The clawed paws of its forelegs were embedded into the soil, ready to propel the cat forward at any moment.

Sariel backed away slowly, keeping his eyes fixed on the large, golden orbs set into the animal's face. If he tried to *shape*, the beast would kill him before he could even take to the air.

The cat lowered its body.

Sariel held his breath.

It sprang forward.

Sariel spun around and ran for the shallow pool where the stream jogged sharply to the east. Leaping across the stream in one giant stride, he turned parallel to the water and sprinted as quickly as his human legs would carry him. He knew he could only stay ahead of the creature for a brief moment, and began scanning the ground for anything that could be used as a weapon. The sound of water and his own footsteps through the damp, compacted soil was all that could be heard. But he knew the animal pursued him, silently and rapidly gaining ground. A quick glance over his right shoulder confirmed this fear. The cat had already closed half the distance between them and was now approaching the stream from the south.

Up ahead, the water diverted around a jagged pile of stone. Sariel surged ahead and grabbed a fist-sized rock from the ground without slowing.

All of a sudden, something large and covered in fur burst from the brush on the north side of the stream.

Sariel lunged forward, bringing his left arm around in a backhanded motion, striking the rock against the creature's snout as it passed behind him.

In that instant, the first cat leaped over the stream and the other animal in an attempt to pounce.

Sariel quickly ducked and rolled forward on the ground. Coming to his feet with most of his speed intact, he continued running. He was now aware of pain in his right shoulder and back that quickly escalated into a searing ache. A few more inches and the cat's claws would have stuck in his flesh and brought him to a halt.

Now that the animals were on the north side of the stream, Sariel jumped across to the south side and kept running, heading blindly into a thick tangle of vegetation. The vines slowed him considerably and he grasped wildly at the tendrils, ripping and tearing through them as he pushed his legs to the limit of their strength.

Unexpectedly, the vines gave way to open air. Sariel had only an instant to notice the stream falling over the edge of a cliff before his body did the same. Instinctively, he *shaped* to his angelic form. Just before hitting the rocks fifty feet below, he extended his massive wings and felt the lift of the air beneath them. As he pulled up, the distorted surface of the pool below him spread outward in the sudden gust of wind. He quickly gained elevation and banked to the south, coming about to see two giant felines standing on the edge of the cliff and a third coming behind them.

The three animals began to shimmer until they took on angelic forms.

Circling back to the top of the cliff, Sariel came to rest on the opposite side of the stream where it widened before plummeting over the edge.

Over the sound of the waterfall, one of them shouted. "Are you a Speaker?" His golden eyes and striped skin tones still held the same appearance as his animal form.

"No," Sariel answered.

"You wear an Iryllur form, yet you can *shape*."

"Yes," Sariel answered. Although it was uncommon for Myndar to serve as soldiers, it wasn't unheard of. The surprise in the eyes of these Shapers indicated that they'd been away from the Eternal Realm for a long time.

The angel on the far left looked more intensely at Sariel than the others. His mouth and nose were covered in blood. "You were not with Semjaza. I don't recognize you."

"No," Sariel replied. "And I take it you're not with him either?"

"Not anymore," the third one spoke. He was slightly darker than the others, though with similar features.

"Who are you?" the first one asked.

Before Sariel could answer the one on the left spoke again. "Why were you chasing us?"

"I didn't intend to. I was looking for the Aytsam. Sorry about the rock," he offered.

The Shaper wiped a hand across his face and looked at the blood in his palm, apparently unaware until this moment that he'd been injured.

"Sorry about the claws," the one in the middle replied. Judging by body language, he was their leader.

Sariel nodded in reply, flexing his back and feeling the associated pain and wetness from the blood. "It'll heal." Even though there were three of them, he could see that they were intimidated in the presence of a soldier. Sariel held up his hands. "Can I come across?"

The leader glanced at the other two, then nodded.

Sariel slowly spread his wings and jumped into the air, then glided effortlessly across the stream to land gently next to the Myndarym.

"We didn't know anyone else was here," the injured one stated.

"Neither did I. I came here on my own. I'm Sariel," he replied, extending his hand.

The injured one looked suspicious at first, then slowly grasped his hand, clearly uncomfortable with the entirely human gesture of greeting. "Jomjael," he replied. "And this is Tamael and Batarel."

"*The* Sariel?" Tamael asked.

"Yeah," Sariel admitted cautiously.

"We've heard of you."

"Oh," Sariel said. "Most of what you've heard is probably exaggerated."

Tamael smiled, his golden eyes now softened with humor. "I know the Iryllurym deal with the enemy on a regular basis, but I doubt they've picked up lying as a habit."

Sariel just raised his head slightly. "Where are you all going?"

The three Myndarym became very quiet and exchanged glances with each other.

Sariel had already pieced together the situation. His question was more of a formality. But they were clearly still trying to keep it a secret. "I'm only asking because you might need another pair of eyes on Semjaza."

Now the Myndarym were still.

"Your falling out must have been pretty bad," Sariel guessed. "Now you're camped somewhere up north and keeping a watch in case he wants to retaliate."

Finally, Tamael gave in. "You're quick," the leader admitted. "We did have a falling out, months ago. He's not to be trusted."

"I can imagine," Sariel replied.

Tamael looked reluctant. "And we could use your help."

"Of course," Sariel answered, folding his wings behind his shoulders. "I'd be glad to help."

Tamael nodded, but was silent for a moment. "What do you want in return?"

Inwardly, Sariel smiled. These angels had obviously spent enough time with Semjaza to learn how things worked within a culture of conflict. "What were your roles under Semjaza?"

Tamael's golden eyes narrowed. "...various things. Why does that matter?"

Sariel smiled outwardly now at the vague answer. He wasn't going to get information from these Myndarym without offering something in return. "Because I've witnessed something quite unusual and I would like to know if Semjaza is the cause of it."

"You'll need to be more specific," Batarel replied this time.

"Did he order you to make contact with demons?" Sariel asked bluntly.

All three of the angels straightened their posture at these words.

"Demons? What are you talking about?" Tamael asked suddenly.

Sariel folded his arms. "What were your roles under Semjaza?"

It was Jomjael who spoke this time. "We *shifted* him and his soldiers here. We helped him understand and control humans. And we built him a fortress."

"Did any of you make contact with demons on his behalf?" Sariel asked again.

"What did you witness?" Tamael asked.

"Alright," Sariel said, holding up his hand in resignation. "I witnessed humans wearing figurines around their necks that gave demons the authority to inhabit their bodies."

"This is not possible," Batarel replied.

"Where did you see this?" Tamael asked.

"First tell me if Semjaza is capable of this. Is he working with demons?"

Tamael shook his head. "I have not seen or heard of this before. And I don't know any angel, Myndar or other, who would do such a thing."

Jomjael, who'd been mostly silent, folded his arms. "If anyone were capable of this, it would be Semjaza. We have seen that his conscience is clouded with many dark secrets."

"Where did you see this?" Tamael asked, getting back to his line of curiosity.

Sariel turned around and pointed. "To the northeast lay two long mountains which run parallel to each other. At the north end of the valley between them is a lake. Along its northern shoreline, there are several demons who are constrained to this realm. Their location is fixed over the remains of dead humans. That's where I found the figurine. I moved one and I observed the power it has over them. The demon was helpless to move beyond the authority granted to it by the figurine."

"But how can such an object take precedence over the will of a human?" Tamael asked.

"That's what I wondered. I believe it has something to do with the human's desire to keep the figurine. They are crafted from gold and humans have yet to discover metals, or the art of working them."[10] In reality, Sariel knew this to be true. After the exorcism of the Chatsiyr man, he understood all too well the nature of the figurine and its control over the human will. But he kept this a secret.

Tamael looked to the north, then back to Sariel. "Can you show it to us?"

"You don't believe me?"

"I believe you," Tamael answered. "But I wish to see this for myself.

"I don't believe it," Jomjael answered.

Sariel slowly nodded. "Alright. I'll take you there. After you see it for yourself, then you'll take me to Semjaza."

"Agreed," Tamael said.

Jomjael and Batarel simply nodded.

* * * *

In the soft morning light, Enoch followed the diverted stream which ran from the Myndar city of Aragatsiyr, until it connected to the nearby river.¹³ He was unsure how long this would take, so he chose a spot under a tree that would provide plenty of shade in the coming hours. The fact was, he didn't really know what he was doing, or if it was possible. But he'd made up his mind to find a quiet place where he could at least speak to the Holy One without interruption. There was no guarantee that his prayers would be answered, but he was confident that the Holy One could hear anything.

Leaning against the smooth trunk of the tree, one that looked more natural than those in the city, he slid down to a sitting position. The sweet fragrance of the tree filled his nostrils, and the constant gurgle of the slow river drifted to his ears. He knew right away that he'd found the right place. Closing his eyes, he breathed deeply.

Holy One. In Your infinite wisdom, You led me to this place. Again I find myself among Your angels. Their ways seemed complicated to me, yet they revealed to me everything that has transpired...

Enoch's thoughts trailed off as he was distracted by a mist that had risen from the river. He watched as it spread outward from the water and began to climb the banks on either side. It continued to climb fast until it enveloped him, blocking his sight of everything except the sky above. He rubbed his eyes to ensure that he was seeing correctly, but the mist remained. He looked up and stared in disbelief as the sun raced across the sky in a giant arc, heading quickly for the western horizon. Suddenly, the sky darkened and the stars and moon passed by with the same suddenness as the sun. Enoch now began to look frantically around him, fearing that something bad was about to happen. Instead, a gentle breeze began to blow. It felt cool against his skin, while the mist began to clear. In a short time, he could see the river again, briefly glittering in the light of the moon. Only a moment later, the moon fell below the western horizon and only the stars remained, speeding across their course in the same direction. To the east, the sky began to change from black to the darkest of blues, then gave way to violet before bursting forth with a brilliant orange. The sun leaped quickly from the horizon and began climbing in the sky again. The breeze had now grown into a fierce wind, and Enoch rose to his feet and walked toward the river, covering his face from the stinging sand that was beating against his skin.

Then, just as the sun touched the western horizon, Enoch felt his body lifting into the air. The same exhilaration he had felt when flying with the Speaker's escorts, he felt now, only it continued much longer as he rose higher and higher into the air. The valley became smaller and Aragatsiyr all but vanished below him as he could now see to the horizon in all directions. He'd never witnessed something so grand in all his years. The thought occurred to him that somewhere below and far to the south, his own village of Sedekiyr was nothing more than a tiny speck on the earth which now appeared as a blue and green mottled sphere, hanging in the darkness, with stars in the distance.

Once again, the sky turned light, but the light came from everywhere and nearly blinded him. He blinked at the harsh transition, then noticed that he was flying over land again, ascending in elevation as if he were climbing a steep mountain. The terrain looked somehow different, foreign and indescribable. As the rocks and trees sped by underneath a great city appeared, white on the mountain peak above him. It was majestic and its radiance illuminated everything near it. Enoch's eyes began to tear, but he dared not cover or close them for fear of missing the beauty that he struggled to comprehend. As he neared, he could make out a flickering movement around the base of the wall surrounding the city, which seemed to stretch so high into the air that the top could not be seen. His rapid ascent was uncontrollable and he shrank back in fear at the sight of fire surrounding the multi-colored foundation of the translucent wall. The tongues of *flame burned white at their centers, with flashes of every conceivable color at their edges. In the center of the wall stood an open gate, wide enough for every member of the Shayeth to walk through side by side. But the fire burned everywhere and blocked the entrance. The dancing colors of the flames were reflected a million times from the wall, which appeared as though constructed of innumerable pieces of transparent stone, as smooth as a lake surface turned on its side. Helpless against his own movement, Enoch covered his face with his arms and flinched, expecting to be burned, but he passed through the flames and the gate unharmed.*

Inside the gate was a vast city stretching to the horizon and beyond. Countless numbers of structures covered the landscape, their crystalline shapes glimmering from the light that seemed to come from all directions. Enoch's pace failed to slow as he approached a structure unlike anything he'd yet seen. Though the wooden intricacy of Aragatsiyr had seemed incredibly fantastic to him only yesterday, this building made it seem like a crude abomination by comparison. Its floor and walls were constructed of the same clear material, exquisitely formed into symmetrical shapes that interlocked.[14] As he moved inside, he saw pillars and arches that supported a ceiling of water which both reflected what was below it and the stars that showed above. Between the arches hovered magnificent and terrible creatures of light. Somehow, though he'd never seen them before and no one had ever explained them, Enoch knew they were called Keruvym. Their bodies, displaying both human and animal characteristics, looked as though they were made of fire. And they hovered in the air, propelled by six wings that moved in a blur.[15] Through the windows, Enoch could see the flames outside and he felt both intense heat and numbing cold at once.

Fear seized his heart and he felt his body shudder, then convulse uncontrollably. The convulsions sent him to the transparent floor where he landed hard on his knees. Collapsing from the terror in his spirit, he fell forward onto his face, but the motion seemed to carry him through the floor in a disorienting tumble until he found himself on his hands and knees in a different place.

Lifting his head slowly, he now saw the entrance to a second structure that was greater even than the first, both in immensity and splendor. The floor and ceiling and walls—if they could be called such, for they seemed as distant as the horizons and sky—danced with flame, but were not consumed by it. Through the pervasive terror, Enoch marveled, and wondered how it was possible for someone to craft such a thing out of fire. Through the entrance, at the center of the building, he could see there stood a throne of the most brilliant blue colors he'd ever seen. Nothing on earth could even compare to it. It hovered above the ground. Its cool light rivaled the intensity of the surrounding flames. Beneath the throne were living creatures that burned with the light of the sun. Shaped as circles standing on end, they were covered with eyes and spinning in all directions so that they appeared as spheres. Enoch knew them to be Ophanym, though he'd never seen them before. And he knew their purpose was to support the weight of the throne.[16] And for each of the Ophanym, one of the Keruvym stood alongside. From beneath the throne and the living creatures, rivers of white fire flowed in all directions.

Enoch shrank back in fear and covered his face from the blinding light. With eyes closed, he could still see the image that was burned into his mind. The One who sat upon the throne was still and immovable as a mountain. Enoch could feel power and majesty flowing in waves from Him. His clothing shone brighter than the sun itself and the fire around his throne prevented any others from coming near. Slowly, Enoch opened his eyes, but dared not look upon the Holy One. Instead, he kept his gaze averted and saw a multitude of angels larger than any number that he could count, for his language was unable to express such a number, neither could he comprehend their quantity. Their ranks stretched from *horizon to horizon. And like him, they were unable even to stand or look at the One upon the throne.*

An omnipresent silence abruptly cut through the air. It was so complete that, until this moment, Enoch hadn't realized the sheer volume of sound that preceded it.

"Come here, Enoch and listen to my voice."

It was the voice of the Holy One and Enoch knew it immediately. His shaking arms and knees suddenly lost their strength and he began to fall. Just before he crashed into the floor, one of the Keruvym caught him and lifted him by the arm. It escorted him through the entrance and into the throne room. Being pulled through the air, Enoch began to panic and dropped his head, suddenly ashamed at his own unworthiness.

"Do not be afraid, Enoch. Your obedience is counted as righteousness in my sight. Come near and listen to me."

The Keruv gently set him down upon the crystalline floor, which was surprisingly cool to the touch, despite the rivers of flame which flowed beneath its glossy surface.[17]

Enoch's fear dissipated entirely in that moment, replaced by an all-consuming love.

In the perfect silence, the Holy One spoke again. "My Wandering Stars have sent a human to intercede for them, but their purpose is to intercede for mankind."

Enoch could hear the sadness in his voice and he began to cry in sympathy.

"Because of their hardened hearts and deaf ears, I will speak to you. For you listen to me. Go and ask them, 'Why have you left the Eternal Realm? Why have you defiled yourself by lying with earthly beings? Why do you take wives like the children of earth and produce abominations as your offspring?[18] *Though you were holy and eternal, you have now defiled yourself with human blood and begotten children of flesh. You lusted after animals and have begotten creatures who were not meant to be. You desired these things as those who die. I have made the flesh of the earth as male and female*

so they may have children to continue their generations. But this is not my desire for you. I did not make companions for you because you were immortal for all generations. And now, abominations of spirit and flesh move throughout the realms. Because they were born of the flesh, the abominations of the Nephiylim will be a curse to the Temporal Realm. And because they were also born of the spirit, their eternal bodies will be a curse to the Eternal Realm. I see what is to come and the sin of the Nephiylim is always before me. They will afflict, oppress, destroy, make war, and work destruction upon my creation. They will rise up against the children of men and women, because they have proceeded from them. The Nephiylim will destroy each other before your eyes and by your hands. You will witness the death of your own children. And in the days of the slaughter and death of the Nephiylim, their spirits will be freed from their fleshly bodies and will continue to persecute mankind until the Day of Judgment in which this age will be consummated.'"[19]

"Now, go and say to the Myndarym, 'You were born in the Eternal Realm, yet all mysteries were not revealed to you. You know only the insignificant ones, and these, in the hardness of your hearts, you have made known to the children of men. Through these, they work great evil upon the earth.'"

"Though they claim to have revealed all things to you, I see their hearts and the things they keep hidden, even from each other. I see the things they have done and the things which they have yet to do. They have asked for peace, but will make war and teach the children of men to do likewise. Tell them, 'You will have no peace.'"

Through this dire message, Enoch could feel the brokenness and utter sadness of the Holy One as if they were his own emotions. Tears streamed down his face, uncontrollably.

"Now Enoch, son of righteousness; I have another message that you will not speak to the Myndarym. You will teach it to your children and they will teach it to their children. Thus, it will remain with your household for generations to come. At

the appointed time, it will be revealed to my Wandering Stars and they will hear and understand."

"Say to them, 'You will see your destruction from afar and will know it is coming. Because of your unfaithfulness, this judgment must come to pass. Therefore, I will raise up one from among those you despise. And I will awaken his eyes to the mysteries which I have hidden from men since the foundations of the world. His feet will I make to tread upon the paths of destruction and his hands to make war. He will uproot the seeds of corruption which you have sown throughout the earth. And then you will know that I am the Lord and my justice is everlasting.'"[21]

The words pierced Enoch's heart and he knew instantly that they would remain with him forever.

"Now Enoch, one who listens; there are many more things which you must see and hear, and write upon your heart and your mind. Things which are yet to come."

One of the Keruvym lifted Enoch from before the throne and began to pull him backwards. Slowly, the throne and multitude of angels withdrew into the distance. But the Holy One never receded. His vast form remained the same size even as the Keruv sped Enoch away.

17

Sariel approached the lake carefully, coming from the east and moving around the north end. Jomjael, Batarel, and Tamael followed close behind. All was eerily quiet in the valley, with only a light breeze stirring the tall grass. Swinging wide around the reeds, Sariel *shifted* his consciousness and saw a pale and sickly creature, its limbs grotesquely long, moving in the grass.

"*Shift* slightly toward the Eternal," he whispered over his shoulder. "You'll see it there in the grass."

A sharp intake of breath could be heard from the other Myndarym.

"You see. It's just as I told you. That's the one that was dragged away from the lake when I threw its statue."

"Indeed," whispered Tamael.

"Do you want to go closer?" Jomjael asked.

Sariel looked back at them. "...if you wish."

"Yes," Tamael said softly. "I'd like to see them up close."

Sariel nodded, then began to make his way forward. Keeping one eye on the lake and one eye on the demon in the field, he stepped carefully through the dense grass.

"AHH!" A scream cut through the silence of the valley.

Sariel stopped.

"I see you, Child of Light. I see you. Do you think you can hide yourself?" The demon in the field frantically jumped and bobbed its head over the grass to get a better view.

Sariel turned his gaze toward the lake, then frowned. His eyes scanned the water and the reeds, but the something was missing. "Where are your friends?" he yelled to the demon across the field.

A small cough was the only reply. Then another. And another. It was laughing.

"Wouldn't you like to know," it taunted.

Sariel pumped his wings and leaped into the air, crossing the expanse of grass while *shifting* his body toward the Eternal at the same time.

The demon scrambled to get away, but snapped backward as if on a leash, unable to leave the statue on the ground.

Sariel came down swiftly on the pathetic creature, pinning it to the wet earth by its neck. In his angelic form, he was more than four times its size. He leaned his head closer to the demon who was now struggling to breathe. "Where are your friends?" he repeated calmly.

The demon wheezed and Sariel let up slightly on his grip.

"No. ...no friends of mine! Ack," it coughed. "...abandoned me."

Sariel looked up to the other angels who were approaching cautiously. Their eyes were wide and their mouths hung open.

"Keep talking," Sariel ordered.

"Yes, of course. ...lots of activity today. It's been so lonely here, but not today. Children of Light and children of men."

"What are you saying demon? You don't make any sense!" Jomjael said, stepping forward.

"Children of Light and children of men. Grabbed our trinkets and carried them away. But I'm not free. No. I'll be here forever," it said sadly, allowing its head to drop back to the ground. Its bulging eyes now swam with an almost human longing.

Sariel slowly released his grip and stood up. In several quick steps, he reached the shore of the lake. He could see now that the once-smooth sand had been churned up as in a great migration of animals. Another few steps brought him into the water.

There, just under the surface, the bones of some unfortunate humans lay in disarray. "Someone's been here," Sariel announced.

The Myndarym came quickly, but stopped just before the water's edge.

"I've never seen one dead before," Batarel said quietly.

"They've taken the figurines. See, the bones have been dug up," Sariel said, pointing. Then, he turned and waded back to the bank where he noted the path of the footprints as they disappeared into the grass to the south.

"Ha ha! THE PEOPLE OF THE TREES! THE PEOPLE OF THE TREES!" the demon screamed hysterically. "They like shiny things and we like war. Now they like war and we like shiny things. Ha! Trees and People. People and Trees. Ha ha!" it screamed over and over.

Sariel's gaze strayed across the lake to the southern horizon. Far beyond his sight, between the peaks of Bokhar and Ehrevhar, was the village of Bahyith.

Sheyir!

Sariel unfurled his wings and burst into motion. The grass beneath him bent low from the sudden downdraft as he climbed rapidly into the sky.

"Quickly, we must move!" he yelled over his shoulder.

* * * *

Enoch opened his eyes. The river below continued to flow peacefully through the land. The sound of the water and buzzing insects were all that could be heard. The canopy of leaves overhead moved gently in the breeze, casting flickering light and shadows down the bank toward the water. Enoch looked to the west and noted that the sun was only a hand's breadth from the horizon.

I must have fallen asleep. I've been here all day!

Pushing against the ground, he struggled to lift himself. His body ached and his limbs felt weak. He grabbed onto the tree trunk for balance and noticed that the skin on his right arm was red and felt quite uncomfortable.

Have I been in the sun too long?

Breathing deeply, he looked toward Aragatsiyr and took a few steps. Suddenly, his vision grew dim and he felt himself falling.

Enoch opened his eyes again when he felt himself being lifted from the ground, but the whirling colors of the sky and trees passing in front of his face only made him dizzier.

"Drink this," someone said in a soft voice.

Enoch could tell by the sound of stillness that he was back inside the city. His head pounded and his body ached worse than when he'd been beaten by the Kahyin. Still not ready to open his eyes, he simply allowed the cool liquid to flow into his mouth and down his throat. The aftertaste suggested flowers and citrus fruit.

Laying his head back, he continued to breathe steadily and deeply until the pounding in his head subsided. Gradually, he felt strong enough to open his eyes. The air was cool. High overhead, the sky was shaded by a ceiling of tree limbs woven together. From somewhere far away, the trickling sound of water came to his ears. Beneath his tender body was a bed of soft ferns, their green fronds looking especially bright against his burned skin. As he looked up, faces began to appear at the corners of his vision.

"Are you feeling better?" Ananel asked softly.

"A little," Enoch replied, his voice sounding harsh.

"Drink some more," a female voice said from the left.

Enoch opened his mouth and allowed more of the refreshing liquid to be poured in. He closed his eyes again, and felt the irresistible pull of sleep. *Haven't I slept enough?*

"Are you hungry?" Ananel asked.

Enoch thought for a moment, then realized that he was famished. "Yes."

Before he could say another word, something smooth and sweet was placed into his mouth, and he began to chew out of habit. Though it was the most delicious thing he had ever tasted, he struggled to chew it for the dryness in his mouth.

Eventually, he worked up enough saliva to swallow it. And after another sip of the flowery drink, he felt strong enough to sit forward.

"I'm sorry. I didn't think it would take all day. I must have fallen asleep."

Ananel smiled. "You've been gone for seven days, little one."

Enoch suddenly lifted his head.

By now, all the spaces around him were filled with the crouching bodies and eager faces of the Myndarym.

"Seven days? But I was just out by the tree—"

"We were watching you from the city. One moment you were there and the next moment you were gone."

Enoch closed his eyes again and tried to make sense of what he was hearing.

"Then we saw you again. We were worried for you, but we didn't want to disturb you. So we waited until you stood up...or tried to."

Enoch rubbed his eyes and when he opened them again, he noticed that his palms appeared to be glowing. A soft radiance shone from the only part of his skin that wasn't in pain.

"You've been in the presence of the Holy One," someone on his left observed.

"It's coming from your face as well. You must have delivered our petition?" another said over Ananel's shoulder.

Ananel leaned forward. "Did you get an answer?"

Enoch simply looked up from his hands. He had neither the words, nor the strength, to have a discussion of this magnitude yet. But his face must have spoken what he was unable to.

Ananel's golden eyes seemed to look through him, but their intensity faded suddenly. "He needs time," he said finally. "Let's get him bathed and prepare him a meal."

"We'll talk later," he said to Enoch.

Enoch was grateful to have some time to compose himself. As the cool water from the stream eased his burned skin and refreshed him, he meditated on what had just taken place. Even while satisfying his ravenous hunger with the most delicious and strange foods, he was lost in his thoughts. He had seen and heard so many things that he knew it would take years before he understood it all.

But now, as he paced by the pond at the center of Kiyrakom, as he called it, he felt confident in what he needed to say to the Myndarym. Overhead, the night sky was dark and clear, revealing gleaming, silver stars that were crowded into every available space. From the perimeter of the Place of Meeting, tall trees reached their foliage toward the center, creating a partial canopy that would offer shade during the day. Their bright, graceful leaves stood in stark contrast to the twisted and knotted trunks that dug into the earth, sending out great roots that traversed the ground in search of water. From above and beneath, it seemed as though the trees were attempting to protect and shelter the inhabitants of the city. Only days ago, this had been the most beautiful place Enoch had ever seen.

That was before the vision.

The image of the White City was still burned into his mind. The vastness and beauty of it was without equal. The Keruvym and Ophanym around the Great Throne seemed as if they were made of light; their strange bodies made to live in a different world altogether. The Throne itself, bluer than the deepest part of the Great Waters, was so large that Enoch couldn't even compare it to anything in this world. And at the center of this display of power and beauty was the Holy One, whom the angels couldn't even approach for it seemed that they would be destroyed by the radiant glory that surrounded Him. Yet, Enoch was invited closer and given a place of honor and privilege.

"Enoch," Ananel said quietly. "How are you feeling?"

Interrupted from his thoughts, Enoch saw now that all the Myndarym were gathered. He could see the eagerness on their faces. Ananel was the only one who appeared to know what Enoch was about to say. His hopelessness was visible. Tears began to form involuntarily in Enoch's eyes as he glanced up to the sky, then down again to the strange beings that had accepted him into their city.

Wandering Stars.

Though once magnificent creatures to behold, their beauty now seemed pale in comparison to those around the throne. Where Enoch used to feel admiration and awe, he now felt sadness and sympathy.

"Minn vanir," he began, calling them *friends* in their own language, which he now understood and spoke fluently. "Thank you for your hospitality. You have been kind to me."

The gathering began to press forward, crowding in to hear Enoch.

"I held your petition in my heart, and I kept your words in my mind. Your repentance went with me as I sat down by the water's edge to speak with the Holy One. I had no assurance that He would hear your plea. Though He always listens, speaking with Him is not the same as it is with you here in this place. Nevertheless, I spoke to Him and waited. Then a vision came to me and this is what I saw."

Enoch recounted everything he witnessed, from the mist to the strange movement of the sun, moon, and stars. He spoke of the White City, the Keruvym and Ophanym, the One upon the Throne and the multitudes around him. Word for word, he repeated what the Holy One spoke, seeking neither to interpret the message, nor soften its rebuke. As instructed, he kept the prophecy of the Awakened and the other visions to himself, but in all other matters, he simply described everything as it had been shown to him.

"...tell them, 'You will have no peace.'" he finished.

The Myndarym were clearly shaken by his words. Some of them dropped to the ground and buried their faces in their hands. Some paced the ground of Kiyrakom. Others simply stood still, their mouths open in disbelief.

Anael was in tears.

Enoch wanted to tell them that he was sorry to be the bearer of bad news. He wanted to be a friend to these magnificent creatures. But these wants were overshadowed by something greater, something deeper. He needed—to be obedient to the Holy One who was now more real to him than ever before. Enoch had never had any doubts about the existence of the Holy

One, as others in his tribe. But if he had, they would have been destroyed by what he had just witnessed. So, with great sadness, Enoch backed away from the gathering of angels, then turned and walked away.

18

Sariel pulled his wings inward and fell from the sky. As the wind ripped past his skin, his large Iryllur eyes could already see that something was amiss. The trees rose quickly to meet him, filling every part of his vision. At the last moment, he extended his wings and flattened his trajectory, coming to a running landing in the grass field near the center of the Chatsiyr village.

Behind him, three massive felines burst through the trees and sprinted into the clearing, their animal bodies heaving great breaths of air as they *shaped* into their angelic forms. Moving rapidly across the field, the group maneuvered around a grass hut and approached the village center, with Sariel in the lead.

As soon as his feet reached bare dirt, Sariel came to a complete stop. Where once was life and movement, all was now still and silent. Everywhere he looked, he saw blood, spears, and the bodies of lifeless humans strewn about as on the countless battlefields he'd experienced in his life. But instead of soldiers, he saw humans who were innocent of the ways of war.

"NO!" he roared, his body shaking.

A flock of birds took to the air from a nearby stand of trees.

When the commotion passed Jomjael whispered, "What happened here?"

"This is Semjaza's doing," Tamael replied with calm assurance.

Breathing heavily, Sariel's eyes scanned the village that had become his home, looking desperately for any sign of Sheyir.

His feet carried his body slowly from place to place, walking him through memories that he would cherish forever. Gradually, the fog of sadness was pushed aside. His trained mind began to suppress his emotions, allowing his senses to collect minute details—footprints, blood spatters, the positions of the bodies— to reconstruct what had taken place. He saw the stone-tipped spears of the Aytsam lying alongside the broken *khafars* of the Chatsiyram. The obvious disparity between technologies only confirmed Tamael's attribution of blame.

"What does Semjaza want with the Aytsam, or the Chatsiyram for that matter?" he asked, never taking his eyes off the gruesome sights.

"He's using them," Tamael answered.

Sariel looked to the cold fire ring at the center of the gathering area. In his mind he saw dancing flames and running children. He saw smiling faces reflecting orange light. He saw bright eyes filled with awe. But with his physical eyes he saw Yeduah's body draped over the blackened rocks with a spear protruding from his chest. Sariel tilted his head and stared at the lifeless form of Sheyir's father. "For what?" he finally replied.

"For years now, Semjaza has been strengthening his resources in the event of a confrontation with the Amatru. He's been using the people to mine materials from the earth. To build his fortress. To make weapons. They're slaves to him. Until recently, his ambitions only extended to the Kahyin tribes. They're more numerous than the others, and physically stronger."

"It looks like he's expanded his efforts since we left," Jomjael added.

Sariel remained quiet for some time, walking slowly from one gruesome sight to another as the Myndarym followed. The picture that he'd been piecing together in his mind was now becoming clear. And the fact that the Shaper's explanation was incomplete only reinforced how dangerous and mysterious Semjaza really was.

Sariel stopped walking as he neared the edge of the village. The trail of footprints left by the Aytsam transitioned from the damp soil into a wide swath of bent grass as it moved south and disappeared into the trees. "If he wants slaves, then why did the Aytsam kill so many? And why did they take all the women and leave behind only men?" he asked, keeping his eyes on the trees ahead.[6, 7]

In the ensuing silence, he could hear the shuffling of the angels' footsteps behind him. He could tell that they were just now becoming aware of the fact that there were no female bodies among the dead. When Sariel turned around, he noticed their slack faces and eyes filled with tears. He could see that they'd never looked upon a battlefield before. And the sight of human slaughter was even more disturbing.

"Look what you've done," he whispered. "You should never have helped him."

Jomjael turned away.

Batarel kept his eyes fixed on Sariel.

Tamael's head slowly dropped. "We never meant for this to happen," he replied, his voice cracking slightly.

Sariel could feel a deep rage welling up inside him now. It was not the kind of emotion that would cause someone to react rashly. Instead, it was the sustained resolution of someone who had spent hundreds of human lifetimes honing his skills of warfare. Slowly, methodically, he pulled a spear from the body of a nearby Chatsiyr man and knelt to lift another from the ground next to him. He adjusted his grip and found the point at which the stone-tipped weapons balanced perfectly in his hands. They were crude and fragile compared to the weapons he'd wielded in the past, but in this place they were apparently still effective.

"You're either with me, or against me," he stated coldly.

Tamael glanced quickly at the others. "We're with you," he replied.

Sariel turned back to the south and unfurled his wings.

*   *   *   *

Sheyir struggled for breath, nearly choked by the tight, animal-hide rope around her neck. She was sitting on the ground with hands behind her back, tied to the inside of a poorly constructed fence of tree branches which encircled hundreds of women. Near her were dozens of other Chatsiyr women and many more from other tribes.

"What do they want with us?" one of the women whimpered.

Across the grassy meadow, on the opposite side of the makeshift corral, were groups of other women that appeared to be arranged by when they arrived at this encampment.

"Gods want children," another woman spoke.

Sheyir twisted her head to find who had answered, but the rope cut into her skin. "Who said that?" she wheezed.

"Take wives to make big men children," the woman spoke again.

From the corner of her eye, Sheyir located the woman only a few feet away. Though her words were arranged oddly, her language was nearly the same as the Chatsiyram. Her face was scarred and she appeared to have survived something terrible in her earlier years. Judging by her clothing, made of plant fibers, Sheyir guessed that this woman was also from one of the tribes descended from the Shayetham, like her own people. Perhaps their tribes even lived relatively close to each other. Not that it mattered anymore. Her own people and way of life had been decimated in a few, torturous minutes.

"What are big men children?" Sheyir asked quietly, just noticing a man with a spear yelling at a group of women on the opposite side of the enclosure.

"God children very big. Mothers every die."

Always die? "The mothers die giving birth because the children are too big?" Sheyir asked, trying to make sense of the women's words.

"Yes. Every die."[9]

Someone screamed from across the enclosure and Sheyir turned to see a section of the fence now resting open, with two massive creatures standing in the gap. A few months ago, she would have been confused and terrified all at once. Now, after knowing Sariel, she was only terrified. These creatures were several feet taller than Sariel as he had first appeared, but they didn't have wings. Their complexion and hair were a light earthen color, and they wore odd loincloths that hung down to the middle of their upper legs in both the front and back. But even with their different appearance, she could tell that they were Baynor.

Are they here to save us?

Just as she began to hope, several men with spears quickly rushed over to the imposing figures and knelt in front of them. The Baynor had not come to save anyone. They were the leaders.

A shadow suddenly moved across the ground.

Sheyir instinctively looked into the sky. Hundreds of feet above, a winged creature circled and descended.

SARIEL!

The winged silhouette grew in size as it banked, eventually dropping gently into the grass inside the enclosure. Pulling its wings inward, it walked toward the other Baynor and began to talk with them. It stood a couple feet shorter, but looked to have authority over them by the way it carried itself. In form, it looked much like Sariel, but with dark brown skin, black hair, and black, feathered wings. After it spoke with the other two, it walked slowly around the enclosure, occasionally pointing at a woman. When it did so, the human guards waded into the group, untied the woman, and dragged her to the center of the prison.

As the trio of creatures made their way toward her group, the last and most recent to come to this terrible place, Sheyir realized that her fingernails were cutting into her own skin. Her fists were clenched and shaking.

One of the taller creatures said something to the dark one.

"Hene, og hene," said the winged one, pointing to two women a few yards away to Sheyir's left.

As the screaming women were untied, the dark one's disinterested gaze swept over the crowd, then rapidly doubled back toward Sheyir. Now his fierce eyes locked onto hers and he slowly took a step forward. "...og du," he said, lifting his upturned hand toward her.

Sheyir couldn't take her eyes off the creature. She was horrified and mesmerized at the same time. Its red eyes held a fascinating intensity, and she could only guess at the emotion behind them. Was it anger? Was it lust? As the rope around her neck dropped to the ground, the violent motion of being jerked to her feet brought her abruptly out of her thoughts.

"Taka dessa konnur ad Semjaza," he told one of the wingless creatures, pointing to the women that had been selected from the crowd.

The men dropped Sheyir to the ground in front of the dark one.

The towering beast looked down to the human males. "You. Go get more," he said in a language that sounded very close to Chatsiyr.

The men nodded and backed away in fear, finally turning and running away when they'd put enough distance between themselves and this fearsome giant.

"And you," he said, turning back to Sheyir. "You will come with me. Semjaza will want you for himself."

Sheyir flinched as the dark one reached down and lifted her from the grass as if she were a child. Holding her with one arm, he stretched out his wings and jumped into the air.

* * * *

The wind rushed by Sariel's face and blades of grass whipped by only feet below him. His great wings propelled him forward, requiring just the occasional downward thrust to maintain his speed. With both hands he gripped the primitive spears he'd taken from the Chatsiyr village; their fragile weight balanced in his palms, adjusted for wind resistance.

Rising slowly over a low mound, he banked slightly to the west and rounded a stand of trees to obscure the sight of his approach. Under different circumstances he would have enjoyed feeling the air move across his wings; the graceful way his body cut through the air above the fields of grass; the way his wings expertly flexed to maintain lift as he banked. But he was not flying for pleasure. It was revenge that fueled him now. A desperate need to bring a violent and swift end to anyone who would dare harm Sheyir.

The stand of trees slid to the right and out of his vision leaving an empty field with a crude circular fence at its center. The two hundred foot diameter was only sufficient to enclose fear-stricken human women, but its height failed to shield the upper body of the single Anduar sentinel standing guard in the middle. Sariel straightened his heading and dropped lower until the blades of grass struck his chest and arms. He covered the expanse of open field in just a few seconds, unseen. At the last possible moment, he adjusted his elevation to glide just over the rim of the fence. In the blink of an eye, the Anduar guard was visible and Sariel thrust the stone-tipped, wooden spears downward. The impact ripped the weapons from his hands and he had to tilt his wings to keep from being pulled down. Just as he passed over the opposite rim of the fence, he started to bank to the left and glanced backward to see the Anduar fall.

Completing his turn, he now approached from the north and could see that Tamael and the others, still in their animal forms, had torn down the south end of the enclosure. The human captors ran in fear from the broken structure and into the fields, leaving their captives.

Sariel slowed his speed and dropped his elevation until he came to a gentle landing in the grass on the south side of the prison. Though he wanted to take the lives of the human men running in retreat, he restrained himself.

They're only acting out of fear of Semjaza!

"I've never seen an Iryllur kill an Anduar before," Tamael said, now wearing his angelic form.

Sariel walked passed Tamael and into the prison without a word.

Scanning the groups of women tied to the perimeter of the wall he could tell in seconds that Sheyir wasn't among them. With a sigh, he stooped to the nearest woman and began to untie the rope around her neck.

She flinched; her eyes wide with horror.

Sariel let go of the rope and put his hands up. "I'm not here to hurt you. You're safe now."

Tamael, Jomjael, and Batarel followed his lead, walking around the prison and untying the women.

As Sariel moved from woman to woman, he asked, "Do you know Sheyir?" He only received blank stares, but he kept working, freeing the women and repeating his question in as many human languages as he knew.

When all were freed, Sariel walked to the center and looked down at the dead soldier. He lay on his side with his legs splayed. One spear had gone through the middle of his chest, while the other hit higher toward his neck. His blood darkened the earth and grass beneath him. It was the first time that Sariel had ever killed someone other than a demon.

"You were looking for someone in particular?" Tamael asked quietly as the others joined him.

Sariel nodded without looking up.

"And she's not here," Batarel stated.

They stood in silence for a moment as Sariel considered what to do next.

"Semjaza?" a quiet voice asked from behind.

Sariel turned around quickly. "What?" he replied in the Chatsiyr language, only now realizing that none of the women had left the enclosure. They remained huddled around the perimeter of the wall. Most were standing while a few were still sitting on the ground.

"Semjaza," a woman repeated.

Sariel now saw who spoke and recognized her from his time at Bahyith, though she probably didn't recognize him in his angelic form.

"A dark one came. He had wings like you," she said, pointing. "He took Sheyir and said Semjaza will want her for himself."

At once, hope and rage collided in his heart. Sariel closed his eyes and clenched his fists until he composed himself. "Thank you," he finally said to the woman, then turned back to the Myndarym.

"I know what you're thinking," Tamael said quickly. "And it's not possible."

"Why?" Sariel probed.

"Because he has an army and a fortress. And you'll never get to her. You don't understand how dangerous he is."

Sariel remained silent and let the words hang in the air for a moment. There were so many responses running through his mind. But only one that would bring him closer to the one he loved. "Then take me there and make me understand."

"He'll kill us before we get within miles of the place," Tamael countered.

Sariel nodded slowly, and could feel the skin on his forehead tighten. "Does he ever leave the safety of his fortress?"

Tamael paused for a moment. "Yes. I guess he does. For years, he used to roam throughout the land, hunting as the Kahyin do. But he tired quickly of that. There are not many things on this earth to serve as a worthy opponent for him. Now, the only time he leaves is to Khanok, the capital city of the Kahyin. He likes to personally check the progress at the mines and to maintain his god-like status among the humans."

"How often?" Sariel asked.

"Since we left? ...monthly. But he is always accompanied by his personal guard—two Iryllurym and two Anduarym."

"I can handle them," Sariel replied with confidence.

"I doubt it," Batarel said in a low voice.

Sariel noticed that the women still hadn't left the enclosure. "You're all free to go."

"We have nowhere. Our villages are destroyed. Our men are dead," the Chatsiyr woman responded quietly.

Now Sariel finally understood the expressions on the faces looking at him. He had been blinded by his own emotions. But now he understood why they weren't leaving.

"We could take them back to our city," Jomjael offered. "They would be safe there."

Sariel slowly nodded in agreement as he plotted his next move. "Yes. You should do that." Then he turned to Tamael and Batarel. "And we should go to Khanok."

"Alright," Tamael agreed. "We'll take you there. But I can't promise you anything."

Sariel turned and walked closer to where the women were gathered, then knelt. "If you are willing, Jomjael will take you to a city. It is a far journey, but you will be safe there." He repeated this phrase in different languages until he saw recognition on every face.

"Thank you, O Excellent One," one of the women replied.

"Call me Sariel," he said with a dismissive wave of his hand.

"I knew it was you," said the Chatsiyr woman. "I could tell by your eyes."

Sariel just smiled. "Go with him," he said, tilting his head toward Jomjael, "...and do whatever he asks of you."

Then he stood and turned to Tamael and Batarel. "Take me to Semjaza."

19

Khanok was a sprawling city that couldn't have been called a village, even in the first years of its founding. What had once appeared as an ambitious project of human construction now bore signs of angelic influence. Intermingled with elaborate wooden structures, built from timber harvested from the towering forests nearby, works of stone were also beginning to appear. Situated between two intersecting ridges of the mountain of Murakszhug, the capital city of the Kahyin was protected by the landscape on three sides. To the northwest, the land sloped downward toward the Great Waters and a massive wall of timbers spanned the widening vale. One either side of the road that passed through the wall, pillars of stone had been erected to form an entrance. Spreading outward from there, it looked as though the timber was being steadily replaced by the quarried material that was sturdier, and required greater skill to craft.

Sariel was perched in the shadow of a cleft, high on the mountain above the city. In their own tongue, the Kahyin called it Mountain of Watching. Sariel smiled at the coincidence, for though it was the place where their gods had first appeared, coming down from their heavenly place of observance, it had now become the vantage point for Sariel's reconnaissance. And so far, it seemed that the gods had become accustomed to looking down on humans. They never thought to look up.

"Seven of each," Batarel growled.

"I thought you said two Iryllurym and two Anduarym?" Sariel countered, turning to Tamael who was just approaching from the west.

"Perhaps he has more to fear as the days pass." Tamael's feline form moved silently over the rocks and sparse vegetation that struggled to grow at this elevation.

For weeks, Sariel and his companions had watched the road leading away from the city toward Mudena Del-Edha, waiting for some indication that Semjaza was on the move. Finally, earlier in the morning, they spotted him coming into the city. But he traveled with two Anduarym to guard him on the ground, and two Iryllurym who flew circles overhead as he moved.[22] There was no opportunity for Sariel to get the Pri-Rada alone. Instead, they watched helplessly as he entered the human city, then they took up a new observation point on the mountain above. But when Semjaza reached the mines at the base of Murakszhug, another five Anduarym and Iryllurym were waiting. Now, there were a total of fourteen soldiers surrounding him. The odds were moving in the wrong direction.

Sariel peered down through the quickly fading afternoon light. "I can see the road, but the entrance to the mines is obscured."

"It's there," Batarel assured him. "All but two Anduarym accompanied him into the mountain."

Tamael nodded in agreement, having observed the same from the western slope.

"How long does his inspection usually take?"

"Perhaps an hour. Sometimes—"

"Wait," Sariel hissed, squinting. "There he is. He's come out already."

"But it's not dark yet," Batarel growled low in his throat.

"This is my only chance," Sariel said with resignation. The situation was less than ideal, but he felt a gnawing panic that the time to act was slipping away.

Tamael was now standing close. "This whole effort was a suicide mission anyway," he whispered. "Whether he's alone or guarded, I fear it will not go well for you, my friend."

Sariel kept his keen eyes fixed on the figures moving hundreds of feet below, but he wondered if this was the last time he'd see the Shapers standing next to him. "If I survive this, I'll meet you at the rendezvous point. Thank you both for your help," he said, then leaped from his hiding place.

Gravity threatened to take control, but his bent wings caught just enough air to steer his silent form between the jagged boulders on each side of the shallow ravine. Hidden in the shadows of the fissure Sariel gained speed as he descended. Seconds later, the walls of rock on either side began to widen and the terrain below changed from boulders to loose gravel. In the pale light of dusk he shot out of the canyon with blinding speed, adjusting his approach as the angle of the slope lessened. To the north, the smooth, dark soil seemed to end abruptly. Somewhere on the other side of that cliff, unseen, was the entrance to the mines. Banking to the right, Sariel followed the contours of the land as it dropped off another steeper slope to the east. He maintained this heading for several seconds, passing to the east and below the mine entrance as he flew parallel to where the road should be. Suddenly, the crevice that he'd spotted earlier came into view. He banked sharply to the left and into the narrow corridor, coming to a landing as quietly as possible on his hands and knees. In the jaws of the earth it was completely dark and he had to scramble upward through the crevice, picking his way across sharp rocks and dirt before he reached a position where he could see the road through the opening on the other end. And there, he waited.

Long moments passed. The sky overhead slowly transitioned from deep blue to black. Cramped into an awkward space, Sariel watched the stars come out and wondered if he'd made a mistake. Perhaps Semjaza went back into the mines. Perhaps he waited at the entrance. Either way, he and his guards should have passed along the road already.

Unless they spotted me.

Sariel quickly ran through the scenario in his mind, picturing the Anduarym moving into position on either end of the crevice. If he were organizing the attack, he'd have the Iryllurym drop in from above.

Looking up, the sky was clear and only the stars were visible.

A faint sound drifted to his ears. Then another. And another.

Footsteps!

Seconds later, three massive figures passed along the road. The two in front carried torches which cast a sudden, flickering light into Sariel's hiding place.

Sariel quickly dropped his head and held still. The moment passed and darkness returned. Then, from the corner of his vision, two silent forms glided through the sky and disappeared behind the north wall of the narrow ravine. Their silhouettes would have been invisible, but for the faint light of the stars.

When only the receding sound of footsteps could be heard, Sariel knew it was time. Easing out of his contorted position, he crawled toward the road.

* * * *

Azael was the first to see the intruder. With black feathers and skin almost as dark, he exceled in the nighttime environment where others struggled. His red eyes were more effective at piercing the shadows than any of the other soldiers that Semjaza had under his command. As he circled back toward the south along his regular search pattern, he noticed something moving out of a crevice along the road. It was behind Semjaza and far too slow for an attack. But its proximity to the road and the fact that he hadn't seen it until it moved, told Azael that it was an enemy nonetheless.

"PA VAKT!" he shouted, alerting the others.

In an instant, he retracted his wings and dropped from the sky, landing swiftly on the road between the threat and his superior.

As the Anduarym moved into position behind him, also putting themselves between the threat and their Pri-Rada, Azael could see the orange light of their torches illuminate the land to the south, as well as the intruder who now stood in the middle of the road.

The sight of an Iryllur was surprising. He was pale, with white and brown coloring, flecked with gold. His eyes were quick and flashed with blue as they reflected the torchlight. His build was thin, but efficiently muscular. Azael could discern from the little amount of movement he'd already observed, and now by the way the intruder stood, that he would be almost an equal match to himself.

Although, the paler ones are weaker in spirit!

A second later, Parnudel dropped to the road behind the intruder, silent until the moment his feet touched the gravel. Although he couldn't see as well at night, his softer feathers and mottled brown coloring made him nearly undetectable by sight or sound, which had proven useful on many occasions.

Now they had the intruder surrounded.

"I apologize for my abrupt entrance," the intruder said, a little too casually. "But your...hospitality was in question."

Azael moved slowly forward, seeing that Parnudel was doing the same. "What is your name, soldier?" he demanded, instantly hating the stranger's attempt at humor.

"Sariel."

"Stand down!" Semjaza ordered, pushing through the Anduar guards.

Azael stopped, and relaxed his grip on the hilts of the *vaepkir* attached to either side of his breastplate at the small of his back. He didn't understand his superior's order, but reluctantly obeyed.

"*The* Sariel?" Semjaza asked.

"Yes," came the simple response.

Azael took note of how the intruder stood with his body slightly turned, keeping Parnudel in his peripheral vision.

"What do you want?" Semjaza asked.

Azael could hear an unusual curiosity in the Pri-Rada's voice.

"Just to talk," the intruder replied.

Suddenly, they were interrupted by a rush of wind as five other Iryllurym passed overhead and doubled back, coming to a landing near Semjaza. Then, the irregular beat of numerous footsteps was followed by the appearance of five more Anduarym, joining Parnudel on the south side of the intruder.

When the commotion subsided, Semjaza's mouth curled upward at the corner. "I hope, for your sake, that you have something very important to say."

Azael watched Sariel hold up his hands in a gesture of peace and move to the side of the road so that he was in the best position for escape. But there was no use. If he chose to flee, he'd be cut down in seconds.

"I think there has been a misunderstanding," Sariel began. The smug humor was gone from his face. Instead, he looked desperate. "My woman was taken from her village several weeks ago. Of course, you had no way of knowing that she was spoken for. So, I came to get her back."

The fact that this Iryllur was standing here revealed that he knew, at least in part, what they were doing with the humans. Azael looked to Semjaza who was now fully smiling. He'd seen this look many times before and it wasn't from joy. It was from amusement at someone's stupidity and usually preceded a violent outburst.

"There are many women," Semjaza said calmly.

"I would be glad to point her out," came the quick reply.

"Yes, I'm sure you would. Tell me. What is a soldier with your reputation doing in this realm?" Semjaza probed, changing the direction of the conversation.

Azael saw the briefest flicker of Sariel's frustration, then it disappeared behind a mask of control. With every passing second, he hated this intruder more and more.

"The same as you, I assume," Sariel replied. "There is more work yet to be done here."

"Mmm," Semjaza mumbled. "...well said."

"So, I came to—"

"I could use someone of your...considerable skills," Semjaza interrupted. "There is indeed much to be done, and much that we could share."

Azael could see Sariel's frustration mounting, and he was enjoying every second of it.

"I'm flattered. But I think we are too much alike, you and I. I can see by the results of your work that you're someone who sets his mind to something and doesn't turn back."

Semjaza nodded, but remained silent.

"I came to this world to escape living under the rule of another. And I'm sure the Amatru doesn't approve of...all this. So it seems you did, as well."

Semjaza nodded once more, but kept his head in a downward position. Azael could see the fury building behind his eyes.

"So it would be wise, I think, not to mingle our ambitions."

"I see," Semjaza replied. "Perhaps I've missed something," he said, glancing quickly aside. "Certainly one who has attained legendary status among the Amatru would possess an intellect superior to most. Strength and skill as well. And if my assumption is correct, as most are, I am confused by what terms you offer."

"Terms?" Sariel now looked confused, but Azael didn't buy it.

"Yes. Terms," Semjaza said, his amusement all but gone now. "If you are not offering your services to me, then what is it that you hope to exchange for the woman?"

"I didn't come here to exchange anything. I came here to speak with you, soldier to soldier. And to tell you that you mistakenly took my woman."

Finally, an honest statement, Azael thought.

"Out of respect for your high position," Sariel continued, "I came here directly to clear up the matter."

Semjaza straightened his stance, which had become increasingly forward-leaning as the conversation had progressed. "This is most unfortunate for you. For this matter will not be *cleared up*. You see, I am no longer one of the Amatru. I've...given up on their archaic ways. I've liberated myself from the shackles of holiness. I'm a new creation now.

You see, I've learned that there is only one thing which produces effective results in both realms—leverage. This is what the Amatru refuses to see and why they will ultimately lose. But this place, the realm that they've abandoned, it's mine. I have authority over it now. And when I see something I want in my own world, I take it. So, when you come to me and demand that I give back something that is rightfully mine, what am I to say?"

"So, you admit you know the woman I speak of," Sariel stated, now clenching his fists.

Azael slowly rotated the hilts of his *vaepkir*, unhooking them from their scabbards, but keeping them sheathed.

"OF COURSE I KNOW!" Semjaza shouted. "I know everything in my world. And now that you've displeased me, I will keep her for myself whether you have something to trade or not."

Sariel looked to the ground and his arms began to shake, muscles bulging beneath his pale skin. He inhaled slowly and when his gaze returned to Semjaza, there was hatred in his eyes.

"I will give you one chance to release her. And if you do not, I swear to you that I will bring an end to your kingdom and your life in this realm."

Azael now saw why Semjaza had tried to gain the soldier's service.

The Pri-Rada's eyes narrowed. "Because of your reputation, I will give you one chance to leave unharmed."

It would be a waste of a potential resource, but Azael unsheathed his *vaepkir*, their ringing sound echoed off the stone hills on either side of the road. Following his lead, the other Iryllurym did the same, while the Anduarym gripped their *vandrekt* in a ready position.

Sariel's quick eyes darted from left to right. He wasn't assessing the situation, for he had clearly already done that. But it appeared that he was now actually considering fighting. Now it was Azael's turn to be amused. The intruder was unarmed and the odds were ridiculous.

Sariel's jaw was clenched and his body tense. Slowly, he extended wings.

Azael and his Iryllurym did likewise.

In the blink of an eye, something passed across the face of the intruder. The reckless abandonment behind his gaze, gave way to reason. Instead of attacking, he lifted his wings. Then, as he leaped from the ground, he brought his wings quickly downward and propelled himself into the sky.

The guards all looked up and watched the intruder go. But Azael turned to his superior, biting back the insubordinate question on his tongue.

Semjaza met the look with his own furious gaze. "He's working with the Myndarym. Take your soldiers and track him. If he leads you to the Shapers, come back and report their location to me. If he doesn't, kill him."

"As you wish, my Rada," Azael replied.

20

Sariel kept low to the earth, moving southwest between Khanok and Murakszhug. As he ascended the portion of the range that protruded to the northwest, he glanced over his shoulder. He couldn't see any movement in the skies, but he knew he was being followed. After cresting the peak, he slowed and dropped into a sparse stand of trees on the western slope. Hidden by the vegetation, he watched the skies and waited.

Sooner than expected, two Iryllurym passed quickly overhead. Their silhouettes revealed long and narrow wings with pointed ends. By design they were capable of faster flight, which would explain how they had managed to catch up so quickly.

When the skies were clear, Sariel took to the air again and turned southeast. Minutes later, he reached the southern slopes of the mountain and noticed two more shapes approaching from the east. Quickly, he banked to the right and dropped into a narrow gorge that led away from the peak. Once again, he passed between jagged boulders, banking constantly to avoid them. With the descending altitude, the gradual presence of trees also helped conceal him, but added more obstacles to his already dangerous flight. When he reached a straight and smooth section of the canyon, he risked a glance over his shoulder.

The two Iryllurym had followed him into the canyon.

Beating his wings harder, Sariel tried to gain some speed, but his pursuers were gaining on him. Up ahead, the ravine bent sharply to the west and an idea came to him. Diving into the turn, Sariel waited until the sheer walls blocked the line of sight between them, then he pulled up and out of the canyon. He skimmed low over the lip of the ravine and shot through a stand of trees. Without a second's hesitation, he doubled back to the north and dropped into another gorge that paralleled the previous one.

Now flying upslope inside a wider gulley, he was heading straight for the peak of Murakszhug and the general direction of his rendezvous point with the Myndarym. Glancing behind, he saw no signs of pursuit. But when his eyes returned to their forward position, he noticed two more Iryllurym moving rapidly across the floor of the canyon, rising to meet him head-on. With hardly a moment to think, Sariel pulled his wings inward and dropped into a roll. As he passed between them, his compressed form pushed itself through the tangle of limbs and feathers, cracking something in the process.

Spinning through the fray, Sariel opened his wings and gained altitude, looking behind him as he made his escape.

One of the Iryllurym was dropping toward the canyon floor, spinning out of control with a broken wing.

The remaining Iryllur banked to the west and came around into pursuit.

Sariel pumped his wings faster and recovered some altitude just as he approached the pinnacle of the Mountain of Watching. Passing by its eastern face, he circled around to the west and came to a landing on a wide platform of rock above a sheer cliff face. His feet touched the mountain at a run and he quickly retracted his wings and stooped to pick up a jagged rock from the scree that covered the entire area.

The Iryllur pursuer was only seconds behind. He dropped quickly from the air and hit the ledge at a run, as well.

Spinning around to face the attacker, Sariel waited, holding the fist-sized rock behind his back.

The attacker was armed with two *vaepkir* and advanced without any hesitation. As soon as he was within range, he threw his right arm forward.

Sariel pivoted to the right and dodged backward, bringing the rock up into the blade, deflecting it just enough to miss his face. Then, he quickly dropped and continued spinning as the carpal joint of the Iryllur's wing passed overhead, also missing its mark.

Sariel pushed to his feet and sidestepped the backhanded slash of the angel's other *vaepkir*. Then he moved in quickly and swung the rock for the Iryllur's face.

But the blow only glanced off the angel's forehead as he dodged to the side of the assault and tackled Sariel who was now too close for weapons.

Both soldiers fell to the ground in a tumble.

Sariel suddenly found himself on his back with the attacker pinning him to the ground. Pushing his wings outward across the rough gravel, Sariel used the added stability to quickly bring his legs underneath the Iryllur. With one powerful thrust, he plowed his feet into the angel's chest and sent him flying through the air.

As they both struggled to their feet, a massive, hairy shape lunged from the rocks to the right and plowed into Semjaza's soldier. In a flurry of wings and teeth, the two creatures rolled across the rocky terrain. A sharp growl cut through the air and the arms and legs that were flailing abruptly stopped.

Sariel rose from his crouching position and walked slowly over to Batarel, who remained still.

The Myndar's powerful animal form stood on top of the other with his massive jaws clamped on the angel's throat. A pool of blood was quickly forming beneath the head of the defeated soldier, whose wingtips now quivered with residual nervous energy.

He was already dead.

"It's done," Sariel said softly.

Batarel released his grip on the enemy, then *shaped* to his angelic form. In the harsh silence, he stood up on two legs and looked down at the soldier. "I've never done this before."

"Killed?" Sariel asked quietly, after a pause.

"I've hunted, but never one of my own."

Sariel put his hand on Batarel's shoulder.

"There was another group farther to the east, but they didn't see anything," Tamael growled, climbing down from the rocks above in his animal form. When he reached the ledge, he came over and sniffed the dead Iryllur, then looked up at Batarel, whose angelic form was marred by the blood that covered his face and chest. "I suppose your meeting could have gone worse," he said to Sariel.

"He takes great pride in having abandoned all the principles that he used to live by. There's no reasoning with him."

"I told you as much," Tamael snarled. "So, what are you going to do now?"

Sariel breathed deeply for a moment, trying to clear his mind so that he could think through his options. The only bargaining tool he had was his own freedom, but that would defeat the purpose of rescuing Sheyir. He wanted to be with her, and trading his own freedom for hers wouldn't accomplish that. He would do it if only to save her, but that was a last resort. No. Bargaining with Semjaza was pointless. Sariel had met his type before, but usually among the Marotru. As he looked out at the western horizon, now illuminated by the moon, he admitted to himself that Semjaza was right about one thing. The only effective tool in this world was leverage. And this left him with only one option.

"Why did the Myndarym come here?"

Tamael turned his feline head, clearly not expecting such an esoteric question at a time like this. "Uh...freedom, I guess," he answered finally.

"After your obligations to Semjaza, what did you hope to do with your earned freedom?"

"Whatever we wanted," Batarel mumbled.

"I suppose that's the point," Tamael answered. "I, for one, spent a great many hours *shaping* this world. And I rather enjoy roaming the land in one of the forms that I *shaped*."

Sariel nodded. "And the others? I assume they would have similar answers?"

"What are you getting at?" Tamael asked finally.

Sariel put his hand on his chin and exhaled. "How will you ever have your freedom when Semjaza sits on his throne? He doesn't even try to hide his aspirations. He will continue to expand his kingdom until it covers the earth. Any freedom you have by running will only end eventually."

Tamael raised his eyebrows. "You want us to go war against him?" he asked. The expression on his face was something between fear and amusement.

Sariel remained silent.

"The Myndarym are not going to risk their lives for your woman," he stated bluntly.

"I'm not asking you to go to war for a woman. That's my reason," he said. "I'm only stating the obvious—Semjaza stands in the way of what you want. So, the question is, what are you going to do about it?"

Batarel now looked up from the body of the dead Iryllur.

Tamael was silent for a moment. "We're not soldiers like you."

Sariel nodded to the angel lying at their feet. "It seems to me that in all your time with Semjaza, helping him build a fortress and prepare his defenses, you learned something."

"They outnumber us three to one," Batarel pointed out. "And they're trained for this sort of thing."

Sariel nodded. "True. But what if you fought alongside someone who was trained in war? What if you outnumbered Semjaza?"

"The Amatru?" Tamael asked. "They want us dead as much as Semjaza does."

Sariel held up a finger. "It's not a question of what they want, but what they are willing to accept. Granted, none of us are on good terms with them any longer. But I suspect that the reason they haven't destroyed Semjaza yet is that they don't have the resources, or confidence that the outcome will be as they hope."

"You've gone mad," Tamael concluded.

"Have I? The Myndarym and the Amatru now have a common enemy. What I'm proposing is actually quite sane."

Batarel looked straight at Sariel, his fearless eyes unflinching. "How is an untrained group of Shapers and an under-resourced army going to defeat Semjaza?"

Sariel smiled at the angel's practical observation. "You and the other Shapers know more than you realize. Your inside knowledge of Semjaza's fortress, capabilities, and strategy is critical intelligence for the Amatru. With your involvement, the resources would be allocated."

"Are you saying that you will go before the Amatru to make this proposal? Because none of us are that stupid," Tamael stated.

Sariel smiled again. "I'll try not to be offended by that. And yes, I'll handle the coordination."

"Very well," Tamael replied after a moment's pause. "We'll take this before the Myndarym and see if they are willing."

"We don't have any more time to waste," Sariel replied. "Semjaza grows stronger by the minute. You must convince the Myndarym while I do the same with the Amatru."

"They will not like us making this arrangement on their behalf. What if they refuse?" asked Batarel.

Sariel stared hard into the unwavering eyes. "Then your freedom will be short-lived."

Batarel looked down to his fellow Myndar as he considered Sariel's words. Then his eyes returned and he nodded his agreement.

"Don't tell the Amatru where we live," Tamael growled. "Whatever agreement you come to, don't betray us to them."

"Of course," Sariel agreed. "And you...travel quietly. Semjaza knows we're working together. The only reason he let me go was so that I would lead his soldiers to the Myndarym."

Tamael nodded.

Batarel *shaped* to his animal form.

Seconds later, as the two Myndarym moved eastward across the mountain face, Tamael turned his head. "Godspeed," he said in farewell.

Indeed, Sariel thought. His mind was already racing with the anticipation of what lay ahead.

* * * *

From beneath the shade of a tree, Enoch watched the rippling water as it left the river and followed the narrow path toward Aragatsiyr. It had become his favorite place since the day he described his vision to the Myndarym.

Or was it more than a vision? Was I really there?

He couldn't be sure. All he knew was that the angels now treated him differently. Not with contempt, but with neglect. It was as if they were choosing to believe that he wasn't there or didn't exist.

And who could blame them?

No one wanted to be confronted with their mistakes, their low standing with the Holy One. And Enoch was simply a physical representation of their judgment. While they had chosen to forget about him, he made it easier by staying on the outskirts of the city. He foraged for food in the nearby forests, but hadn't yet received any indication that he should leave.

Holy One, I am confused. I do not know why You asked me to come to these creatures. I have not been able to prevent them from doing what is against Your desire. I once believed that You sent me to befriend them, but I think they wish to be rid of me now. I pray that You give me wisdom. Reveal to me what You want of me. I am useless now, going about as an animal in the forest. Though I have little contact with them, each day I feel their discomfort growing. What should happen if they choose to be rid of me forever? What then? It would be nothing for creatures of such power. I just—

"Prophet," a voice spoke softly.

Enoch jumped at the sound. Turning, he noticed Ananel standing a few paces off.

"I'm sorry to startle you."

"It's no trouble. What can I do for you?"

Ananel smiled. "...talk with me?"

"Of course."

Ananel walked closer and bent down, leaning his angelic form against the same tree so that they were almost back to back, but could see each other if they turned their heads. "You know," he began. "I like you. You are an honest man. When I look at you, there is nothing of deceit or falsehood."

Enoch continued to stare out at the river, not knowing what to say in response.

"That's why you should come back."

"Back? To the city?"

"Yes," Ananel answered.

"But the Myndarym would be troubled by my presence," Enoch protested.

"True. ...for a little while. But your honesty will put them at ease in time."

"Hmm," Enoch mumbled, feeling like he was speaking to his wife, Zacol. She always seemed so sure of everything. Enoch rarely felt sure of anything, unless the Holy One revealed it to him.

"With you living out here, away from us, it gives us too much time to think of only the bad things."

"You mean, when I speak for the Holy One?" Enoch quickly clarified.

"Yes. He speaks through you and sometimes His words are difficult to hear. But that is not your fault. You are not to blame for our decisions. It was our choice to come here, to disobey. The longer you stay out here, the easier it is for us to blame you instead."

Enoch turned his head and looked up at the angel who towered over him, even in a sitting position. "The ways of your kind are complicated."

"And the ways of your kind are simple," Ananel added. "But I admire that. I know you don't wish to deceive anyone. I'm only suggesting that you continue to live among us. It is safer for you to remain familiar."

A murmuring sound to the north had now grown into a commotion. Enoch leaned forward and looked past Ananel toward the city, but he couldn't determine the reason for the noise.

Ananel rose to his feet and looked north, holding his hand to his brow to block the afternoon sun in his eyes.

"What is it?" Enoch asked.

"It's Jomjael."

"Who is he?"

"We sent him and a few others to spy on Semjaza. It looks like he's returned and there are human women."

Enoch stood up and came around the tree.

"Lots of them," Ananel added. "Come little one. It's time to go back."

21

The pungent odor came suddenly to Batarel's feline nose, bringing him to halt.

A few yards ahead, Tamael lowered his nose to the grass and a quiet growl escaped his throat. His head turned suddenly, then he began to move toward a hiding place nearby where a dense tangle of vines cascaded down from the limbs of a massive tree.

Batarel followed his friend into the bright, green strands of concealment. Crouching low to the damp earth, they both waited.

After a few seconds, a tall figure moved out of the trees on the other side of a clearing. His dark and muscled form was difficult to see against the background of jumbled branches and leaves, but even at a hundred yards they could tell it was one of Semjaza's Anduarym. He was moving quickly by virtue of his enormous stride, but didn't seem to be in a hurry. Neither did he appear concerned about moving with stealth.

When the soldier had retreated into the distance, Batarel turned to his friend. "Spy?" he whispered as quietly as his animal vocal chords would allow.

Tamael nodded. "We will have to be more cautious from here on out."

Slowly, the two rose to their paws and crawled out into the open. Despite the confidence they had in their animal forms, which gave them a sensory advantage over anything else in the forest, they continued with caution to the north.

In the gathering mist of the afternoon, the two creatures came to the last of a series of mountain peaks just south of Senvidar. As they began their ascent from the foothills below, the breeze shifted slightly, bringing warning of a nearby threat. Batarel looked to Tamael, whose fierce golden eyes were narrowed, while the whiskered skin of his face twitched.

Tamael growled and bared his teeth.

Batarel knew instantly what it meant. For years, they had hunted together and their coordinated efforts had always been successful. Communication was no longer necessary, it had become habit.

The two animals, whose agile and powerful bodies were designed for silent movement and rapid attack, moved in opposite directions.

Tamael crept slowly, straight up the incline toward the enemy. His striped fur faded into the mist and the mottled brown and green colors of the forest.

Batarel turned westward and trotted quickly through the trees, leaping from clearing to clearing. When he'd gone a safe distance, he turned north and headed up the incline much faster than Tamael had done. Using the soft pads of his feline paws, he moved silently through the labyrinth of vines. As he climbed, the mist grew denser, reducing visibility and distorting the way sound traveled through the air. Batarel smiled inwardly as the environment began to favor his superior sense of smell. After long minutes of cautious footing, he topped the ridge and paused as a shift in the air took the scent of the enemy away. But a low sound to his right told him that he was very near his objective.

With unmatched agility, he scaled the thick, twisting trunk of a nearby tree. Between the digits of his supple feet, deadly claws dug into the bark, steadying his movement along a thick branch that intertwined with that of another tree. In this way, he moved across the remaining distance of the ridge to find his enemy almost directly below him.

There were four of them—all Anduarym. They crouched before a low mound with a clearing to the north, watching the Myndar city which was partially obscured by the mist rising from the earth.

Batarel quickly estimated the distance he would have to jump, and found it to be well within his ability. When the breeze shifted again, he picked up Tamael's scent mixed with that of the Anduarym. Knowing his friend was in position to the east of the soldiers, the time had come to attack. He focused on the nearest of the group, crouched low, and readied his powerful legs for the leap.

Out of the mist, Tamael came at a full run, so quickly as to have appeared from nowhere. By the time the soldiers recognized the movement, they only had time to turn slightly in his direction and bring their arms up in defense.

Just as Tamael lunged to take the nearest soldier by the throat, Batarel launched himself through the air and landed on the back of the Anduar nearest him. Immediately digging his claws into the soldier for leverage, he bared the ten inch daggers in his deadly mouth and thrust forward, clamping down on the back of the Anduar's neck.

The soldier instinctively dropped and rolled, using Batarel's momentum against him.

Struggling to maintain his grip, Batarel felt his body fly through the air as his claws and teeth slid easily through the Anduar's flesh and were suddenly free. There was a second of weightlessness, then the crushing impact of the ground as he landed awkwardly on his side and rolled onto his back.

From the corner of his vision, he saw Tamael pushing one of the soldiers backward, violently wrenching his head from side to side. The soldier's throat tore and splattered blood on the ground and leaves as Tamael's growl filled the forest.

Batarel rolled over onto his feet and came up in a pouncing position. Without a second's hesitation, he jumped forward and caught the Anduar by the front of the throat.

From the other direction, Tamael continued to press forward, swiping with his powerful claws and ripping flesh as he pushed the next Anduar backward. But the third soldier swung around his right flank with a *vandrekt* in hand. Tamael didn't have time to react or even regret his terrible oversight. With a single powerful thrust, the spear punched through his chest and stole the air from his lungs.

When the first Anduar fell before his powerful jaws, Batarel turned toward the remaining soldiers. One was holding a spear that extended from his two-handed grip through Tamael's chest. The fierce, massive cat had already gone limp and was dropping to the ground.

From somewhere inside him, rage welled up and clouded every other thought. Bursting forward, Batarel collided with the legs of the unarmed soldier and knocked him to the ground, then jumped for the next one.

Seeing sudden movement from the corner of his vision, the Anduar released his grip on his now immovable spear and turned slightly, bringing his hands up in front of his face.

But Batarel wasn't aiming for the soldier's face. Instead, he tilted his head and opened his mouth as wide as his jaws would allow. Slipping underneath the Anduar's arms, Batarel dug his teeth into the muscled abdomen, feeling a grinding sensation as he bit into the angel's lower rib cage.

The soldier fell backward, just as the other one had done.

Operating by the instinct that came naturally to his animal form, Batarel used the momentary leverage to jerk his head from side to side. The powerfully muscled core of the ground soldier easily gave way to sharpened teeth, and the flesh was shredded in seconds.

Batarel released his grip when the soldier hit the ground. Then he spun around to face the final soldier who had now regained his footing and was holding a *vandrekt*.

The Anduar crouched low, holding the butt end of the spear against his right hip, with the bladed tip pointing menacingly at Batarel.

Without the benefit of surprise, Batarel was now at a disadvantage to the soldier's sturdy position and weaponry. Moving carefully to the side, he watched the Anduar simply pivot to keep the bladed tip of the spear between them. The silence of the misty forest returned, and Batarel could now only hear his own harsh breathing and that of the enemy.

The Anduar pivoted on legs bloodied by Tamael's claws.

Batarel stepped to the side, circling his enemy.

The soldier lunged forward and thrust his spear.

Batarel dodged to the side and attacked instantly. The soldier's blade grazed his neck and shoulder as he leaped forward and moved quickly inside the soldier's defense, biting down hard on his fleshy upper leg. When his feline paws came to the ground, he twisted with all his might in an attempt to throw the soldier off balance.

But the Anduar didn't budge. Ground warfare being their specialty, their massive size and low center of gravity made the Anduarym nearly invincible in hand to hand combat. Instead, the soldier fought through the pain to retract his spear and shove it through the animal's shoulder.

A yelp of surprise escaped Batarel's throat as he released his jaws and snapped instinctively at the weapon, shearing the wooden shaft from its metal tip. The searing pain spreading through his shoulder was almost lost amidst the choking weight that now fell on him. Pinned to the ground, Batarel looked up to see the cold stare of a battle-hardened warrior. Both of the Anduar's hands were firmly grasped around his throat. The soldier now had his full weight on top of Batarel, with his legs spread wide for balance.

Sensing the nearness of death, and the uselessness of his animal form, Batarel *shaped* into his angelic body and allowed his consciousness to drift toward the Eternal Realm. His vision began to darken as he reached out toward the face of his enemy. Whether in the physical realm or the small fragment of the Eternal that clung to it, he couldn't be sure what part of creation he now saw. The face and arms of the Anduar began to swirl with colors, their shapes undulating as if underwater.

So many times, he'd stared into faces during the Shaping— both human and animal. But most had been unaware of his presence. This time, the face wore a different expression. This time, the form in front of him wasn't being *shaped*; it was choking the life from him. As a feeling of euphoria came over his body, Batarel closed his eyes. In the absence of vision, a melody came into his mind. It was Myndlagid, a Song of Shaping. He smiled at the familiarity and comfort and began to sing in his imagination. His frantic, grasping hands slowed and his fingers began to pulsate with the melody. But the melody turned and took on a discordant sound, driven in a different direction by the anger that was swelling inside him. He thought of Tamael; his spirit being pulled into the Eternal and kept in the Place of Holding for the Final Judgment. He thought of Semjaza and his obedient soldier who now threatened to take everything away. He realized that the melody in his head came from the song in his heart. And the song in his heart now desired, more than anything, to destroy all that Semjaza had worked to establish.

Batarel opened his eyes and saw the straining face of the soldier, the knotted muscles now rippling along the Anduar's forearms. He saw his own hands and arms extending upward into the air, no longer grasping at the face of the enemy, but waving along with the melody instead. Looking deep into the soldier's form, seeing both his existence in this realm and the other, Batarel allowed the melody to grow and fragment into a complexity that only the Myndarym knew. He felt the discordant notes running counter to the melody and saw a unique beauty in them. Focusing all his attention, he realized that the melody was now sounding in reverse, a Song of Unshaping. Despite the realization that it was a tactic of the Nin-Myndarym, he sang in his mind and used his hands and fingers to direct and focus the notes.

All of a sudden, the chest of the Anduar exploded outward.

Batarel flinched, quickly closing his eyes as he felt something wet splatter against his face. The air came suddenly into his lungs again as the grip on his throat relaxed. Lying there in the stillness and silence Batarel breathed deeply of the moist, jungle air. He opened his eyes and saw leaves and branches overhead, obscured by the mist and fading light of dusk. When he sat forward, he found a ghastly scene.

The force of the explosion had thrown the body of the Anduar backward and to the ground. His ribcage was torn open and exposed. Blood and entrails were everywhere.

A sharp stab of pain in his shoulder quickly reminded Batarel of his whereabouts. Reaching around with his right hand he removed the long metal object from his shoulder and held it up in front of his face. The twelve-inch, double-bladed point was dark with his blood. Some of the shaft remained, shredded and broken on the end from the bite of his animal form. As he stared at the weapon in his hand he remembered the soldier that had passed by earlier, likely carrying the knowledge of Senvidar's location back to Semjaza.

Batarel exhaled a deep breath and looked over to the limp animal form of Tamael lying nearby. His fingers involuntarily tightened around the weapon in his hand. "Farewell, my friend," he said aloud.

Climbing slowly to his feet, Batarel turned south and looked into the trees in the direction of the Anduar he'd seen earlier in the day.

If Semjaza wants war, we'll bring it to him.

* * * *

Sariel watched the brilliant colors of the terrain pass below him. The luminescence merged into a blinding whiteness that blurred his now dim vision. It was painfully obvious to him that he had changed since the last time he moved through the Eternal Realm. His body, which used to shine with the light of the Spirit, now appeared dull against the backdrop of territory controlled by the Amatru. But he shook off these feelings of regret which threatened to cripple him. If he'd learned one thing during his service as a soldier, it was to focus on the objective.

Instead, he chose to feel relieved that he had guessed right. It was critical for his success that he crossed over into the Eternal in just the right place. If he did so behind enemy lines, he'd instantly be captured or killed. And showing up in the wrong place within territory held by the Amatru might have produced the same result. What he needed was Amatru territory that was no longer occupied, to give him the best chance of reaching his objective with the least amount of resistance. And that was exactly what he found.

Despite the dull colors that now formed his eternal body, he still felt the same as he glided over the waving grass, moving east toward the battle line. Behind him, miles of flat, peaceful land spread out, covered in bright, green vegetation that swirled with traces of multi-colored light as the breeze moved through it. It brought a smile to his face. But only briefly, as he rounded a hill and descended into a valley of rolling knolls. In the distance, the dull reddish smear of horizon told him that he was approaching Marotru territory. Nearer and slightly to the north, a large tent structure covered a hilltop. The ranks of Anduarym and Iryllurym encamped at the base of the hill told Sariel that he had found what he sought. As he approached the temporary command post of Fer-Rada Danduel, he slowed his speed and landed gently. Folding his wings inward, he walked with arms out to either side, his hands open in a gesture of peace.

Already, the ranks of soldiers were stirring into formation.

Sariel's heart beat loudly in his chest, coursing with the life-giving Spirit that sustained all holy things in this realm. But now, he could feel its hesitation. The flow of life was restricted by his altered body, which now seemed opposed to the Spirit.

When the Anduarym were assembled into a defensive line, three rows deep, the Iryllurym flew forward and dropped to the grass in front of Sariel.

"HALT!" one soldier commanded.

"Sariel?" another Iryllur said, his eyes narrowing.

Sariel kept his hands spread outward. "I wish to speak with Fer-Rada Danduel."

One of the seven aerial scouts immediately took to the air and headed back to the camp. The other six stayed behind. Their bodies were tense and their eyes squinted.

"How goes the battle?" he asked them.

"That is no longer any concern of yours," their leader stated. "We heard that you crossed over into the Temporal."

Sariel nodded slowly.

"It's not every day we hear of such an honored soldier deserting."

Sariel's head dropped. As confident as he was about his decision, the words still cut through him like a blade. But he wasn't about to discuss the matter with these soldiers. While he understood their feelings and knew their perspective was necessary, he also realized that their single-mindedness was part of the problem. He didn't see himself as a *deserter*, but there would be no convincing these soldiers of that.

After an awkward silence, the seventh Iryllur returned, hovering above the fields. "The Rada will see you now."

The remainder of the Iryllurym took to the air.

Sariel waited, as a matter of protocol, before following his escorts across the field.

The command post, though a temporary structure, was still more sophisticated than anything humans were capable of building. Its rigid skeleton of exquisitely crafted posts and beams spread over the hilltop, with numerous wings that met each other under a vaulted, central area. Its gleaming white walls and ceilings fluttered in the slight breeze, like a massive hand made of shimmering water.

The Iryllurym touched down just outside the central vaulted area, where they parted on either side of a doorway.

Sariel landed cautiously and walked between them. As he passed through the opening, he braced himself, expecting at any moment to be ambushed once inside. To his pleasant surprise, he entered without incident, though his position was flanked by a pair of Iryllurym in full battle armor. Large, quick eyes glared out of sleek helmets. Chests and arms were protected by plates of light, expertly crafted to conform to their thin, muscled bodies. With their arms crossed at the wrists, they displayed their *vaepkir* with pride. The long blades ran upward, along the outside edge of their forearms, ending at their shoulders.

Unarmed, Sariel felt quite vulnerable. Though it would have only made his task more difficult, part of him wished he had a *vaepkir* of his own.

Straight ahead, the Rada stood at the center of the tent near the primary support column. His wingless form was surrounded by other Anduarym, also in full battle gear.

Sariel bent low and placed one knee on the ground. "Fer-Rada Danduel," he said in greeting.

The Rada, who had been speaking with the Anduarym, now turned. "For one who has abandoned the Amatru, your courtesy is absurd."

A sarcastic response immediately came to mind. But Sariel bit his tongue and waited.

"I assume you realize that you can't make it out of here alive. And I'm sure you didn't come to surrender yourself, so you must have something important to say. Make it quick!"

Sariel exhaled the breath he'd been holding. "I understand Pri-Rada Ganisheel sent a Speaker to Semjaza. And the welcome was less honorable than expected."

The Rada took a few steps forward. "Are you working for him?"

"No," Sariel replied quickly.

"Then how did you come upon this information?"

"Your visit only provided the catalyst for a confrontation that was already in the making."

"Between who?" the Rada asked, clearly intrigued.

"Semjaza and the Myndarym who recently came under his leadership."

"Go on," Danduel replied.

"The Myndarym are no longer under his rule. They have established their own city in hopes of attaining the independence that motivated them to cross over to the Temporal in the first place."

Danduel lifted his head slightly, but remained silent.

"...but their independence is fragile," Sariel continued.

The Rada crossed his arms while shallow creases formed above his eyebrows. "...how so?"

"As you can imagine, Semjaza is not happy with losing such a key component to his plans. And to have this happen just as the Amatru reveal their knowledge of his operations—very inconvenient timing for him."

The Fer-Rada thought for a moment. "This is an interesting development, and nothing more," he said dismissively.

Sariel raised his eyebrows. "If I didn't know better, I'd say that was a lie."

The Rada scowled at the rebuke, but didn't deny its truth.

Sariel continued. "Clearly, you are aware that they were integral to helping him establish his kingdom there. But you don't know exactly what they were doing. You don't know how strong Semjaza is, what resources he has, or his ultimate goals."

"And you do, because you are working with the Myndarym," the high-ranking officer stated.

Sariel smiled. Though he had been prevented from higher-level leadership while he served the Amatru, he understood the strategic aspects of war better than most. This discussion was simply a different form of battle and he knew it was time for a direct attack, to exploit the Fer-Rada's own sense of inadequacy.

"You've been ordered to destroy his kingdom. But without weapons and armor in the Temporal Realm, and deficient intelligence concerning your enemy, you are unable to fulfill your orders. The message from Ganisheel's Speaker was a bluff, and Semjaza knows it."

The room was silent now, as all the Anduarym and Iryllurym listened intently to the conversation.

Sariel realized that in all his years as a soldier, he hadn't ever spoken so bluntly to someone in authority. And the difference this time was just that. Though a Fer-Rada, Danduel wasn't in authority over him because Sariel had removed himself from the authority structure.

"What are you proposing?" Danduel asked finally.

Sariel squinted. "You and the Myndarym have a common enemy, complimentary needs, skills, and supplies."

"Are you saying that they will fight for me?" Danduel asked.

"No," Sariel stated, rejecting the idea outright. "I'm saying, if the Amatru can produce the needed quantity of trained soldiers, the Myndarym will fight alongside you, as equals."

Danduel's face turned red.

The assault on his sense of pride was effective. As the Fer-Rada attempted to stifle his anger, Sariel knew that the officer was off-balance and would move to protect his weakness.

The crowd of soldiers immediately began to whisper and murmur among themselves.

When the color drained from his face, the Rada took a deep breath. "So, they have agreed to provide us with weapons and intelligence?" he asked finally.

"Only with a sufficient show of force on your part," Sariel replied, pleased that this Fer-Rada was able to see the big picture. "If you fail to do so, they will not be willing to risk their own lives, no matter how temporary their newfound freedom may be."

Danduel slowly shook his head. "How did someone of your reputation get mixed up in all of this? How did you go from being what you were, to standing here in front of me, in all your...dimness, speaking these things? Why are you doing this?"

Sariel straightened his posture. "I have my reasons. So, do we have an agreement?"

The Rada put one fist in the other hand and flexed his grip, but kept silent.

Sariel took the opportunity to tip the scales in his favor. "If you know my reputation, then you understand a fraction of what I'm capable of. Side with the Myndarym and I give you my word that I will kill Semjaza myself."

At this, the Rada looked up from the ground. "Very well. Give me until the second full moon from today to muster my forces. My Iryllurym will take you to Fim-Rada Nuathel. You can discuss the initial strategy with him and he will make the arrangements."

"Good," Sariel replied.

"...one more thing. Where shall we meet?" the Rada asked.

"You can cross over at the eastern end of the Dalen a-Sorgud," Sariel instructed.

"Is that where the Myndarym are?"

"No," Sariel replied with a smile.

22

Enoch rushed along the twisting corridors of Aragatsiyr. Though their creations were beautiful, they seemed to appreciate beauty more than functionality and he had a difficult time learning his way around. By the time he reached Kiyrakom, Ananel and the others were already assembled.

Pressing through the circle of angels, like a child trying to participate in the conversation of adults, Enoch saw a Myndar standing at the center near the pool of water. He didn't look familiar. But the gigantic, striped cat lying dead at his feet looked somewhat like the form a Myndar might take. Suddenly, Enoch realized what he was witnessing.

The one standing had blood oozing from a severe wound in his left shoulder. He had cuts and scrapes all along his arms and a deep gash that cut across his cheek from his mouth to his temple.

"...there were four of them," he was explaining.

Enoch was upset with himself that he'd missed the first part of the discussion.

"They were spying the location of our city. Tamael and I attacked them. We thought, with the advantage of surprise—"

The room was silent as he composed himself.

"I went after the last one and caught up with him before he could deliver his message."

"Surely there are more. Perhaps he already knows where we are," one of the Myndarym suggested.

"Perhaps," the stranger replied. "Perhaps those were only the first spies."

The crowd murmured with fear.

"But I do know something else. As much as we'd wish to forget about him, he will not forget about us. I saw the look in the eyes of the Anduarym. ...their blind obedience. Semjaza must be dealt with sooner rather than later."

"How can we possibly—" someone began from the back of the room.

"But they're soldiers—" another interrupted.

The stranger held up his hand. "I know. I know."

"Batarel," a voice rang out clear among the chatter.

Enoch looked up and noticed Ananel who now stepped forward from the gathering.

"You killed several Anduarym, so it is not impossible."

"They outnumber us three to one," someone shouted from across the circle.

"Sariel has gone to address that issue," Batarel argued.

"But the Amatru cannot be trusted," someone else suggested.

Batarel shook his head. "I think they would say that we are the ones who cannot be trusted. And who can argue with them?"

At this, the gathering of angels quieted.

Batarel continued. "I see now that Semjaza will not stop until he owns everything. I was blind to this while under his authority. I wanted to believe that he would honor our agreement once our duties were completed. But we will never have our freedom while he sits enthroned in his fortress, growing stronger every day. If the Amatru agree to this plan, I will be the first to join in."

"Who is this Sariel?" someone asked. "Perhaps he is a spy of Semjaza."

Batarel made a low noise that Enoch thought sounded like an animal. "He is an Iryllur who has come to this world for his own reasons. He is not working for Semjaza. I can assure you of that," he answered.

One of the Myndarym with a female form stepped forward. "I suppose any more discussion is pointless until we hear whether the Amatru agree."

"No!" Batarel almost barked. "I say, decide for yourselves whether or not you are willing to fight! Reach this conclusion before the Amatru agree. Then you will know in your spirit where you truly stand."

* * * *

Sariel approached the Myndar city from the east, finding it exactly where Tamael had said it would be. Circling around to the south, he observed it from the afternoon sky, marveling at its construction. Though far from finished, it had a gracefulness to its design that seemed directly opposed to the functional battlefield structures he'd left behind in the Eternal Realm. A low trumpet sounded and Sariel smiled. Not only were they sounding his arrival, but they were doing so with instruments. It seemed the Myndarym couldn't help themselves when it came to creating things.

Sariel glided slowly toward the fields to the south of the city. As soon as he touched down, he allowed himself to feel the fatigue in his wings and chest muscles that he'd been denying for days. Only once had he ever journeyed so far, and the soreness in his muscles confirmed it.

Batarel, who had been waiting as planned, came walking through the grass. His face bore an odd and unreadable expression as he extended his hand in the human greeting that Sariel had used on their first meeting. "Welcome."

Sariel looked over his shoulder. "Where's Tamael?"

Batarel stood motionless and closed his eyes for a moment. When he opened them, tears spilled down his face.

Sariel opened his mouth, but suddenly couldn't think of anything to say.

"We came across some of Semjaza's spies, but we took care of them," Batarel said finally.

"Spoken like a true warrior," Sariel replied, placing his hand on Batarel's un-bandaged shoulder. "And Jomjael?"

"He made it here with the women. They're all fine."

Sariel nodded, not knowing how to offer his condolences.

"The rest are waiting to speak with you. Come on," Batarel said, nodding toward the city.

As they began walking, Batarel turned his head. "Before we get in there, how did it go?"

"As planned," Sariel replied, enjoying the walk through the soft, short grass.

Reaching the city, Sariel was now able to compliment his aerial understanding of the city with a different perspective, appreciating it all the more. Inside the wide, arched passage, the trees seemed to be intertwined without any cutting or destruction of any kind. It was as if they had simply grown into this configuration from seedlings, seamlessly woven together like threads of a tapestry. In certain locations, leaves formed a decorative ornament or served some functional purpose, like providing light to a dark corridor with their luminescent veins. It was as if the trees had agreed to provide their foliage for the whims of Myndarym design. Sariel smiled at the beauty, realizing that the Shapers would always find some way to exercise what they were created to do.

"What do you call this place?" he asked.

"Senvidar."

Twisted Trees, Sariel thought to himself, interpreting the name in the angelic tongue.

The winding hallways eventually opened into a central courtyard where the massive trees created a partial canopy around the perimeter, while their roots snaked out across the ground toward a large pool of water at the center.

The Myndarym were already gathered and waiting.

Out of habit, Sariel quickly assessed the threat level of any new location he entered, starting with the number of other individuals—a quick estimation that revealed a discrepancy. "They're not all here," he noted.

"When we left Semjaza, some wanted to take their chances on their own. The rest of us thought it safer to stick together, at least for a while."

"I see," Sariel said, still counting in his mind. *Thirty nine, forty, forty one...*

Walking to the center of the courtyard, Batarel turned to the gathering of Shapers, while Sariel knelt and dipped his hands into the pool and brought the cold liquid up to his face. The water was refreshing on his hot skin and seemed to wash away some of his weariness.

"I present to you, Sariel of the Iryllurym," Batarel announced.

Sariel stood, water dripping from his face. He was exhausted, thirsty, and hungry. But he could see that these angels were anxious to hear what they'd been waiting for. So, he ignored his tiredness and addressed the gathering.

"My friends, I've just returned from a long journey—"

"Who do you think you are?" someone shouted out. "...speaking for us. What arrogance!"

Sariel scanned the group of angels, but couldn't tell who spoke. Most of them appeared in the forms which were the natural equivalent to their eternal bodies. But some obviously preferred the forms that had been given to humans, wearing muscular bodies with beards and other male attributes. "If you have something to say to me, step forward and say it openly."

An angel stepped carefully out of the crowd. It wore a female body and looked decidedly different than the rest.

Sariel laughed at the sight, but his weariness was too great to prevent the swell of anger that followed it. "I'll tell you who I am. I am a Myndar."

Gasps could be heard all around, while the female took a step backward.

"And the fact that you wear the form of a female human only confirms what I already know to be true. You," he pointed to the woman, "...and all the rest of you. You want to live in freedom. You want to take forms of things without answering to anyone. You want to roam this world without fear for your lives. You desire a world without Semjaza."

The crowd was silent now.

"I met with Fer-Rada Danduel who commands a division of Anduarym for the Amatru. He's been tracking Semjaza's progress for a long time."

"How long?" asked a colorful Myndar in the front.

"Ever since he left the Eternal Realm. And lest your own arrogance rival that of Semjaza's, he knows all about you as well. The Amatru were not fooled by anything Semjaza did to cover your tracks. We are all their enemies now."

"Then why would they let you leave?" a tall one in front asked.

"Because I am also a soldier and I understand how they think. We have leverage in this situation." Sariel couldn't say the word *leverage* now without hearing the repulsive way it fell from Semjaza's tongue. "Semjaza is their primary target and we have information and resources they need."

"Why to do you say *we*? You are not one of us!" someone yelled.

"That implies we are the secondary target," another added.

Sariel ignored the first statement. "Yes. But that doesn't become a concern until the primary target is dealt with. This is the way of the Amatru. They are disciplined in the prioritization of their tasks," he explained. "For the meantime, we each need the other."

"And afterwards?" the female asked, more humbled than the last time she spoke.

"We only have need of the Amatru until Semjaza and his armies are destroyed. After that, I would advise going somewhere far away, as quickly as you can."

"Why is this human woman so important to you?" the female asked with a grin.

"Does it matter?" Sariel replied. "My problem and your problem are only symptoms of the same disease. We both want something that we cannot have while Semjaza rules. And that is what must be changed."

Batarel, who had been facing the crowd, turned to Sariel. "How many soldiers will Danduel bring? And when are they coming?"

"He commands one division, but he asked for us to wait until the second full moon so that he could muster additional forces. I assured him that he would need to bring enough to convince you all that this fight would end the way we want it to."

Batarel grinned. "So, they will be needing weapons—"

"Will they fight on our behalf?" someone interrupted.

Sariel turned. "No. They will fight alongside you," he answered

"But how are we to go against Semjaza's armies untrained?"

Sariel held up his hand. "I will gladly train you with the time that is available. But I've seen many times over, the most effective way to fight is to use what you already know. So, let me ask you, what do you know?"

"...how to fight like an animal," Batarel quickly responded.

"Yes," Sariel said. "You understand forms and how to use them.

"We know Myndlagid," another added.

"Yes. You must think of what it is that you understand better than anyone. Then think how to use it to your advantage," Sariel suggested.

"...Songs of Unshaping," Batarel said under his breath.

Only Sariel heard this comment and he turned to the Myndar with wide eyes.

Batarel shrugged his shoulders. "It was an accident, but very effective."

Sariel grinned, then turned back to the rest of the Myndarym. "So what do you say? Shall we take the opportunity that is before us? If not, think carefully about how the next years of your life will turn out."

"I'll fight!" Batarel announced.

A long moment of silence passed. Sariel began to worry that his carefully constructed plan may fall apart before it ever began.

"I'll fight," said another. This one had a human standing next to him.

"I will," said the female.

One by one, they all chimed in, adding their commitment to the effort.

"Very well. Myndarym, we have a tough road ahead. But my hope is that on the other side of this momentary trouble we will be greeted by freedom. Think about what you offer; what you're capable of. We will reconvene in the morning to discuss preparations."

The mood of the gathered angels seemed elevated as they turned to leave, but the ache in Sariel's heart persisted.

This is all taking too long! Hold on, my love. We'll be together soon!

* * * *

As the group began to disperse, Enoch looked up at Ananel. "I want to speak with him."

Ananel looked down and nodded. "You don't need my permission."

Stepping from side to side to avoid being crushed by the giants around him, Enoch worked his way through the exiting crowd and approached Sariel.

The winged angel had returned to a kneeling position to refresh himself from the pool at the center of Kiyrakom. His head turned slowly as Enoch approached.

His brilliant blue eyes seemed to look straight through Enoch, just like the first time he met Ananel. But this angel reminded Enoch of the ones who guarded Semjaza in his throne room. He was roughly the same height as a Myndar, but more muscular, with coloring closer to that of the Speaker's winged escorts.

"Can I help you?" he asked in a ragged voice.

"You lived among the Chatsiyram," Enoch stated.

The angel closed his eyes for a moment, the extended blink of a weary traveler. "One of the women told you about me?"

"No," Enoch answered truthfully.

Sariel turned his head slightly. "There is something different about you. Who are you?"

"I am Enoch."

Sariel lifted his head as if he'd just pieced something together. "That's why they let you in here. What can I do for you?"

"Well," Enoch paused. "If you're all Shapers, why can't you just take a form that is more powerful than Semjaza? ...something big."

Sariel's face curled into a lopsided grin and his eyes quickly lost their intensity. "Taking a form is not as simple as you might think. When we do so, we are bound by its limitations. Everything must be considered. What food will it eat? How will it use the food for energy? How will it breathe? How must the body be constructed and in what environment will it live? And many more considerations, all of them far too complicated to explain. It takes years to learn a form; generations of your time to master it. Forms are not chosen lightly."

"Oh," Enoch mumbled.

"Most Myndarym take the forms they are most familiar with. There simply isn't enough time to do what you suggest. But it is a good question."

"I see," Enoch said softly.

"Now what did you really want to say to me?" Sariel asked, scooping up some water and drinking from his hands.

Enoch smiled, realizing that his ploy of easing into conversation had been completely transparent to the angel. "I've seen you before."

"You've probably seen many of my kind," Sariel replied, sipping more water from his hands.

"No," Enoch said, shaking his head. "You. When I was child. The Holy One showed me."

Now Sariel straightened to a standing position. "Me? Why?"

"I don't know," Enoch replied, looking up into the sky above the angel's head. "But He sees you."

Sariel turned his head and looked up as well. When his face returned, his eyes looked distant. "Yes. I suppose He does," he mumbled. "So, He speaks to you?"

"He does."

"And you speak to Him?"

"I do," Enoch admitted.

"What does He think about me?"

Enoch rubbed his hands together, carefully considering the question. "I don't know yet."

Sariel raised his chin and looked down at Enoch. "What do you think of me?"

The words were already on the tip of Enoch's tongue. "Though you have abandoned your home and have disobeyed your elders, you still believe that you are doing the will of the Holy One."

Sariel looked at the ground for a moment. "I hadn't thought of it that way before, but yes. I suppose you're right."

Enoch nodded, then turned slowly and began walking away.

"It wasn't just a vision," Sariel called after him.

Enoch stopped and turned.

"When I met with the Fer-Rada, I overheard some soldiers speaking of a rumor. It hasn't happened since the first of your kind, but the Holy One apparently allowed a human into His presence. The soldiers were quite offended. A human. Can you imagine that?"

Enoch couldn't help but grin at the answer to the question that had plagued him for weeks.

"Good evening," Sariel offered, then walked past Enoch and left the Place of Meeting.

23

Four hundred miles southeast of Senvidar, at the eastern end of a narrow channel of water, Batarel stood in a small clearing amidst a dense stand of trees. The soldier in front of him was also a Shaper, but had been operating as an Anduar for many years, not unlike the direction Batarel had been heading before Semjaza found him. The soldier was looking down at the bundles of weaponry lying on the ground, taking inventory in order to relay the Myndarym's state of readiness to the Amatru.

"Fifty *vaepkir*. Fifty *vandrekt*. Thirty *vanspyd*. Fifty light *keskyd*. Thirty heavy *keskyd*. And forty *skoldur*," the angel mumbled to himself. "This is not enough. How many more are being made?"

"...two, maybe three times what you see." Batarel assured him. "They are en route now.

The soldier looked up to midday sky in search of the moon, which was nowhere to be seen. "How far away? We only have one day left."

Batarel noticed the way the soldier's eyes darted back and forth along the grass, looking for other information that may be useful. Most likely, to identify the location of the Myndar city. The arrangement with the Amatru was fragile, and Batarel didn't think the answer to the question was relevant to their mission. At least, not their primary mission.

"We'll worry about that," he replied. "You just make sure you bring enough soldiers to get the job done."

The Shaper suddenly turned his head toward Batarel.

Behind his eyes, Batarel could almost see his disgust at having to work with unholy traitors.

But the soldier held his tongue.

"And next time you cross over, do it here. Not in the open again. Semjaza's eyes are everywhere."

Again, the Shaper held his tongue. But his displeasure at taking instruction from someone outside the Amatru was obvious. Finally, the soldier nodded. Then, the objects around him appeared to distort. Trees and vines bent inward. The grass bowed toward him. But it was only an illusion. It was the light from these objects that was warping, fragmenting into bands of color as the Shaper *shifted* his existence out of the Temporal Realm.

And then, he was gone.

In the following silence, Batarel smiled. The plans were moving along quickly. Soon, Semjaza's fortress would be infiltrated. And the wicked Pri-Rada would be overthrown.

A faint scraping noise rapidly brought him out of his thoughts. At once, his heart sunk in his chest, for he knew the sound to be abnormal. Perhaps it was a residual benefit of spending time in an animal form. Even in his angelic form, he could almost feel the rhythm of life in his surroundings—their sounds and smells.

Shifting his consciousness toward the sliver of Eternal existence which clung to the Temporal, he looked outward with different eyes, seeing beyond the orderly structure of this realm. To the west, he counted fourteen spirits, spread out into a loose crescent-shaped formation. The fiery nuclei, visual representations of the spirit within each temporal being, hovered just above the ground, moving cautiously toward him. As they passed over the earth, they came closer to each other, converging upon Batarel's location. Judging by their size and movement, they were Semjaza's Anduarym.

Batarel stepped quietly to the north and began making his way out of the clearing, hoping to lead the attackers away from the stash of weapons and armor. Instead of *shaping* himself, he stayed in his angelic form. It was slower than his animal form, but he wasn't planning on trying to escape. Instead, he felt a mixture of fear and hatred building in his heart, and he allowed it to grow and consume his thoughts and actions. As his feet moved more quickly with each step, now running over and around the thick vegetation, a discordant melody wove itself into his mind. It produced a sense of pride and pleasure that intertwined itself among the other emotions, taking control of them. From his lips, which were now curled into a grin of delight, a Song of Unshaping began to emanate.

* * * *

"...and what are those?" Enoch asked, pointing ahead to the bundle of weaponry hoisted on the back of a nearby Myndar.

"*Vandrekt*," Ananel replied. "...for the Anduarym. They are the closest approximation of the weapons they use in the Eternal Realm. They hold the wooden shaft and thrust the sharpened, metal point toward the enemy."

Enoch couldn't keep his face from wrinkling at the thought of such violence.

"I know. Your kind is not familiar with war," Ananel stated. "...or the art of working with metals."

"How long has your kind been at war?" Enoch asked, looking up.

Ananel stepped high over a rock and kept moving ahead. "Since before humans were created."

Enoch looked ahead to keep from tripping over a bush. "Why can't the Amatru bring their own weapons?"

"That's a good question," Ananel replied. "When the Myndarym *shift* from one part of creation to another, it comes naturally, for that is how we were created. It is much like when humans learn to walk. Once the skill is mastered, it is rarely given much thought afterward. But clothing, armor, and weaponry—these objects are not part of us. So, it takes a great deal of practice to *shift* these things with us. And when creation was sundered into our two realms, this task became infinitely more complex. But the weapons and armor used by the Amatru are a different matter altogether. They are not like other objects. They are purer, crafted solely from the light of the Spirit. And only the most skilled Shapers even know how they are made. Such objects have no Temporal equivalent. They cannot exist in this realm. So, when the Amatru arrive, they will be without weapons and at a great disadvantage against Semjaza."

Enoch kept his eyes forward, but nodded, trying to take in the wealth of information that Ananel seemed pleased to offer. When he looked up again at the angel, who was now smiling, he realized suddenly that he had made a friend. It was something that Zacol had been trying to get him to do for years among the Shayeth, but somehow it never worked.

How strange to befriend an angel, but feel so distant from my own kind!

After a long silence, Enoch spoke again. "If it is so difficult to *shift* objects other than yourselves, then how did you bring Semjaza and his soldiers here? Surely another living being is more complex than clothing. How did the Speaker and his angels come here? How will the Amatru be brought here?"

"The Speaker and his angels were Myndar. But to *shift* others, well, it is quite complicated," Ananel admitted. "Few among the Amatru can do it. In fact, when we *shifted* Semjaza, there was only one among us who was capable. Ezekiyel. He is a master Shifter and Shaper. It is he who taught the rest of us."

"Hmm," Enoch mumbled, trying to concentrate on Ananel's words. But his thoughts were drifting to Zacol and Methu.

Ananel continued. "Each of us had to sing a Song of Naming to comprehend all the individual pieces which comprised the angel we were *shifting*. Then, in order to move the pieces, I had to find suitable forms for each one to take as I brought them across. You see, this realm operates differently. So, if I were to just move the pieces here, they would perish. They had to be constructed properly to exist within the laws which govern this realm. Then I had to reassemble the pieces into yet another structure that could exist and function here as intended. And all of this had to be done at once, in transit. For the very moment one piece is changed, it is also no longer able to survive in the other realm. And so, the ever changing location and complexity—"

Enoch looked up at Ananel who had trailed off.

The angel was looking out across the fields. His eyes were narrow with suspicion.

Enoch followed his gaze and could barely make out something lying in the field, just before the shoreline of the water they were approaching. He couldn't see what it was, but immediately felt that something was wrong.

* * * *

Sariel dropped the bundle of armor he'd been carrying. In one swift movement, he unfurled his wings and leaped into the air. Seconds later, he glided to a running landing, then slowed as he reached the dead body.

Batarel's angelic form lay on its side, with arms stretched out in front of him. Two spears had been run through his chest, and another protruded from the side of his ribcage, sticking into the air like a standard carried before an army. His pale skin was covered in blood from head to toe. And though his fatal wounds had obviously been gruesome, Sariel's trained eyes could see that not all the blood was his own.

"Check the weapons!" Sariel yelled, pointing into the nearby forest as the other Myndarym came running.

A few dropped their bundles and ran away from the crowd, while the remainder of the angelic population of Senvidar approached Sariel with caution.

Before they arrived, Sariel followed the trampled grass westward along the shoreline. A short distance away, he found a blackened Anduar lying on his back. The skin on the front of his body had been burned so that it seemed to peel backward away from its bones. On either side of the dead soldier, two swaths of bare soil extended to the west for thirty feet. At their edges, the charred roots of dead vegetation jutted upward to the sky, while the surrounding grasses bore the unmistakable wilting and discoloration of proximity to fire.

Sariel continued walking west, finding two more dead Anduarym a hundred yards away. One was completely missing his upper body, while the other looked as if something had exploded inside his chest cavity. The gore was scattered for several yards in a half-moon shape in front of the body. Bare ribs were exposed to the air, like fingers of an open hand.

"They're gone. All the weapons are gone!" someone yelled from behind.

Sariel turned and walked back to the group which had gathered around Batarel's body.

Most of the Myndarym stood motionless while several knelt close to their fallen friend.

Ananel, who always seemed to be accompanied by Enoch, pushed his way through the crowd. His face looked grim, but there were no tears in his eyes, unlike the others. "Were they watching us the whole time?" he asked in a low voice.

"I don't think so," Sariel answered him. "It was probably just a scouting party. But if they get back to the fortress with the weapons, we'll have lost the element of surprise. Semjaza will have time to prepare for the attack."

"And they'll know we're working with the Amatru," Ananel added.

"What can we do?" one of the females asked. "The Amatru will not arrive until tomorrow."

"By the look of things," Sariel said, glancing back to where the dead Anduarym lay. "..Semjaza's soldiers have a half-day head start. Maybe more."

"We can't afford to wait," Ananel concluded.

Sariel noticed that the expressions on the faces of the other Myndarym began to change. No one said another word. But he could see their sadness over Batarel's death being replaced by fear, and he spoke quickly to put an end to it.

"Like it or not, we are already at war with Semjaza. Hiding from him is no longer feasible. So we have two options. We can wait for the Amatru, forfeit the majority of our weaponry to the enemy, and give up our element of surprise. Or, we can go after the weapons and risk our lives to keep the plan intact."

"But how many soldiers are we talking about?" one of the Myndar asked.

"Three of them are dead. But they were able to carry off the weapons, so it was probably more than one scouting party," Sariel answered. "If it was two parties, then there should be eleven left."

Ananel turned to face his fellow angels. "I say we go after them. We can catch up with them. They'll only be walking on two legs."

"But what will we do when we catch up?" another asked.

Sariel ran through the scenarios in his mind, then quickly verbalized his thoughts. "Those of us who can fly, can probably catch them within an hour, if we push hard. Those who travel by land...perhaps two or three times as long. If any of you wear forms accustomed to water, you'll be somewhere in between. But I'm the only one who knows how to use these weapons, so we may only be able to slow them down."

"If we're going to go after them, we'd better do it quickly," Ananel pointed out.

Sariel looked from angel to angel, still seeing fear in their eyes. But now, at least they realized the gravity of the situation and the consequences for waiting. From years of battle, he knew this look. He'd seen it on countless faces. Many times, it was the last he ever saw of the soldiers. But he also knew that action must be taken. And sometimes, the only way to initiate it was to make the decision for them; to push their wavering courage over the edge.

"Alright. Those of you who can fly, follow me. We'll move fast and try to slow the Anduarym down when we reach them. The rest of you, catch up as quickly as you can. The greater our numbers, the better chances we have. Where's Enoch?"

"Right here," the human said, stepping out from beneath the crowd as a child among adults.

Sariel knelt to the ground. "Wait here for the Amatru. When they arrive, tell them what has happened. Give them the weapons and tell them to follow us. Do you see this mountain range here," he asked, pointing to the south.

"Yes," the prophet answered.

"Semjaza's fortress is beyond the western end of this range. If they head in that direction, they'll find us."

The short man's fingers wound nervously through this dark beard, but he nodded anyway.

Sariel reached over to the nearest bundle of weapons and untied the cord that bound them. The pale, fibrous cloth unrolled across the ground. From the pile, he chose two *vaepkir*, then stood up, feeling their comforting weight resting in his hands and the cold metal lying against the outside of his forearms.

"Take what you need and let's move."

"...just my teeth," Ananel replied. His voice already sounded like the canine outline that his shimmering form began to take. When the process was complete, a massive grey wolf raised its head into the air and loosed a deep howl which spread across the valley. Then, with his snout to the ground, the Myndar burst into motion, running swiftly through the deep grass to the west.

One by one, the Myndarym *shaped* into their preferred forms, some as creatures of the air and some as creatures of the sky. Before he took to the air, Sariel noticed several Myndarym who were still in their angelic forms, wading into the nearby water. Seconds later, they began to shimmer, as well.

Sariel looked back to the odd assortment of flying creatures scattered across the field. They were waiting for his lead. He pulled his weapons to his chest and spread his wings. "Try to keep up!"

24

A massive bird of prey came to a quick, but graceful landing on the ground beside Sariel. The group of winged Myndar parted to make room for his sleek, brown form. With massive talons embedded into the soft earth, the bird's head swiveled toward Sariel and its golden eyes fixed on his. Then its form began to shimmer.

"You were right—eleven Anduarym," it said, as soon as it wore its angelic body. "They're moving quickly across the plains to the west, about two miles away."

Sariel breathed deeply, readying himself for the last charge. "...and the weapons?"

"Each one of the brutes is carrying at least two bundles," the Myndar replied.

Sariel nodded. *The Anduarym are made for this sort of thing.* Then he looked around at the peculiar assortment of winged creatures that made up his untrained group and was struck by the contrast. All of them were large, even in their animal forms, but none were designed for war. Few were even capable of a meaningful attack. It would be a challenge to make use of them all in a capacity that wouldn't result in their deaths.

"Alright," he said to the group. "We'll have to move together and attack as one. We'll only get one chance. After the first strike, they'll change formation to ensure they're protected on all sides. With their weapons, we won't be able to do anything; it'll become a waiting game. So, the first priority for you is to disarm them. Grab those bundles and anything else they're carrying. If you can do that, they'll be vulnerable for when the others arrive."

"What about you?"

Sariel looked to the one who had scouted the Anduarym. His golden eyes were bright behind disheveled, brown hair. He almost looked like an Iryllur. "You and I have weapons," he replied. "I want you to sink those talons deep into Anduar flesh and not let go until your prey is dead."

The Myndar squinted, but remained silent.

"Let's go," Sariel said, taking to the air once more.

Vast plains stretched to the horizon, bordered on the south by mountains and water to the north. Sariel led the flying Myndarym swiftly across the terrain, staying close to the ground to keep their outlines visually obscured for as long as possible.

At the center of the thirty-mile wide flatlands, a small cluster of shapes could be seen moving due west. Their silhouettes were barely visible against the harsh backdrop of the setting sun, frequently disappearing as the fleeing soldiers moved in and out of the trees. The occasional glint of light reflected from the metallic weapons slung across their broad shoulders. The long and muscular legs of the Anduarym carried them quickly across the land and it appeared that they were trying to reach Semjaza as fast as possible.

But they were no match for the swift wings of the Shapers. As the Myndarym came upon the soldiers, Sariel pulled back slightly to tighten the formation and give the signal to attack. Then, he dove and pumped his wings furiously to gain speed. He brought his hands together and flexed his arms until his *vaepkir* were at their fullest extension. With silent precision, he targeted a space between two Anduarym and quickly retracted his wings at the last moment before impact. His narrow outline shot through the gap, but the weapons collided with the back of the soldiers' legs, chopping their sturdy footing from underneath them. With most of his forward movement coming to an abrupt halt, Sariel instantly tucked into a ball and rolled as he hit the ground.

A flurry of sound followed.

Wet earth pounded his body.

Blades of grass lashed at his skin.

The bright colors on the horizon whipped past in a blur.

Sariel pushed his legs outward and came swiftly to his feet with *vaepkir* ready, facing the enemy.

The nine remaining soldiers were already breaking formation as the Myndarym fell upon them.

The grasslands erupted into a chaotic explosion of movement, color, and sound.

Piercing shrieks cut through the air amidst the clang of metal.

Great wings of dappled brown beat frantically as the giant eagle wrenched one soldier away from the group and attempted to drag him across the ground by the bare flesh of his back.

Another Anduar pitched forward and slid through the grass, holding tight to the cord that fastened his bundle. A ripping noise emerged from the uproar as a white, feathered creature rose into the air, still clutching a piece of coarse fabric. Spears scattered along the ground in its wake.

Sariel's eyes darted from the two Anduarym he'd cut down, to another two who were coming at him now, both carrying *vandrekt*. He advanced slowly upon the larger angels, wary of their deadly strength and proficiency with bladed objects.

The one on the left stepped wide, while the other came straight at him.

A sudden flicker of movement in the sky to the left prompted Sariel to rush forward, keeping the soldiers' attention on him. Raising his right arm, he feigned an attack and watched the eagle descend again.

It came from the northeast and plunged its talons deep into the back of the Anduar on the left.

The soldier fell forward without a struggle. His body went limp the moment his heart was punctured.

The eagle, with talons still embedded in its prey, flapped its giant wings to keep from being pulled to the ground.

To the right, a brightly-colored flurry of wings drew Sariel's attention as another bird descended.

But the other Anduar was quicker. He turned and thrust his spear upward, plunging it through the bird's chest. With a swift, pivoting motion, he brought the bird crashing to the ground and leaned on the spear to keep the animal's desperate spasms from becoming a liability.

With the soldier's attention diverted, Sariel lunged forward and brought his *vaepkir* to bear, cleaving a deep gash into the angel's upper arm and chest.

The Anduar instantly released his grip on the spear and fell backward, spinning as the force of the bladed attack drove him to the ground.

Looking up from the immediate confrontation, Sariel was disappointed to see that the discipline of the ground soldiers had taken over. The six remaining Anduarym now had spears in hand and were assembled into a ring formation with their backs to each other.

The element of surprise was gone. The infantry were now ready to repel any further attacks.

* * * *

The moon shone brightly against the night sky, illuminating the fog that had settled into the shallow valley to the west. A short while ago, Ananel had passed over the bodies of four soldiers and one Myndar. Though the mist prevented him from seeing anything beyond a few yards, he knew by scent that the Anduarym and his fellow Shapers were close. With his paws churning up the wet soil, he descended into the valley while the rest of the pack struggled to keep up with his rapid pace.

Trees and shrubbery slipped silently past. Only the swish of grass and his own breath could be heard. The scent of the soldiers gave Ananel direction, while his canine reflexes responded to the terrain that came out of the mist. Suddenly, the gray shroud lifted and a wide clearing could be seen. The air was moving to the south now and pushing the fog against the mountains.

Two hundred yards ahead, a cloud of frantic shapes swarmed in the air above a tight cluster of shadows moving along the ground. The Anduarym were on the move. The winged Myndarym were following from above, but seemed reluctant to prevent the movement of the soldiers.

As the pack neared the confrontation, Ananel realized why. The six remaining Anduarym were moving at a steady pace. Each one kept a hand on the shoulder of the next, while holding a spear outward with the other hand. The two at the rear were nearly running backwards, but their defense seemed effective.

To Ananel's right, a feline broke away from the pack and charged ahead. Ananel wanted to loose a howl to bring Jomjael back, but he kept silent to maintain the advantage of surprise. His fellow Shaper must have seen a weakness and immediately responded to his animal instincts. As Jomjael swung wide and disappeared into the taller grass to the north, Ananel identified the weakness.

One of the soldiers held his spear in a different hand than the others. It restricted his forward movement and the awkwardness seemed to command more of his attention.

Before the soldier even had time to react, Jomjael burst from the deep grass and slipped under the blade of the spear. With all his might, he bit down hard on the Anduar's upper leg. As the two dagger teeth on either side of his mouth sank into the muscled flesh, Jomjael brought his front claws around and gripped the lower body of the soldier. He pulled his rear legs off the ground and allowed his weight to drag the soldier downward.

But the Anduar ran on with incredible strength, and maintained his footing. With a silent grimace, he retracted his spear and drove it through Jomjael's stomach.

The feline's left claw slipped free, but he bit down harder and refused to release his prey.

Another soldier stepped out of formation and thrust his *vandrekt* through Jomjael's chest.

Immediately, the Shaper's animal body went limp and fell to the ground and the Anduarym continued their relentless march to the west.

* * * *

With his higher vantage point, Sariel saw Jomjael long before the enemy did, but still too late to prevent the attack. When the second spear punched through Jomjael's chest behind the shoulder, Sariel banked to the right and positioned himself between the enemy and the other land animals fast approaching. He came to a hover above the ground and waved his hands erratically, trying to draw their attention. He knew it was pointless to attack the Anduarym, and Jomjael's senseless death only proved it.

Running low and swift across the plains, the four-legged Myndarym came through the tall grass. When they noticed Sariel, they slowed their approach.

"Don't attack," Sariel called out. "It's useless."

"What can we do?" Ananel growled.

Sariel came to a landing in front of the pack. "Surround them. Stay close enough to harass them and probe their defense. But don't commit to an attack. We'll do the same from the air. All we can do now is try and slow them down."

Ananel's wolfen snout snarled in frustration. "And what if they reach Semjaza?"

"Let's hope they grow weary and make a mistake before then," Sariel replied.

The sky grew light in the east.

Sariel took to the air again, just as one of the winged Myndarym landed. Earlier in the evening, he had implemented a rotation to allow one member of the winged group to rest every fifteen minutes. The four-legged Myndarym had also followed this example, but were still showing signs of exhaustion.

The Anduarym, wounded and carrying the extra burden of weapons, showed no signs of slowing. Their race was remarkable in situations like these and it saddened Sariel that they had abandoned their original purpose. It was truly a shame to have to fight against them, rather than at their side.

As the sun crept from behind the eastern horizon, the mountains to the south gave way to flatter terrain. From high in the air, the peak of Murakszhug could be seen along the southwestern horizon, a hundred and fifty miles away. And somewhere to the northwest of that mountain was Semjaza's fortress.

Time was running out.

Moving into position over the Anduarym, Sariel reversed his grip on his weapons. Holding the blades of the *vaepkir* out in front of him now, he considered the price of an attack. Their range with spears far exceeded that of the weapons he held. And each attempt to attack would surely cost the life of at least one Myndar. He could attempt to throw his weapons, but the *vaepkir* weren't designed for that. It would likely be a waste of good weaponry.

Slowly, he breathed a sigh of exhaustion and looked to the sunrise. Somewhere out there behind the mist, dozens of miles across terrain already covered, new weapons lay scattered among the trees and grass. Unfortunately, Sariel had neither the strength, nor the time, to retrieve them.

Just as all hope seemed lost, he noticed a dark cloud moving quickly across the land. He watched in fascination as it sped over the trees, constantly changing in color, while its shape became more evident with each passing second. Alternating flashes of dark and light were interspersed with the glint of reflected sunlight.

As soon as Sariel recognized the narrow, pointed column formation, he smiled. For he knew the terror induced by the charge of an armored wing of Iryllurym. He remembered his years of flying at the head of such formations; the feeling of exhilaration at the first strike; the look on the faces of the enemy as they realized, too late, what they were up against. And before they even arrived, Sariel knew that the Anduarym below were now breathing their last breaths upon the earth.

"To me!" he shouted. "All of you! Come to me!"

The Myndarym looked confused, but were too weary to object. Slowly, the creatures peeled away from the running soldiers and came toward Sariel's hovering form.

Moments later, the air was thick with the drone of wings. Fer-Rada Danduel's soldiers came like lightning across the fields. With armored chests and bladed forearms, two wings of Iryllurym, ninety-eight in all, engulfed the tiny Anduar force and broke them into pieces. Spearheads were sheared from their shafts, along with the limbs that held them. Heads rolled across the ground as the lifeless bodies were scattered across the plains. The formation of winged angels poured over, around, and through the enemy as would a wave hitting a rocky shoreline.

In the aftermath, Sariel descended to the grass and waited while the soldiers of the Amatru circled back to land gracefully among the carnage they had just created.

"The prophet said we'd find you here," said one of the Iryllurym, stepping forward and removing his helmet.

Sariel recognized Fim-Rada Nuathel from his recent visit to the Eternal Realm. "You're early! Thank you for your assistance," he replied, inclining his head slightly. "We weren't making much progress against their defense."

Nuathel wore a scowl on his face and remained silent.

Sariel was a traitor in his eyes, and this meeting was simply something he had to endure. Under different circumstances, the disappointed look would have been unbearable. But Sheyir was in danger. Every other emotion—regret, shame, even fear—was swallowed up by his love for her.

"Where is Danduel?" Sariel asked, dismissing the cold reception of the officer.

"The Fer-Rada...sent us ahead," Nuathel replied, emphasizing the fact that Sariel hadn't used the officer's proper title. "He and his Anduarym will be here by the day's end."

"Very well," Sariel replied with equal coldness.

25

After giving the weapons and armor to the soldiers of the Amatru, Enoch watched them go their separate ways. The Iryllurym took to the air while the Anduarym ran through the fields to the west. The holy Myndarym, who had *shifted* the soldiers into this realm, disappeared just as the Speaker had done in Haragdeh. The Vidirym, who seemed the most secretive, had come from the Eternal Realm directly into the nearby water. Enoch didn't get a good look at them, but did manage to catch a glimpse of bluish green skin. As they slipped beneath the water, something trailed behind them, disturbing the smooth surface.

When they were gone, silence descended like a thick blanket, the likes of which Enoch hadn't experienced in months. Stranger than this abrupt change was the fact that Enoch now felt quite lonely. Though he'd always been a recluse by nature, he'd been living with the Myndarym for quite some time and had grown accustomed to their presence. Looking now across the water and the patches of fog swirling over the grass, he wondered what he should do. Aragatsiyr was vacant now, as all the Myndarym had gone to war. And Semjaza's stone city, which he named Malakiyr, was soon to be a battlefield. Neither place held any purpose for Enoch, which led him to wonder if his responsibilities had been fulfilled.

Immediately, his thoughts turned to his family. He missed Zacol and remembered now the way her eyes filled with tears the day he left. And little Methu, the way he was fascinated by something he'd found on the ground. Enoch even missed his tribe; the usual mild disdain with which they treated him, now seemed comfortingly familiar in light of everything that had occurred since he had left. He missed the feeling of peacefulness that he experienced when sitting in the fields at night, watching from a distance as families huddled together around fires, staring into the flames. He missed the sound of the animals that grazed in the fields of Sedekiyr. And, as strange as it seemed, he even missed the smells that went along with them. It was the smell of home. The air in this place was cleaner, with more pleasing fragrances, but he could almost smell the loneliness beneath it.

Enoch slowly closed his eyes. *Holy One. Once again, I find myself alone. You have allowed me to see such strange and marvelous things, but now I am reminded of the ache in my heart. I miss my family and my home. Is there more that You require of me? For greater than any other desire of mine is that which seeks to obey Your voice. You know what my needs are. You know what is best for me and my family; for this world. Is there more that You require?*

When Enoch opened his eyes, he saw water covering everything as far as the eye could see. He stood on a rocky fragment of land, looking north. And yet, without turning around, he knew it was connected to a larger landmass behind him. It was different, yet reminded him of the land he passed over when traveling toward Aragatsiyr for the first time. He had named it Sahveyim, for there had been water on all sides.

Then the vision passed away and he saw only the swaying grass, dancing in the morning breeze. In his mind, a few words remained—echoes of something that he was certain he hadn't heard in the first place. They repeated themselves, so quietly as to make him wonder if they were not his own thoughts.

For a time...
One more thing, my faithful child.
One more thing...

* * * *

The incoming waves thundered against the rocks, breaking through the narrow slit that separated The Great Waters from the secluded gorge where the officers of the Amatru now sat. On the cliffs high above, two wings of Iryllurym were joined by two companies of Anduarym, keeping watch over the surrounding land. And somewhere beneath the vast stretch of water to the north, two companies of Vidirym patrolled the depths. Though Semjaza's fortress was still nearly a hundred and fifty miles away, the officers were not about to take any chances at being discovered by Semjaza's scouts.

As promised, Fer-Rada Danduel had arrived the previous day. His Anduarym had picked up the remaining weapons and armor left behind by the attack on Semjaza's soldiers. After spending the night in the fields, the soldiers of the Amatru and the Myndarym moved northward to the coast of the Great Waters. Along the way, they met up with the remainder of the water-going Myndarym whose progress had been severely slowed when they were forced to take on their angelic forms in order to cross over the land to the south.

Now that all parties were accounted for, the leaders held their war council in the secrecy of the rocks along the coast. Though it was almost noon, the sun's rays only illuminated one side of the steep cliffs, while the remainder stayed cloaked in shadow. By the time the waves entered the tall and narrow fissure, they were calmed considerably, reduced to soft ripples which wet the rocks beneath their feet.

Sariel crouched low on his perch so that he was, more or less, looking into the eyes of the others.

"Semjaza's fortress is situated on a small peninsula at the center of a cove," Ananel began, having taken the leadership role for the Myndarym by default. "It is very large. Its center tower rises above the height of the surrounding cliffs, giving his Iryllurym visibility for miles in every direction."

"So his Iryllurym occupy the upper level?" asked Danduel.

"Yes. Its tetrahedron shape incorporates three levels—one for each segment of his army. The widest, base level sits below the waterline and houses his Vidirym. The next level sits even with the peninsula of land leading to its main entrance. This, of course, houses his Anduarym. And the narrowest, top level houses the Iryllurym. Each level is also crafted from different substances based on the needs of its environment."

Danduel suddenly looked disinterested.

"Generally speaking, the lower level is *shaped* from heavier, denser materials, with the upper level from lighter, porous materials," Ananel added quickly, trying to convey anything that may be useful.

"You said a peninsula. It's connected to the land around the bay?" Danduel asked, changing the direction of the conversation slightly.

"Yes."

"I assume there is a trail or passageway that his Anduarym move along? How do we get in?"

Ananel looked off into the water for a moment. "The route along the peninsula connects to a path on the mainland which traverses the foothills of the surrounding mountains. It leads to a pass through the cliffs on the east side of the cove. It is the only entrance by land. The other terrain is far too steep and dangerous for anyone to climb. That is how Semjaza wanted it—to prevent a land-based infiltration. On the west side, the mountains descend into the ocean before they're able to form a complete circle, creating the equivalent entrance from the sea."

"Perfect," Danduel said with a smile.

Ananel cocked his head slightly. "Each pass is flanked by a pair of watchtowers with a wall between them. The passages are long and narrow—"

"Reducing the effectiveness of larger invading armies," Fim-Rada Erethel jumped in. He commanded one of the two divisions of Anduarym.

Ananel merely nodded at the interruption. "And each side of the passage has multiple narrow corridors leading in from an angle. I'm not sure of the purpose for this."

Danduel's eyes narrowed.

Fim-Rada Evanel spoke up this time. "While the invading army is thinned out through the entrance, defending soldiers can approach both flanks from the rear. It's brilliant, really," the other Anduar officer admitted.

Beneath the water, something large moved. A broad and flat shape broke the surface of the water, followed immediately by a brief puff of air escaping from a blow-hole on the top of what looked like a hairless head. Its smooth skin was dark blue, with a tint of green. The wide-set eyes were black and menacing. "And this is the same for the sea entrance?" came the eerie voice of Kai-Niquel, Fim-Rada of the Vidirym.

"Yes," Ananel replied, a look of disappointment on his face. "Only, it's under water."

After seeking clarification, Kai-Niquel's head dropped just below the surface and he remained there, hovering effortlessly. The gills along either side of his neck expanded and contracted methodically, pulling oxygen from the water. The dual methods of breathing enabled the Vidirym to exist in multiple environments, though water was their primary domain. Beneath his colossal figure, several flattened, snake-like appendages undulated, gracefully holding him in position.

Sariel turned to Danduel. "It looks like the Iryllurym will need to provide cover."

"Exactly what I was thinking," the Fer-Rada replied. Then he turned to Ananel. "Being an Anduar himself, I assume we'll find Semjaza in the ground level of his fortress?"

"His throne room is actually one story above the ground level."

"Alright," he mumbled to himself, then turned to the other officers present with both hands clasped in front of his chin. "In order to defeat him, we'll need to concentrate our ground forces there. Which means we have to get them through that land entrance. So, the Iryllurym will need to provide air cover, striking quickly at the gate defenses just before our Anduarym arrive," he said, looking directly at Nuathel.

"Once through, our land forces will be vulnerable to a flank attack from the bay by Semjaza's Vidirym. And that means our own will need to have breached the sea entrance first. We'll all meet in the middle," he said, stopping to look up at Sariel. "And that's when you fulfill your promise to kill Semjaza yourself."

Sariel nodded.

"If we strike fast and make it through the gates, we should be able to use Semjaza's fortress design against him. Then it's just a matter of numbers; I have twice the soldiers he does."

Sariel looked to Ananel who had been silent for a while. The Fer-Rada had not only dominated the conversation, but had also made no mention of how the Myndarym would fit into the strategy. As expected, the soldiers had taken control of the direction of this battle. Sariel was disappointed that the Shapers, it seemed, were content to allow it.

26

Kai-Niquel's sleek body cut through the water with little resistance, requiring only a slight rippling movement of his rear fins to propel him forward. At this depth, the ocean was completely black. But Kai rarely used his eyes for much of anything. Instead, he generated a series of clicking sounds from an organ behind his blow-hole. The returning sounds brought a detailed understanding of the terrain as his resonating jawbone interpreted the echoes.

But the information had stopped hours ago. With the ocean floor thousands of fathoms below, there was nothing to return the sound waves. Now, the only other presence in the water was his division of Vidirym, followed by a handful of Myndarym. In the silence, they pressed on, having traveled for nearly twenty four hours without stopping.

Gradually, Kai began to pick up a presence below him. The faint echoes grew stronger as the ocean floor rose. Now, only a thousand feet lay below him, and the distance was closing fast. He released a louder pulse of sounds, a blend of moans and chirps, telling his soldiers that they were approaching the target. The floor continued to rise by hundreds of feet per minute, gradually tapering off into a gentle upward slope. With the coastline a mile away to his left, Kai altered his southern course a bit to the east and searched the shelf for a change in texture. As expected, a smooth delta of sand spilled out into the deeper water, signaling that Semjaza's fortress was near.

Halfway across the wide sandbar, Kai turned directly east and slowed his approach. Just as the Myndarym described, he could feel the jagged mountains rise from both sides of the delta, while directly in front was a flat wall, spanning the hundreds of feet that separated the ocean floor from the surface, blocking their entrance to the cove. Descending to the sand below, Kai came to the base of the wall and waited for his team to catch up. Then, he rose slowly, bouncing sound waves off the wall, scanning the front surface for the passages that the Myndarym described. It took only seconds to locate the first one, but to his surprise, it was blocked by a lattice of metal bars.

Kai could sense the confusion from the Myndarym, but remained silent while resuming his work. Using a methodical serpentine pattern to scan the wall in ascending passes, he found one barred passage after another. Finally, he backed away and drifted toward the Myndarym who had been hanging back. "Any other ideas?" he whispered.

"There's one more at the top," one of them replied.

Kai nodded, then brought his rear fins together, propelling his body upward toward the surface. He came to a stop fifty feet below the rippled ceiling. At this depth, the miniscule amount of light coming from the starry skies above allowed his eyes to add visual information to his understanding of the obstacle. He could now make out the bottom of an unblocked passage. But his sensitive ears, if they could be called such, picked up something else—subtle vibrations coming through the passage. Someone was on the other side, waiting.

* * * *

Sariel came up silently over the rocks, riding the gentle updraft that was forced against the mountains from the wind blowing across the Great Waters. The back of an Iryllur sentry came into view and Sariel glided toward the enemy with one *vaepkir* ready. Without a sound, Sariel tackled the soldier from behind, simultaneously clasping a hand around his mouth and driving the *vaepkir* beneath his right forewing and into his chest cavity.

The two soldiers tumbled forward across the rocks, locked in a deadly embrace.

Sariel gritted his teeth as his body slammed into jagged stone and slid across the mountaintop. Refusing to release the sentry until the task was complete, he held fast with his arms and legs wrapped tightly until they came to stop. Silence returned once again and Sariel slowly let go. When he regained his footing, he resheathed his *vaepkir* and walked to the edge of the cliff, giving the signal that the last of the sentries had been removed.

Overhead, the night sky was full of stars which shed soft, silver light across the mountains. On the other side of the deep ravine, Fim-Rada Nuathel and his Iryllurym slowly rose from their hiding places, still clinging to the shadowed crevices like bats. Hundreds of feet below, the front lines of the Anduarym marched quietly toward the pass, the only obstacle separating the ground soldiers from the cove that housed Semjaza's fortress.

As the silent forms of the Iryllurym dropped from the cliffs, Sariel could barely make out their outlines against the dark terrain. He waited for them to cross the ravine, then jumped from the cliff to join their formation as they turned north and made their way further up the pass. The flight lasted only seconds before they turned toward the cliffs again. Sariel followed and retracted his wings, inverting himself beneath an overhang. When he came to a stop, he was only a few feet away from the Fim-Rada.

"To that outcropping," whispered Nuathel.

Again, the Iryllurym took to the air and headed for a larger section of rock that jutted from the cliff at a higher elevation. As soon as he reached it, Sariel had a line of sight to the land entrance of Mudena Del-Edha. Its stone wall stood nearly one hundred feet tall and spanned the width of the pass. It was flanked by a pair of angular, pointed towers that loomed ominously over the gorge. As Danduel's army crept closer to the gate, keeping to the shadows on the southern side of the pass, Sariel's eyes darted between the towers and the passage leading through the center of the wall.

"I don't see any movement," he said quietly.

Nuathel leaned out from the cliff slightly to get a better view. "Nothing yet. Hopefully they won't know until we're upon them."

Through the eye holes in his helmet, Sariel scanned the ranks of the Anduar army below. They were within a few hundred yards now—almost to the signal point.

"Get ready," Nuathel announced quietly.

Sariel quickly inspected the towers one last time, surprised by the absence of guards or scouts.

"They're at the signal point. Go. Go. Go," Nuathel commanded.

Sariel jumped from his place of concealment and stretched his wings. When he felt the lift of the air underneath him, he thrust himself forward and into position behind the other Iryllurym. The angels were superbly trained, quickly assembling into a column with their leader at the point. Dropping a few hundred feet in elevation, their speed increased as they covered the distance to the defensive structure. The column of winged angels flowed gracefully over the steep terrain, condensing and expanding with each outcropping and fissure.

Sariel reached to either side of his breastplate and pulled his *vaepkir* from the sheaths crisscrossed along his back. Banking slightly to the west, he followed the formation out of the cliffs to come directly over the top of the wall. Now only twenty feet below them, the length of the battlements seemed to pass by more swiftly.

The formation broke into six-person teams, one for each of the eight corridors on both sides of the passage. As one, the whole column rose, banked, then inverted to come straight down into the channels, with the lead groups taking the nearest.

Bringing up the rear, Sariel followed the last group into the final corridor on the western end of the passage. The dull starlight was instantly blackened within the confines of the stone structure. Pulling his wings inward, he pressed forward into the formation which now spanned the entire width of the corridor.

Shapes moved in the darkness before them; colorless patches of random forms, shifting in the shadows.

The Iryllurym approached rapidly, breaking into the mass of bodies as a wave of sharpened metal. The blades of Sariel's *vaepkir* jolted in his hands and rammed into his forearms as they sliced through the flesh of the enemy. Following the narrow channel around a bend, the winged angels pulled up and out of the corridor just before their forward motion stalled, pumping their wings to propel themselves into open air.

Looking out across the cove, Sariel could see the tower of Aryun Del-Edha rising from the center of the water like a multi-pronged spearhead.

The Iryllurym quickly banked to the east as the other groups did the same, each having made their first pass. Now approaching from behind the gate, the Iryllurym descended once more, positioning themselves for a second pass. On the ground below, a mass of bodies swelled behind the gate, filling the side corridors and blocking the main entrance. But something looked strange from this new vantage point.

"THEY'RE HUMAN!" Sariel shouted.

Atop the wall, at the base of the northern guard tower, a low horn sounded, blanketing the cove with an unmistakable warning call.

"Pull up! Pull up!" Nuathel commanded.

At once, the formation leveled out.

Sariel looked down in disbelief as they passed over the entrance while human soldiers gathered behind the gate. Not only did Semjaza know they were coming, but he had enough foreknowledge to amass an army that the Amatru weren't authorized to kill.

"We can't attack them!" Nuathel shouted only a second later.

"We have to warn the Anduarym!" Sariel shouted back.

Following Nuathel's lead, the Iryllurym dropped into the mountain pass and banked to the south, following the road leading away from the gate. Quickly, they came upon the Anduar army and dropped to the ground in front of the soldiers.

Fer-Rada Danduel ran from the front lines to meet them.

"A human army guards the gate," Nuathel explained quickly.

"Humans?" Danduel asked. "Are you sure?"

"Yes. Hundreds of them."

"But we're not authorized—" Danduel began. His once wide eyes suddenly narrowed and he spun around to address his approaching army. "The gate is guarded by a human army!" he shouted above the din of marching footsteps. "We are not authorized to kill humans, even under Semjaza's leadership. But we must breach that gate!"

The army halted.

"Push them out of the way. Throw them to the ground. Injure them if you must. But do not kill them. We will take this gate tonight! Semjaza's deception cannot stop the Amatru."

"Rada Talad!" came the unified response.

Danduel turned back to Nuathel. "Can you carry them away from the gate without killing them?"

The Fim-Rada thought for a moment. "It will be much slower, but yes."

Sariel replaced his *vaepkir*, safely tucking one under each wing. A sudden noise brought his attention back to the gate where hundreds of humans now came pouring out of the entrance, massing in front of the wall.

"We'll take care of these," Danduel said. "You just concentrate on those corridors so they're clear by the time we reach the entrance."

"Yes Fer-Rada." Nuathel replied, then turned to his own soldiers. "Back to the gate!"

Sariel unfurled his wings and leaped upward to join the other Iryllurym.

* * * *

With Danduel at the point of a tight wedge formation, the Anduarym advanced quickly upon the gate. Semjaza had formed an army from the Kahyin, the tallest and strongest of the human species. But they were no match for the Anduarym, who were approximately twice their height. The wedge concentrated the force of the Anduar strength at the center of the opposing army, dividing the humans into two groups who were now faced with a solid wall of shields. With each flank protected, the soldiers marched quickly to the wall and entered the main passage.

Once inside, Danduel and the others at the point of the wedge pulled back and formed a line, while the flanks of the wedge pulled inward to create a column.

Despite the efforts of the Iryllurym, humans continued to pour out of each corridor and attack the flanks of Danduel's formation. They came forward with reckless abandon, throwing their spears which shattered harmlessly against the shields of the Anduarym. The few unfortunate souls who ran at the angels were easily turned away or knocked down.

Within minutes, Danduel's ground forces had driven through the passage and were now only yards from breaching the land gate of Mudena Del-Edha. As the Fer-Rada crested the hill and caught sight of the bay glittering in the moonlight, he saw Semjaza's Anduarym waiting.

"AMBUSH!" he yelled.

No sooner had the words left his mouth than the stars were blotted out by shadows from above. At the same moment he recognized the enemy Iryllurym, one of the soldiers at his side fell, pierced through the neck with a spear. Danduel quickly realized that he was trapped.

More of Semjaza's Anduarym were arrayed along the top of the wall, casting their spears down into the mass of vulnerable angels, who were unable to protect themselves from multiple directions at once. Danduel gritted his teeth. If he pressed forward, he and his soldiers at the head of the column might be cut off from the bulk of their force still outside the passage. With the objective so close, yet unattainable, he shouted in frustration.

Suddenly, the humans pulled back into the side corridors while Semjaza's Anduarym advanced down the center passage, picking up speed.

Danduel knew that at any moment, he would see them coming from the side corridors as well. And then the battle would be over. He was now faced with the painful realization of Semjaza's strategic brilliance. There had been almost no information available on the Pri-Rada, which meant that his missions were classified. From the design of this fortress, to his deceptive strategies and efficient utilization of soldiers, Danduel could now see clearly that Semjaza was a master of battlefield tactics. Danduel was out of his league.

"Dreg aftur! Dreg aftur!" Danduel yelled, moving his shield over his head.

His orders were relayed along the column of Anduarym, and slowly, his army backed out of the passage, leaving behind the bodies of fallen comrades.

The front line of enemy angels came forward, marching quicker than the retreating army.

Danduel knew that they wouldn't make it out of the passage in time. "Varnir, horfa!" he shouted.

The column, responding immediately to his orders, pulled themselves into a denser formation, interlocking their shields to present themselves as an armored wall with protruding spikes. The column continued moving slowly backward, using the standard retreating front defense formation.

Semjaza's soldiers crashed into the front line and used the high ground advantage to push the invading force out of the gate faster than they could retreat.

One by one, Danduel's soldiers were thrown off balance and either trampled or impaled as soon as they fell to the ground. Danduel flinched as his left shoulder was thrown violently forward, followed by a sharp pain. Grazed by a spear from above, he now felt warm blood flowing down his arm.

"Dreg aftur!" he shouted again.

* * * *

At the rear of the column, Ananel heard the command to pull back being passed from soldier to soldier. Semjaza's Anduarym were now atop the wall, casting their weapons down upon the confused Amatru. The Iryllurym on both sides of the conflict were swarming overhead. Inside the passage at the center of the wall, a frenzy of movement was taking place. The original plan was being abandoned. Semjaza had been prepared for their coming.

As Ananel looked around at the other Myndarym huddled within the protective lines of Anduar soldiers, another idea came to mind—one for which Semjaza would surely not be prepared. He could now see Danduel exiting the passage with his shield over his head.

"Step aside," he shouted. "I have to speak with the Fer-Rada!"

27

The sky began to lighten in the east, while shouts of retreat could be heard across the battlefield. Having fought for hours to break through the angelic force holding the land entrance to Semjaza's fortress, Danduel's soldiers had sustained much damage. Though they originally outnumbered Semjaza's forces two-to-one, the high ground and arrangement of the passage gave a considerable advantage to the enemy. Danduel's numbers had been steadily whittled down to roughly sixty Anduarym and he was no longer able to maintain the attack. His Iryllurym had sustained even greater casualties.

"Horfa! Horfa!" he commanded.

As his soldiers backed away from the wall, cheers rose up among the enemy force. The ground forces raised their spears and shields high in the air, while the humans laughed and made crude gestures. The winged angels hovered in the air above the gate, while the holy Iryllurym backed away, covering the retreat of their counterparts on the ground.

Danduel shook his head in frustration, then turned to lead his army down the road, away from the gate. Trying to maintain some semblance of order, his Anduarym lined up and began marching. Within minutes, the retreat was in full force. The Fer-Rada quickly made his way to the head of the retreat and led them around a sharp bend.

A smile came to his lips as he saw Ananel standing to the side of the road, waving to him. Danduel marched toward the newly formed hole in the side of the eastern-facing cliff.

"Are you ready?" he asked the Myndarym as he approached.

"They'll punch through as soon as you're in position."

Danduel nodded, then ducked into the cave. Without anything to light the way, he held his shield in front of him and marched as quickly as his legs would carry him. Luckily, the tunnel was level and smooth, having been *shaped* by the Myndarym. If it had been dug by any other method, the debris alone would have made it impassable.

Semjaza will never be expecting this!

"Fer-Rada?" came a voice from the darkness.

"I'm here. Just wait until the tunnel is full," Danduel replied, coming to a stop. He felt another presence behind him as his soldiers packed themselves into the passage beneath the mountain. "Come in and make room for the others," he commanded.

Though completely dark, he could nevertheless hear a change in the way sound traveled through the tunnel. After waiting patiently for several minutes, he heard the message being relayed from the back of the line.

"We're ready," the soldier behind him stated.

"Go ahead," Danduel told the Myndarym. "Make it as fast and wide as you can."

After a moment's pause, a low note sounded, accompanied by another, then another harmony. The music filled the tiny space until the very rock seemed to resonate with it. As each harmony was layered onto the growing force of sound, Danduel had to cover his ears to keep from losing his balance. His head began to ache and his hands shook.

A sharp pulsing sound threatened to burst his eardrums and he wondered how an angel could produce such a noise. The pulsing resonance increased in volume and tempo until the very earth beneath them rumbled. Finally, the rhythm merged into a single note and the Myndarym shouted with a violent burst.

Instantly, morning sunlight flooded into the passage as the rock in front of Danduel seemed to flee in fear. Large boulders, dirt, and small rocks alike, flew away from the Shapers with such force that the air was filled with a cloud of debris. Danduel removed his hands from his ears, and stared out in fascination. He could now see the whole of Semjaza's city at a glance. A great tower stabbed upward from the surface of the water. Its height was beyond anything Danduel had ever seen, and was clearly a monument to Semjaza's pride. A road traversed the descending terrain before him. One direction led west along the bay toward Semjaza's fortress. The other led east to the back side of the entrance that they had unsuccessfully attempted to infiltrate.

Danduel rushed forward.

The Anduarym followed, emptying from the tunnel beneath the mountains as a chaotic mass.

"Ad a tarn! Delas! Foran aras! Aftan varnir!" he yelled to his soldiers.

The Anduarym quickly assembled into a formation with half the soldiers facing forward and half facing to the rear. Then, they moved as one to the west, heading for the peninsula leading out to Semjaza's fortress. A feeling of excitement came over the Fer-Rada as he saw his objective in such close proximity. Somewhere inside the tower, cowering in fear was the disgraced Pri-Rada. No doubt he realized that the odds had just shifted.

To the east, Semjaza's Anduarym were just realizing what had happened and were abandoning the gate, while the Iryllurym were advancing quickly along the road in Danduel's direction.

As their dark silhouettes moved closer, Danduel brought his shield up high and held his *vandrekt* tight. "Iryllurym!" he yelled to his soldiers.

Semjaza's defense was playing out just as he wanted. Looking now to the still waters of the cove, he could already see the smooth surface being disrupted. A loose grouping of triangular waves was coming quickly from around the peninsula. His Vidirym were already inside the cove and moving into position to cover the rear of his advancing formation.

This time, he allowed himself to smile.

The water continued to swirl and the wakes grew in depth. But gradually, they changed direction and began to come straight at his soldiers on the shore. Danduel's momentary feeling of superiority evaporated as he realized what was happening.

"Varnir! Halda! Snua rett!" he commanded.

The sixty Anduarym quickly stopped their forward movement and morphed their frontal attack formation to a defensive posture, aimed toward the water. The right side of the column now became the front line, interweaving their shields to form a barrier along the shore line, while the rear lines held their shields overhead.

The first wave of Iryllurym arrived. With a flurry of wings, the airborne enemy dove and rammed into the shields of the two rear lines. One of Danduel's soldiers went down, while another lost his shield.

As soon as the formation passed overhead, the water along the shore bulged upward as massive shapes came from the depths. Instead of Danduel's underwater soldiers, it was Semjaza's Vidirym who broke through the once tranquil surface. Their sleek, aquamarine bodies glistened in the morning light, as the water slid from their skin. The angels' upper bodies rose above the surface, supported and propelled by the long appendages still under the water. They were all armed with *vanspyd* at their sides, which they quickly transferred into an overhanded grip. In one fluid motion, they loosed their spears and sent them flying through the air with deadly accuracy.

"Vidirym!" came a cry from the rear of his forces.

At the left side of the front line, Danduel was nearly pushed over by the force of a spear hitting his shield. His arm twisted violently, trying to maintain his grip on the protective barrier. Three of his Anduarym went down—two from the same spear which had gone clean through the first soldier. The third fell forward out of formation when the Vidir pulled on the cord that attached his barbed *vanspyd* to the metal gauntlet on his forearm.

Danduel had never seen this use of the famous Vidirym weapon and struggled to think clearly in the chaos of the moment.

"Varnir! Skyv vinstri!" he yelled.

His soldiers maintained their formation, but began side-stepping along the road to the west. As Semjaza's sea and air forces took turns at the invading army, Danduel's company pressed on, slowly losing one soldier after another. By the time they reached the peninsula, his force of sixty had been reduced to forty-three. And now that he faced a narrow strip of land with water on each side, his optimism was all but depleted. It was a gauntlet and the casualties were sure to be severe. His own Vidirym were nowhere to be found, and he knew he would need additional numbers to reach the fortress alive. Looking up to the southern cliffs, he thrust his spear into the air and gave the signal for half of the Iryllurym to join the fight.

Semjaza's winged soldiers must have seen the signal, because the next attack came not in unison, but as random individual assaults. The soldiers of the water quickly followed this change in strategy, and now it was impossible to predict where the next attack would come from.

Suddenly, the soldier next to Danduel lost his shield to a diving Iryllur who carried it away, nearly ripping the Anduar's arms off. In the next instant, a long spear punched through the soldier's chest. The Anduar turned to his Fer-Rada and grasped at him, with a pleading look on his face. Then he was violently wrenched out of formation as the enemy retracted his weapon.

Danduel pulled his own shield tight to his body and simply watched, helpless while the soldier was dragged into the water.

* * * *

Clinging to the shadowy cliffs above the southern side of the bay, Sariel watched as Danduel's forces below were taking a beating from the air and sea. And at any moment Semjaza's ground force would reach them, as well.

"...change of plans," Nuathel said, looking down at the signal from his commanding officer. "It looks like he needs half of us."

Sariel nodded.

"You stay out of sight," the Fim-Rada continued. "Wait for the signal. Then go for the tower...fast!"

Sariel nodded.

"It's time," Nuathel announced to his soldiers. "Let's go."

Half of the Iryllur force jumped from the cliffs and took to the air.

As soon as they left the concealment of the high position, Semjaza's Iryllurym took notice, and immediately pulled away from Danduel's soldiers to meet the new threat.

Sariel and the other half of the winged angels remained hidden in the quickly shrinking shadows of the cliffs. With his *vaepkir* ready, Sariel looked out over the battlefield. The enemy ground soldiers who left the eastern gate had now reached the right flank of Danduel's formation. Even though the Fer-Rada no longer had to worry about an attack from the sky, he still had to protect himself from the sea and land. The odds still didn't look good, which only put more pressure upon Sariel for what they expected from him—what he had promised.

Without warning, an immense grinding noise blanketed the bay and surpassed all other sounds, shaking the very ground beneath their feet.

Sariel looked down, wondering if the mountain was collapsing on the tunnel that the Myndarym had created.

"There!" one of the Iryllurym said, pointing to the west.

Sariel followed his outstretched arm to see the water near the ocean gate surging. The leftmost tower began to lean inward. Then, the wall between the towers sunk below the water line.

As soon as they realized what was happening, Semjaza's Vidirym pulled back from the water's edge and slipped below the surface, speeding away to meet the new threat.

"Our Vidirym have joined the battle," he told the other angels clinging to the rocks.

*   *   *   *

Fim-Rada Kai-Niquel hung back with his division of Vidirym while the Myndarym huddled near the ocean floor at the base of the stone wall. He could feel the movement in the water before anything was visible, but it seemed sudden nonetheless. First a rumble sent vibrations through the water. Then a shudder. Then a jolt. The water began to swirl as a great surge drew them all inward, threatening to suck them into the void that the Myndarym had *shaped* beneath the defensive barricade.

As sea water rushed in to fill the gap, it displaced a mass of air that exploded outward and shot toward the surface in a blinding myriad of bubbles. The upward rush of air was so extensive that it blocked all sight. It wasn't until the vast migration of tiny air pockets all jolted to the right as one that Kai realized the wall was moving behind it.

The center of the wall dropped first, dragging the stone on either side with it. This was followed quickly by a ripple effect as the destruction spread outward from the point of attack. Within seconds, a cloud of debris spread outward and upward, choking the water and blocking all light from the surface.

Through the chaos, Kai sensed a safe passage over the center of the wall, and surged forward, signaling his soldiers to follow. Thrusting his fins down, he shot toward the top of the wall, then leveled out a few feet below the surface. Through the cacophony of sound vibrations moving in all directions through the water, Kai could still make out the chatter of his soldiers' echo-location. With the large obstacles cleared from their path, nothing stood between them and the fortress.

"Stay alert. We're not the only ones in the water," he told them.

Cutting swiftly through the sea, Kai could sense the western-most turret of the fortress, rising from the floor of the bay. Farther in the distance, rounding the peninsula point, he could also sense many shapes moving through the water toward him. Fortunately, his forces outnumbered Semjaza's two-to-one.

"Delas! he called to his soldiers. "Foran loka! Aftan, sakra ingangur!"

Immediately, Kai and half of his division banked slightly to the north to meet Semjaza's sea force. When they reached a position between the western tower and the incoming Vidirym, they halted and assembled into a vertical wedge formation.

Semjaza's soldiers came quickly, spreading out at the last moment in an attempt to get around the defensive force.

Kai's formation allowed the soldiers at the top and bottom of the wedge, who were positioned farther back, to fan outward and contain the enemy maneuver.

On instinct, Kai dodged to the side and brought his *vanspyd* forward, quickly deflecting an enemy spear. The triple-bladed tip hung in the water, inches from his face. Then, without warning, it shot backward and returned to its owner. It took only an instant for Kai to understand the deviation from the standard Vidirym tactics. In the Eternal Realm, it was a last resort for a soldier to cast his weapon, for it meant giving away his only defense. But it seemed that, as in many other ways, Semjaza had taught his soldiers to abandon their previous training. Without taking his eyes off the enemy, Kai's echo-location told him that he'd already lost a few soldiers to the devious change in weaponry, but the rest had learned quickly

Slowly, Kai's force began to give water while moving backward in an attempt to contain the enemy's forward progress.

Another spear shot forward and Kai deflected it. In frustration, he moved backward again. He wanted to sink his trident into the flesh of a traitor, but Semjaza's Vidirym were staying just out of reach, using their longer-ranged attacks to their advantage.

Despite his disappointment, the Fim-Rada took pleasure in the fact that his primary objective had been met. As their backward defensive formation finally reached the turret, Kai sensed that the other half of his force had secured it.

"Ad a ingangur," he called out.

Immediately, his soldiers lunged backward and converged upon the triangular doorway at the base of the turret. One by one, his Vidirym slipped through until he was the last. Quickly backing into the entrance with a double-handed grip on his spear, he watched the movements of the enemy morph into a column formation with their leader at the rear.

Kai exhaled a quick mouthful of water, disgusted by the blatant rebellion of the leader's actions. Among the Amatru, it was standard protocol for the leader to be at the front of an attack or the rear of a retreat. It was a mark of character for the leader to position himself between his soldiers and the enemy. To do otherwise was a tactic of the Marotru. And it seemed that Semjaza had adopted this method as well. Though such confirmation wasn't necessary, Kai was now fully convinced that Semjaza was beyond redemption. If he could align himself with the tactics of the demons, then he deserved to die.

Inside the triangular tunnel, the sound waves changed from the great, lonely echoes of open water to short and bright sounds. The lower ranking enemy soldiers came first, advancing quickly, aggressively.

Too aggressive!

Kai watched with tranquil confidence the sloppy movements of the enemy soldiers entering the narrow passage. Slowly, he continued to move backward into a wider section of the tunnel and noted the angular, stair-stepped design of the corridor as it led inward.

The nearest soldier came forward and cast his *vanspyd*.

Kai dodged to the left and jabbed his own weapon, striking with precision and perfect timing that had been honed over ages of conflict.

The enemy's spear was pushed sideways, around the corner of the stone passage. When the soldier attempted to pull it backward its bladed end caught on the stone.

Kai instantly surged forward and thrust his weapon in a single-handed attack. The trident glanced off the Vidir's armored gauntlet and pierced the center of his chest, meeting with more resistance than expected. As he wrenched the bladed weapon from the victim, Kai watched the water cloud with blood.

Two enemy soldiers drifted limply to the floor of the stone passage.

28

"Ad a tarn! Aftan varnir!"

Danduel's command rang out clear. Now that Semjaza's Vidirym were occupied beneath the water, the peninsula was no longer a dreaded road, but a clear passage to his objective. With the low and bright rays of the morning sun casting long shadows across the water, Danduel's disciplined ground force began to advance, changing their defense structure to protect the rear of their formation.

"It's time," Sariel announced to the remaining Iryllurym. Then he leaped from the shadows of the cliffs.

Half of Semjaza's Iryllurym peeled away from the conflict and rose into a wide, staggered line formation. Clearly, the hours of constant battle had sapped their energy and it was beginning to show.

The soldiers flying with Sariel began to spread out to meet the line of defense.

The sounds of battle below fell into the distance, replaced by the wind rushing past Sariel's ears. As he looked forward, his gaze settled on the enemy soldier directly in front of him.

His hands clenched the hilts of his *vaepkir*.

The muscles in his arms tensed, readying for the coming impact.

Closer and closer the two forces sped toward each other.

Each soldier eyed his counterpart in the opposing line.

Just before impact, Sariel's horizontal formation pivoted, with the left flank banking upward and right while the right flank dropped and banked left. The abrupt change was mimicked by the enemy, but with a slight delay. As the two forces spiraled into one another, Sariel and the right flank were too quick for Semjaza's soldiers and passed beneath them without contact.

The piercing ring of metal on metal sounded behind him as Sariel and eight other Iryllurym left the diversion and raced for the peak of Semjaza's fortress. They quickly exchanged glances; there was no time for words now. They'd worked out the plan ahead of time and all that was left to do was carry it out. Sariel had hoped for a few more Iryllurym to make it through the initial charge, but the group of nine would have to do.

Reaching the southern face of the fortress in just seconds, Sariel pulled his wings inward and dove toward the triangular window that sat just above the crown of turrets encircling the apex. Hoping that the Myndarym had given an accurate description of the building, he banked to the left until his wings were vertical, then dropped through the window.

Flying more by instinct than sight, Sariel felt a rush of stone and soldiers pass quickly by as his body plunged through the open shaft running down through the center of the tower. As the shaft widened, he spread his wings to slow his descent, noticing several of Semjaza's guards descending the spiral staircase which ran along the inside walls.

Making a quick correction, he paralleled the staircase and rammed into two of the soldiers, knocking them from the stairs and into the open air. Down below, and approaching quickly, the floor of the throne room was filled with more enemy Anduarym. Having already passed several guards on the way in, Sariel was now surrounded. But his fellow Iryllurym would have to take care of the enemies behind him, because his attention was focused ahead.

Sariel came to a running landing on the last few steps of the staircase. Tucking his wings behind his shoulders, he quickly changed his grip on the right *vaepkir* and held it with the blade pointing forward, like a spear.

With the shadows of the descending Iryllurym passing over their tall and muscular forms, the enemy Anduarym tightened into an attack formation and came forward.

* * * *

"The north and east towers are secure, my Rada," the soldier announced quietly.

"Good," Kai-Niquel answered, looking upward at the distorted surface of the water. The light, rippling and bending with each wave, revealed to his trained eyes the interior of the first floor of Semjaza's fortress. Piecing together the refracted images, he could see two enemy Anduarym standing guard. There was water on the stone floor in front of a metal triangle set into the ground.

"Hold this position," he told his subordinate. "If Semjaza or any of his soldiers try to escape through the water, don't hesitate. Kill them instantly."

"Yes, my Rada."

Kai looked up again, then slowly rose toward the surface. As his head broke silently through, the airborne sounds assaulted his sensitive ears. Instead of clearing the water from his blowhole in one violent burst, like usual, he quietly allowed the water to leak out as he began to rely on his lungs for breathing.

The two Anduarym kept their gaze fixed through the massive, triangular doorway facing south. They couldn't hear the silent enemy rising behind them.

Though his weak eyes couldn't see far enough, Kai assumed that Danduel and his ground forces would be advancing along the peninsula by now. And with this distraction keeping the attention of the soldiers, Kai raised more of his upper body out of the water. Holding two *vanspyd* and his arms close against his sides, the water shed from Kai's skin to run silently down his body instead of dripping. When the weapons had cleared the surface of the water, he leaned forward. In one swift movement he threw both weapons with deadly accuracy.

The bladed shafts buried themselves in the unprotected flesh of the Anduarym, as both soldiers pitched forward. They were dead before their bodies crashed to the floor.

Quickly, the Fim-Rada rose from the passage and spread two of his lower appendages across the rough stone. Both unfurled from his body outward along the ground until they could bear his weight. Then, he pulled himself up onto the floor as he pushed with the other appendages behind him. In a fluid, but unearthly motion, his body slid across the stone until the majority of his fourteen foot height stood before the crude, metallic triangle on the floor.

Its design was more primitive than the rest of the fortress, and looked as though it had either been constructed hastily, or by a lesser craftsman.

Kai reached down and wedged his flattened blade of a hand between the stone floor and the metal. With all his might, he gripped the edge and pulled upward. As he suspected, the crude doorway opened, revealing a staircase of descending steps disappearing into water. Without hesitating, he moved down the passage and into the water.

Immediately, he could tell that something was wrong. His echolocation revealed that the tunnel was clearly constructed for land creatures to pass through. But the water, cloudy and choked with debris, told him that the passage had recently been flooded. Whether accidentally or intentionally, he wasn't sure.

The tunnel extended for thousands of feet to the south, directly beneath the peninsula. Kai, swimming rapidly and reading the terrain as he went, came to where a pile of rocks and sand rose from the floor almost to the ceiling. The debris was higher on the right side of the passage, where he could sense open water through a crack in the wall. Immediately, he knew the passage had been flooded on purpose. Which begged a question.

What are the soldiers trying to keep hidden?

Rising to the top left of the passage, Kai pulled rocks away from the pile and pushed beyond the rubble. The tunnel continued directly south, and the Fim-Rada now swam with more urgency, feeling that he was about to discover something important.

Thousands of feet later, the tunnel ended again at a staircase which rose from the water, much like the one leading into the passage from the fortress. Cautiously, Kai ascended and slipped quietly into the air once more.

Darkness and silence greeted him.

Judging by the distance and elevation of the passage, he believed himself to be somewhere beneath the mountains on the southern side of the cove. With his eyes useless in this environment, he attempted echo-location. What returned to his ears was an indiscernible cacophony. The echoes were harsh and erratic, quickly overwhelming his senses. But when the initial wave of sound passed, he realized that all the sounds were not his own. He heard screaming and moaning. Slowly, the dizzying barrage of noises began to make sense. Though it was only a rudimentary image, he began to sense a large cavern. Huddled at the far end were numerous humans crawling over each other in the darkness. He waited a few more seconds and tried to make sense of the sounds bouncing off the walls. Slowly, he realized that most of the figures were female.

There were others whose outlines were confusing to him. Initially, he thought it to be the result of his severely disabled senses. But as he tried desperately to adapt his ability to this strange environment, he became more confident of what he saw.

They were large creatures—human in shape, but some nearly as tall as the Anduarym. They were also huddled in fear against the wall of the cavern, indicating that they wouldn't be a threat.

"Do not fear," Kai spoke softly.

The sudden presence of sound only terrified the group more. But eventually, their screams lessened.

"I am here to rescue you. Do not fear," he assured them.

This time, they heard him and kept silent.

* * * *

Sariel's *vaepkir* dripped with Anduar blood.

The two remaining ground soldiers stepped cautiously backward down the stairs from the throne room. With their shields overlapping, their eyes darted back and forth between Sariel and the other three Iryllurym behind him.

Sariel advanced, choosing his footing carefully on the steps.

Suddenly, one of the soldiers glanced to the side.

It was only a split second of opportunity, but Sariel was ready. He burst forward from his crouching position and swung his right *vaepkir*. The blade sliced through the air just above the Anduar's shield and caught the soldier on the bridge of the nose, forcing his head sideways from the impact.

The angel on the left quickly stood tall and arched his back.

The motion was startling and confusing, until Sariel saw the spear. It was only when Semjaza's angels fell to the ground that Sariel realized there were several Vidirym in the room.

Coming down the last few steps, he looked around the first-floor of the fortress and saw the glistening, aquamarine shapes of the water angels, forming an intimidating perimeter of protection. Around the backside of the staircase, was a triangular-shaped doorway in the floor. Three human women sat on the ground beside it and hugged each other. Their clothes were soaked and dripping. Crouched on the ground in front of the women was the sleek and muscled form of Fim-Rada Kai-Niquel.

"What's going on here?" Sariel asked

The officer turned his head and inspected Sariel, his eyes scanning up and down. "Where's Semjaza?" he asked.

"We just came through the throne room. He's not there," Sariel answered.

Kai rose up and turned around. Over his shoulder, Danduel and his soldiers could be seen through the massive doorway. They had just reached the fortress from the peninsula.

"Where did these women come from?" Sariel asked again, hearing the desperation in his own voice. He knew that Danduel would control the conversation when he arrived and his time to get information was running out.

Kai looked quickly in the direction of his superior, then back to Sariel.

His black eyes were unreadable and Sariel feared that he wouldn't cooperate.

Finally, the officer answered. "This passage leads to a cavern beneath the mountains to the south. Many women are being kept there. The passage was flooded and we're trying to get them out."

"One of the women is named Sheyir. Make sure she gets out alive?" Sariel asked.

"I will," Kai answered in a whisper.

"WHERE IS SEMJAZA?" Danduel shouted as he walked briskly across the stone floor, accompanied by Nuathel.

"He's not here," Sariel answered.

"My Rada," Kai called out. "This passage leads underground to the mountains south of here. It was flooded by his soldiers. But there is a cavern at the end, above the waterline."

"Semjaza?" the Fer-Rada asked quickly.

"No. It is full of humans. And something else—"

"Where is that traitor!" Danduel said through clenched teeth.

"There has to be another passage into the chamber...for ventilation," Sariel blurted out.

Both the soldiers turned their heads. Danduel's face looked like it was about to explode in anger.

"Was there another?" Sariel continued, now that he had control of the conversation.

Kai thought for a moment. "Yes. In the ceiling, but—"

"Semjaza's escaping," Sariel interrupted. "He's probably on the other side of the mountains by now."

The color drained instantly from Danduel's face as he realized what was happening.

"We must fly quickly," Sariel added, looking now at the Iryllur commander.

"My Rada," said Nuathel, stepping forward. "We'll accompany him."

"Very well," the senior officer answered. "Take whatever remains of your forces and go quickly. As soon as we've cleared this fortress, my Anduarym will give chase by ground as well."

"Yes, my Rada," came the quick and trained response. Then, Nuathel looked to Sariel. "You lead the way...and do what you promised."

Sariel nodded. "Let's go."

29

The southern cliffs of Mudena Del-Edha disappeared behind the Iryllurym. Below, grassy plains stretched all the way to the coast of the Great Waters. A faint trail of disturbed vegetation passed beneath the angels as they tracked the former Pri-Rada. Far ahead, only a few miles before the forests of Murakszhug, something was moving over the land. It was only visible for erratic moments between patches of mist rising from the earth.

"Is he riding something?" Nuathel called out.

Sariel turned his head. "...his hunting beast. ...some abomination the Myndarym *shaped* for him."

Nuathel nodded. "We'll take it out from under him. The rest is up to you."

Sariel looked back to the south and squinted as the Iryllurym pulled ahead and began their descent. He dropped into formation behind them, but allowed them to create some distance. Less than a minute later, the winged angels caught up with Semjaza.

The creature beneath him was powerful and fast, propelling itself and its oversized master on eight long, muscular legs. Its elongated head and snout were topped with a mane of chestnut hair which matched its fluttering tail.[23]

Fim-Rada Nuathel split his Iryllurym into two groups which spread apart from each other as they approached the flanks of the retreating commander. Dropping to within a foot of the waving grass, they approached fast and silent from behind.

With *vaepkir* extended to their sides, they cut the legs from underneath the unfortunate beast in a rapid succession of glancing blows.

The animal instantly dropped to the ground and tumbled, end-over-end, while Semjaza dove sideways and did the same.

Sariel pulled up and slowed to a hover before dropping to the ground.

Ahead, the grass was parted into a wake behind the steaming body of the flailing creature. Blood was scattered everywhere from the severed limbs. To the right, the dark outline of the Pri-Rada rose from the grass. Shrouded in a drifting patch of mist, his condition was unknown. But judging by his unhindered movements and the fact that he still held both a shield and a spear, Sariel guessed that he was not injured by the fall. In fact, he appeared to have expected it.

Slowly, the mist passed to the southeast.

Semjaza's massive form remained still. Standing a full head taller than the typical Anduar soldier, he towered head-and-shoulders over Sariel. The burning embers of his eyes were fixed on Sariel.

The returning Iryllurym dropped to the field on all sides, forming a perimeter of two hundred feet to enclose the pair of combatants. The wailing sound of the dying creature came to an abrupt stop as one of the winged angels put the abomination out of its misery.

Semjaza didn't even flinch. He just stood with *vandrekt* and *skoldur* hanging at his sides. His body was tense, ready, but unmoving.

"The last time we spoke, I made you a promise." Sariel's voice seemed to disappear into the vast openness of the plains. He removed his helmet and cast it aside, so that Semjaza could see him clearly.

"...if you didn't release my woman, I would bring your kingdom to an end."

Semjaza quickly brought his shield up and burst forward into a run. Lunging, he thrust his spear at Sariel's chest.

Sariel pivoted to the side and diverted the attack with his left blade. The sound of clanging metal rang out over the grass.

Semjaza came forward again, stabbing repeatedly as he advanced.

Sariel quickly blocked each left-handed strike, moving backward with each one.

Again Semjaza lunged forward and stabbed.

This time Sariel stepped to the right of the *vandrekt* and brought his *vaepkir* across to parry the attack. In the same motion, he brought his right forewing around and drove the carpal joint over Semjaza's outstretched arm and into his face. An audible smack accompanied the impact.

The Pri-Rada flinched at the surprise counter-attack and stumbled backward a few steps.

Sariel instantly surged forward and followed with a left cross, running his forearm blade across Semjaza's exposed ribcage.

Immediately, the massive Anduar commander brought his shield around from the right side of his body and slammed it into Sariel.

Sariel was stunned and thrown backward by the force of the blow. Before he had time to recover, a sharp strike glanced off his bladed forearm and tore through the flesh of his upper arm. The pain brought him back to his senses immediately. Seeing the next spear thrust coming, Sariel dodged left and grabbed the shaft of the spear. As Semjaza pulled it back, Sariel rode the momentum and jumped forward, bringing his left blade over the top of Semjaza's shield.

But the Anduar was too quick and strong, quickly ducking below the attack and using the momentum and the leverage of his shield to throw Sariel over his shoulder.

Unable to control himself, Sariel drifted twenty feet through the air before crashing to the ground. The wind was knocked from his lungs and he struggled to get his feet beneath him.

Semjaza was on him instantly, following the throw with a running jab.

On instinct, Sariel ducked under the spear and rolled forward, striking with his left forewing to take the Anduar's legs from underneath him. But the blow only caused Semjaza to lose his balance just long enough for Sariel to get to his feet.

Now, the two enemies faced each other, both breathing heavily.

Semjaza's face and chest were covered in the blood that flowed from his nose. And he was also bleeding heavily from the cut on the left side of his abdomen.

Sariel's right arm was covered in red, as well, and dripping from the elbow. His face felt numb and he was sure he'd broken some ribs.

Before this fight, Sariel had been confident in the advantage of his speed. But the Anduar commander was nearly as fast, and much stronger. As Sariel studied his opponent, Semjaza came forward again, relentless in his aggression.

The spear came for Sariel's face. He ducked and swung his left *vaepkir* as hard as he could. A sharp, metallic sound pierced the air as Sariel's weapon shattered and Semjaza's spear flew sideways, torn from his grip.

With his only weapon wielded by a wounded arm, Sariel was nearly helpless against Semjaza's following charge. Struggling to bring his right arm up quickly enough, he was unable to stop the shield that smashed into his face and drove him backward. His feet slid across the damp grass, unable to find traction. Sariel was helpless against the ground soldier who had both a weight and height advantage.

As his strength was being rapidly depleted and the threat of being crushed to death neared, Sariel quickly pulled his feet inward and dropped to his back.

The sudden release of opposing force sent Semjaza stumbling forward.

As the Anduar's shield passed overhead, Sariel rolled onto his left side and raised his right blade. Supporting it with his unwounded left arm, he shoved the point of the elbow blade upward through the bottom of Semjaza's belly.

The next instant, Semjaza's knee slammed into him, forcing him to the ground just as a foot came down and crushed the wind from his lungs.

Semjaza tripped forward and fell over Sariel to land face down in the damp soil.

The resulting silence was deafening as Sariel writhed in pain, fighting for a breath. It seemed his lungs wouldn't obey him, as if they were afraid of the stabbing pain in his chest that threatened to kill him for the effort of breathing.

Rolling onto his back, Sariel felt the pain lessen slightly. A few seconds later, his body agreed to take a shallow breath. And then another spasm of pain, followed by a short breath. Slowly, he opened his eyes, realizing only now that his pain had been so distracting that he had left himself vulnerable to attack. Turning his head quickly, he was relieved to see the motionless form of Semjaza, lying face down in the grass with a pool of blood spreading around his dead body.

Slowly. Cautiously. Sariel rolled onto his right side and rose to his hands and knees. The stabbing pain in his chest remained, but he was now able to breathe steadily. Gritting his teeth, he pulled his feet underneath him and readied himself to stand, while Nuathel and his Iryllurym came near.

The Fim-Rada nodded.

Sariel returned the gesture, then began to *shape* himself to repair the damage.

* * * *

In the highland forests north of Murakszhug, Azael dodged the point of a *vaepkir*. Rushing inside the Iryllur's range, Semjaza's second-in-command grabbed the other angel by the throat and lifted him off his feet. Using his superior size and strength, he hefted the soldier of the Amatru and slammed his face into the side of a tree. When one blow failed to produce the results he wanted, he repeated it again, and again, each time harder until the soldier's face became an indistinguishable mass of bloody flesh. Then, he tossed the soldier's limp body aside.

Pale weaklings, he thought to himself with disgust.

Suddenly, he felt a shift in his spirit. Where once was an oppressive force, requiring submission, there was now only a void.

Not a void, he corrected himself. *Freedom!*

Without seeing it or hearing it, he knew instantly that Semjaza was dead. Smiling a wicked smile, he looked through the dense tangle of tree trunks to see his two remaining subordinates approaching. It was clear that they had also dispatched the last of the Amatru Iryllurym who had tracked them after they escaped from the fortress.

The dark angels stared back, feeling a similar sensation in their own spirits, though their immediate authority was still alive.

"The battle is over for us," he told them.

"Yes, my Rada," they both responded.

"To the mines," he said, then spread his black wings.

30

Just as Sariel's body regained its whole, uninjured form, he felt the hands of two Iryllurym slip beneath his arms and gently lift him to a full standing position. "Thank you," he muttered, grateful for the assistance.

The angels' grip tightened.

"I got it," he complained, shrugging his shoulders.

They held fast to his arms and their grip quickly became forceful and rigid. In the next moment, two more angels grasped his wings from behind, and he felt the blade of a *vaepkir* press against his neck.

Nuathel and another Iryllur walked forward.

Sariel assumed the last two were somewhere behind him, out of sight, likely with their weapons drawn.

"What are you doing?" he hissed through clenched teeth.

"We have to take you back," the Fim-Rada answered.

Sariel stared hard at the soldier.

"You will stand trial and receive judgment for your disobedience," Nuathel continued. "These are my orders."

Sariel opened his mouth to respond, but quickly decided to keep silent. He had known deep down that this was a possibility. He'd even cautioned the Myndarym about it.

The Iryllurym pulled hard on his upper arms and turned him around to the north.

Instead of fighting, Sariel complied and walked with his captors, trying instead to remain calm, breathe carefully, and think quickly.

I could just shift out of their grasp, but they know where I'm going. They'll just follow me. I have to kill them.

Sariel immediately began to run through hand-to-hand combat scenarios in his mind.

Two in front. Two beside. And two behind.

He'd been surrounded before, but never in this close of proximity. As each imagined battle came to an unacceptable end in his mind, his thoughts were slowly overwhelmed by the despair of never seeing Sheyir again.

What will happen to her? Who will protect her? Love her? No one.

She had no one in this world now. She was alone. And Sariel had come through too much to be with her.

Too much for this to stand in my way!

The blade pressed into his neck as they walked. He felt a warm trickle of wetness down his skin.

Nuathel and his second-in-command walked in front now with their backs turned. Their body language suggested they were confident that any threat had been neutralized.

Sariel had unwillingly come to the same conclusion. Tears began to form in his eyes. He thought of the coming trial, and the eternal judgment that would proceed from it. He was an enemy of the Amatru now, but not just a demon to be slain. He was special kind of enemy—a traitor.

As the hopelessness of his situation became more and more evident, something came alive inside him. Something that had been dormant for ages. Within his spirit, a mournful melody was born. It was the nature of a Shaper to hear and feel the Songs of Creation that flowed through everything; sustaining everything. And it was the nature of a Shaper to hear the melodies within his own spirit, and respond to them. But Sariel had followed a different path for so long that he had begun to wonder if his nature had changed; if the ability even existed any longer.

In his sadness, he heard the words of a friend.

It was an accident, but very effective.

In that moment, Sariel realized that the melody was the language of his spirit—the expression of his heart. And as his sadness translated into anger, he felt the melody twist and writhe inside him. What once would have frightened him, he now welcomed, for it brought with it a tremendous power that began to surge through his body. He felt invigorated, as in the early days when he had *shaped* creation. But this was more powerful. All consuming.

And darker than anything he'd experienced before.

He allowed the melody to grow and contort. To multiply into numerous, uncontrollable strands. His body began to shake with rage. His mouth opened. But instead of silence, a Song of Unshaping came forth. His anguish came out as a scream that blanketed the plains with its frightening power. Screams of fury were mixed with wails of sorrow; each dissonant tone woven together into a tapestry of darkness.

Sariel felt his body jolt as a spherical wave exploded outward from him. The sky and land seemed to distort as the pulse expanded and eventually dissipated into the vast openness of the plains.

Silence followed.

With eyes instinctively closed, Sariel waited, afraid to see what he'd done. One by one, his senses began to perceive his surroundings. The sound of the breeze moving through the grasses in the distance. The sound of insects buzzing nearby. The damp feeling of mist as it passed over his skin. The smell of the damp earth.

Sariel opened his eyes.

He was standing in a shallow depression of land. The grass underfoot was smashed into the soil, barely recognizable. All around him, the tall stalks of bright green vegetation were pushed on their sides, pointing outward. Sariel walked up the side of the earthen bowl and looked out across the plains. The effect of the pulse seemed to lessen with distance. The stalks of grass gradually transitioned from horizontal to vertical over a radius of two hundred feet. And randomly scattered within this diameter of Unshaping were the motionless forms of the Iryllurym. Sariel couldn't tell if they were dead or just stunned. But the curiosity was fleeting.

He was free. And Sheyir was waiting.

Spreading his wings high into the air, he brought them down with all of his might as he jumped upward. One day, when there would be time to meditate on such things, he would think about this moment. He would consider what had happened and the implications of it. But not now. Now, he sped north, faster than he'd ever flown in his life.

*   *   *   *

Fer-Rada Danduel stared at the abominations of flesh before him. They were huddled together with the women, and despite their size they cowered behind the tiny females. "Come here," he commanded the largest one.

The creature glanced nervously about, but remained crouched behind the mothering presence of the humans.

One of Danduel's soldiers stepped into the huddle and put a spear to the creature's neck. "Get up!" he ordered.

Finally, the creature stood and began to make his way over to the Anduar officer.

As it came forward, Danduel inspected it. It was male. It moved upright on two legs. Judging by its facial features and body construction, it seemed to be a hybrid of Anduar and human. He estimated its height to be fifteen feet tall. And though it was larger than an Anduar, its gangly movements gave the impression that it was young, not yet fully grown.[18]

"Do you speak?" the Fer-Rada asked, having to look up at the youth.

The other Anduar stood near, still pointing his spear at the creature.

"Yes," he mumbled.

What is Semjaza doing? Danduel mused as he circled slowly around the revolting beast, examining its smooth, hairless skin and muscular build. Then, his eyes drifted across the soil of the peninsula to the rest of Semjaza's slaves. There were several other such creatures in the small crowd, all of various sizes. One infantile beast was even being held across the breast of a woman, and was already twice the size of a newborn human. Danduel felt the bile rise in his throat at the detestable image.

"My Rada," a quickly approaching soldier called out.

Danduel turned away in disgust. "Yes?"

"The fortress is secure, but the Myndarym are nowhere to be found. It's as if they disappeared."

The Fer-Rada felt his face grow hot. "Send out your most skilled trackers. I want them found. The rest of us—let us be away from this place of wickedness! Nuathel will be needing our help by now. Move out."

"Rada Talad!" the obedient soldiers shouted.

* * * *

Breathing heavily, Sariel hid in the shadows of an overhang and looked from the cliffs northward along the peninsula road. The Fer-Rada and his Anduarym had evacuated the fortress and were marching now toward the eastern gate. Behind them, a small group of women were gathered near the entrance of Aryun Del-Edha. Among the women were several larger creatures who appeared human but for their angelic size. Sariel's trained eyes took in everything at a glance, but his will was focused on only one thing. One person.

There she is! Sheyir's alive!

He jumped from the cliffs and kept his wings only partially extended, dropping quickly toward the cove below. The jagged rocks passed by in seconds and the bare soil of the peninsula rushed up to meet him. Sariel extended his wings further and pulled up to flatten out above the road, which was now only a blur beneath him. The wind whipped at his face as his wings cut through the air with rapid efficiency. Everything on the horizon disappeared and all he could see was Sheyir.

Banking quickly right, then left, he maneuvered around several women wandering along the road. Their screams of surprise began to fill the air in a rolling succession as each one took notice of him.

"SHEYIR!" he shouted.

She quickly turned her head.

In that moment, as Sariel's wings shot outward and abruptly slowed his Iryllur body, it seemed as though time itself came to a crawl.

Sheyir's eyes widened.

Sariel inhaled.

She squinted.

He reached out his hands.

Her face softened as she reached forward.

He glided gently toward her and lifted her from the road.

She grasped him tightly.

With both arms around her, Sariel pulled Sheyir to his chest as his wings thrust downward and lifted them both into the sky. "It's alright," he told her. His calm voice was a stark contrast to the straining of his body. "I have you now. It's alright," he kept saying.

The tower of Aryun Del-Edha dropped away below them as Sariel flew north over the cliffs. When the mountains passed beneath them, he leveled out and banked to the northwest. Through the rush of air passing by, he heard a faint voice.

"Is it really you?"

"I'm sorry, my love" he replied, looking down into Sheyir's glistening eyes. "I'll never leave you again."

Sheyir closed her eyes and leaned her head against his chest.

Her clothes and hair were still wet from the flooded passage. Her skin displayed numerous abrasions and she looked thinner than normal. "Did he hurt you? Did Semjaza hurt you?" he asked.

Sheyir kept her face buried, but her head moved from side to side.

Sariel exhaled deeply, trying to expel the dread and anxiety that had lodged itself in his chest the day his love was taken captive. As he looked out now to the horizon, tears came to his eyes and rolled back across his temples, driven by the wind beating against his face—the liquid manifestation of his overwhelmed soul, beginning to drain away. "I'm sorry about your family...your people. I'll never leave you alone again."

Now Sheyir lifted her head. Wisps of hair flew wildly about her face. She squinted at the bright sunlight, but her mouth was curled up at the corners. "Where are we going?"

Without taking his eyes off her, Sariel answered. "...away. ...far away!"

* * * *

"Look!" one of the Anduar called out.

Danduel spun around and glanced over the marching formation of soldiers to see an Iryllur flying rapidly along the peninsula. "Who is—?" he trailed off as he realized what he was witnessing. "No," he said quietly.

The Iryllur came to a hover and plucked one of the women from the road, passing over the waters of the bay before gaining altitude.

"NO!" he screamed. "Where is Nuathel? He's getting away!"

"My Rada," another soldier said, pointing toward the eastern gate.

Danduel turned around to see an angel standing in the road directly in front of the Anduar formation. He was wingless, a Speaker from the Eternal Realm. One of his arms was missing, but despite his odd, incomplete look, he carried an aura of authority.

"Pri-Rada Ganisheel sent me to check on your progress. Semjaza is dead and it looks like congratulations are in order."

Danduel's heart quickened in his chest at the words of the Speaker. Sariel must have been successful in honoring his promise, but now he was escaping. Fim-Rada Nuathel and his Iryllurym hadn't returned. And the rest of the Myndarym had vanished without a trace. All of these thoughts rushed through his mind in an instant, stealing the sense of satisfaction that should come with victory.

"You can forget about tracking the Myndarym," the speaker continued.

Suddenly Danduel's thoughts and emotions converged upon a single point. "But my mission is not complete. Semjaza's kingdom has fallen, but there are many more who must be brought to justice."

"Yes, I understand," the Speaker replied dismissively. "But that is another task...for someone else."

Danduel paused for a moment, not quite believing his ears. "But... Surely the Pri-Rada knows that we have evidence of their cooperation with the demons? And it may not have been Semjaza himself."

The Speaker drew in a breath, then exhaled slowly. "The Pri-Rada is aware of this. But you are ordered to return. Rest assured, Fer-Rada, that alternate plans are underway. Nothing goes unseen from the gaze of the Holy One."

"Indeed," Danduel replied quickly, bowing his head immediately in submission. "We will return at once."

31

Three months after the army of heavenly soldiers passed through Dalen a-Sorgud on their way to catch up with the Myndarym, Enoch found himself sitting on a rocky point looking northward over the vast expanse of the Great Waters. The sunlight danced along the gentle surface glittering with a million points of silver light. The journey had taken him just over two weeks and, as he had done every day since his arrival, he wondered why he was here. After he had met with the Amatru and told them of the Myndarym's whereabouts, he'd followed the vision that the Holy One had given him. It had led him to this place, but as he'd learned over the years, the next step of obedience wasn't always obvious. Sometimes, it didn't become obvious to him until after it had already happened. He hoped that was not the case this time.

Holy One, I miss Zacol and Methu. I have not seen them in over a year. Methu must be so big by now. My heart longs to be home, among them. And even among my people. Forgive my questions, but what do You require of me? Why have You brought me here? It is empty. Truly these waters are great, but as far as my eyes can see, I am alone. What is left for me to do, but to sit and stare at Your creation? I should be back in Sedekiyr. My people need me. They do not hear Your voice unless I tell them what You speak. They are lost without me. My voice is silent among them now and I fear that everything You have accomplished among them will have to be repeated.

The weight of this responsibility falls heavy on me and all I can do is wait for You. Please forgive my questions. Please answer me!

Back in Sedekiyr Enoch used to sit along the shores of a nearby river. The sight of the trickling water and the constant, gentle sound was soothing to him. It was his place of refuge and a time to listen for the voice of the Holy One. The Great Waters felt much the same now. His ears were fed a banquet of sounds, from the low and steady murmur of distant, crashing waves, to the sharper sound of the water colliding with the rocks beneath him. For his eyes, large patches of reflected light swayed with the movement of water; blending, then separating. On the horizon the light seemed to meld together into a blanket that covered everything, eventually merging with the orange sky above. Enoch smiled as he thought about the predominant belief among his own people. That somewhere out there, at the edge of the world, the sky reached down into the water and the water reached up to the sky. Until his journey into the Eternal Realm, it had also been his belief—that the sky was simply the waters above. But in that disorienting moment when he was lifted from the earth, he saw the world as he moved away from it. What began as a limitless horizon quickly bent downward at both ends. What he perceived to be an endless expanse of flat terrain changed into a sphere which hung in the darkness. And all around it, a soft blue haze was gathered like a mist. It now seemed obvious to him. If the sky was simply the waters above, why didn't it shimmer like this?

With these thoughts spinning through his head, Enoch noticed a sudden change in the shimmer on the ocean surface, several hundred yards out. The light swirled, then broke into two intersecting lines. The point where the lines converged was moving quickly to the southeast, coming closer to the land as it moved across the path of his vision.

Enoch rose from his position and put a hand to his forehead, trying to block the glare from the setting sun. Now that it was close enough, he understood that something large was moving through the water, just under the surface. When it passed beyond the point on which he stood, it began to curve to the south and out of sight.

It's circling, Enoch thought. Stepping down off his rock, he started to run through the tall grass, trying to keep up with it. He dodged to the side of a sprawling tree and pushed through a hedge of brush just in time to see the massive wake move beyond another point to the east. Enoch ran once more, down into a shallow valley and up the other side. When he crested the hill, he had to climb through a tangle of thick branches that seemed to be competing with one another for territory.

Finally, pushing a vine aside, Enoch could see a tiny cove with steep, rocky terrain on its western side gradually merging with the flat, sandy terrain in the east. On the sand, just before the water's edge, a group of tall figures was gathered. Enoch was suddenly choked by the lump in his throat. His heart, already beating quickly from the exertion, now thumped powerfully in his chest, as it did anytime he felt fear. Even at a distance of a hundred yards, Enoch could tell that the figures on the shore were the same as those he'd lived with in Aragatsiyr. However, something was quite different about their appearance.

Cautiously moving closer, Enoch began to see the difference. Some were smaller than before, wearing the forms of humans. Most were large, like the armies of the Amatru. Animal features had been blended with human and angelic features, while some wore their animal forms altogether. The water in the bay swirled and rose to outline a round shape. As it lifted from the water, strands of dark blue light ran down from its spherical surface. Then Enoch saw the eyes, glowing like fire, but blue and green in color. He was seeing only the head of the massive creature with long hair flowing down into the water. When its pale blue neck and shoulders came out, Enoch realized the enormity of the beast with human features.

These are the gods whom the Kahyin worship!

It was as if a veil had been removed from his eyes. He remembered in that instant how these magnificent creatures had first appeared in his sight, before their splendor was eclipsed by the beauty of the Throne, and the One who sat upon it.

Ananel was not among them. Neither was Sariel. And as soon as he thought of the winged soldier he remembered something Sariel had once said to him.

It takes years to learn a form; generations of your time to master it. Forms are not chosen lightly.

Enoch was now struck with a realization—the Myndarym had been lying to him all this time. While they had played the part of the victims of Semjaza's oppressive rule, they had been studying and mastering these forms the entire time. And if they wore these forms now, why hadn't they made use of them during the battle with Semjaza? It was obvious now, as he looked upon the motley assortment of intimidating creatures, that their forms held no other purpose than to put themselves in positions of control over this world. And they had been so committed to keeping the depth of their iniquity a secret they had allowed hundreds of holy angels to fight and die on their behalf.

Enoch ground his teeth together.

Through the loud pounding in his chest a firm conviction cut like a blade, immediately silencing all doubts. It left little room for question or uncertainty about its origin.

Go Enoch.

Go and speak to my Wandering Stars.

With immediate obedience, Enoch stepped away from the trees and began to walk along the top of the ridge that swung down to the beach. With fear still coursing through his veins he approached the creatures who could smash him like an insect in one swift movement. But greater still than his fear of the Myndarym's new forms was his wonder of the Holy One. He would never forget the sight of Him sitting upon His sapphire throne, encircled by countless multitudes of Keruvym. He could still feel the heat from the tongues of fire which surrounded the crystalline city. And he knew that as long as he lived, nothing would ever surpass the feeling of power and majesty that he felt in the presence of the Holy One. Though he walked now into a situation that would have caused other men to tremble, he was confident that he would be protected.

"...burden of authority," someone said as Enoch neared.

"Semjaza is defeated and his kingdom overthrown. The Amatru have returned to the Eternal Realm," someone else answered.

Enoch continued walking toward the group, wondering when he would be noticed.

"Now we find ourselves here, unrestrained, ruling over the land, sea, and air. No longer do we have Myndar, Anduar, Iryllur, and Vidir—the classifications of the Amatru. This is a new world. We are all equals."

"But only some of us are here," another offered.

"Yes," another replied. "I propose that this new era demands the establishment of a leadership with these principles in mind."

The enormous sea creature moaned with what seemed to be disapproval. "We came here to escape such things," it said with a booming, lonely voice. "...to live in freedom, in whatever forms we wished. Now you want to establish more tyranny?"

A tall, winged creature raised his hand. His skin was black as the night and his wings were featherless, with skin stretched over a framework of thin bones. "Not tyranny," he argued. "...but a gathering of equals. Of course we all desire to roam from place to place and live as we please. And we will do that. But eventually, we will run into issues of jurisdiction, ownership of land and people. I suggest that we start this discussion now. To meet at some regular interval to work out these matters before they become problems. Not tyranny, but a council."

Enoch continued walking toward the group, now conscious of the sound of his steps padding across the soft sand. He couldn't stand to be silent any longer, disgusted by what he was hearing. "How dare you!" he shouted.

The Myndarym, in their multitude of forms, turned in unison, eyes wide with surprise.

Enoch looked now from one grotesque creature to the next. It was a much smaller group than before and he wondered if many had been killed in the battle, or if these were simply the only ones who hadn't gone their own way.

"How did you get here, Prophet?" asked a tall and beautiful woman. Her skin was pale and perfectly smooth and she glared at Enoch with piercing green eyes.

"Why does it continue to surprise you that nothing is hidden from the sight of the Holy One?" Enoch shot back. He'd never spoken to them in this way before, but the days of being friends with such creatures were over.

"This is a private meeting," a wolf-headed creature growled. His oversized human body now seemed tense, as if he were expecting to attack at any moment. "It has nothing to do with you!"

Enoch shook his head slowly without removing his gaze. "When will you learn? You have all come here to discuss how you will divide this world that is not yours to begin with. You believe this meeting is part of your plans. But you are wrong. The Holy One brought me here months ago. And now I see that you have been gathered to me to hear your judgment."

To his left, the air swirled and twisted in such a way that Enoch knew another Myndar was present, floating along in the form of the thing that it had sustained at one point of its life, and *shaped* at another. At the back of the crowd, toward the sea, Enoch recognized the one who had taught the others to bring Semjaza from the Eternal Realm. His angelic form began to shimmer as he started to *shape* himself into something else.

"Here is what the Holy One has to say to you. *'If you desire, in the hardness of your hearts, to live in a place that is not meant for you, then so be it. You will have what you want. ...for a time!'*"

As soon as the words came out of Enoch's mouth, he felt a sudden relief. A weight lifted off his shoulders and he knew immediately that his task had been fulfilled. He turned away suddenly, eager to begin the long journey home. As his feet took their first steps across the sand, he could hear the laughter just starting to crop up among the rebellious angels.

First one.

Then another.

Finally, all of the Myndarym joined in, laughing heartily at the powerless words of a tiny human.

By the time Enoch had taken twenty steps, the laughter came to an abrupt end and Enoch thought he heard choking.

"I...can't...*shape*," someone grunted, sounding as if they were in great pain.

Enoch didn't bother turning around. He didn't need to. Whatever judgment the Holy One would bring about was no business of his. He no longer had to concern himself with their disobedience or their punishment. Instead, he felt only great anticipation. He envisioned the day when he would look out across the grassy plains and see Sedekiyr in the distance. He couldn't wait to pick up Methu and embrace him; to stare into Zacol's eyes once again. This was all that was on his mind now. And it brought a smile to his face.

* * * *

Sheyir walked slowly, looking downward. Her left hand rested on the growing bump of her belly, unconsciously rubbing it.

"Do you see it?" Sariel asked from up ahead.

Sheyir suddenly pulled her hand away and looked up. She smiled quickly, hoping that Sariel hadn't noticed, but her heart pounded with fear.

Sariel was facing ahead and only now turned around. His human form, though tall, was far less intimidating than his angelic form. His bright blue eyes looked out through the mist with compassion, while his shaggy, white hair and beard gave him the distinguished look of a tribe elder. "There, just where the mountains come together. Do you see it?"

"Yes," she answered this time. Her throat was constricted and the panic in her answer sounded obvious to her own ears.

"They are a peaceful people," he continued. "Like the Chatsiyram, they are also descended from the Shayetham. Their language is nearly identical to yours. We'll be safe there."

Sheyir smiled again and Sariel turned around, continuing to make his way along the rim of the canyon. When he wasn't looking, she exhaled the breath that she'd been holding, but her heart continued to beat—so loud that she wondered if it was audible. When Sariel had first rescued her, he asked if Semjaza had hurt her. And she indicated that he hadn't. It wasn't a lie. But neither was it the whole truth.

Sooner or later, he's going to find out, she thought with disappointment. *What will he think of me then?*

Sariel abruptly stopped walking. One of his hands reached back toward her, while the other went to his forehead. He stood there for a moment, wavering on unsteady feet. Slowly, he crouched to the ground.

"My love!" Sheyir exclaimed, rushing forward.

Sariel was now down on his knees in the dirt. One hand was clutching his stomach.

"What's wrong? Are you alright?"

Sariel looked up with a sad resignation in his eyes. "Something has changed. I... I can't *shift*." He squinted as if he were exerting himself. "I can't *shape* either."

Sheyir knelt down and picked his hand up from the ground, feeling the damp soil between their intertwined fingers. "You can't go back, can you?"

Sariel shook his head from side to side. Slowly, the lines of concern running across his forehead softened and seemed to change places, moving to the sides of his eyes as his expression turned to a smile.

"I wouldn't, even if I was still able," he assured her.

BOOKS BY JASON TESAR

THE AWAKENED SERIES

Over five thousand years ago, a renegade faction of angels abandoned the spiritual realm and began their inhabitation of earth. Worshiped as gods for their wisdom and power, they corrupted the realm of the physical and forever altered the course of history.

Amidst the chaos of a dying world, a lone voice foretold the awakening of a warrior who would bring an end to this evil perpetrated against all of creation. But with the cataclysmic destruction of earth and rebirth of humanity, the prophecy went unfulfilled and eventually faded from the memory of our kind—until now!

In his debut series, Jason Tesar delves into the heart of an ancient legend, embarking on an epic saga that will journey from earth's mythological past to its post-apocalyptic future, blending the genres of fantasy, sci-fi, and military/political suspense.

BOOK ONE

The physical dimension is fractured. What remain now are numerous fragmented worlds moving simultaneously through time, sharing a common history, connected only by a guarded portal. On a parallel earth, in the city of Bastul, Colonel Adair Lorus disappears while investigating the death of an informant, triggering a series of events which will tear his family apart and set in motion the resolution of an ancient struggle. Kael, sentenced to death after rising up against the cruel leadership of his new step-father, is rescued from prison and trained in the arts of war by a mystical order of clerics. Excelling in every aspect of his training, Kael inwardly struggles to give himself fully to the methods of his new family, or the god they worship.   Maeryn, bitter over the disappearance of her husband and supposed execution of her son, fears for her life at the hands of her newly appointed husband. Finding comfort and purpose in her unborn child, she determines to undermine his authority by reaching out to an underground social movement known as the Resistance. After being forced from his home, Kael's former mentor, Saba, uncovers a clue to Adair's disappearance. Sensing a connection to his own forgotten past, Saba begins an investigation which leads to the discovery of a secret military organization operating within the Orudan Empire.

BOOK TWO

Returning to his home city of Bastul, Kael finds the Southern Territory of the Orudan Empire under invasion. As he races to unravel the secrecy of the enemy's identity, he becomes entangled in a brutal conspiracy to gain control of the government. After years of collaboration with the Resistance, Maeryn coordinates the covert exodus of the entire slave population of Bastul. Along their treacherous journey to the capital city of Orud, she is faced with the pressures of leadership as she attempts to protect her daughter and ensure the survival of her companions. Saba, held captive by a mysterious military force, escapes after years of solitary confinement. Propelled by an elusive memory, he chases after the hope of rediscovering his past and learns that everyone's future is in jeopardy.

BOOK THREE

After fighting his way back from a paralyzing defeat, Kael resolves to bring an end to the enemies of the Orudan Empire. Enlisting the help of his family and most-trusted friends, he faces off against an ancient evil and embraces his destiny. As Maeryn rises through the ranks to attain a command position within the Resistance, she learns of a conspiracy in her organization and realizes the enormous resources at her disposal. Determined to set things right, she seizes control and sets a new course for the movement. Reacquainting with his closest friends, Saba pieces together the identity and motive of the enemy. Bringing his vast knowledge to bear, he collaborates with Orud's High Council to force the enemy into the open, while waiting to reveal a secret of his own.

BOOK FOUR AND BEYOND...

Watch Kael's destiny unfold with the continuation of the *Awakened* series. Visit www.jasontesar.com for behind-the-scenes information and release dates for future books.

THE WANDERING STARS SERIES

Deep in the recesses of the human soul, echoes and shadows survive—remnants of a time long-forgotten. These memories refuse to die, striving for existence by taking the form of myths and legends which continue to shape human history across the boundaries of time and culture.

This is their story—where it all began.

In this riveting prequel to the Amazon bestselling *Awakened* series, Jason Tesar sets in motion a sweeping fantasy epic birthed at the very foundations of humanity when our prehistoric world collided with supernatural forces, spawning an age of mythological creatures and heroes.

INCARNATION: VOLUME ONE

Since the ages before time was measured, the angelic races have existed. Unseen by our eyes, they move through creation, shaping our world, sustaining our existence, and battling demonic hordes. But the war is changing; the battle lines are expanding into new frontiers and the next epoch is emerging.

Seven hundred years after the first humans were exiled from their home, their descendants have pushed eastward into a prehistoric wilderness. In a land shrouded by mist and superstition, primitive tribes struggle to establish new civilizations, unaware that their world is about to change forever.

Weary from unceasing conflict, Sariel, legendary warrior of the Myndarym, crosses into the Temporal Realm in search of the only one who can bring him peace. But he is not the first; others have already begun their inhabitation. As the dominance of their kingdom spreads, threatening to engulf all of humanity, Sariel finds himself standing between his own kind and the one he loves and must embrace the life he abandoned in order to secure her freedom.

VOLUME TWO AND BEYOND...

Follow Sariel's journey as the *Wandering Stars* series continues. Visit www.jasontesar.com for behind-the-scenes information and release dates for future books.

ABOUT THE AUTHOR

Jason Tesar lives with his wife and two children in Colorado. He works in the microelectronics industry improving and developing processes, and writing technical documentation for integrated circuits manufacturing. In his personal time he enjoys graphic design, playing guitar, reading books, watching movies, and doing anything outdoors with his family. To learn more about Jason and get behind-the-scenes info on *The Awakened* and *Wandering Stars* series, visit his blog (www.jasontesar.com), like him on Facebook (jasontesar.com), and follow him on Twitter (@jasontesar).

GLOSSARY
AND PRONUNCIATION GUIDE

The following is a glossary of names, titles, terms, places, and characters that are used throughout this and subsequent books of the Wandering Stars series.

The *vowels* section below contains characters, or arrangements of characters, which are used in the pronunciation section of glossary entries. Each vowel sound is followed by an example of common words using the same sound.

The *additional consonants* section also contains characters, or arrangements of characters, which are used in the pronunciation section of glossary entries. These sounds are not used in the English language, but examples are found in other languages and are listed for reference.

Glossary entries contain the word or phrase, its correct pronunciation (including syllables and emphasis), the translation of the word or phrase, its culture of derivation, and a description. The format for each entry is as follows:

Word or phrase \pro-**nun**-ci-a-tion\ *translation* [Derivation] Description

Vowels

[a]	apple, sad
[ey]	hate, day
[ah]	arm, father
[air]	dare, careful
[e]	empty, get
[ee]	eat, see
[eer]	ear, hero
[er]	early, word
[i]	it, finish
[ahy]	sight, blind
[o]	odd, frost

[oh]	open, road
[ew]	food, shrewd
[oo]	good, book
[oi]	oil, choice
[ou]	loud, how
[uh]	under, tug

Additional Consonants

[r]	roho (Spanish)
[zh]	joie de vive (French)
[kh]	loch (Scots)

Glossary

Ad-Banyim \ad-**ban**-yim\ *First Between Waters* [Shayeth] The first narrow strip of land between two bodies of water which Enoch crosses during his journey to Nowd.

Ad-Rada **ad**-rah-dah\ *First Rule* [Angelic] The first, or highest position of rank among the Amatru.

Aden **ey**-den\ *Pleasure* [Shayeth] The first place of human habitation on earth.

Amatru **ah**-mah-trew\ *Faithful* [Angelic] The combined military forces of Eili who have remained faithful to the Saerin. The holy, angelic military. The Amatru is comprised of three original branches—Anduar, Iryllur, and Vidir—with a fourth branch, Saman—being added later in response to enemy tactics. Each branch is comprised of seven disciplines: Draepa, Vorda, Braegda, Vaeka, Frysla, Viytur, and Smyda.

Amthardel **am**-thahr-del\ *Unknown* [Angelic] The last member of Sariel's special operations team, whom Sariel carried from the battlefield to Laeningar.

Ananel **a**-nah-nel\ *Unknown* [Angelic] The first angel to befriend Enoch, whom he encounters after being taken captive by the Kahyin. Race: Myndar. Size: approximately 10 feet tall when in angelic form. Age: unknown. Appearance: golden eyes; pale gray skin; pale to dark-gray hair.

Andomur \an-doh-**mewr**\ *Final Judgment* [Angelic] A future event occurring at the end of the age of Tima, when Saerin will pronounce judgment on all beings, whether living or held in Saekra, and place them in the location where they will spend eternity.

Anduar **an**-dew-ahr\ *Land Force* [Angelic] The singular name for a member of the land force of the Amatru.

Anduarym **an**-dew-ahr im\ *Land Forces* [Angelic] The plural name for members of the land force of the Amatru.

An-Rada **an**-*r*ah-dah\ *Second Rule* [Angelic] The second position of rank among the Amatru.

Aragatsiyr **ah**-*r*ah-gaht-seer\ *Woven Trees* [Shayeth] The name that Enoch gives to the city of the Myndarym, which they established after their rebellion from Semjaza. See also Senvidar.

Arar Gahiy \ah-**rar** gah-hee\ *Valley of the Curse* [Chatsiyr] The valley to the north of Bahyith where several Chatsiyr men became ill. See also Armayim.

Armayim **ahr**-mah-yim\ *Lake of the Curse* [Chatsiyr] The lake in Arar Gahiy, north of Bahyith, where several Chatsiyr men found figurines and subsequently became ill.

Aryun Del-Edha \ah*r*-**yewn** del-ed-hah\ *Eyes of the Gods* [Kahyin] Semjaza's fortress or tower within Mudena Del-Edha, so named for its peak, which rises above the surrounding mountains and allows the gods to observe the actions of man.

Aytsam **eyt**-sahm\ *People of the Trees* [Chatsiyr] A human tribe, descended from the Kahyin, which occupies the land east of Bokhar.

Azael **a**-zey-el\ *Unknown* [Angelic] Fim-Rada of Semjaza's Iryllurym, and one of Semjaza's personal guards. Race: Iryllur.

Size: approximately 10 feet tall. Age: unknown. Appearance: red eyes; charcoal-gray skin; sleek, black feathers.

Baerlagid \bey-air-**lah**-gid\ *Songs of Creation* [Angelic] The comprehensive, musical language used by Saerin to bring all things into existence out of nothing. A small subset of Baerlagid was taught to the Myndarym for the purpose of reshaping Tima to make it self-sustaining after its separation from the Eili. See also Myndlagid, Navlagid, Skalagid, Tanklagid, Vinlagid, and Vislagid.

Bahyith \bah-**yith**\ *House, Dwelling* [Chatsiyr] The village of the Chatsiyram, situated between the mountains of Bokhar and Ehrevhar.

Batarel **bah**-tah-*r*el\ *Unknown* [Angelic] One of the three Myndarym, whom Sariel encounters while searching for the Aytsam. Batarel is the slowest to befriend Sariel, but later becomes a fierce companion. Race: Myndar. Size: approximately 10 feet tall when in angelic form. Age: unknown. Appearance: orange eyes; dark-golden skin; tan to dark-orange hair.

Batna **baht**-nuh\ *Recover* [Angelic] An organization in Eili, coordinating with, but not subject to the Amatru, whose purpose is to collect the bodies of fallen soldiers and return them to the territory of Saerin.

Baynor **bey**-nohr\ *Children of Light* [Chatsiyr] Beings from Shamuyim, named for their luminescent appearance. See also Shamayim, Del-Szhinda, and Eili.

Bokhar **boh**-kha*r*\ *Morning Mountain* [Chatsiyr] The mountain to the east of Bahyith, named for its association with the rising sun. See also Ehrevhar.

Braegda **breyg**-dah\ *Transport* [Angelic] One of the seven disciplines within each branch of the Amatru. The Braegda specialize in transportation of combat resources, sensitive information, and non-military personnel.

<u>Chatsiyr</u> **kat**-see*r*\ *Grass* [Chatsiyr] The singular name for a member of the small, human tribe, descended from the Shayetham, which occupies the valley between Bokhar and Ehrevhar—the residents of Bahyith.

<u>Chatsiyram</u> **kat**-see*r*-am\ *People of the Grass* [Chatsiyr] The plural name for members of the small, human tribe, descended from the Shayetham, which occupies the valley between Bokhar and Ehrevhar—the residents of Bahyith.

<u>Dalen a-Sorgud</u> **dey**-len ah-**sohr**-goot\ *Valley of Sorrows* [Angelic] In Eili, the site of an infamous battle between the Amatru and Marotru. In Tima, it corresponds to the narrow channel of water that extends eastward from Sahveyim.

<u>Da-Mayim</u> **dah**-mah-yim\ *Unmoving Waters* [Shayeth] The large body of water west of Sedekiyr, named for its contrast to other moving waters, such as the numerous streams and rivers throughout the vast plains.

<u>Danduel</u> **dan**-dew-el\ *Unknown* [Angelic] Fer-Rada of the Anduarym. Race: Anduar. Size: approximately 12 feet tall. Age: unknown. Appearance: light-brown eyes; tan skin; dark-brown hair.

<u>Dathrah</u> **dahth**-*r*ah\ *Knowledge, Sight* [Chatsiyr] Unexplainable or supernatural wisdom or ability.

<u>Del-Szhinda</u> \del-**zhin**-duh\ *Place of Always* [Kahyin] The world of spirits, or the sky, where the spirits are said to dwell. See also Shamayim, Shamuyim, and Eili.

<u>Draepa</u> **drey**-pah\ *Attack* [Angelic] One of the seven disciplines within each branch of the Amatru. The Draepa specialize in attack operations for the purpose of gaining territory and/or defeating enemies.

<u>Ehret</u> **e**-*r*et\ *Earth, Land* [Shayeth] Dirt or soil, or the earth where physical beings live, in contrast to Shamayim. See also Ehrut, Ehrudah, and Tima.

Ehrevhar **air**-e-vahr\\ *Evening Mountain* [Chatsiyr] The mountain to the west of Bahyith, named for its association with the setting sun. See also Bokhar.

Ehrudah **e**-rew-duh\\ *Place of Never* [Kahyin] Dirt or soil, or the earth where physical beings live, in contrast to Del-Szhinda. See also Ehret, Ehrut, and Tima.

Ehrut **e**-rewt\\ *Earth or Land* [Chatsiyr] Dirt or soil, or the earth where physical beings live, in contrast to Shamuyim. See also Ehret, Ehrudah, and Tima.

Eili **ey**-i-lee\\ *Eternal* [Angelic] The portion of the creation Spectrum that is eternal, in contrast to the portion that is temporal. See also Tima, Del-Szhinda, Shamayim, and Shamuyim.

Enoch **ee**-nahk\\ *Dedicated* [Shayeth] Husband of Zacol; father of Methushelak; prophet of the Shayetham. Race: Shayeth. Size: 5.5 feet. Age: 65 sun-cycles. Appearance: pale-green eyes; ruddy skin; black hair and beard.

Erethel **air**-eth-el\\ *Unknown* [Angelic] Fim-Rada of the Anduarym. Race: Anduar. Size: approximately 12 feet tall. Age: unknown. Appearance: reddish-brown eyes; medium-brown skin; dark-brown hair.

Evanel **e**-van-el\\ *Unknown* [Angelic] Fim-Rada of the Anduarym. Race: Anduar. Size: approximately 12 feet tall. Age: unknown. Appearance: golden eyes; light-tan skin; blonde hair.

Ezekiyel **e**-ze-kee-el\\ *Unknown* [Angelic] A master Shifter and Shaper of the Myndarym who taught others how to move beings and objects from Eili to Tima.

Faera **fey**-er-ah\\ *Shift* [Angelic] The ability of a Myndar to move its body, consciousness, or another object from one point to another along the Spectrum of creation.

<u>Fer-Rada</u> **fair**-*r*ah-dah\\ *Fourth Rule* [Angelic] The fourth position of rank among the Amatru.

<u>Fim-Rada</u> **fim**-*r*ah-dah\\ *Fifth Rule* [Angelic] The fifth position of rank among the Amatru.

<u>Frysla</u> **frees**-lah\\ *Rescue* [Angelic] One of the seven disciplines within each branch of the Amatru. The Frysla specialize in search and rescue operations within hostile territories.

<u>Gadol Har-Marah</u> \\gah-**dohl hahr**-mah-*r*ah\\ *Greater Mountain of My Vision* [Shayeth] The taller mountain range as seen from Enoch's vision, situated southeast of Mudena Del-Edha and Khanok. See also Murakszhug.

<u>Gadolyim</u> \\gah-**dohl**-yim\\ *Great Waters* [Shayeth] The large, connected bodies of water to the west and north of Mudena Del-Edha. See also Meyaveem, and Malakiyr.

<u>Ganisheel</u> **ga**-ni-sheel\\ *Unknown* [Angelic] Pri-Rada of the Anduarym.

<u>Gongur</u> **gahn**-gewr\\ *Wandering* [Angelic] The home city of the Kahyin. See also Khelrusa and Khanok.

<u>Gongurhiyd</u> **gahn**-gewr-eed\\ *Wandering Mountain* [Angelic] The mountain above Gongur. See also Gadol Har-Marah and Murakszhug.

<u>Haragam</u> **ha**-*r*ah-gam\\ *Murderers* [Shayeth] A derogatory term for the Kahyin tribe.

<u>Haragdeh</u> \\hah-**rahg**-duh\\ *Killing Fields* [Shayeth] The fields between Khanok and Malakiyr where the Speaker's escorts were slain.

<u>Hauta-Lara</u> **hou**-ta-**lah**-*r*ah\\ *Speaker* [Angelic] A messenger of the Amatru. Typically, a Myndar who is capable of *shifting* to any point along the creation Spectrum.

<u>Himel</u> \\hi-**mel**\\ *Unknown* [Angelic] Pri-Rada of the Iryllurym.

Iryllur **eer**-i-lewr\ *Air Force* [Angelic] The singular name for a member of the air force of the Amatru.

Iryllurym **eer**-i-lewr-im\ *Air Forces* [Angelic] The plural name for the air forces of the Amatru.

Jomjael **johm**-jey-el\ *Unknown* [Angelic] One of the three Myndarym, whom Sariel encounters while searching for the Aytsam. Jomjael leads the freed captive women back to Senvidar. Race: Myndar. Size: approximately 10 feet tall when in angelic form. Age: unknown. Appearance: golden eyes; pale-golden skin; tan to dark-orange hair.

Kahyin **kah**-yin\ *Possession* [Kahyin] The largest of the human tribes, descended from a man named Kahyin, of the second human generation. The Kahyin inhabit the land of Nowd.

Kai-Niquel **kahy**-ni-kwel\ *Unknown* [Angelic] Fim-Rada of the Vidirym. Race: Vidir. Size: approximately 14 feet tall when in angelic form. Age: unknown. Appearance: black eyes; blue-green skin.

Katan Har-Marah **kah**-tan **hahr**-mah-*r*ah\ *Lesser Mountain of My Vision* [Shayeth] The shorter mountain range as seen from Enoch's vision, situated southwest of Gadol Har-Marah.

Keruv **kair**-ewv\ *Unknown* [Angelic] The singular name for a member of the Keruvym.

Keruvym **kair**-ew-vim\ *Unknown* [Angelic] The plural name for the six-winged creatures, with human and animal features, surrounding the throne of the Holy One, as seen in Enoch's visitation to the Eternal Realm.

Keskyd **kes**-keed\ *Center Protector* [Angelic] Singular and plural name for the chest armor of the Amatru. The lightweight version is used by the Iryllurym and the heavyweight version is used by the Anduarym.

<u>Khafar</u> \kahf-**ahr**\ *Dig* [Chatsiyr] An arm's-length, wooden pole with one end tapered to a spade. Used by the Chatsiyr males as both a building tool and a weapon in times of defense.

<u>Khanok</u> **kan**-ahk\ *Dedicated* [Shayeth] The home city of the Kahyin tribe. See also Khelrusa and Gongur.

<u>Khelrusa</u> \kel-**rew**-sah\ *Dedicated* [Kahyin] The home city of the Kahyin tribe. See also Khanok and Gongur.

<u>Kiyrakom</u> **keer**-ah-kohm\ *Place of Meeting* [Shayeth] The open-air courtyard or meeting area at the center of the Aragatsiyr.

<u>Laeningar</u> **ley**-nin-gahr\ *Valley of Healing* [Angelic] In Eili, the valley where Sariel recuperates after times of war. In Tima, it corresponds to the valley where Sheyir goes to sing.

<u>Laevidar</u> **ley**-vi-dahr\ *Tree of Life* [Angelic] One of the two trees at the center of Aden, which exists in both Eili and Tima and represents the Eternal Realm.

<u>Malakiyr</u> \mal-a-**keer**\ *City of Angels* [Shayeth] Semjaza's city. See also Mudena Del-Edha and Pardeya.

<u>Malrah</u> **mal**-rah\ *Evil One* [Angelic] The Evil One. The Commander-in-Chief of the Marotru.

<u>Marotru</u> **mah**-roh-trew\ *Unfaithful* [Angelic] The combined military forces of Eili who have rebelled against Saerin to follow Malrah. The unholy, demonic military.

<u>Methushelak</u> \me-**thew**-she-lak\ *Man of the Dart* [Shayeth] The firstborn son of Enoch and Zacol; also called Methu.

<u>Meyaveem</u> **me**-yah-veem\ *Great Waters* [Kahyin] The large, connected bodies of water to the west and north of Mudena Del-Edha. See also Gadolyim and Sturvat.

<u>Morkum</u> **mohr**-kewm\ *Borderland* [Angelic] In Eili, the portion of the creation Spectrum just before Tima, where that majority of form and structure has been lost.

Mudena Del-Edha \moo-**dee**-nuh del-**ed**-hah\ *City of the Gods* [Kahyin] Semjaza's city. See also Malakiyr and Pardeya.

Murakszhug \moo-**rahk**-zhoog\ *Mountain of Watching* [Kahyin] The mountain above Khelrusa. See also Gadol Har-Marah and Gongurhiyd.

Mynd **mind**\ *Shape, Form* [Angelic] The ability of a Myndar to change its form, or the form of another being or object.

Myndar **min**-dahr\ *Shaper* [Angelic] The singular name of a member of the Myndarym.

Myndarym **min**-dahr-im\ *Shapers* [Angelic] The plural name of the angelic race that was entrusted with a small subset of Baerlagid, for the purpose of reshaping Tima to make it self-sustaining after its separation from the Eili.

Myndlagid **mind**-lah-gid\ *Song of Shaping* [Angelic] One of the Songs of Creation used to alter the form of an object or being. See also Baerlagid, Navlagid, Skalagid, Tanklagid, Vinlagid, and Vislagid.

Nagah \nah-**gah**\ *Mountains of Reaching* [Shayeth] The mountain range east of Sedekiyr, named for its appearance to be reaching toward the sky.

Navlagid \nahv-**lah**-gid\ *Song of Naming* [Angelic] One of the Songs of Creation used to identify or determine the structure of an object or being. See also Baerlagid, Myndlagid, Skalagid, Tanklagid, Vinlagid, and Vislagid.

Ne-Banyim \ney-**ban**-yim\ *Second Between Waters* [Shayeth] The second narrow strip of land between two bodies of water that Enoch crosses during his journey to Nowd.

Nedaret **ned**-ah-*r*et\ *Beneath the Earth, Land* [Angelic] The subterranean force of the Marotru—distorted versions of the Vidirym. They resemble squid, with multiple snake-like appendages on the lower half of their body, the ends of which are equipped with talons used to penetrate and push aside the soil.

<u>Nephiyl</u> \nef-**eel**\ *Fallen* [Shayeth] The singular name for the offspring of angelic-human or angelic-animal copulation.

<u>Nephiylim</u> \nef-**eel**-im\ *Fallen People* [Shayeth] The plural name for offspring of angelic-human or angelic-animal copulation.

<u>Nidur</u> \ni-**dewr**\ *Great Turning-Away, Descent* [Angelic] The period in creation's history, preceding Omynd, when the first humans ate from Skynvidar. This act allowed death to enter into a portion of creation, causing a division from Eili, thus giving birth to Tima.

<u>Nin-Myndar</u> **nin**-min-dah*r*\ *Unshaper* [Angelic] The singular name for a member of the Nin-Myndarym.

<u>Nin-Myndarym</u> **nin**-min-dah*r*-im\ *Unshapers* [Angelic] The plural name for the demonic counterparts to the Myndarym, who have misused and distorted Baerlagid for the purposes of destroying Eili, the Amatru, Tima, and humans as well.

<u>Nowd</u> **nohd**\ *Wandering* [Shayeth] The land settled by Kahyin and his descendants.

<u>Nuathel</u> **new**-ah-thel\ *Unknown* [Angelic] Fim-Rada of the Iryllurym. Race: Iryllur. Size: approximately 10 feet tall. Age: unknown. Appearance: pale green eyes; light-tan skin; dark-brown hair.

<u>Omynd</u> **oh**-mind\ *Reshaping* [Angelic] The period in creation's history, immediately following Nidur, when the Myndarym used Baerlagid to shape Tima so that it could become self-sustaining after it began separating from Eili.

<u>Ophan</u> **oh**-fan\ *Wheel* [Angelic] The singular name for a member of the Ophanym.

Ophanym **oh**-fan-im\ *Wheels* [Angelic] The plural name for the spinning, wheel-shaped, creatures beneath the throne of the Holy One, seen during Enoch's visitation to the Eternal Realm.

Pardeya \pah*r*-**dey**-uh\ *Pride* [Angelic] Semjaza's city. See also Mudena Del-Edha and Malakiyr.

Parnudel **pah***r*-new-del\ *Unknown* [Angelic] One of Semjaza's personal guards. Race: Iryllur. Size: approximately 10 feet tall. Age: unknown. Appearance: golden eyes; mottled-brown skin and feathers.

Pri-Rada **pree**-rah-dah\ *Third Rule* [Angelic] The third position of rank among the Amatru.

Rada Talad **rah**-dah ta-**lahd**\ *Rule Has Spoken* [Angelic] An exclamation among the Amatru, commonly used in response to an order from a superior.

Ruaka **rew**-ah-kah\ *Spirit* [Angelic] The life-giving essence of the Holy One which sustains all created things in the Eili and Tima.

Saekra **sey**-k*r*ah\ *Place of Holding* [Angelic] The place where spirits are held until Andomur.

Sahveyim \sah-vey-**yim**\ *Water On All Sides* [Shayeth] The section of land, narrowly connected to larger land masses on the south, east, and west, which sits in the middle of Gadolyim.

Saerin **sey**-eer-in\ *Holy One* [Angelic] The Holy One. The Commander-in-Chief or Ad-Rada of the Amatru.

Saman **sah**-mahn\ *Joint Operations* [Angelic] The joint operations branch of the Amatru, comprised of Anduarym, Iryllurym, and Vidirym, added later as a response to enemy tactics.

Sariel **sah**-ree-el\ *Minister Appointed by God* [Angelic] Formerly a Myndar, who became a soldier after Omynd. Race: Myndar. Size: approximately 10 feet tall when in Iryllur form, 6.5 feet tall when in human form. Age: unknown. Iryllur appearance: bright-blue eyes; light-tan skin, white feathers flecked with gold and reddish-brown. Human appearance: bright-blue eyes, light-tan skin, white shaggy hair and beard.

<u>Sau-Rada</u> **sou**-rah-dah\\ *Seventh Rule* [Angelic] The seventh position of rank among the Amatru.

<u>Sedekiyr</u> \\sed-e-**keer**\\ *City of Justice, Righteousness* [Shayeth] The home city of the Shayeth tribe. From a root word meaning level or flat, named for its location on the vast flatlands or plains and not as an indication of moral value.

<u>Semjaza</u> \\sem-**jah**-zah\\ *Unknown* [Angelic] Formerly a Pri-Rada of the Saman, until his invasion of Tima. Size: 13 feet tall. Age: unknown. Appearance: dark orange eyes, reddish-brown skin, black hair.

<u>Senvidar</u> **sen**-vi-dahr\\ *Twisted Trees* [Angelic] The city of the Myndarym, which they established after their rebellion from Semjaza. See also Aragatsiyr.

<u>Set-Rada</u> **set**-*r*ah-dah\\ *Sixth Rule* [Angelic] The sixth position of rank among the Amatru.

<u>Shalakh Akhar</u> \\shah-**lahk** ahk-**ahr**'\\ *After Exile* [Shayeth] A reference point for measurement of time; also abbreviated as S.A. The first humans were immortal prior to being exiled from Aden, therefore, the passage of time was irrelevant. The practice of referring to events or objects in the past-tense only came into being when there was a noticeable difference between their past and present states. This occurred during the time of their banishment and the translated phrase after exile came into use.

<u>Shamayim</u> **shah**-mah-yim\\ *Waters Above* [Shayeth] The sky, or the kingdom of heaven; where spirits are said to dwell. See also Shamuyim, Del-Szhinda, and Eili.

<u>Shamuyim</u> \\shah-**mew**-yim\\ *Waters Above* [Chatsiyr] The sky, or the kingdom of heaven; where the Baynor are said to dwell. See also Shamayim, Del-Szhinda, and Eili.

Shayeth **shey**-eth\ *Compensation* [Shayeth] The singular name for a member of the Shayetham.

Shayetham **shey**-eth-em\ *People of Compensation* [Shayeth] The plural name for the second-largest of the human tribes, descended from a man named Shayeth, of the second human generation. The Shayetham inhabit the land between Da-Mayim and Nagah.

Sheyir **shey**-eer\ *Song* [Chatsiyr] The youngest daughter of Yeduah. Race: Chatsiyr. Size: approximately 4.5 feet tall. Age: 19 sun-cycles. Appearance: light-brown eyes; earthen skin, black hair.

Skalagid **skah**-lah-gid\ *Song of Understanding* [Angelic] One of the Songs of Creation, used to communicate thoughts, emotions, and ideas among multiple angels simultaneously. See also Baerlagid, Myndlagid, Navlagid, Tanklagid, Vinlagid, and Vislagid.

Skoldur **skohl**-dewr\ *Shield* [Angelic] Singular and plural name for the heavyweight shield used by the Anduarym.

Skynvidar **skeyn**-vi-dahr\ *Tree of Wisdom* [Angelic] One of the two trees at the center of Aden, which exists in both Eili and Tima and represents the Temporal Realm.

Smyda **smee**-dah\ *Build* [Angelic] One of the seven disciplines within each branch of the Amatru. The Smyda specialize in the design of weaponry and armor and construction of fortifications.

Straeka **strey**-kuh\ *Stretch* [Angelic] The spectrum of creation. In the beginning, all created objects and beings existed in close proximity in one eternal world. After the rebellion of Malrah, he and the Marotru were cast out of the presence of Saerin. The violence of this judgment stretched creation into a continuum of existence. On the opposite end from Saerin, the stretching was more pronounced, causing a separation of environmental qualities. What resulted was a realm that lacked enduring light and sound—which would later become Tima—followed by a realm that lacked form and structure—which would later become Morkum.

<u>Sturvat</u> **stewr**-vaht\\ *Great Waters* [Angelic] The large, connected bodies of water to the west and north of Pardeya. See also Gadolyim and Meyaveem.

<u>Svvard</u> **svahrd**\\ *Unknown* [Angelic] The singular and plural word for an experimental weapon being developed by the Amatru. Similar to a *vandrekt*, it features a shorter handle and longer blade. It functions as a stabbing or swinging weapon in close-quarters combat.

<u>Tamael</u> **tah**-mey-el\\ *Unknown* [Angelic] The leader of the three Myndarym whom Sariel encounters while looking for the Aytsam. Race: Myndar. Size: approximately 10 feet tall when in angelic form. Age: unknown. Appearance: golden eyes; pale-golden skin; tan to dark-orange hair.

<u>Tanklagid</u> **tahnk**-lah-gid\\ *Song of Idea* [Angelic] One of the Songs of Creation, used to steer a being's thoughts toward a conclusion that will reveal a truth which Saerin wishes to communicate. See also Baerlagid, Myndlagid, Navlagid, Skalagid, Vinlagid, and Vislagid.

<u>Tarsaeel</u> **tahr**-sey-el\\ *Unknown* [Angelic] Sariel's former friend in Viytur. Formerly a Myndar who became a soldier after Omynd. Race: Myndar. Size: approximately 10 feet tall when in Iryllur form. Age: unknown. Iryllur appearance: golden eyes; mottled brown, red, and tan skin and feathers; chestnut hair.

<u>Tehrah</u> \\te-**rah**\\ *Dark Knowledge, Dark Sight* [Chatisyr] Evil thoughts or actions.

<u>Tima</u> **tee**-mah\\ *Temporal* [Angelic] The portion of the creation Spectrum that separated from Eili and became temporal, in contrast to the portion that remains eternal. See also Ehret, Ehrut, and Ehrudah.

Vaeka **vey**-kuh\\ *Search* [Angelic] One of the seven disciplines within each branch of the Amatru. The Vaeka specialize in surveillance & reconnaissance.

Vaepkir **veyp**-keer\\ *Arm Blade* [Angelic] The singular and plural word for the arm-blade weaponry used by the Iryllurym. When held in the standard position, it functions as a ramming weapon during air-based attacks. When held in a reverse position, it functions as a stabbing weapon during ground-based, or hand-to-hand combat.

Vandrekt \\vahn-**drekt**\\ *Air Spear* [Angelic] The singular and plural word for the short spears used by the Anduarym. Each *vandrekt* is fitted with a 12 inch, double bladed tip. It functions as a stabbing weapon in close-quarters combat, or a swinging or casting weapon on the open battlefield—though casting is typically a last resort.

Vanspyd **vahn**-speed\\ *Water Spear* [Angelic] The singular and plural word for the long spears used by the Vidirym. Each *vanspyd* is fitted with three short, double-bladed, staggered tips on the front end and two at the rear. It functions as a stabbing weapon in close-quarters combat.

Vidir \\vi-**deer**\\ *Sea Force* [Angelic] The singular name for a member of the sea force of the Amatru.

Vidirym \\vi-**deer**-im\\ *Sea Forces* [Angelic] The plural name for members of the sea forces of the Amatru.

Vinlagid **vin**-lah-gid\\ *Song of Force* [Angelic] One of the Songs of Creation, used to modify dense materials after they've become unresponsive to shaping. See also Baerlagid, Myndlagid, Navlagid, Skalagid, Tanklagid, and Vislagid.

Vislagid **vis**-lah-gid\\ *Song of Withering* [Demonic] A distorted version of one of the Songs of Creation, used by the Nin-Myndarym to corrode or deteriorate an object or being. See also Baerlagid, Myndlagid, Navlagid, Skalagid, Tanklagid, and Vinlagid.

<u>Viytur</u> **vee**-tew*r*\ *Wisdom* [Angelic] One of the seven disciplines within each branch of the Amatru. The Viytur is a cross-branch force, specializing in the gathering and analysis of information and controlled implementation of its conclusions.

<u>Vorda</u> **vew*r***-dah\ *Defense* [Angelic] One of the seven disciplines within each branch of the Amatru. The Vorda specialize in defense operations for the purpose of holding territory or protecting personnel or resources.

<u>Yeduah</u> **ye**-dew-uh\ *Unknown* [Chatsiyr] The elder of the Chatsiyr tribe and father of Sheyir. Race: Chatsiyr. Size: approximately 5 feet tall. Age: 312 sun-cycles. Appearance: dark-brown eyes; earthen skin, black hair.

<u>Zacol</u> **zah**-kohl\ *Strong Voice* [Shayeth] The wife of Enoch and mother of Methushelak. Size: 5 feet tall. Age: 41 sun-cycles. Appearance: dark-brown eyes; ruddy skin; black hair.

REFERENCES

1. ...the angels which kept not their first estate, but left their own habitation, he hath reserved in everlasting chains under darkness unto the judgment of the great day...wandering stars, to whom is reserved the blackness of darkness forever (Jude 1:6, 13a, KJV).

2. And Cain [*Kahyin*] went out from the presence of the LORD, and dwelt in the land of Nod [*Nowd*], on the east of Eden [Aden] (Genesis 4:16, KJV).

3. And Adam knew his wife again; and she bare a son, and called his name Seth [*Shayeth*]: For God hath appointed me another seed instead of Abel, whom Cain [*Kahyin*] slew (Genesis 4:25, KJV).

4. And Enoch lived sixty and five years, and begat Methuselah [*Methushelak*] (Genesis 5:21, KJV).

5. ...for the Lord God had not caused it to rain upon the earth... But there went up a mist from the earth, and watered the whole face of the ground (Genesis 2:5b-6, KJV).

6. And it came to pass, when men began to multiply on the face of the earth, and daughters were born unto them, that the sons of God saw the daughters of men that they [were] fair; and they took them wives of all which they chose (Genesis 6:1-2, KJV).

7. And it came to pass when the children of men had multiplied that in those days were born unto them beautiful and comely daughters. And the angels, the children of the heaven, saw and lusted after them... (The Book of Enoch 6:1-2)

8. And they were in all two hundred; who descended (The Book of Enoch 6:6-8).

9. And all the others together with them took unto themselves wives, and each chose for himself one, and they began to go in unto them and to defile themselves with them... (The Book of Enoch 7:1)

10. ...taught men to make swords, and knives, and shields, and breastplates, and made known to them the metals of the earth and the art of working them... (The Book of Enoch 8:1)

11. ...Enoch was hidden, and no one of the children of men knew where he was hidden, and where he abode, and what had become of him (The Book of Enoch 12:1-2a).

12. And they besought me to draw up a petition for them that they might find forgiveness, and to read their petition in the presence of the Lord of heaven. For from thenceforeward they could not speak with Him nor lift up their eyes to heaven for shame of their sins for which they had been condemned (The Book of Enoch 13:4b-6a).

13. And I went off and sat down at the waters... And behold a dream came to me, and visions fell down upon me... (The Book of Enoch 13:7b-8a)

14. ...in the vision clouds invited me and a mist summoned me, and the course of the stars and the lightnings sped and hastened me, and the winds in the vision caused me to fly and lifted me upward, and bore me into heaven. And I went in till I drew nigh to a wall which was built of crystals and drew nigh to a large house which was built of crystals... (The Book of Enoch 14:8b-10a)

15. As for the likeness of the living creatures, their appearance [was] like burning coals of fire, [and] like the appearance of lamps: it went up and down among the living creatures; and the fire was bright, and out of the fire went forth lightning. And the living creatures ran and returned as the appearance of a flash of lightning (Ezekiel 1:13-14, KJV).

16. The appearance of the wheels and their work [was] like unto the colour of a beryl: and they four had one likeness: and their appearance and their work [was] as it were a wheel in the middle of a wheel. When they went, they went upon their four sides: [and] they turned not when they went. As for their rings,

they were so high that they were dreadful; and their rings [were] full of eyes round about them four (Ezekiel 1:16-18).

17. And before the throne [there was] a sea of glass like unto crystal: and in the midst of the throne, and round about the throne, [were] four beasts full of eyes before and behind. And the first beast [was] like a lion, and the second beast like a calf, and the third beast had a face as a man, and the fourth beast [was] like a flying eagle. And the four beasts had each of them six wings about [him]; and [they were] full of eyes within... (Revelation 4:6-8a)

18. There were giants [*Nephiylim*] in the earth in those days; and also after that, when the sons of God came in unto the daughters of men, and they bare [children] to them, the same [became] mighty men which [were] of old, men of renown (Genesis 6:4, KJV).

19. ...whose height was three thousand ells, who consumed all the acquisitions of men. And when men could no longer sustain them, the giants [*Nephiylim*] turned against them and devoured mankind. And they began to sin against birds, and beasts, and reptiles, and fish, and to devour one another's flesh, and drink the blood... (The Book of Enoch 7:2-6)

20. ...and as men perished, they cried, and their cry went up to heaven... (The Book of Enoch 8:3)

21. Therefore, I will raise up one from among those you despise. And I will awaken his eyes to the mysteries which I have hidden from men since the foundations of the world. His feet will I make to tread upon the paths of destruction and his hands to make war. He will uproot the seeds of corruption which you have sown throughout the earth. And then you will know that I am the Lord and my justice is everlasting (The Writings of Ebnisha).

22. ...two wolves which he has... The ravens sit on his shoulders and say into his ear all the tidings which they see or hear... (The Prose Edda)

23. These are the names of the Æsir's steeds: Sleipnir is best...he has eight feet (The Prose Edda).

ACKNOWLEDGEMENTS

I would like to thank Carly Tesar, Jeff Boutwell, Becca Day, Cathy Walters, Chris Walters, Luke Flowers, and Mike Heath, for their creative energy in developing an art concept for cover design on the *Wandering Stars* and *Awakened* series.

I would also like to thank Carly Tesar, Cindy Tesar, Becca Day, Marcia Fry, Joyce Paige, and Ronda Swolley, for donating their precious time and expertise in editing the *Incarnation* manuscript.

Made in the USA
Columbia, SC
18 August 2020